THE SOUTHERNMOST STAR

THE INNISFAIL CYCLE
BOOK TWO

Published in the United States by Burnt Leaf Press.
www.lmriviere.com
Cover design by L.M. Riviera

Burnt Leaf Press is an independent publisher of digital and printed fiction.

Visit https://www.burntleafpress.com/ to discover our full library of content online.
eBook ISBN: 978-1-914152-13-9
Paperback ISBN: 978-1-914152-13-9
Hardcover ISBN: 978-1-914152-12-2

THE SOUTHERNMOST STAR

The Innisfail Cycle
Book Two

L. M. RIVIERE

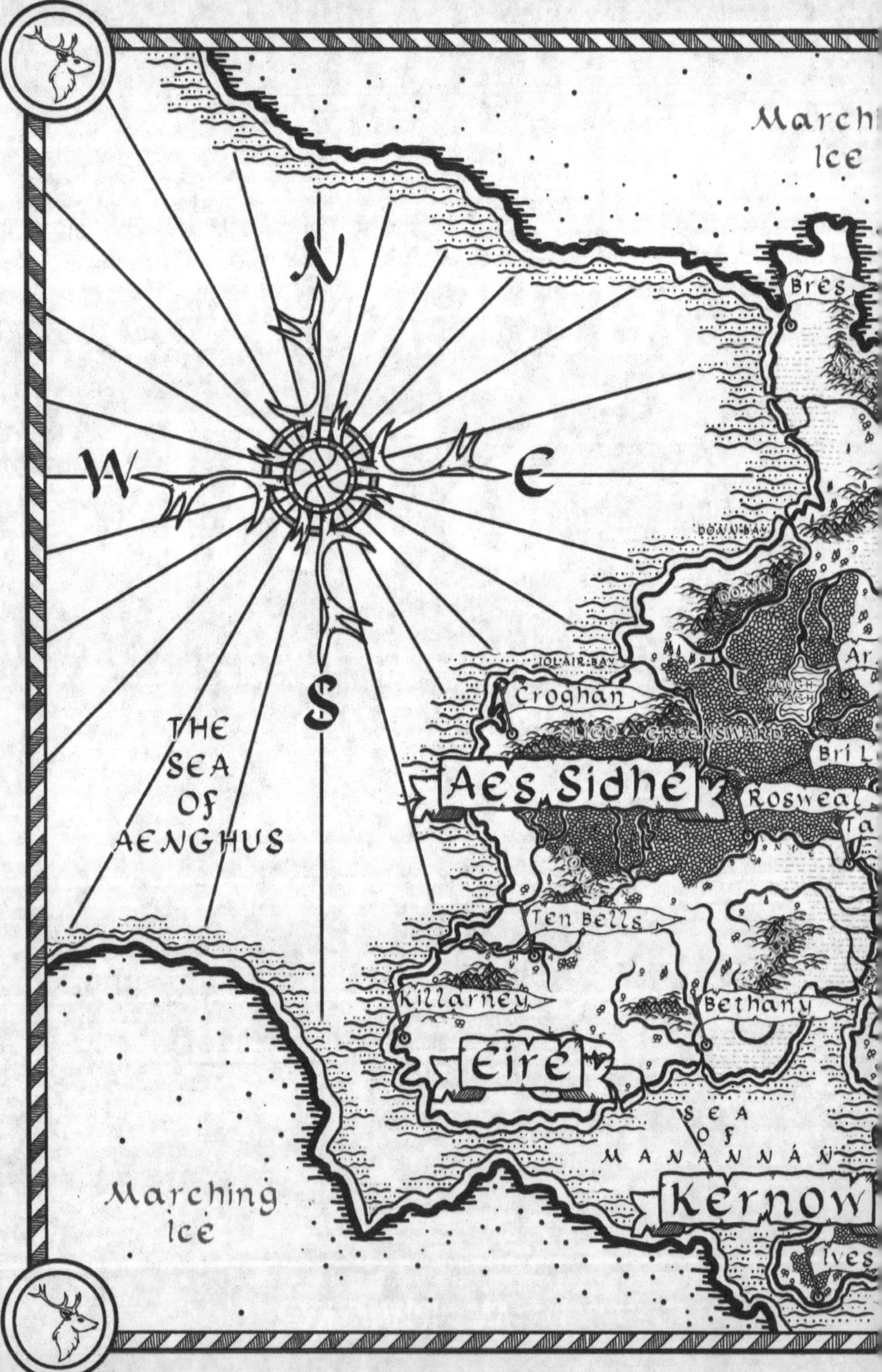

N
W
E
S
THE SEA OF AENGHUS
Marching Ice
March... Ice
Brés
Aes Sidhé
Éire
Kernow
Croghan
Killarney
Ten Bells
Bethany
IOLAIR BAY
SLIGO GREENSWARD
Roswea
Brí L
Ta
Ar
LOUGH NEACH
DOWN
DONAGHAN
SEA OF MANANNÁN
Ives

The Land Of
Innisfail
Scotia
Marching Ice
THE NORD SEA
Alba
The Wastes
BRITON
Mann
iannon
Mru
THE SEA OF REEDS
The Briton Fields
Derby
DORSET
Marching Ice
TAGN SEA
Created by Talesfromfarcliff

Contents

1
SOUTH

N.E. 508
04, DOR ORAS
EIRE

Una wished she was dead. Every breath was a losing battle. Any air she managed to squeeze into her lungs burned through her airways like acid. The pounding in her head might have been a thousand-pound bell, pealing back and forth for hours. The furs she lay beneath were as heavy as a two-ton stone. Something rattled within her chest, as if one of her ribs had come loose and was attempting to work itself into her gut. Is this what suffocating felt like? She couldn't be sure, but if this went on much longer… death would be a blessing. Every inch of her hurt, from the tips of her bruised toes to the bleeding hollows of her shrinking gums. She was an aching husk of herself: a parchment stretched taut over disintegrating bones.

"What's wrong with her?" asked a gruff voice from far off.

"Spark drag, I'll wager." *That* voice, she knew. She'd have gone cold at the sound if she had any blood to spare. "She's used too much."

The unknown speaker whistled. "Reason. Too bloody right there. If I hadn't seen what she did with my own eyes, I'd never believed any of this was possible. Is she dying?"

As another tremor galloped along her nerves, bowing her swollen spine, Una also wanted to know the answer to that question. She heard the scrape of a boot near her ear. The air drew close as a hulking figure bent over her. Why couldn't she open her eyes? If her last living act on earth was to spit in his face, she would count her stars. She tried to move her head, but the effort sent spears of lightning down her throat. She might have choked if she had the strength. Instead, she sucked tiny ribbons of air into her taxed lungs and trembled with the urge to weep. The familiar voice cursed. "Not if I can help it. *No*! Don't touch her."

A flurry of movement. "I meant to—"

"If you touch her now, she'll likely kill you without meaning to. Siorai of her skill level are forbidden to fuel themselves this way, but it can happen."

"I see," said the heavier voice, clear revulsion in his tone.

Gloved fingers probed her face from brow to jaw. Only Damek Bishop would have the gall to lay hands on her so boldly. Pity, she was unwell, for she would have loved to drain the arrogant bastard dry.

"No help for it, I'm afraid," Damek sighed, smoothing back her hair. She hoped he'd be stupid enough to remove his glove. "Bring me one of our prisoners. Someone healthy, but not over-strong. Martin, *discreetly*, please. The men are already terrified of her."

"Yes, My Lord." Now she recognized that deep, oak-rich voice. Martin O'Rearden, her father's Commander at Arms. Though she hated the circumstances, she was glad of his presence all the same. She had nothing but fond memories of the old soldier and prayed she wouldn't have to harm him to escape. Distracted by distant memories and unbearable pain, she hadn't quite heard Damek's order. What had happened? How had she come to be here? She couldn't glean the details, simply snippets: flashes of brilliant orange flame, men and horses screaming, a cottage consumed by oppressive emerald eyes, Rian's small body limp against a filthy wooden floor, a black beast with an appetite as bottomless as the sea— Kaer Yin, the erstwhile Ben Maeden, silver eyes half-lidded, pale hair laying limp over his collar, lips still and cold as wax— and the dead, so many cold creatures she could never count them all.

How long had she lain here? Frustration nearly outpaced her pain.

Where was Kaer Yin? Was he alive?

Had Rian survived what Una had done to her? How had Damek gotten hold of her?

"Una," Damek whispered. "Can you hear me?"

Yes! She wanted to scream. *Tell me what happened! Where are my friends? Where is Kaer Yin? What did you DO, Damek? What did I do?*

"I'm sorry for this, but neither of us has a choice." His breath dusted her cheek.

Was that genuine regret she detected in his tone? Why? Not the Lord of Clare, surely?

Her mind wandered. A flower bloomed in bright spring sunlight. A garden filled with birdsong, damp green things, and warm male laughter. She knew this place, didn't she? The first brush of infatuated longing, small pleasures, fleeting as the sun in winter. Then, she felt the cold stone at her back, the sharp sting of betrayal. A mouth full of teeth and animal hunger chewed through blood and sinew to her thundering heart. Slow-simmering rage chased this vision away, cloaking her girlhood fancy in blackest hate.

Oh, Damek, come closer. Press your lips to mine, I beg you.

"My lord," Martin reappeared, bearing unhappy resignation in his voice. Someone new whimpered beside him. "This one killed a man trying to escape. Best I could find."

"Good," said Damek. "Bring her over."

The whimpering melded into panicked gasps.

Una's broken body flooded with dread.

Oh no... no, no, no, NO!

A silent scream bubbled within Una's chest, raising icebergs in her already frozen blood.

Siora! Forgive me!

HOURS OR DAYS LATER, SHE COULDN'T SAY WHICH, UNA WOKE FROM A doze to find herself tied to a creaking saddle. Disoriented, she shook herself to clear her head, though it did little to help her gain her bearings. From beneath the rim of a heavy cowl, she spied the hard-worn road below her horse's hooves. Steady rain bounced back up to her knees from deep puddles on either side, and a host of stripped trees fell away from a broad river snaking past on her right. *The Shannon*, she knew at a glance. Those blue hills she spied over the horizon told her all she needed to know. This was the Taran High Road, and soon they would hug the river at Dumnain and then trek South-by-South-west to Bethany. She was headed home. Damek was taking her to her father. They were leaving her life, friends, and freedom behind in the North. When they crossed at Ten Bells, she would be her father's subject once more.

Princess of Bethany.

The words soured like spoiled milk in her throat.

Patrick Donahugh's kingdom.

The one place in all the world she'd rather die than spend a day. She gnashed her teeth in silent loathing. Una held one power there, one worth. Her value was measured by the potential fruits of her body and whatever price might fetch for the most ambitious man in Innisfail. There was no worse fate she could imagine for a liberated Tairnganese woman, autonomous in her own right, than the one that awaited her in Bethany.

The Duch would marry her off as soon as he was able. Should she dare use her gifts against any would-be suitors, innocents would suffer in her place. That had ever been the way between Una and her father. She hardly believed anything would have changed, saving maybe the brutality of his vengeance. She'd defied him for fourteen years already.

He didn't care about her, who she was as a person, who her mother had been, whom she loved, what she believed, nor what was best for her. Patrick cared about *Tairngare*. He lusted for an Eire unified under his rule. His interest in her terminated with the claim she held in the North and the viability of the meat between her legs.

Patrick Donahugh wanted to be a king.

He would sell her a thousand times over to achieve that goal.

Una must escape before it became impossible. She was not chattel to be bought and sold for anyone's gain, least of all Patrick's. Setting her jaw at a determined angle, she slid her eyes forward and aft. She was surrounded by Souther knights, but none paid close attention to her. Walking their horses at a gentle clip, many were engaged in hushed conversation or leaned over their horse's necks, sound asleep. A knight beside her held her reins loosely, gnawing at a browning apple with a haunted, faraway mien.

Everywhere her eyes came to rest, she saw men worse for wear. Some were missing digits from appendages swaddled in unsanitary bandages. Many sported cuts and bruises that no one had bothered to tend. All wore expressions loaded with disbelief, pain, or numb horror. Una felt little sympathy for them; they were murderers, all. Led North by lust and greed, these men were no less guilty than her duplicitous cousin in his quest for power.

Maybe one of them would lean down to grab her if she slipped quietly from her saddle? No, too public. Perhaps she should demand a nature break, and when led away, she could…

"I can hear the cogs turning in your head from here, cousin," Damek laughed from behind her.

She didn't bother to crane her neck to look at him. Why waste the effort on such a useless view? "Mmm," she hummed. "Afraid yet?"

He kicked his mount forward and drew up beside her. She looked away, fuming. "Not really. Though, seeing you now after all these years, I wonder how I never noticed that *you* are. Always have been, too, I gather. How charming."

She ground her molars together.

The only words with the power to sting bore truth.

You are not cowed, she told herself.

He will make a mistake eventually, and you'll be free again, one way or the other. She squared her shoulders and raised her chin as high as it would go. "Perhaps all these armored men frighten me. Will you hold me?"

He rewarded her with a throaty chuckle that was much deeper than the one she remembered. She stole a glance at him from the corner of her eye and wished she hadn't. His smirk made her want to rip his jugular out with her teeth. "Not yet, *Lady Donahugh*. I won't presume until you ask me seriously, of course."

"I'd rather drink crushed glass, Lord Bishop."

His smile bordered on the lascivious. The years had been kind to her cousin. He was taller, broader through the chest and shoulders, and the flesh of his cheeks had settled into the sharp bones of his face. Arching black brows swept over his violet and green eyes.

He was very handsome. She hated him the more for it.

"Oh, I don't know about that. One day I may grow on you, my Lady Donahugh."

"My *name* is Una Moura. I am Prima of the Cloister of the Eternal Flame and a free citizen of Tairngare. You have no right to hold me against my will."

He shook his head with that annoying, affable grin. "Reason, but you're beautiful in a temper. Even covered in filth and scrapes... hm," he hummed a sound that made Una burn with rage.

Don't get angry. That's what he wants.

"What do you think, Martin? Is she not the loveliest woman you've ever set eyes upon?"

Don't get angry. Don't get angry. Don't.

"My lord," Martin cleared his throat. "Perhaps not?"

Damek was having the time of his life at her expense. Her nostrils flared. "I am not some tavern-wench, Damek. I am the Doma's granddaughter and heir."

"For all your education, your sense of direction is rather pathetic, isn't it?"

His men, save Martin, chuckled around her.

"When my grandmother hears of this—"

As if he'd been waiting for this threat, he pulled a rolled bit of vellum out of his tunic and wagged it under her nose. She looked away, taking deep breaths. Recognizing Nema's seal at a glance, she could guess what it read. "Should I read it for you?"

"No." She knew where this must be headed.

"Oh, what a shame," he said, waving the scroll back and forth. "It's such a fun yarn. Old Grandmama has been deposed. It seems the Red City is under new management, and this," he paused to read the name, "Vanna Nema is now Doma. Want to know what the new Doma thinks of you and your family, my love?"

"Fuck yourself."

"Whatever My Lady advises, of course."

"You've made your point!"

"Have I?"

"Yes!" she hissed, fighting tears. Her grandmother... her family. She didn't know how they'd come to this pass so quickly but had no doubt who had orchestrated the coup. Nema had tried to kill Una three times already, and only Siora knew what she'd been doing in Tairngare since. Though Una had been oblivious to the trouble brewing within the Cloister while she remained within its walls, now that she was out in the world, she'd been disabused of that ignorance rather quickly. The Red City had chafed under Drem's rule for some years. Hells, half the North cried out for Moura blood. Forty years of heavy-handed doctrine and policy had stripped the poorest in Innisfail of taxes they could ill afford and resources they could hardly spare.

Furthermore, Una bore her share of responsibility on that score. Her untimely disappearance revealed a chasm of weakness within the Cloister that had surely fanned these flames. The people sought new leadership, justly or no.

It seemed the scales had finally tipped in Nema's favor.

Una didn't want to know anymore.

Her heart couldn't process so many tragedies at once.

Damek threw the scroll at her. She let it bounce off her wounded arm and roll into the mud from her horse's flank. "Unless I march up there and force the issue, your mother's name means nothing now. Your inheritance, your power, and your titles: *nothing*. That missive declares you a heretic and traitor, Una, anathema. Your beloved city would have you burn. The way I see it, I've saved your life. When you're done playing the selfish child, you might see sense one day." He watched her closely while she swallowed wave after wave of misery. She averted her gaze, blinking back the hot tears boiling in her eyes. The men around her, making no bones about their disapproval of her, curled their lips and shook their heads.

How many of their number were now dead because of her?

"Lost your tongue?" he pressed on.

While the blame couldn't wholly be lain at Una's feet, neither could she deny she'd played her part. If she hadn't trusted Nema's creature, Gan. If she hadn't tried to run away... before that, if she hadn't buried herself in her studies and shirked her duty to her family, perhaps none of this would have happened. If she'd stayed in Tairngare, would things have been different? Could Nema have been thwarted, or the Moura Clan have presented a unified front?

Who knew?

There was an equal chance that Una would have been murdered in her bed, and the same result achieved, regardless. She might never know, but that wouldn't dispel her guilt, in either case. She was an outcast now. *Anathema*, precisely as Damek had said.

"Una," his tone softened. "Did you really think that old miser in Aes Sidhe would help you? The Sidhe couldn't spare a tinker's fart for any of us. So long as we pay our taxes, keep off their lands, and steer well clear of their kind, they don't care what we do to each other here in Eire. We're all you have, cousin. I hope you come to see that before it is too late." Rather than allow her to spoil his speech with a rebuttal, he kicked his mount into the forward line.

He didn't look back—an old trick, this, but effective.

Una was left alone in a sea of creaking leather and hostile glares.

Friendless, unmoored, and insolvent, she bit her lower lip until it bled and suffered in silence.

As they led their mounts close to the river two days later, Una's chances to escape thinned by the mile. Damek had thought of everything, of course. She was bound day and night. No one spoke to her unless directed. No one touched her or came near her without a thick pair of gloves. No one even looked her way except to feed her, cart her to the privy, or tie her to her cot every night. The first time she attempted to talk to someone, Damek had the poor fellow digging latrines that evening. When she tried to wander deeper into the woods to relieve herself, Damek had her escort replaced with prisoners, each given a lash for every yard she had dared stray.

Una was fed with wooden spoons and drank from wooden dippers. If she drifted too far when they stopped, struggled with her handlers, or made any moves that appeared suspicious in the least, Damek punished the innocent to spite her. After a few days of this, Una had retreated within herself. She moved when and where she was told, kept her eyes resolutely forward, and never opened her mouth but to accept food or water. She might have been a doll for all the trouble she caused. If he wanted her docile, so be it. She would wait, watch, and plan.

Damek made none of the mistakes she'd hoped he would. He didn't converse with her except to impart orders or inquire about her wellbeing. He spent little to no time in her immediate vicinity and scarcely looked at her save when necessary. So much for thinking she could tempt him to lower his guard. She knew escape wouldn't be easy, but Damek was going out of his way to make it impossible.

When the gulls called from the bay and the smoke from Ten Bells rose in the distance, Una swore she wouldn't be trounced. She would get out of this, even if it killed her.

Kaer Yin, she thought.

Please be alive. Please be safe.
I will come back for you.

A GIBBOUS MOON WAS HIGH IN THE LATE AUTUMN SKY WHEN DAMEK'S men wound their way through Ten Bells' twisting lanes. Una was in the lead group, strapped to her saddle as usual, and Damek himself held her reins. Another hope dashed. She had thought of creating a ruckus in the street and praying the townsfolk would intercede long enough for her to get away—no such luck. If the Lord of Clare held her leash, no one would dare challenge him for his prisoner. They were in the South now; Damek's influence held far more weight here than hers. Not many of these folks would even know who she was on sight. Tairngare was a faithful trading partner here, but few Siorai ever made the trip. Merchers and students of the Libellum were the few Tairnganese faces she spied. Her people tended to congregate around the university in the West Moorings, while here in the North End, there were primarily local farmers' stalls, taverns, and stately inns astride the Taran High Road. She imagined they'd cross the Limerick Bridge at first light tomorrow and from there travel due south along the Mallow High Road to Bethany.

It wouldn't be long now. She had but a few days left to get away. Once she was in her father's Keep, she might be chained to a wall for the rest of her days.

Her mind worked so furiously to uncover a solution to her situation that she barely noticed they'd stopped until Damek pulled her into his well-covered arms. Without ado, he set her down, grasped her shoulders, and wheeled her toward an impressive three-story building. *The Ferryman,* its beautifully painted sign read, was easily one of the most well-appointed inns she'd ever clapped eyes upon. This was no surprise. Ten Bells had fainne to spare. Though it wasn't as large a city as Tairngare or Bethany, 'twas likely richer than both. Ten Bells was a thriving commercial hub overflowing with more rich trade guilds, labor unions, and banks than anywhere else in Innisfail. Ten Bells' Mercantile Union traded as far away as balmy Francia in old Europa, and its banks held a fair monopoly over the bustling Tairnganese colony in Cymru. If she wasn't mistaken, the Cymrian Winemakers Guild's Home Office wasn't far from their present position. Just over the Limerick and down the docks, or so she recalled from her studies. Ten Bells owed much of its success to that Guild's founding charter.

Additionally, the city was neutral. It took no sides in any conflict continent-wide. Since almost every other town in Innisfail depended upon it for crucial trade, there was very little danger of that changing anytime soon. When someone makes you rich, you tend to leave them to their business. Sure, men had made the mistake of sacking the city in the past— her grandfather, for one— but when the fainne ran dry, and those men couldn't replicate the Guild's results, Ten Bells' Charter was returned, and their Merchers left well alone.

Only madmen and zealots bite the hand that feeds.

Damek led her over swept cobbles in perfect repair toward the expansive covered veranda yawning from the Inn's northwestern façade. A lamplighter on stilts tapped his way down the street, brandishing his matches like a well-trained magician. A snap, twist, and flare, and another glass bauble would cast ambient light over this charming thoroughfare. Though the rooftops climbed too high to view properly from her angle, every structure's architecture was pre-Transition. Stone rowhouses lined each side of the street with corniced windows and exquisite gabling. *The Ferryman* took up the majority of the southernmost corner.

They were met at the door by a fussy majordomo who led them through a series of candlelit alcoves to a private dining area beneath a sweeping grand staircase. Damek nodded to Martin, whose job it would be to sort the men and see to their accommodations for the evening. The majordomo bent almost double in obeisance to the Lord of Clare before Damek waved him away. A few wealthy patrons were seated inside the dining room. These diners tucked themselves deep within their booths to avoid the attention of so many armed men.

On the opposite side of the vast double-hearth lay a larger taproom occupied by the general public. If the fire wasn't so hot, Una could almost squeak through to the other side and out the front door before anyone could stop her. Her cousin noted the direction of her gaze and wagged his finger, 'no.' Soon, she was unceremoniously shoved into a tall wooden booth near the rear wall. Damek took the seat beside her. Chewing her cheek raw, she faced the polished window to observe the lamplighter's progress; she didn't turn when others squeezed into their booth. Upon his return, Martin, as always, took the seat on his lord's opposite side. Damek's hand found Una's shoulder, his pressure firm.

"Keep your hood up. Speak to no one and try not to let anyone see your face."

She shrugged his hand away.

"Martin," he said aside. "Have you ordered?"

"Yes, My Lord. Whatever was best for our officers in here—soup and bread for the boys outside. Room and board are sorted, too. Fellas will head to the waystation next door, brass upstairs two to a room. You are to have the suite on the top floor as soon as its tenant is vacated. I had them send out for, erm, ladies' things, as well."

"Excellent. What's for supper then?"

Martin shrugged. "Didn't ask. I could eat a bloody horse."

Damek leaned over Una. "Are you thirsty?"

She didn't look at him. A serving girl carried over a heavy tray laden with bread, salted butter, and five tankards of ale. The men leaped at the tray like starved hogs. Damek slapped one fellow's hand and set his tankard in front of Una. "Wait your turn, Ridley. Ladies first."

Una rolled her eyes but didn't waste her breath to argue. She *was* parched. Living in patriarchy was Ridley's bloody problem. Even with her hands bound, she managed to lift and pour half of the heavy vessel's contents down her throat in two gulps. The spiced ale warmed her from her throat to her toes. She hadn't had a decent meal in days; though she was becoming somewhat accustomed to roughing it outdoors, she could hardly refuse one when offered. Amused, Damek slid his trencher of bread and butter toward her. It, too, did not last long. She stopped chewing long enough to take a sip of her ale before returning to work. Damek passed her a second helping, then his own tankard.

She didn't complain.

Siora bless the Brewer's Guild in Ten Bells.

Only *The Hart* in Rosweal had had better ale, and she was working very hard not to think about that at all. Damek wore an odd smile on his face while he watched her cheeks puff out like a chipmunk. Chuckling, Martin also slid her his bread and the hunk of cheese he'd pilfered from another table.

Bless Martin O'Rearden, too, she thought.

"How'd you meet him?" Damek asked, pressing his chin against his knuckles.

"Meef hoo?" she managed around a mouthful of cheese.

"Kaer Yin Adair, of course."

She would not rise to Damek's bait. Not now. She kept her eyes on her food. Torturing herself wouldn't help anyone. Swallowing, her bread went down her throat like a lump of coal. "Does it matter?"

"Yes, damn you. He killed over two-dozen men trying to take you back— one of my best lieutenants, a man of no mean skill. I've never seen someone move like him," Damek frowned at the air as if conjuring Kaer Yin's face. "His reputation was understated, you ask me."

Una said nothing, her heart racing.

He'd come for her? Tried to save her?

After that... *thing* tore a hole in his chest the size of Lough Neagh, he'd come to take her back? She couldn't believe it, not Ben— er— Kaer Yin. He wasn't the type. Yet, Damek had no reason to lie. It certainly didn't make him look the grander for having said anything, did it? She hesitated. "Did— I mean, was he killed in the attempt?"

Damek's smile was cruel. "You first."

The serving girl brought another round of tankards. Damek claimed two more without breaking eye contact. Una reached for hers, but he held it shy of her fingers. She groaned. "If you're asking why he wanted to help me, I don't have an answer for you. He happened by when I was dragged behind a horse and almost beaten to death, and this after I'd managed to escape Rawly and his men."

"You're lying about Rawly. He and his boys were killed by the same man that killed those two beasts in Ferndale and a cadre of armed Corsairs on the road. Come on, cousin. Try showing me at least a fraction of the respect I deserve."

"I don't know what you want me to say. He saved my life, and we traveled together. That's all there is. He thought he might help me over the border, and I intended to help him reclaim his title. We met in the middle."

Damek took a sip of his ale and snorted into his tankard. "You're in love with him."

Una went still as a stone. She didn't respond for quite some time, but when she did, her tone aimed to kill. "*What of it?*"

Damek's hand paused over his trencher, eyes glowing cold murder. "Oh, good. I hoped I'd have the pleasure of watching your heart break."

"My lord—" Martin attempted from his left elbow.

"What do you mean?" Una asked, trying in vain to keep the fear from her voice.

Damck's grin was a knife-slash in the firelight. He toasted her. "The Crown Prince is dead, Una. I watched him fall myself. You're on your own now, love. I hope you're ready for what follows."

2
SIORA'S MERCY

N.E. 508
10, DOR ORAS
TAIRNTARE

Vanna Nema's brilliant golden robes snapped in a bracing northerly wind. She could address the people en masse from her newly constructed pulpit above the Grand Arcade. They came in their thousands, an ocean of faces breaking against the Citadel in unending waves. Nema's smile was like the sun after a storm. She held out her hands to hush her audience, her black miter flashing onyx in the sun. On either side stood Nema's favorites, the Cloister's newest Alta Primas, Pors Yma, and Kalen Hamma. Each wore the blazing scarlet of an office neither had earned nor deserved. They were here for the same reason everyone else on the terrace was today: Nema was now Doma, and they each had played their parts. Further back, a line of newly minted Primas in their bone-white robes and a smattering of grey-cloaked Secundas knelt with their heads bowed in prayer. Parliamentary Judges and representatives of the Union of Commons occupied the dais once reserved for members of the Libella, most of whom stood below Nema's pulpit, nude and covered in filth.

So many people were gathered within and around the Grand Arcade, yet none spoke a word. The only sounds were collective breathing, the gulls crying over the Citadel's high walls, and the occasional whimper from Nema's aristocratic prisoners in the Gallery. Among them, Aoife narrowed her eyes at the Tenma Judge in the next row. Twisting her bruised and bleeding mouth into the darkest sneer she could manage, Aoife shot the sniveling woman a withering glare.

Have some dignity, you milksop bitch.

Feeling Nema's imperious gaze upon her shorn and seeping scalp, Aoife faced forward and raised her chin. Naked as a newborn child, with oozing slashes tearing over her back, buttocks, and arms, she shivered in the chill morning air. Her spine was as straight as she could make it. Although beaten, burned, cut, and humiliated, she would not give her ruthless grandmother the satisfaction of seeing her cowed.

Let the soft-bellied whores around her make a fuss; Nema would get no such pleasure from Aoife.

Did Nema's mouth quirk a bit at the corner? *Good*.

If the old witch wanted a show... by Balor, she would get one.

Aoife's one consolation stood three rows back, reams of snot dribbling down his fleshy chins. Quivering like gelatin, Fawa Gan was too weak to stand beneath Nema's judgment. Rather, he knelt in a weeping, pitiable mass of torn flesh. Aoife didn't have to look at him to know he'd pissed himself recently. She could smell it from her place at the front, in the very terminus of Nema's vengeance.

If Aoife was going to die today, she could but pray she got to watch that fat pederast meet his maker first. How he came to cower among the condemned had everything to do with the woman in the center of their company. Basa Alvra, easily the oldest amongst them and by far the most powerful, had fingered him as Drem's erstwhile informant. Basa was the former Doma's cousin and was once the most influential politician in Tairngare. Aoife had to hand it to the ancient hag; she had a pair of bollocks that would shame any man in Innisfail.

Basa hadn't been whipped or scourged as Aoife, and so many others had been— she was far too old. Instead, she'd been stripped of her clothing and forced to carry her daughter's severed hand around her neck like a trophy.

Basa and Ana had been caught on the docks at Drogheda, attempting to flee to the colonies for aid. Ana had died under interrogation, and Basa had been present for the occasion. Even with her daughter's rotting flesh resting against her sagging collarbone, she did not bend. She stood tall and as straight as she could make herself at seventy-four years of age, her wild white curls blowing around her head like a stormcloud. Basa revealed nothing but condescending contempt for these proceedings, the new government, and especially the new Doma. Nema ignored her, but Aoife knew... deep down, she seethed. For Basa's arrogance, Nema would kill every Alvra supporter in this crowd before she granted her adversary the mercy of death.

"Good people of Tairngare," Nema's voice carried far and wide without embellishment. This was more than simple acoustics, as presence had ever been one of Nema's foremost gifts. "We stand here at the birth of a new era. Too long have we suffered the whims and rages of an elite caste with little regard for the lives of those they were ordained to serve. In Siora's name, we abjure them. In Siora's name, we strike their works from the Register. In Siora's name, we seek justice."

Aoife gritted her teeth.

Get on with it. I'm ready.

The people outside murmured the appropriate prayers, though she could tell their hearts weren't committed. Until recently, Tairngare had been one of the world's safest, most privileged cities. Since the coup Aoife had herself helped foment, every possible change was occurring much too fast for many to keep up. Last month, they'd had a thriving elite class and a Doma who rarely interfered in the commoners' lives. Now, everything was different. Nema's reformist government was made possible for the love she inspired among the merchants, guilds, and the poor... but many of them had no idea how far she'd planned to go. In just a few weeks, the nobles had been ousted from the Libella, and The Union of Commons had taken over Parliament. What few nobles remained in the Red City were gathered here, condemned by the new Doma and her cronies in the Commons. When news of Drem Moura's escape from the Cloister swept through the city, the rioting and mayhem had reached such a fevered pitch that it had taken the Cohort nearly a week to put down the mob and douse the fires. A week after, people were dragged from their homes and imprisoned by the fledgling government, not all of them loyalists, either. Indeed, the general public appeared to be reeling from the violence and disarray that trailed in Nema's wake. Her rise to power had been a painfully swift but bloody affair. Aoife didn't doubt many folks who supported the new Doma a half-month before had discovered they'd bitten off far more than they could chew.

Nema had been waiting for this for almost fifty years.

She had no intention of leaving any dissenters alive to challenge her later. As for Aoife, well... she had failed Nema for the last time. Allowing the Moura Domina to escape was the final nail in Aoife's coffin.

She's dragging this out to spite me.

"If any among you wish to speak for the condemned, please step forward." Nema gestured to the knot of nude flesh on display. "Without their fine clothes and dazzling jewels, they no longer seem so untouchable, do they? These slavers— these base, corrupting idolaters— see them *as they are*. They are not beautiful, powerful, strong, or superior. They are weak, simpering mortals with more flesh than honor. Who among you pities these sad creatures? Which of you bears compassion for those who spare none?"

Here it comes, Aoife thought with an irritable smirk.

Basa Alvra threw back her head and laughed. Her audience scarcely moved a muscle save to gawp at the old Alta's manic outburst. Aoife hadn't expected this, and from the expression on Nema's pinched face, neither had she.

"Well? No one has anything to say, hm?" taunted Basa.

Nema folded her hands. "Of course, the accused has the right to a last word in my court. Though I warn you, old schemer, you'll find few sympathetic ears here."

Basa looked around. "Oh, I dunno. It seems to me plenty stand behind me."

To Nema's intense ire, Aoife knew, that statement earned several chuckles from many places in the Grand Gallery, even from among Nema's supporters. Basa, massive sagging teats swinging in the breeze, spat for the Commons' benefit. "That scrawny bitch up there would have you idiots believe she has your interests at heart. Tell me, short of the few corrupt witches that supported her rise to power, how much richer are any of you that have laid us low? Hm? Do you feel safer, more respected, and better protected? I hope so since the streets are filled day and night with her foot soldiers."

"Basa Alvra, you stand accused—"

"You said your piece, you withered old cunt. You have us standing out here in the cold in naught but our skins, waiting to die. Where is the *justice*?

Without evidence, trials, or representation, you have declared us guilty. The wealthier our families, the greater our guilt." Basa tugged her chin at the horrified Merchers gathered far below the dais. "She'll be after you all next, mark me. History's full of over-reaching despots like your new Doma. Her 'reformist' smell will sour, and you'll all realize what a terrible mistake you've made today."

"*Basa Alvra, this is—*"

"Executing anyone with the power to challenge her on her coronation day?" Basa sucked her teeth over a wry grin. "Best of luck, you bloody gorgeous fools."

"Captain, if you please?" Nema gestured, and a Cohort officer reached over and punched the old woman in the gut. She staggered to one liver-spotted knee. Before she could gasp out another blistering reproach of the new Doma, the Captain wrenched her head back while a second officer pried her mouth open. Amidst her gurgles and grunts, they dug into the open cavity with a pair of iron tongs, stretched her tongue out as far as it would go— and severed the offensive muscle as if carving mutton for luncheon.

Aoife stood very still, watching the spectacle without passion, even as those around her moaned and fidgeted in fear. She, for one, had seen worse... had *done* worse.

This was merely a prelude.

When a lump of hot coal was shoved against the bloodied stump between her teeth, Basa fainted in a pool of her own blood and piss. Aoife looked up to meet her grandmother's eye. Nema was smiling. "Alta Alvra is such a brave woman, despite her many failings. This Court believes that she would best serve Siora as a living but silent reminder of idolatry's folly. Take her below," she purred.

The Captain and his assistants hauled Basa up and carted her somewhere within the Citadel's black bowels. Aoife imagined she would likely be trotted out at every gathering and paraded before the masses. If Basa had kept her mouth shut, she might have escaped such a macabre fate. Surely, it would have been better to watch her friends put to the Spark than rot in the public eye.

"Now," said Nema, beaming at Aoife. "I think we've had enough entertainment for one day, don't you? Pors?"

Pors Yma stepped forward on the dais. She raised a fist, and suddenly, Aoife and everyone in her company crumpled to the ground, twitching and writhing in unimaginable pain. The veins in Aoife's neck seized, and the blood halted mid-course. She felt her eyes and nose drain of fluid— of oxygen. No air would enter or leave her lungs, frozen in place as she was, a spider in a jar.

"As Siora's representative on earth and Doma of The Cloister of the Eternal Flame, I condemn you all to die by emulation. We are not so crude as to draw out your suffering for our amusement. Kalen?"

The Hamma Alta Prima sidled up beside Pors, whose brow was damp with perspiration. Manipulation was hard work, especially for women who had no business pretending to have truly mastered it. Kalen mumbled under her breath. A slow serpent of flame undulated beneath Aoife's flesh. First, it uncoiled itself from her core, then slithered beneath her ribs. Inside her chest, she knew her ribs blackened. She exhaled smoke as her eyes filled with blood. Choking on cinders, she gurgled uselessly, unable to move far enough to claw out her own throat. From the inside, she burned. Though she couldn't see beyond the thickening red haze nor hear anything save for the fat popping in her ears, Aoife was aware that those behind her had already succumbed to Hamma's Spark. Moaning, they collapsed as charred smoldering sticks against the flagstones.

The pain was exquisite, but Aoife did not die.

Her skin popped open at every joint, releasing torrents of steam and hissing fluids. What was left of her hair caught next. The kiss of these flames seemed almost a relief in contrast with the raging inferno within. She heard the crowd whisper, and felt their eyes on her, disbelieving and petrified. Then, as suddenly as the assault began, it stopped. Cold, clean air hit the wreckage of her lungs with startling clarity. At last, the cauldron in her airway subsided, and she coughed up bits of black she knew had once been lung tissue.

Doubled over, Aoife could squeeze out the barest wail.

Nema's laughter rang throughout the open-air chamber.

Aoife titled her working ear toward the sound. One of her eyes had burst from its socket, but the other merely swam with blood and soot. She could see the sky above her grandmother's saffron robes. It seemed to have snowed in the Grand Arcade that morning. Great ribbons of ash swirled overhead. She turned her face away. Her nearest neighbor disintegrated beside her. This formerly important someone was a whirl of dust flirting with the wind. Aoife croaked a half-scorched scream. Everywhere she looked, human beings were reduced to piles of ash; even their bones were no match for Hamma's flames.

Dazed, Aoife pushed herself up to her elbows. Behind her, she heard a familiar wheeze. Summoning her last ounce of strength, she took a peek beneath her blistered forearm. Gan, singed and bloodied from the crown of his steaming scalp to the soles of his formerly corpulent feet, looked back at her in shock. His eyes, too, had been spared the worst.

The better to see, my dear, Aoife knew.

Every condemned prisoner but she and Gan floated on the morning air; whether to Gods or grace, she didn't care to know. The nobles of Tairngare might drift toward the heavens, but they would never gain entry. Their every thought and feeling, their very lives, were fodder for storms. She was reminded of an ancient quote: '*But the devils cannot interfere with the stars*' and wanted to howl with laughter.

If only she could. The ruin of her throat had other ideas, alas.

Unto dust thou wilt return.

Aoife admired the perversity of Nema's justice. The crone might have been a Kneeler for the poetic brutality of this moment.

The horror of this scene was not lost on the witnesses above, either. Aoife was beyond caring how the complicit bastards in the Gallery covered their mouths or fainted away in revulsion. She wasn't moved by their cries of protest or the chorus of weeping that chased the desecrated into the atmosphere. She wasn't even afraid. After a while, she could focus on Nema's triumphant leer. Pors and Kalen had crumpled and were now being carted away to enjoy their imminent—and, Aoife hoped, fatal—Spark drag. Their task done, Nema had no further use of either. Such a vulgar display of power might very well cost Hamma her life. Nema wouldn't mind, of course. She certainly hadn't chosen Hamma because she cared a whit for the odious lickspittle's wellbeing. She'd selected her for this purpose alone.

Aoife's hatred burrowed deeper and burned hotter than any part of her that an inferior Milesian had Manipulated. Why *had* Nema spared her and Gan? She didn't have much time to ponder her dubious luck when her forehead struck the slate beneath her with a hollow thud.

Before the night claimed her, she was granted a final thought.

What a joy it is to be Grandmama's favorite.

3
THE ART OF NECESSITY

n.e. 508
13, ÐOR ORAS
ROSWEAL

Rian took several deep breaths at the door. She had no time for this. With half a dozen critical patients downstairs awaiting her attention and a total deficit of sleep, she'd rather have left Kaer Yin's cronies for later. Though, as always, she was not asked for her opinion. She groaned, resting her forehead against the painted jamb. What she wouldn't give for a hot cup of tea, a bit of bread, and a week-long nap. The blond oak tree standing behind her cleared his throat. Rian spared him a bit of curled lip. Niall was this one's name, or so she thought she'd heard him called. Honestly, she didn't care. These Dannan brutes looked much the same. Scowling, Niall pushed the door open and none-too-gently nudged her forward. She immediately nosedived into someone else, who grunted and knocked her into yet another oversized Sidhe. Clawing herself upright in the crush of towering males crammed into the shrinking room, Rian growled and dug her nails into the next fool who tried to step on her.

The big bastard flinched as if a favorite kitten had scratched him.

She'd had about enough of this, truth be told.

"There she is," remarked a rich, deep voice. Rian tried not to sneer. "Let her through."

Beneath an exaggerated portrait of a stout but curvaceous woman of middling years was the subject herself. With her greying auburn hair coiled over one round shoulder and her bandaged fingers clutching her favorite bone-handled pipe, Barb Dormer leaned against her massive fox-footed desk with a pinched expression. Beside her sat Robin, shirt open to the waist, while Rose fretted over the seeping wound around his midsection. He was working on a dwindling bottle of Gilcannon's best uishge while the Prince of Connaught held him fast to his chair with a firm hand. The faintest irascible frown marred the cold perfection of Tam Lin O'Ruiadh's face. Robin's stitches had come undone.

In true Innish fashion, he'd sooner drink himself into a stupor than admit he was in pain.

Rian blew a lock of hair out of her eyes. "Wonderful. Who let him get like this?"

Barb took a long pull from her pipe. "No one *lets* Robin Gramble do anythin', love."

Robin burst into song on cue, tone-deaf as a toad in a bucket.

"Wonderful," Rian repeated with a sigh. "Well, hold him down."

Tam Lin waggled his fingers. Three blond mountains shuffled over with persistent irritation. The largest of them, Tam Lin's lieutenant Shar Lianor, slunk behind Robin's chair while Rian rolled up her sleeves. A dangerous gleam flashed in Robin's eyes, and upon the next breath, he had his dagger up and swinging about.

Barb artfully dodged away when the knot of Dannan males descended upon her stammering mate. She shook her head. "Ye'll have to brain him, ye know? He'll fight till he's minced."

Robin's grunts and thrashing limbs did little to advance their cause. Through the muddle of elbows, knees, and shouts, Rian could see the gash in his side seeping anew. "Easy, Siora, damn you! He's bleeding all over the floor."

Tam Lin shot her an unkind glare with his face having gone as red as his hair. "We have your permission then, Mistress Dormer?"

Barb shrugged. Robin's dagger drew a scarlet line down Niall's forearm, and he guffawed in unintelligible victory. "Don't see as ye have a choice."

Tam Lin wasted no more time; drawing himself up to his full height, he brought his fist into Robin's clenched jaw. Robin slumped a bit, but the blow did not finish him. Sluggish as a newborn colt, he turned to grin at his attacker, a thin line of bloody spittle dangling from his swollen lower lip. "*Herne!*" Tam Lin barked and struck again. This time, Robin crumpled to the floorboards. Shaking his aching fist, the Prince of Connaught laughed. "Great Gods, that's one Milesian I'd rather not tangle with in the dark."

Everyone laughed at his astonishing wit... save Rian, of course. "If you've broken his jaw to boot, I'll have you know, you're going to be the one feeding him through a tube. I have enough to do, thank you."

His smile flickered as he blinked back at her, his long golden lashes sweeping against his impossibly high cheekbones. He was beautiful, as all Sidhe were—outwardly, anyway. His build, height, and lovely violet eyes did not impress her in the least. Rian despised her blood enough not to value its benefit in others. Her mother had always warned her that *a serpent is most colorful when venomous.* "Mistress... ah, I'm sorry. What was your name again?"

Rian was too tired to project any outward emotion, even irritation, though he'd been told her name half a thousand times already. She'd been running back and forth for days, stitching cuts, mending bones, and treating myriad burns since they'd all returned from the Greensward more than a week before. Indeed, if she didn't return to it soon, she'd probably faint. "Rian Guinness," she said, her voice bland as her mental acuity at the moment. "You summoned me, remember?"

He snapped a finger as if in sudden recollection. "Of course. Master Gramble here needs fresh stitching, I find. I fear Mistress Dormer here is unequal to the task. She asked for you, not I. You know one another, I take it?" His eyes slid between them like a child seeking to instigate a brawl.

"We've met," offered Barb helpfully. "Wasn't under the best circumstances, ye might say."

"A shame," he remarked without a shred of warmth. "Now would be a perfect opportunity to mend impressions, moving forward. Don't you agree? Now, Mistress... ah, damn it. What was your name again, girl?"

Rian bit her tongue. "Guinness."

"Right. Master Gramble and I have many matters to discuss and prepare for. That will prove impossible if he falls feverish. Also, though she has refused, I'd like it very much if you would also see to our hostess' hands."

"What happened?" asked Rian dispassionately.

Barb pursed her lips. "Struck a wall when I saw what them Souther cunts did to my *Hart*. Bout a temper, nothin' more."

"Hm," Rian sniffed. "That finger looks broken. Needs a splint."

Barb took one look at Rian's face and snickered. "I don't need nursin', thanks very much. 'Sides, ye'd sooner bleed me than mend me. Wouldn't ye, girlie?"

Rian raised a brow at her. "I don't let my dislike of someone affect my practice, Barb. Lucky for you."

"I don't need charity, little miss."

"Suit yourself. Now, if you will set Master Gramble upright in that window seat, I'll see what I can do about these seeping wounds." She gestured to Robin's snoring carcass on the floor. She'd already stitched him together twice. She silently swore this would be the last bloody time. Whoever kept giving him uishge could tend to him themselves from here on out. She reached into her bag for a clean needle, thread, and what few bandages Rose had managed to scrounge from the laundry a few hours before.

Tam Lin's brow darkened. "I'm asking to be polite. Would you prefer an order?"

"This is not Aes Sidhe, and I am not your subject. Now," she held up her fingers to tick off items one by one. "I'll need boiling water, oil of lavender, and more clean linens. There should be some left hanging on the line in the alley; if not, petticoats will do. We may have run through most passable material at this point already. Let's see. I'll need more thread... I left some on the bar downstairs... uishge, though not for bloody drinking, mind. He's had plenty. Also, for Siora's sake, a pot of tea if your men can manage it?"

If she didn't get some into her soon, she might fall down dead.

Tam Lin just stared. Barb laughed herself purple. Rian couldn't see what was so funny. There was a bleeding man on the floor who might now be wholly concussed. What was so funny about that? Tam Lin's men shuffled their feet, searching for anything else to fix their attention upon. The prince sighed. "Anything else, *Mistress* Guinness?"

Rian thought about it for a moment but ultimately shook her head. "The tea first, if you please? I haven't slept in some time."

Barb wiped at her eyes. "Siora, girl. Ye, I like fine."

Tam Lin didn't turn. He glared at Rian for an indeterminable length as if she were a peculiar sort of insect he could not identify. "Shar?"

"*Mo Flaith*?"

"See to Mistress Rian's requests."

Ah, so he did know her given name after all. *Bastard*.

Shar dipped his blond head and strode through the door, wearing a poorly concealed grin. He, at least, Rian found moderately tolerable. Tam Lin crossed his arms while Rian confiscated Robin's discarded bottle of uishge. Niall and Derck hauled Gramble from the floor and worked him into the worn cushions of Barb's window seat. Rian made a face when she got a closer look. His bandages were filthy, and he'd lost half a dozen stitches at first glance. She was beginning to wonder why she bothered sewing these fools back together if they were just going to get drunk and destroy all of her hard work.

She had a mind to go to bed for the next week and let them all sort themselves.

"How fares my cousin this morning?" Tam Lin asked jovially.

She prodded Robin's wound and frowned. "He, too, will live. Though I daresay, I'm not sure how with that hole in his chest."

"That would be Diarmid's handiwork. I'm amazed the old codger bothered. I suppose the question of favorite nephew has been summarily answered." Rian had no idea what he was on about, but she assumed he meant that Diarmid— whom she'd met as Faris, the man who'd trapped her and Una in the Otherworld on Samhain— had used some sort of dark magic to heal the majority of Kaer Yin's wounds. She couldn't be sure what a spell of that sort would cost— and all magic costs, she understood— but she'd be willing to bet the Dannan sorcerer was equally as wounded as Kaer Yin. "Anyway," Tam Lin continued," I suppose I'm asking if he'll be worth a shite in the foreseeable future?"

She pried a pair of tiny scissors from of her hem and squinted over Robin's bare ribs. "Was he ever? I'm not sure what you'd like me to say."

Tam Lin threw back his head and laughed. "Fair enough, Mistress! I need to know if I should plan an extended stay in this, erm, charming hamlet?"

She rolled a shoulder. "Ben's in a terrible temper since you ask, but I have at least a hundred patients gathered beneath this roof that shares his mood. He's alive. Best I can tell you."

LATER, AFTER HAVING SEWN ROBIN'S CUTS BACK TOGETHER AND begrudgingly changing the bandages on Barb's hands, Rian scarcely looked up when Tam Lin gently steered her into Kaer Yin's room by the elbow. She was too tired to complain of his touching her and far too emotionally drained to argue. She had a heap of tasks to see to after this, and her lack of sleep was taking a heavy toll. If Tam Lin noticed her reticence, he refrained from comment. In the doorway, a slight sound from within the chamber snapped Rian's head up. The sight she beheld there sent a fresh surge of furious vitality straight to her brain. Kaer Yin lay on his back, overtaking the small bed and its homely flower-patterned coverlet. Rose, who'd been charged with caring for Rian's remaining patients for the day while Rian was busy tending to their betters upstairs, had tucked herself against him, feeding him spoonfuls of raw, stinking uishge.

"Ben!" Rian barked, spilling her fifth cup of tea down the remnants of her once presentable homespun skirt. Her head pounding, she slammed her empty cup down on the larder so hard that it cracked. "*You*," she pointed to Rose, who bloody well knew better. "Out. *Now.*"

Rose simpered beautifully; she'd had years of practice. Too bad Rian was a woman and not over-fond of anyone much, least of all a hard-worn prostitute of Rose's ilk. "I came to see if Ben... I mean, His Highness, needed anything while ye were occupied. It's a wee bit of uishge, Rian. Nothin' to get upset over."

Tam Lin leaned against the doorjamb, watching Rian intently. "I think you've poked the bear here, cousin. Not enamored of drink, this one."

Kaer Yin, the bloody stupid Crown Prince of Innisfail, squirmed under Rian's murderous gaze. "Ah, right. Rosie, love?"

"Hm?" Rose breathed, unable to tear her eyes away from his moronic face.

Rian narrowed her eyes to slits.

"They need you downstairs. Would you mind leaving the bottle?" He asked, fidgeting.

Rian stamped her foot. "No bloody uishge, damn you. Take that bottle with you and bring no more in here, or I swear to Siora, you'll regret it, Rose."

Rose winced from the venom in Rian's tone.

Kaer Yin patted Rose's knee. "Best do as she says, Rosie."

She pouted, but you don't become a favorite in a place like *The Hart* by arguing with your patrons. She got up with exaggerated sloth, leaning appreciably forward here or suggestively flouncing there. By the time she made it out of the damned door, both males in attendance had long forgotten Rian. With a vicious jerk, she pulled Kaer Yin forward by his collar to mash another pillow behind his head. Not for comfort, mind; she needed to change his dressings. "Ouch!" he cried, reaching out to curb her manhandling.

Rian slapped his hands away as she would a child of five and set a stare on him that would boil water. "Sit still, or I swear, I will make this hurt."

Tam Lin hovered behind her. She ignored him and went about unraveling yesterday's bandages. Being comprised of laundered burlap and scraps of linen hose, the dressing was far from ideal, but given what they'd all been through in the past two weeks, they might have been spun of gold and rainbows. There wasn't much left in *The Hart* but splinters and broken glass these days. Ben winced under her fingers. "*Créatúr fíochmhar, an ceann sin.*" Tam Lin remarked dryly.

"*Olc, go fírinneach,*" answered Kaer Yin.

"*Ní haon ionadh nach bhfuil fear céile ann.*"

"*Aye, bheadh sí marbh air.*"

More laughter. Rian's cheeks burned.

Tam Lin cocked his head. "*Fós, tá sí thara bheith álainn le haghaidh faerie.*"[1]

That did it.

"*Gabhaim buíochas leataraon le cuimne a thabhairt go bhfuilim sa seaomra, agus níl aon rud cearr le mo chluasa.*"[2] She spat in rapid, fluent Ealig.

Tam Lin's mouth snapped shut. Ben gave her a knowing smirk. He'd never asked her if she spoke his language, but the discovery didn't seem to surprise him in the least. He didn't mind Tam Lin's obvious embarrassment either. "Fine." He tactfully looked away from Tam Lin's lowered brows. If the Prince of Connaught didn't already know that his cousin was a bit of an ass already,

---

1   Tam Lin: 'Fierce creature, that.'
Kaer Yin: 'Evil, truly.'
Tam Lin: 'No wonder she doesn't have a husband.'
Kaer Yin: 'She would have killed him.'
Tam Lin: 'Still, she's quite lovely for a faerie.'
2   Rian: 'I'll thank you both to recall that I am in the room, and there's nothing wrong with my ears.'

he certainly did now. That would teach him to talk over others as if they didn't exist, wouldn't it? "To business then. What's your diagnosis, Rian?"

"Well," she took a breath. "You've two broken ribs, a cracked breastplate, damage to your collarbone— I pulled teeth out of that, thank you for the nightmares— a fracture in your left forearm, three broken fingers, and of course, a massive hole in your chest that should have killed you. Aside from that, millions of scratches, several concerning cuts and contusions... and that's just your torso. Not to worry, though, as fast as you purebloods heal, I'll have to rebreak whatever doesn't heal properly and reset it for you."

Kaer Yin grimaced. "Saying what, exactly?"

"You're lucky to be alive right now. Why push things any further, you blithering idiot?"

"Now now, Mistress," cooed Tam Lin. "Don't fall in love with him. He's a scoundrel, you know. The very worst sort."

Roundly ignoring Tam Lin, she inspected the nearly fatal wound in Kaer Yin's chest. The skin was puckered pink and red, but it looked and smelled better than it had the day before. He *did* heal remarkably fast, thank Siora. She knew what he was waiting to hear, and maybe, just maybe, she had better news today. She sighed. "Two months, at best."

"No bloody way am I going to lay here that long."

"You don't have a choice. What good will you be to her riddled with holes?"

A muscle kept time in his jaw. "I can't wait that long, damn you!"

Tam Lin took a seat on Kaer Yin's right, cleaning his nails with a jeweled dagger. "Is this about that bloody woman again? I've told you repeatedly, it will come to no avail. Your father will never—"

"*Clúdaigh do bhéal*, Tam Lin."[3]

Tam Lin pointed the dagger at him. "You wouldn't be so pissy about it if I wasn't right. Forget her. She's but a Milesian sweetmeat anyway. When we go home, you can have your pick of far more suitable women."

Kaer Yin slapped the dagger out of Tam Lin's hand, his eyes gone a terrible silver. "Say that again, *ceathrar*, and I'll cut your tongue out with your own blade."

Rian, sensing another pointless brawl on the horizon, moved between them. Her mother always told her the Sidhe burned hot as a brushfire then cold as the wind through a cairn. She never believed such extremes were

---

3   Kaer Yin: 'Shut your mouth, Tam Lin.'

possible until she witnessed so many together at once. There were fights nearly every night; almost all resulted in bloodshed, and few were ever started over something worthwhile. Oddly, despite the heat of every disagreement, no friendships ever suffered from the violence. Indeed, as if the roughhousing and discord brought them closer together. Rian struggled to equate her calm, sweet mother with this gang of overgrown brutes. "Will you two *please* be better behaved than your men downstairs? I swear. I've seen wee bairns with better temperaments."

Tam Lin rolled his eyes. "It's our way, little one. Yours too, if you aren't too lofty for self-reflection?"

She opened and closed her mouth like a goldfish.

Kaer Yin guffawed and tried not to hiss when the movement jostled his ribs. "He's got you there, Rian."

She flushed. "*Tá tú an dá leathcheanns.*"[4]

A round of chuckles did little to cool the heat in her cheeks. Clearing her throat, she patted Kaer Yin's wound with the nettle and honey salve she'd brought from home all those weeks ago. He was a mute patient for a while. A faraway look settled in his storm-bright eyes. She pursed her lips. "She's alive, Ben. That's what matters. They need her too much to harm her."

"For now," he said, swallowing hard.

"You did everything you could. You can't blame yourself."

"I don't. I blame Bishop, and when I see him again, I'll make him pay for it."

"No woman is worth so much trouble, Yin. I beg you to let this go," argued Tam Lin, more cautiously this time. "You're finally free to return home after all these years. Let's leave the Milesians to themselves."

"I am the Crown Prince of Innisfail, Tam Lin. The Milesians are my people too. Bishop broke the Ard Rí's law to take Una back. Even if I didn't care for her, it would nevertheless be my responsibility to ensure my father's justice is done. I don't understand why you're fighting me so hard on this."

Tam Lin sheathed his dagger with a sullen shrug. "The last time you went South, I didn't see you for nearly thirty years. I don't want to lose my cousin again over some Milesian girl," he paused, tugging his chin at Rian. "What's your opinion of this lunacy, then? Surely you don't think it's wise to march on

---

4   Rian: 'You're both idiots.'

Bethany with a handful of Sidhe, especially for such an absurd reason? What do *you* think?"

Rian blew a lock of hair out of her eye. "Well, you don't know, Una, Your Highness."

"What does that have to do with my extremely rational argument?"

"None of us would be alive now if it weren't for her. Everyone in Rosweal owes her. Me and Ben, especially."

"So, you support his cockamamie plan, then?"

She gave Kaer Yin a long look. "Yes, I do."

"For *Herne*'s sake, why?"

She twisted her lip sideways at him. "Because I love her too."

"Is she sleeping?" Barb asked from the crack in the doorway.

"Yes, finally." Kaer Yin replied, motioning her and Dabs forward. "Though, I'd hide that teapot somewhere she'll never find it. If she realizes you've drugged her again, I'll never hear the end of it."

Barb giggled. "Poor mite. She'll work herself to death one day, won't she?"

"Probably."

Barb patted Rian's flaxen head where it lay against Kaer Yin's mattress.

Tam Lin had no clue what to make of all this. "Why not go and rest?"

"Och," Barb blew smoke at him. "Rosweal don't have a proper doctor, ye know. After them Southers came and went, we have lots o'folks needin' care. This tiny slip o'a girl takes it all upon herself. Won't hear o'rest until all have been seen to. She's a bleedin' Kneeler's angel, ye ask me, no matter how sharp her tongue. There ye are, Dabs, be careful with her now! Make sure ye give her Tansy's quilt. She wanted her to have it."

Even with the fair-haired Dannans clogging the room like hulking tolls, Dabney's bulk was impressive. Gentle as a giant with a tiny bird, he plucked Rian into his arms and carefully laid her over his shoulder. Her long thin fingers trailed down his back as he ducked through the open doorway and into the hall with her, passing several curious Dannan faces along the way.

Tam Lin stared after them for a while, as if the mystery of her character would materialize in the darkened alcove like smoke. "What a strange girl."

"Lin, you have *no* idea," Kaer Yin chuckled while slowly resettling himself against his mound of pillows. He was ash-pale and weak, but there was a glimmer in his silver eyes that Tam Lin was happy to see returned. Maybe the girl did know what she was doing.

"How did you meet her again, cousin?"

"Oh, well, it's a *very* long story...."

"Never mind all that now," Barb interjected, lighting another wad of witchroot in her pipe. "We have matters to discuss. Robin, bless his larcenous heart, won't be fit for much for a few days. Has almost as many marks on him as ye do, Ben."

"I know. I gave him most of them," Kaer Yin snickered.

"Well, that's as may be, but my sweet man don't have yer constitution, Yer Arseness," she blew another cloud of smoke and pointed. "It's Robin ye need to see all this through, ye know?"

"I do. He's my best friend, no matter how many times he's tried to kill me in recent weeks. We're of the same mind on this issue."

"Good. Now, can we count on ye lot?"

She was asking Tam Lin directly. He held up his hands. "Under protest."

Kaer Yin groaned. "Let it bloody go, already!"

Barb tapped her teeth. "Does that mean yer in or out?"

Tam Lin folded his arms and exhaled heavily. "In. My men too, as promised."

Her smile was macabre in the poorly lit chamber. "Well then, gather close, and I'll tell ye everythin' ye want to know about the Machine City, starting with her brothels...."

4

MY BROTHER'S KEEPER

n.e. 508
15, dor oras
bethany

Henry caught his son in a bear hug, once more amazed by the breadth of the lad's shoulders. Had he grown again so soon? It had been less than two months since they'd met in the cellars below the Great Hall, yet it might have been years. Henry patted Micah's broadening back with an appreciative smile. Was he taller too? By the Lord! Micah's brilliant golden curls hung low over his beaming face. He wore the cobalt and scarlet of Donahugh's house, and Henry was proud to see they suited his handsome son quite well. Henry stepped back a pace. What was Patrick feeding his sons to effect such a marked change? He forced the expected knot of bitterness that always rustled when he was allowed to speak to his own children, deep down. There would be time enough for all of that later.

For now, he must not show Micah one ounce of doubt or fear. God had plans for Henry's boys... for them all.

"There now, let's have a look at you, lad! You've grown a mile since last I saw you. Where are all these bloody muscles coming from?"

Micah gave him a sheepish grin. "I've been training with Carrigan and Grimley, father. Six hours a day. The few reprieves I'm allowed are on Feast Days and at table in the evenings."

His diction was much improved as well. Henry's heart swelled with pride. "That is wonderful news, my son. Isaac? Is he training also?"

"Not yet. Uncle says he must learn his letters and table manners before he'll be allowed the tiltyard. He's doing quite well, though he can't wait to swing a sword of his own. You should see him, father. He's already Uncle's height."

The second knot of bitterness was more difficult to swallow than the first.

"Is he? Well, that's as God would have things. Please send him my love and tell him we'll be reunited again before long."

Micah ruffled his hair, clearly anxious that he'd inadvertently wounded his father. "He misses you too, Da. Old Grimshaw speaks of your many victories all the time. Isaac lives for them."

Henry waved this placation away and steered his son toward the stairs, which spilled out of the dungeons above and into the river below their feet. In the dark, the River Lee slapped lazily against the castle's stone moorings. This cavern was an underground port designed to ensure deliveries of goods and services were private and out of the way. For Henry's purposes, it served as his sole means of transport in or out of the Keep. That Micah could visit with him here was an artfully engineered prospect that had cost Henry several hundred fainne to procure.

Though, this was neither here nor there.

"No matter, no matter, my boy. Now, let us sit here together and have a chat. Hm?"

Micah's smile faded but allowed himself to be led. No doubt, he was already acutely aware of what his father wished to discuss, as anyone within a hundred leagues of the city knew Una Moura Donahugh was on her way home. Micah gulped. "Father, I know what you would say, and I would like to remind you that—"

"Micah, if you mention Damek again, I shall strike you. You are not some defenseless weakling, are you? Or is your uncle training you for nothing?"

"No, father."

"Well then, what is there to remind me of?"

"I should like to be friends with my cousin. I don't wish to be enemies. I would like to serve at his side, as you did, with my uncle. Why is that wrong? Doesn't the Lord wish for families to support one another?"

Micah had been practicing this speech.

Henry tried not to chuckle. How innocent were the young? "Micah, I've told you already. Damek Bishop will not allow any man, especially not a legitimized Donahugh man, to share his dais for long. You were enemies the moment my brother discovered you and will be so until one of you is dead. Don't forget this again. It is not just your life and safety you must protect. Isaac will be Damek's prey after he's sunk his talons into you."

"I don't see why things should be so. She's a godless wanton, from what I hear. They say the Siorai in Tairngare f-fornicate with the inferior males of their order during their rituals. Jasper told me that my cousin was even with child once, but she sacrificed the infant to her goddess for power."

Henry chewed the interior of his lip. He could not tell Micah that Una and Damek had been twice married and divorced by her father in pursuit of other wealthy lords, willing to exchange armaments for her dowry. "The customs in Tairngare are not your concern, Micah. Nor hers anymore, by the by. She's a Donahugh. I don't care if she has a hairlip and walks with a limp; you're going to marry her and sire an heir of your own. This is your duty, and you *will* accept it or die. You can't go back."

"It's not—"

"No one said life was fair, Micah."

Micah groaned. Henry prayed for the strength not to abuse his son physically.

"Look, boy. She's rumored to be beautiful. Hells, my nephew, has been obsessed with her all of his life. From what I hear, she's kind, intelligent, and honest. What more do you want? She's the most desirable woman in Innisfail, and you're whingeing because she isn't a virgin."

"Father, God forbids us to f-fornicate before marriage."

"Aye, so? She's not of our faith. It will be your responsibility to teach her how about our God and his mighty works. Can't you see what an opportunity this is?"

Micah hadn't thought about Una converting to their faith. Again, Henry could tell what he was thinking. He really must do something about the boy's face. Every thought Micah had was visible as the sun in a clear blue sky. "I suppose when you put it that way... but what about Damek? He's handsome, they tell me. Rich in his own right. Powerful. The people love him. How do I steal any woman from someone like him?"

Henry couldn't help but snort. "Don't you worry about Damek, son. She hates him. All you need do is be kind to her. Speak to her. Treat her with respect and admiration, and she'll be yours in short order." He did not say that she had been so mistreated by her father, by Damek, and every man in either's service that she'd cling to any act of kindness like a lone buoy in a roiling sea. "Be her friend, Micah. Her confidant. Trust me, Damek could never be either."

Micah was quiet for a moment. "He hurt her, didn't he? Before?"

Henry turned around to look at him. "If she's a witch, what do you care?"

"God won't like it, but I can use it if it's true. Can't I?"

By God.

There might be some Donahugh in the lad, after all.

SHANLEY, PATRICK'S NEWEST STEWARD, SET THE SCROLL IN PATRICK'S open palm. The sheaf was heavier than Patrick expected. Unwinding its leather stays, he frowned as a wad of crudely inked vellum sprang free from the binding. He didn't need to read any of these pages to know what writ upon the heading of each leaf was.

He Knows What Lies In The Darkness...

Patrick tossed the papers aside with a snort. "What nonsense is this?"

The fellow's yellow eyes bulged from his pinhead. "These were confiscated in the Mercantile district only yesterday. Someone has been proselytizing treason to the poor, it seems."

Patrick snapped his fingers with an impatient sigh he did not feel. His groom returned to his throat with a cautious razor. "Many men and women attempt to convert Bethonair citizens every year. It never holds. Southers have no patience for dogma. We're guided by Reason and the True South, remember? We require no creed."

"Yes, My Lord," said Shanley, attempting to moderate his tone. He would have to work on that, or Patrick would see him swinging from the Mahon Gate one of these days. "But these were not crafted by an outsider. My source insists they were written by your brother and distributed by Lord Warrick and his retinue."

Warrick, eh? Now that *was* a surprise to Patrick. Sure, he'd had Warrick's Colonial Commission revoked a few years back, but he'd never have expected such a stalwart man to fall under Henry's thrall. How interesting. "Nonsense. Warrick wouldn't dare cross me in public. Like all rodents, he will always seek the path of least resistance. You sure it wasn't Hamley, Knockburn, or Morton who've been abetting this drivel?"

"No, My Lord. This morning, Lord Warrick's squire was caught with the documents in his valise. The lad has confessed all, without torture."

"How convenient," Patrick quipped while his groom grinned up at him. "No doubt his master will prove equal to the lad's cowardice. See to it that he and his family are stricken from the registry. I'll give his lands to Lord Bander, and Warrick's coffers will help finance my eager nephew's latest campaign North. Well, is that all?" Shanley squirmed. Patrick growled. "I asked, is that all?"

"No, My Lord..."

"Reason, one would think I were a patient man."

"More documents have been procured in Lord FitzDonahugh's apartments. They are... well, they're of an incendiary nature, My Lord. In his own words, he condemns the Barony, women's freedom to buy and own property, trade with the colonies and the 'unholy' Sidhe, the lavish lifestyles of those at Court, and your own indolence and erm, 'depravity,' My Lord. He's taken issue with everyone in Bethany, it seems. What's worse, he's garnered quite a loyal following among the poor working class and an alarming number of stolid sorts from among your courtiers. He's dangerous, My Lord. My servants have heard him praised as a martyr to your ambition."

The razor's course stopped mid-swipe. Patrick's groom flushed and backed away. Patrick sat up. "Where is Henry now?"

"In his quarters, My Lord. Confined there, under my orders."

Patrick made a face. "Release him."

Shanley blanched. "Forgive me, My Lord, but he has committed treason."

"Shanley, do you know how martyrs are made?"

"N-no, My Lord. I believe they must be persecuted and scourged by their rulers?"

"Exactly so. What do you suppose will happen if I imprison my brother again?"

"I take your point." Shanley genuflected but persisted, chalk-white cheeks ablaze. "We can hardly allow him to sow discord in the city with his vitriol, can we?"

"No, we cannot. I want his followers arrested and their property and funds confiscated. I will make an example of every one of them. As for my brother, I believe we'll honor him with lands and a bevy of titles, which previously belonged to his flock."

"You'd reward him?"

"Hardly," Patrick smirked. "I'll make a hypocrite of him. His sons are fine boys who will one day be peers of the South. I'll lavish them with gifts, accolades, and feasts while Henry's followers are ground into obscurity beneath the Barony's yoke. Hard to believe in a man who embodies the opposite of his professed ideals."

"I... see, My Lord." He didn't, but Patrick wouldn't bait him further. Maybe he should have Shanley here replaced? The fellow was thick as butter.

"What else, Shanley?"

"Well, My Lord," he cleared his throat. "While investigating this business with the letters, your housekeeper had some rather disturbing things to report."

"Meaning?"

"Several reports of manhandling and molestation upon the serving girls in the East Wing. The housekeeper has applied for a general ban on female servitors in that part of the castle."

Patrick cursed. "How many girls have been tampered with?"

Shanley fidgeted. "Three, My Lord. One was so badly beaten that her family filed a formal complaint. They mean to apply to you personally, in full view of the Court."

"That absolutely cannot happen. Pay them off and move them to Clare or Kerry as quietly as possible. The others?"

"One is with child. The other has been reassigned to the North Wing."

Patrick covered his half-damp face with one hand. "Reason. Grant the housekeeper's request. I want no women below the age of sixty servicing the East Wing. My brother will have to make do with boys and old women for sport. Is that all?"

"Ah, well... no."

Patrick stomped to the fireplace and leaned against the mantle. His groom handed him a flagon of wine, though his stomach had turned far too sour to drink anything. "What?"

Shanley wrung his hands, stealing a nervous sideways glance at Patrick's impassive groom. "Two girls are missing, My Lord."

"From the East Wing? Why didn't you say as much before?"

"Not from the East Wing. From the Central Keep. They didn't report to their chambers after the Feasts last week."

"Gods damn that pig-fucking pederast!" Patrick threw his flagon against the wall over Shanley's quivering scalp. Dark red Cymrian spattered the drapes and carpet near the steward's feet. The poor steward blubbered. "I want him watched at every feast. He's to have two bodyguards dogging his heels at all times. Fuck's sake! Why wasn't this brought to my attention when the first girl complained?"

"Lord Fitz Donahugh vows he has never laid a hand on any of them, My Lord. None of the girls' families wished their names dragged through the muck in opposition to a peer, the Duch's own brother. They're all terrified of him. Respectfully, My Lord, I restate myself: your brother is dangerous. I represent all of your household staff when I urge you to reconsider his liberties. Please, Your Grace. This could easily spin out of our control."

Patrick was silent for a while, mulling it all over. He'd known there would be trouble when he'd released Henry but perhaps not this much, so soon? How that gnarled old predator managed to get it up high enough to force himself upon his maids, one could hazard a guess. Perhaps, the violence did the trick for him? Patrick couldn't say it didn't hold a certain appeal, but he'd never been aroused by a screeching female before. He liked his women soft and pliant, excluding his late wife, of course. That bitch had earned her stripes in the best way possible.

"All right. Restrict his access to all but the East Wing and the Keep, though I want him followed as I said, and there are to be guards in his hall day and night. See that the staff are alerted to steer clear of him, and even the housekeeper is to remand her duties to a male servitor for the time being. I want him lavished in food, furs, gifts, and books in the meantime. If allowed, he'll pretend to this preposterous notion of martyrdom at every opportunity. I want him kept clean, well-fed, his sons admired and coddled, and his coffers growing. This is imperative, despite his less-public urges."

"As you wish, My Lord, but, well...."

Patrick's nostrils flared. "For your sake, I would suggest you spill every ounce of information at the start from now on. Speak, damn you!"

"He, ah, has been meeting with the young Lord Donahugh, as well. They met this very afternoon in the Moorings."

Patrick's right eye twitched to a painful degree. "Have I not commanded that I am to be informed immediately should the lad be unaccounted for at any point during the day?"

Shanley backed up a pace. "Yes, My Lord. We were—"

"Your excuses mean less than nothing to me, Shanley. Today, you will take ten lashes for this failure. On the next occasion, it will be your head. Do you understand me?"

Shanley knelt, weeping openly. Patrick's former steward currently dangled from the North Tower, a sack of bones plucked white by crows. That fool had failed to prevent Damek's rebellious march North and elected to run rather than inform Patrick of his nephew's perfidy. Patrick had executed a fair share of stewards in his time. Motioning for the guards to remove Shanley to the courtyard, he took a seat at his desk and sighed. His groom waited patiently by the fireplace, Patrick's towel dangling from his forearm.

"I swear," Patrick grumbled, scribbling furiously over a fresh sheaf of vellum. "It is *so* hard to find good help these days."

Having no tongue with which to comment, Patrick's groom nodded vacantly.

NOTING THE GUARDS WAITING BEFORE HIS CHAMBER DOOR, HENRY slowed his pace slightly. He might have known Patrick would have been told already. He chuckled under his breath. Much that the old fool could do about it. Henry wouldn't be cowed. Holding his head high as it would go with a bent spine, he strolled past his brother's stolid guards to discover the Duch of Bethany rummaging through his personal effects. It didn't matter. He was welcome to look. Henry waved at his brother as he shrugged out of his heavy outdoor cloak. With an eyebrow raised toward his balding pate as he read through the notes in his left hand, Patrick scarcely looked up.

"Evening, brother," said Henry, noisily taking a seat to remove his shoes.

Patrick chortled through his nose, tossing the wad of papers into the fireplace. "'Licentious tyrant,' am I? Dear me, Henry, but you've lost your talent for wordplay."

"I'm out of practice. Don't worry, I'll find my rhythm again."

Patrick took a seat, tucking the tankard in his right hand against his chest. He fixed Henry with a cool glare. "Oh, I've no doubt. If you'd half the talent for sermons as you do for rape and violence, I say you'll corner the market in no time."

Henry wasn't cowed. "Ah, a servant has been telling tales, I see? They're nonsense."

"Are they? It's funny. I'd have figured you were impotent, given the general state of your health." He tsked. "Ironic, considering that you're soon to be a father again."

"The girl lies. Ask your housekeeper. A few weeks ago, she was found with one of the grooms in the stables. She means to fleece me for a living. As you know, I am in no state to inspire scandals."

"Huh. That is quite a tale. And the others? I suppose they're all lying too."

Henry flashed his wooden teeth. "Of course they are. You've given me quite an allowance, and a title always attracts this sort of chicanery. As I recall, you fended off dozens of these accusations in your youth?"

"In my case, none were true."

"Suppose this is where you'll warn me to hold my tongue about that girl's heritage, then?"

Patrick went very still. Henry had seen that same iron-edged glare many times in his life, and when he'd been a younger, more cautious man, it would have concerned him. "Is that why you're forcing yourself on my staff? To threaten or insult me?"

Henry shrugged and leaned back on his knobby elbows. "If I had done any of the horrible things they say I've done, I imagine it would be a compulsion outside of my control and very little to do with you. Yet, you'll concoct your theories, regardless."

"Una is *my* daughter, Henry."

"If you say so, little brother."

"I know so." The blood rushing to Patrick's cheeks blazed violet. "And if you ever—"

"No need. I intend to marry my eldest son to your peerless daughter, don't I? Why would I ruin that perfect Donahugh union with ancient rumor, hm? Besides, it's not as if she would wish to know that her impotent father kidnapped and raped her mother under the advice of a Fir Bolg witch, only to fail in her conception time and again. I imagine she might feel rather put out when she learns I was the one who—"

"That's enough. You are not her father, Henry, and you are not Duch, despite your imagination. You have no power over her or your son. Let me be clear."

"It *is* a sin to tup one's siblings, but in our family, that line's always been a bit murky. Hasn't it, Patrick?"

"I said that's *enough*, damn you!" Patrick had gone a rare shade of puce at this point. Henry didn't bother to conceal his smirk. "Shall I have your tongue torn from your head? Perhaps your hands, from the wrist down?"

"Why not pitch me over the Mahon Tower, like our beautiful Alis? It must have been quite infuriating to see her belly swollen with another man's child, though you never seemed to mind with Arrin, did you?" Henry's tone was acerbic with an ancient enmity. "Ah, I vowed I'd pay you back for our sweet sister one of these days, Patrick."

Patrick leaned forward. "So, you'd have me believe you're a reformed man but would happily condone an incestual union between two of your children? Pah. Arrin was kept in seclusion and well away from Court when Una was conceived. You were not even there, but truly— a fair attempt, brother."

Henry gave a mock bow. "God will forgive me for wedding my children together if it purges this city of your filth."

"You're insane, you know?"

"Does it keep you awake at night?"

"Your lunacy?"

"No, Alis' son?"

Patrick didn't answer, as Henry knew he wouldn't. Instead, he got up and stalked around Henry's bed to the windows. "Yes. I lie awake at night, but not for the reason you suspect. I worry he will make me kill him."

Now seated on his bed, Henry tucked his hands behind his head and settled against his mountain of pillows. The finery in his chamber increased by the day. Since Patrick saw fit to reinstate him to the peerage, he had coin to spare. After a decade in a dank, dark cell, he didn't mind the added comfort.

"You should have adopted him when you had the chance. Now, he's your greatest liability. Not that I care overmuch. I'll be happy when Micah sits on my father's throne, and the Damek Bishops of the world are gone."

"I thought you had a care for Alis' son, brother?"

"He's a half-breed, Patrick. Brilliant he may be, but you know his kind run to madness more often than not. Or do you suppose he will march in here with his prize and allow you to pretend to power for much longer? The fate of your kingdom hinges upon the decisions you make when he returns. You're wrong if you truly believe he'll make a grand ruler."

Patrick took a long pull from his tankard and belched. "Why not? His being in your way does not lessen his worth in my eyes. Forgive me if I don't take succession advice from a man convicted of high treason." He paused with a heavy sigh. "Never mind all that. I'm not here to discuss Damek, Henry. I want your word that you'll cease interfering with my staff."

"I've already given it."

"Have you?" Patrick turned. "Do you know what awaits me in the cellars at this very moment? Two girls had gone missing from the Central Keep last week. Both were fished out of the river this afternoon. The things done to those girls turns even my stomach, Henry."

Henry's brow furrowed together. This was news. "Where were they found?"

"A dozen yards shy of the bay. Swept downstream on the outgoing tide. My surgeon believes they were killed at the same time and dumped into the Lee from the Moorings. The very same spot you've been taking meetings for the past month, including with Micah, whom you've sworn to avoid upon penalty of death. Is the image I'm painting for you vivid enough, or do you require further illumination?"

"I did and do take meetings there, yes. To sermonize, which you've allowed me to do at my discretion. As for Micah, to encourage him not to shy from his duty to you and this House. I will not be shamed by my sons, no matter what Damek might conjure for them. Otherwise, I have kept to my word, Patrick. I know nothing of any girls."

"Right. Just as the complaints from my staff here must be lies, let me tell you what's going to happen now, brother dear. You will be under guard from the moment you wake until you close your eyes at night. You will never take another meeting that isn't officially approved in full view of the Court, and you will never be given the opportunity to harm any of my staff again. Starting today, only men and old women shall serve in this tower, and you are restricted from any feast that I am not attending. I want no more of this. Am I clear?"

"As glass, brother. Though I'm afraid, you are censuring the wrong man. One of the maids, yes. I— how did you put it? — 'interfered' with. God will forgive me for that weakness. The others are bald liars, especially that slut from the Narrows. Her child is her own business. Now, as far as these slain girls are concerned, there's simply no way it *could* have been me, Patrick. I am not as deft a sneak as I once was. I am already guarded at every feast, led to and from the Hall, with no exceptions. To accuse me of this, you're assuming I'm capable of walking over a half-mile, going up and down four flights of stairs, passing through several brightly lit halls and hordes of workers... at night, in the dark, with these knees." He tugged his robe up so Patrick couldn't mistake the gout, which bloomed green and purple over his knee joint. "Walking, standing, lying down, or sitting on my bed... there's no relief."

Patrick visibly turned off his ale, set it down on the larder. "Yet, you're still able to maltreat a girl half your age. No matter what you say, brother, no one else in this castle has your history. Those girls were gutted."

Henry covered his knees with his long black robe. "I *am* a reformed man. Beyond that, I've never done such things to a woman. I've taken from them, sure, but murder? One throttled thief a lifetime ago does not make me a butcher. Besides, I struggle to hold my bread knife these days." He held up his gnarled, arthritic hands. "I'll take your point on the one serving girl and accept my punishment without further argument, but I don't know the first thing about the others. That is God's truth."

Patrick didn't believe him. Well, Henry expected that. "Una returns in a week or less. If you attempt to fill her ears with any of your nonsense, I'll kill one of your sons. I vow it."

Henry clenched what was left of his teeth. "So you've said, and I have consented. Visiting Micah was a necessity you may thank me for later. The boy is smart but needs prodding to do his duty. What use would he be if he didn't provide a rational alternative to our brash young nephew?"

"Then we are agreed. Please don't make me restate this for a third time, Henry. Mind yourself. Whatever machinations you think you're hatching in secrecy, remember, you can conceal nothing from me for long. Two young men are relying upon you to keep them alive."

Patrick shrugged his cloak tight. Having said his peace, he moved toward the hidden staircase in the east wall. Henry's voice caught him short at the bottom step. "How were they done?"

Patrick paused. "What?"

"The murdered girls. How were they found?"

Patrick looked very small in the torchlit passage. "Throttled, beaten, and slashed."

Henry felt a chill creep down his spine. "Raped?"

"No."

"Virgins?"

"No. It is the opinion of the coroner that the killer might be impotent."

Ah. "You suspected me, naturally?"

"Until you admitted to raping one of my servants, yes."

"I hope he is found quickly."

"I've no doubt of it, Henry." The passage closed behind him, leaving Henry to sweat in the dark, alone.

5

LADY DONAHUGH

Una chewed hard-tack and pretended not to see any of the men riding around her. She wasn't shaking anymore, which was a vast improvement. Though she'd long since given up hope of escape, she did keep an eye roving for any potential scenarios she might utilize to regain *some* agency over her person. Being strapped to a horse all day and tied to her cot every night, she was running out of ideas. A day's ride south of Ten Bells, the single change to her situation was the view. Having left the river valley behind, they were now marching through reconstituted forest, which led through the bogs at Skiberdeen, then over the low hills of Blane. Not long now. The snow-kissed forests and knolls of the North had given way to the rolling greens and browns of the Southern plains. She could taste the sea on the western wind and smell the peat burning in the city, a few miles away. The road yawned up at her, muddy, malodorous, and merciless. Her mount's hooves beat her doom into the earth.

Every step brought her that much closer to a fate worse than death.

Here sits the property of Duch Patrick Donahugh and any male he might have a mind to share her with.

She spat, not caring if she hit anyone in the process. Served these bastards right, believing a woman should surrender her fate to the males in her family. As far as Una could reckon, the only thing men managed to be better at was violence, and some were *infinitely* more skilled than others. She ignored the sharp pain in her gut. She wouldn't think of him now. She must not. Damek would love nothing more than to berate and belittle her for her feelings, so, she would display none. She kept her face as impassive as marble while her insides bled.

"What did you study, My Lady? In the Cloister, I mean?" Martin leaned in from her right side. His affable, grizzled cheeks did give her a tiny pang of guilt for her generalizations. Some men were kind, too. Though, in her experience, Martin O'Rearden was one of a very select few. Martin didn't have a cruel bone in his body, though he served the worst of men. That he was so loyal, despite this, softened her regard. She would speak with no one else.

Damek, blissfully, ignored her.

She stole a peek now and then to make sure he remained well outside her vicinity and had yet to see his head turn, nor his shoulders uncoil. That was fine by her. He *should* stay well away. If he got close enough, she'd relish the opportunity to feed him his teeth. She spat out another seed. This time, a nearby soldier swiped the offensive missile from his cheek with an irritable grunt.

Ha! she thought. *I'll take what I can get.*

"Particle theory and practicum."

Martin chuckled. "Peapods and pigpens? There's a smile! Haven't seen that in an age."

Una tucked her lip back into place. "Well, don't get used to it."

"Ah, now. Try not to be like that, My Lady. I know how you feel about your Da, but I vow it won't be as bad as you believe." He tugged his chin at Damek's rigid back. "He'll never let any harm come to you. Nor will I."

Una felt a bit like a fly under glass. "Martin, I would appreciate it if you wouldn't peddle my cousin's wares to me. We are enemies. That's all there is to it."

"Hogswaddle."

"Excuse me?"

"You heard me, missy. That lad's loved you since the day you were born."

"That is not my problem."

"You're right. It's your privilege."

Something burst behind Una's eyes. "Say that again, one more time. I dare you, Commander. Tell me how lucky I am that a man I want nothing to do with believes he has the right to hunt and take me captive against my will." She held up her bound wrists. "Is this your definition of a lucky woman?"

Martin didn't flinch. "These fetters you earned by running away from your own family. Tell me, in your grand matriarchal city, how often were you free to do as you pleased? Did your grandmama allow you outside of the Cloister to exercise your 'free will' very often, ever? In the decade or more that it's been since I last saw you, how many trips did you take to the surrounding towns? The markets? Hells, the opposite end of the Citadel? No need to answer, for I already know, Una. None. That old hag kept you under lock and key, day and night."

"I wanted to be where I was. You don't understand the Cloister, Martin. Freedom is a relative term."

Martin shrugged, scratching his scarred chin. "Once you were free, did you run home?"

She flushed to the roots of her hair. "That is none of *your* business."

"Kaer Yin Adair, no less." He shook his head. "When we first began to suspect that your protector might be Sidhe, we immediately assumed the tale a ruse to foil your father's plans by spiriting you across the border. I was loudest among that set. When we discovered his identity... well, the shock hardly dispelled that notion. We believed he meant to use you to earn his father's forgiveness."

She would not cry. She *would* not. "He did. All of that is true."

Martin gave her a long look. His eyes held a modicum of pity. "I heard how he fought for you, lass. We all did. That man will have my respect till the day I die, no matter which side we stand on. I'm sorry it came to this pass. Truly, I am."

She hadn't expected his sympathy. "Why are you saying this to me?"

"He's gone now, My Lady. Make do."

She saw Damek's head swivel slightly in her direction. "I will never have him, Martin."

"You loved him once. He fights for you, though you're too self-absorbed to see it now. Many good men died to bring you home. Don't give me that face. Listen, imagine this from our perspective. You are heir to our kingdom and greatly beloved by the people, no matter how you revile them. Your grandmother has kept you locked in a tower for over ten years, and once you were freed, we believed you were kidnapped by a rogue Sidhe agent, then hunted and scourged by your chosen people. We set out to save you, and what do we find? Murderers and cutthroats on your trail, a hive of villains, resolved to sell you for profit, otherworld beasts and nightmares seeking your flesh... and through it all, a man who should have been dead ages ago, seeking to use you for his own gain."

He paused to let the words sink in, deep.

"How are we the villains in your mind? As far as Damek is concerned, he saved your life and your dignity and did so at great personal cost. Your father is frothing at the mouth to disinherit him for disobeying a direct order to march to your rescue, young lady. He has a fight ahead of him you cannot be bothered to conceive of, all because he refused to let you die in the wilderness or be swept over the border, never to return. You have as much to account for as Damek in this, and you know it."

She fell silent for a long while, fuming. She wanted to rail at these accusations, to berate O'Rearden as a ruthless patriarch with little understanding of the world or her situation, but she couldn't. Though lobbed without much insight, his statement rang with more than one note of truth. She stared at the trees around their limping band, her jaw burning. "I never asked any of you to come, and I certainly never wanted anyone to die in pursuit of me. I am no victim, but neither are any of you. Damek knew before he marched that I would reject his help. I didn't want him there, and I don't want to be here now. You don't chain someone you value, do you?"

Here Martin squinted a bit. "You do have a point there, My Lady. However, sometimes to save someone, you must drag them out of harm's way by the hair. In this case, you are right that you never asked for our help, but we determined you owed it all the same. You didn't wish us to intervene on your behalf, but you are alive because Damek fought for you. You might have wished to remain by this Sidhe lordling's side, but you were almost killed many times for that desire. To protect you, we were forced to drag your nearly lifeless body from a horror no Souther has ever seen. I am not saying you should find all of this fair, but you should accept that we have your best interests at heart. We *are not* your enemies, and though you have a right to be angry at Damek for his impulsive youth, you do not have the right to punish him for his affection for you. Reject him as you please, but don't avoid your share of this mess."

"You know why I ran away, damn you."

"Aye, and I never blamed you for it either. Given the events of the last few months and all the unrest in your Grandmother's city, it's time to come home, Una. You have responsibilities that other women, even the nobles in the Cloister, can never match. Your father isn't as evil as you'd paint him, and the future of our kingdom rests with you. If you truly mean to improve the world, how about you start where it would matter most, hm?"

Her ears burned. Upbraided *again*.

She watched the trees slip past her in nondescript uniformity and willed her retort back down her throat. She wouldn't win this debate, and she knew it. He was brushing over many essential details, but neither was he wrong. Damek sent her one searching glance over his shoulder, and she glared back until his neck twisted forward again. He always did have the ears of a bat, damn him. Martin had a point about the men and their sacrifices to save her against her will, but she would be Siora damned if she'd buy any of Martin's drivel about love.

Damek didn't love her. He needed her.

He wanted what she represented more than anything in the world. She knew this better than anyone. Una would never allow him to manipulate her again. Whatever her father had planned, Damek could be certain: she'd never accept him.

"Fine. When my father dies, and I'm Duchess... I wonder how I'll repay your Lord Bishop for his kindness?"

"Una, don't be like that," Martin sighed. "One kind word from you would mend all breaches. If you'd let him, he will be your greatest ally in the trials to come."

She opened her mouth for a stinging rebuke, but Damek's fist popped up, and the company halted to a man. From the thicket on Damek's right side, Una thought she caught the flash of something bright. Martin saw it too. His sabre sang as he slid it from his scabbard. The men, as a unit, followed suit.

"Double cover," said Damek, walking his horse backward to place himself between the woods and Una's mare. His knights drew their shields around her in a semi-circle. Martin's own blade deflected the first arrow. "Killian, Dawes! Bowmen to right rear flank!"

The archers rushed behind Una's knot of protective swords and shields while pikemen hammered their halberds into the earth before them. "What's happening?" She hadn't realized she asked aloud. Damek grasped her mount by the reins.

"Bandits, no doubt. They'll have been informed that a woman matching Una Donahugh's description is among our party," he whispered back, eyes moving furiously. "Our numbers are depleted enough that we appear vulnerable. Your ransom would be their goal."

She groaned. "Damek, untie me."

He glanced sideways at her. "Not a bloody chance, Una."

Motion through the shrubbery ahead was the least of their concerns; they were likely surrounded, as Damek surely knew. The brigands would attack all at once, from all sides. To make a move this bold, there must be dozens of them.

"Untie me! I can help, you arrogant idiot."

He made a face but slipped his dagger out of his vest all the same. "Dawes, if Lady Donahugh attempts to run, you have my permission to break one of her legs."

"My lord." Dawes saluted.

"Lord Bishop," a voice cried from somewhere unseen while Damek sawed into Una's bonds with a meaningful glare. She was unamused. "Surrender the lady, and yer men may leave in peace. Refuse, and every one of ye will die here today."

Damek waved the dagger at her. "I mean it. No tricks."

She took the dagger from him by the blade. "I heard you the first time."

With a wry smirk, Damek cupped his free hand over his mouth. "Come and get her, you lowborn dog!"

Una didn't see what he had to smile about

Then every hell broke loose at once.

DAMEK HAD NEVER BEEN HAPPIER TO HAVE SOMEONE TO KILL THAN HE was at that moment. Weeks of frustration bottled up inside him burst forth in bright red spray. Every look, every gesture, every ounce of Una's derision came pouring out of him in a hacking, slicing, gouging surge. Gods, how he hated her. If there had ever been a more selfish cunt in all the world, Damek would never believe her worse than his sweet cousin. A fellow leapt upon his horse from an overhanging tree bough. Damek nearly cut the fool in half. The warm spatter of blood was a soothing bath. Martin roared from the road ahead, taking on three poorly armed bandits at once. Damek spun, slashed, ducked, and sidestepped so many rusty weapons he might believe every peasant in the South had the gall to try for the Duch's daughter.

Well, come one, come all.

He very much needed the distraction. Somewhere further down their line, Una was hard at work defending her honor. He could tell from the resulting horrified screams. Dawes remained close by to hold her back up, but from what Damek saw, she hardly needed his help. Indeed, they'd be in serious trouble if she decided to use her abilities on any of his men. When did she gain such power? Once, Dawes was distracted by multiple assailants, and Damek thought he would guard her back himself. He needn't have been concerned. Wielding his dagger expertly in one hand, she set the other against any flesh that reached for her with divine retribution. He watched two men melt from the inside out before realizing he must stop. What had her grandmother made her? Surely, she was no longer human... what human woman held such a cursed gift? With that shock of white at her temple and the golden gleam in her eyes— she looked like an avenging goddess from the Age of Heroes: the Morrigan herself, lady of death, astride a mountain of corpses.

The longing that kindled in his gut at the sight made his arm work harder. More death. More pain. More vengeance.

More, more, more.

He wasn't sure when he'd run out of things to cut through until Martin found him gasping against a tree, where he ground a bandit's guts to sausage with the point of his sabre. "Reason, Damek! Leave off!" Damek didn't object to being shoved away from his kill. Martin's eyes were round as saucers. "You think he's dead?"

Winded, Damek squinted. "Report?"

"All dead or fled. Most took one look at our lady and sped away screaming. Damek," Martin struggled to articulate his thoughts. "She's..."

"I know."

"Now you're hurting my feelings, Martin." Una stepped over Damek's piled victims, wiping her hands on her soiled skirts. She didn't appear the least winded. Damek almost flinched from her newfound glowing health. Had there ever been a woman this beautiful? Her dark skin, bronze in the dappled sunlight; her wild silken curls, full mauve mouth, and high cheekbones... he longed for more things to kill. "I thought you wanted to know what I studied in the Cloister, Commander?"

Dawes, Damek noted, maintained a respectful distance. None of his men seemed over-eager to approach her again, for that matter. While Martin searched for something to say, Damek cleared his throat. "Dawes, her bonds, please."

Those golden eyes flashed at him, and Damek's blood rushed into his ears. "If he touches me, he will regret it." Dawes shrank away. Damek cursed. Slamming his sabre into the earth, he marched over to retrieve her manacles from his cowardly aide-de-camp. She said nothing as he dragged her to him by the elbow. Brow raised, he lashed her hands together and clicked the irons shut over her wrists. She rolled her eyes at him. "You're welcome?"

Next, he moved to clip one end of her chain to the manacle around her ankle. "Don't be cute, Una. It doesn't suit you."

"I didn't run, did I? This is hardly necessary."

Once her bonds were fixed, Damek tied the other end of her chain to his belt with a vicious jerk. "I will not have you believe that I'm going to forgive you so soon. Fenley, Bors— our mounts, if you please. The rest of you, back in line."

"Forgive *me*? Did you hit your head? What in the *Nine Hells* do you think I owe you, Damek?"

He ignored her, dragging her behind him while he stomped around his bustling men. Martin followed at a sedate, tactful pace. Damek's pulse beat so loudly that he thought Martin probably heard it from a yard away. "Your life, for one."

"As I recall, all of you would be dead now if it weren't for me. The Sluagh would have taken you a man at a time. We're even now, as far as I'm concerned. Untie me already."

She wasn't wrong, but that didn't make him feel better. He wanted to snap her wrists like kindling. He wanted to wring the column of her throat in both hands. He wanted to crush her against him and never let go. He had never hated anyone so much in all his life, not even her father. "Let's get something straight. You are not in control of this situation. I am. You will be given no privileges, and I will hear none of your whimpering."

"Whimpering? You blockheaded son of a whore—"

She planted her feet, which yanked him backward. In a trice, she used her meager bodyweight to fling him to the dirt, arse-first. The next thing he knew, she was on top of him, digging the heels of her hands into the exposed flesh at his chest. Teeth clenched, she held on tight though he should have bucked her easily. His men pooled around them with their weapons drawn, though they clearly struggled between fear and uncertain duty. To which did they truly owe fealty? Even Martin wrestled with this conundrum as Damek and Una rolled around in the dirt like two hissing cats. Una got the upper hand once and nearly dragged Damek's dagger out of his belt, but he pulled her leg from beneath her and crushed her into the soil. Her hand shot out, quick as a snake, and struck him hard enough to make his nose bleed. He swiped the red line against his sleeve and ground his elbow into her chest. Her breath came out in a rush, but her right knee pounded into his kidney.

Throwing his head back on a bellow, he tried to stand, but her temple smashed into his chin, and he howled, "Gods damn it, you little witch! Stop!" He turned aside to hold her down with his flank while he tightened the iron at her wrist. Kicking like a mule, she hooked both arms over his neck and dragged him backward by her manacles. Choking, Damek rammed his head as hard as he could into her nose. Slightly dazed, her grip slipped, and Damek was free to hoist her up and slam her into a nearby trunk.

"Lord Bishop, that's enough!" cried Martin, though he might have been a gust of wind. All Damek could see through the red haze of his vision was Una.

"You're pretty brave with an unarmed, bound woman, Damek," she mocked, straining against her iron bracelets. "Take them off, and then we'll see how you do."

"Fine," Damek decided with sudden inspiration. Nose streaming, he maintained eye contact while removing her restraints. They bounced off his knee and into the dirt with little fanfare. With his free hand, he loosened his collar for her. "Go ahead. I'll give you the first shot."

"Damek, you bloody fool!" growled Martin.

Grinding her canine teeth together, she dug her nails deep into the flesh at his throat. Damek didn't move a muscle. "I'll kill you, you know?"

"I doubt it," Damek smiled. "Go ahead and try, you spoilt, selfish cow. *Do it.*"

Her nostrils flared, but she removed her hand long enough to shove her fist into his eye. Her knee came up, missing his bollocks by an inch as he staggered away, swearing. "No need. Patrick will do it for me, you blithering braggart."

Damek marched toward her with murder blazing from both eyes like a lantern, but Martin's heavier shoulder caught him midstride. "That's plenty, that is. The two of you."

"I will wear no more restraints from today on, Commander O'Rearden," said Una, spitting out a wad of blood. "I will return to Bethany with you, as ordered, so there is no further need for these theatrics. If that strutting peacock comes near me again," she pointed at Damek, who grumbled low in his throat. "You'll have yourselves to blame for his death."

Spine straight as it would go, Una took her reins from Fenley without another word. She remounted and waited at the fork in the road while Damek collected the remnants of his dignity. His men looked anywhere but at him, and he couldn't blame them a whit. Martin watched him reseat himself with a concerned eye. "What in the Kneeler's Hell do you have to grin about, boy?"

"She still loves me."

Martin covered his face with both hands. "Reason help me... why would you imagine such nonsense?"

Dawes passed Damek's sword up to him with an uncomfortable grimace. Damek flashed his teeth as he snapped his blade home. "I gave her the chance, and she didn't take it."

"She didn't kill you, so she has to care for you. Are you mad?"

"She didn't take my life when she had the chance, and after what I've done... not wanting me to die is the same as a confession to me, Martin. Una is as fatalistic as I am and always has been. I'm so bloody relieved right now, the next town we stop at, all the ale and women any of you wants is on me."

The round of cheers he expected did not come to pass. The woods reeked of bloating corpses, but if one were to judge the situation by Damek's grin, they would have reason to be utterly confused.

FOR THE FIRST TIME IN WEEKS, UNA WAS ALLOWED THE COMFORT OF A bed without restraints. Having bathed and washed her matted hair, she lay down in a clean tunic, a bit sore but blissfully free of roots, damp soil, and the snores of sleeping men. The fire blazed, and her belly was, for once, full of something more substantial than hard-tack and cold tea. Despite these comforts, she could not sleep. Part of her wanted to run downstairs to Damek's quarters and pop his head off like a top, while the other longed to weep herself into oblivion. Perhaps she'd made the wrong decision? Maybe she should take the feeble trust she'd earned by not killing the idiot Lord of Clare and climb out that window to her freedom, after all? It would take some time, but she could make it back to Rosweal before the heavy Dor Cromna snows. Once the roads became impassable, she'd have to wait until spring to find out whether or not Damek's claim held any truth. She couldn't imagine Kaer Yin dying so easily after all that they had been through together, all that she'd seen him survive.

He couldn't be dead. He *couldn't* be.

Why would Siora open her heart this way, only to rip it from her chest so soon? Surely the Ancestor could never be so cruel?

Now that she was alone, she couldn't stem the flow of her tears. Great racking sobs had soaked her bedding clean through by the time she collapsed atop them, spent. Hours later, her mind offered no ease, and she still could not sleep. Rian? What had happened to her? Did she linger in Rosweal, alone and afraid in a strange, hostile place? Would that horrid old bawd try to sell her again, now that Una and Kaer Yin were no longer there to keep her safe? What happened to the townsfolk after Samhain? How had they come down the mountain in one piece?

Not knowing was the most onerous burden to bear.

Kaer Yin's face flashed in her mind, in repose, blood spattering his fair cheeks. She could never forget the look in his eyes as her lips came away from his that terrible night as if she'd told him a secret he'd never imagined possible before. She would hold that image in her heart and pray every day that he made it home to mend ties with his father. He would live inside her now, if nowhere else.

He must. She owed him that much, at least.

A thud against her door forced her upright. Damek, battered from the fight earlier but otherwise clean, entered with a lantern and a small tray of something hot and peaty poised atop it. He did not smile, nor did he sneer. His features might have been carved of stone. He took a seat between her and the fire without asking. She wiped her nose and looked away.

"Why are you crying?"

"None of your business."

She heard his plodding, indrawn breath. "For Kaer Yin Adair?"

"For many things lost to me now."

He was silent for quite a while. She heard his Adam's apple bob in his throat, his hard exhale. "It will get easier, Una."

"I don't want to hear that from you."

"Why not? It's true."

She turned, unable to blink fast enough. "Why are you here? To gloat? To fight? I am in the mood for neither."

"To tell you that I'm sorry. For everything."

She almost forgot to breathe. "How *dare* you?"

He did not flinch from the fury in her eyes. "Again, it's the truth."

"You unbelievable bastard," she laughed. The sound held very little mirth. "Did you think this would make me forgive you, huh? Meaningless words? Or perhaps you thought you'd come up here and I'd welcome you into this bed? You're dreaming either way."

He leaned forward so she couldn't escape the cold sincerity in his gaze. "You came to me of your own accord, and I made love to you, my *wife*."

"*Get out.*"

"Not until you listen to sense. I'm the greatest ally you're going to have, Una. Wield me as you see fit. I will make no complaint. I owe you that."

"I'm going to kill you if you don't leave."

"No, you won't."

Her head swiveled round. "Are you daring me?"

His eyes were huge and liquid dark in the firelight. "Begging you. If you can't forgive me, then use me. I mean it. Do you know what he has planned?"

"Of course, I do. I'll be a first-rate prize for the highest bidder... or three."

His fists clenched and unclenched. He licked his lips. "He's discovered our uncle had two boys. They are, even now, awaiting our return. He will use you as a lure for rich war enthusiasts while he pits our newfound cousins and me against one another. This will be purely for his amusement, and you will never have a say in it."

"And you can stop him?"

"I can stop them all. If you'll trust me?"

She tucked herself into bed again, facing the window and away from him. "I've heard you. Now, leave."

He fought to get to his feet without retort. Una could tell from his breathing. She refused to look at him again. "Una... what... happened to our daughter?"

She felt like her insides were suddenly screaming. She tried and failed to keep the waver out of her voice. "Damek, if you don't leave this room right now, I *will* kill you."

She didn't notice when the door shut behind him, for the burning hole in her chest.

6
THICKER THAN BLOOD

N.E. 508
20, DOR ORAS
TAIRNGARE

How long d'you think it's been, Aoife?" Gan's breathy trill issued from somewhere in the dark. Aoife could just make out the hint of his prone form, where he lay in the farthest corner of their spartan cell. He was wrapped head-to-toe in stained linens and reeked of spoiled medicinal salve. He'd never be whole again, considering most of the flesh and fat had been melted from his bones, but he might heal someday. He'd be even more revolting to look at than he had been before, but he would live, which annoyed Aoife more than her aching scabs.

"Stop asking, damn you," she spat. "Why Nema didn't see fit to remove *your* tongue instead of Alvra's, I'll never understand."

He issued a rasping cough that might have been a laugh. "She spared both of us. That's something."

Aoife stopped scratching at her throat long enough to snort in his general direction. Her wounds were terrible, to be sure, but she would heal, given time and effort. Being half-Bolg sometimes had its benefits. However, the maddening itch she'd developed in the meantime was its own hell. "Gan, you nonce, she *did not* spare us. Only a spoilt, selfish, simpleton like yourself could even dream such a stupid thing."

He was blissfully quiet for some time, pondering the leaking ceiling over his cot as he was wont to do for most of each day. Aoife mostly filled the cacophonous silence with scratching. "She'll kill us eventually, then?"

"Of course. Once we've served whatever purpose she intends for us, yeah." Gnashing her teeth, she strained for a particularly hard-to-reach spot. "You'll go long before me, I'm afraid. She'll wait until you've debased yourself by every conceivable standard, then save your death for the moment you believe its possibility has long passed. I've seen it happen many times."

He didn't respond immediately, but when he next spoke, his voice lacked any trace of the old fear. "Good, then it will be the sweeter to disappoint her on that score. Aoife? You want to kill me, don't you?"

That gave her pause. Her leg shackles rattled as she sat up. "I'm not going to steal Nema's prey, Gan. Though, I admit, I've often longed to."

"How old are you?"

She couldn't recall anyone ever having asked her such a question before. She stammered a response, "O-one hundred and sixty, or thereabouts."

"For how many of those years have you served Vanna Nema?"

This line of inquiry was getting a bit intolerable. "That's—"

"None of my business, right? Do you know how long I've served her?"

"Forty years, give or take?"

"Yes. Nearly the whole of my life. You've quadrupled my record if you're one hundred and sixty years old. Is that not fair to say?"

She stared at his dim white outline. "Yes, it is."

"We've both become terrible in her service. Haven't we? I, a degenerate popinjay, and you, a vicious henchwoman who loathes the wide world, perhaps only slightly less than you loathe yourself."

A hot tear ran down her cracked cheek. "*Shut up.*"

"Aren't you tired, Aoife? I know I am. I won't live near as long as you might, yet forty years in blind obeisance to that beast is quite long enough. You won't have to do it yourself. You might hand me that broken bit of grating dangling from the window there, and I'll—"

"*No.* Stop sniveling."

Again, the silence stretched long in their dank hole in the Citadel's deepest bowels. One would expect to hear the ravings of fellow prisoners, guards' gruff admonishments, or at least footsteps and clanking metal. Here, however, it seemed Nema had tossed her former favorites in an oubliette so far removed from every living thing a whale might have swallowed them. Aoife knew this sojourn couldn't last. Nema had a purpose for them that was sure to be far from pleasant. Her grandmother might have spared their lives, but they were hardly forgiven.

"Don't you want to be free?"

Of course, she did. She'd never wanted anything so much in all of her life. To have her *geis* broken was her tiny black heart's fondest, deepest wish. There'd been a moment when she'd lain on the cold flagstones outside when she thought it was finally over. Aoife wasn't sure what she hated Nema for most: holding her *geis* and forcing her to poison, manipulate, corrupt, and kill in her name; or that Nema hadn't let her die when she'd had the chance? Aoife had been ready to die for most of her miserable life. Not that she'd share such information with a traitorous pervert like Gan. Be that as it may, as much as she loathed him, he did look tiny and pathetic in his cot.

Surely, he hadn't always been an opportunistic ferret, any more than she'd always been a hateful, murderous minion? They were each as circumstance has made them: useful, bitter, and cruel.

"If you would hold my head down, I think I could swallow my tongue," Gan wept.

Aoife exhaled slowly. She didn't want to feel sorry for Fawa Gan. He didn't deserve anyone's sympathy any more than she did. "If I did, Nema will take her revenge through any or all of your remaining family. You know this, Fawa," her tone was softer than she'd expected. "She won't be deprived of her toys. Why did you betray her in the first place? I know you loved her. No point denying that now."

"Eva Alvra discovered my... arrangements with the Third Floor stewardess and reported me to the Doma. If I hadn't informed on our mistress, Drem would have fed my family's Patent of Maternas to the fire and had them all shipped to the Colonies. After she had my bollocks sewn into my mouth, of course."

"Point's moot now, isn't it?" scoffed Aoife. Gan's family had been decimated in the Reformist Purge. Now his mother and two sisters yet lived, and both were bound for indenture in Swansea. They would live short, terribly hard lives gathering Sulphur in the Wastes. "You should have told Nema what you were up to years ago. You might have escaped with a reprimand. Now, look at you."

"You're not in much better straits, yourself."

"No, but I'll heal. Well, eventually, anyway. She counted on that, I'm sure."

"I'm sorry, Aoife."

She flinched as if he'd struck her. "*What?*"

"I wonder what sort of girl you were before she dug her teeth into you?"

Aoife would *not* weep. Not in front of Fawa fucking Gan. "I've always been this way. Your problem, Fawa, is that you can't help assigning desires to each person you meet. This one wants something forbidden that one craves the success of others, and on and on you run. Me? I want one thing alone, and it isn't something you can rub your greasy palms together and profit from. In this, you are powerless as I am. I'm compelled to serve, so I serve. That is all. You'd be better off seducing the wall to your side."

"She'll burn Innisfail to bedrock, Aoife. She means to kill every man, woman, and child in Eire."

"I know."

"Faeries, too."

"I *know.*"

"How can you accept that?"

"Because I have no choice. Free will is a luxury, Fawa."

"I could never face this with your calm. How you can consent to such a terrible fate."

Aoife leaned her head against the damp wall, watching a tiny sliver of light creep across the roughhewn ceiling. "Because nothing truly lasts forever."

FAWA WAS REMOVED IN THE NIGHT. WHERE TO, AOIFE HAD NO IDEA. His screams pealed through the labyrinthine halls for hours, it seemed. Sometime later, when Aoife's heart had stopped pounding enough for her to get some sleep, they came for her as well. Unlike Gan, Aoife wasn't afraid. If Nema had meant to kill her, she would have let her burn. Now it would merely be a matter of punishment, and frankly, Nema grew less enthusiastic for torture with time. Aoife could bear whatever Nema threw at her.

She'd had lifetimes of practice, after all.

She was led through narrow, close passages by either arm. Limp as a wet leaf, she didn't bother to struggle—no bloody point. Aoife refused to fear. She wouldn't give the ancient bitch the satisfaction. Once you've been roasted from the inside out, nothing much could compare. Up endless flights of stairs, through myriad nondescript halls, and over countless thresholds lit by dusty, flickering sconces, she was dragged into a room constructed of nothing but pure, uncut onyx and flung against the slick, polished floor. Aoife knew where she was, even if she'd never set eyes on Drem's throne room. She scrabbled upward, ignoring the pain. Any move she made opened a partially healed sore. The Doma's throne was a magnificent architectural marvel. Every square inch gleamed with dark magnetism, unadorned and opaque as a starless night. She felt consumed by its dark grandeur. She supposed the woman in yellow at the far end of that ocean of ink was meant to appear as if she were suspended in the pupil of some cosmic beast.

Siora's Eye, indeed, Aoife thought.

Nema reclined in the center of that seamless hunk of obsidian, plucking at the edges of an open map and smiling at her. Off to the side, dwarfed by the mammoth throne, sat a younger woman cloaked in the unassuming grey robes of a newly minted Secunda.

Grainne.

Aoife had almost missed her. She wrinkled what was left of her nose.

If that bitch is here, something is happening.

Grainne dipped her head to the slightest possible degree. "Aoife Mac Sionnovar."

Aoife sketched a mocking bow. "*Bhean Tiarne.*"

Grainne made a rude sound and tossed her lustrous braid, her violet eyes dismissive. "Pleasant as always, *isasáeligh.*"

"I'm sure you can see it's been a rough fortnight, cousin."

Grainne *did* see. She failed to limit the horror in her expression. "Balor, *seanmatháir*, what did she do to deserve this?"

"She let Drem's little abomination escape to the South, unscathed," answered Nema dryly.

"Perhaps 'unscathed' is too mild a term for kidnap and unlawful incarceration? There's a future rape in there somewhere too, let's not forget," replied Aoife, without a shred of irony.

"Those blessings are owed to my grandson's efforts, stupid girl. Not your own," Nema snapped, folding the map and passing it back to Grainne. "She'll be ready. She doesn't need to be beautiful to be useful."

Grainne frowned at Aoife as if she were a prized mare suddenly afflicted with mange. "I don't know that I agree, *seanmatháir*. *Deartháir* has given me this task in the strictest confidence. I must not fail him on account of one mad faerie."

"Now, now. We're blood-related, princess. Let's not be rude." Aoife brandished her perfect teeth. Hoping the effect earned the discomfort she was aiming for. When Grainne shivered, Aoife chuckled and turned her eye on Nema. "Your Eminence, why am I here? For what dread purpose did you spare my life?"

Nema was wise enough to know that Aoife had been pushed as far as she would allow. They had a long, long history together, hadn't they? "I mean for you to aid your cousin in the Midlands."

"In what capacity?"

"Whatever I bloody well require, you insolent bitch!" snapped Grainne.

Nema raised a hand, and she stilled. In all the Mac Nemed Clan, only Aoife had the bollocks or license to speak out of turn to Nema. What else could Nema do to her that hadn't already been done? Soft, *precious* Grainne would never know. Would she? "Child, you are my best soldier. I want to grant you the opportunity to prove yourself worthy of my service again."

Aoife's opinion of that was plain. "Who am I to kill for you now, old woman?"

Grainne sucked down a breath, but Nema clenched her fingers, and her voice evaporated. Nema's eyes glittered a fierce emerald. "I'll allow your acerbic attitude, Aoife... though you know I won't forget it. Now, don't you have anything else to say?"

Aoife attempted a mock curtsy. "Congratulations on your new office, My Lady."

Nema frowned at Aoife's disrespectful tone and clapped her hands. A handful of Fir Bolg Warhammers entered the chamber from a hidden door concealed along a glossy black wall. However, they weren't wearing the typical black cuirasses stamped with the Red Bull of Armagh. They wore the white and silver cuirasses of An Fiach Fian: The Wild Hunt of the Tuatha De Dannan. They were dressed as the Ard Ri's guards.

Ah, mused Aoife with a grim smile.

So that's to be the game this time, is it?

"You'd better not let me down again, girl. You are sorely mistaken if you've convinced yourself that nothing worse could happen to you."

Aoife knew better.

There was very little left that the Dowager Queen of Armagh could threaten her with now. Every pain, every fear, every loss, every ounce of despair; Aoife had lived through them, time and again. A queer sort of furious hope kindled anew in her duplicitous breast. She would beat Nema yet. She would simply outlast her.

"As you command, Eminence," said Aoife, pressing her fist into her blistered chest with perfectly feigned obedience.

7
THE ERSTWHILE PRINCE

n.e. 508
21, ÐOR ORAS
Rosweal

"You're rushing this." Tam Lin shook his head at his cousin through the glass. Shar was busy helping Kaer Yin shove his feet into his boots, and neither flinched at Tam Lin's complaint. They'd both heard it more than once today already. "I received my father's orders only yesterday, I might add. I'm in no great hurry to disobey him. It wouldn't be the first time he's banished me to the Oiche Ar Fad for listening to one of your rash schemes."

Kaer Yin finally glanced up; his face nearly healed save for a few yellow bruises. "They were always *your* rash schemes, Tam Lin, and your father never minded when you behaved like a boorish fool. You two are one of a kind. No, it is *my* father you're referring to and *my* frequent banishment for not discouraging you from being yourself."

Tam Lin pursed his lips. "That's not how I remember it at all."

"*Pft.* As you say. Anyway, how many men is he sending to Rosweal?"

"Two hundred."

"So few?"

Tam Lin shrugged. "I think they're meant to keep you here until the Ard Ri decides what to do with you, and of course, Diarmid will have filled his ears with your tomfool plan to raid the South. I'm telling you, this is a terrible idea. There are better ways to handle this."

Upright and fully dressed for once, Kaer Yin *did* look a lot better, but that hardly meant the idiot was fully healed and ready to march on the Souther capital. "I'm all ears when you come up with one, cousin. Hand me my swordbelt, will you?"

Tam Lin passed *Nemain* over with an intense frown. "No woman is worth dying for, you horse's ass. I don't care if her teats leak honey and she can crack a man's spine with her thighs. She's Donahugh's own daughter. Let it go."

Kaer Yin said nothing but clapped him on the shoulder on his way past. Shar shrugged, and Tam Lin rolled his eyes as he followed him downstairs. The semi-renovated *Hart and Hare* was filled top to tail with exhausted, worn-down Roswellians and their elegant Sidhe counterparts in their white and silver cuirasses. The madam leaned over the bar, nursing a dram of skinny Colm's newest batch of uishge. Tam Lin's mouth watered at the sight. There had been a decided deficit of spirits in the last week since Robin ordered Gilcannon's remaining stores cellared. Tam Lin doubted this batch would live up to the standard, but he wouldn't mind the effort in the least. Ale and cider simply wouldn't do any longer.

Robin caught Tam Lin's grim expression over Kaer Yin's head and sniggered. He, too, rolled his shoulder as if to say, 'Well, I told ye.' Why did it seem that only Robin and Mistress Dormer had any bloody sense? This stupid Souther girl was going to get his cousin killed, and for what? Love? Fat load of twaddle, that. "Thousands of gorgeous Sidhe women await your triumphant return to Bri Leith, Yin. Did she cast a spell on you? What?"

Kaer Yin shook hands with a few well-wishers and pulled Gerrod in for a brief embrace. The lad winced at Tam Lin's scowl. "Och. What's that all about then?" Gerrod asked Kaer Yin.

"Wants to know for the thousandth time: why Una?"

"Oh," said Gerrod. "Well, me and Robin think it's cuz she scares him."

"That is not even funny," groaned Tam Lin. "She'd better be the most beautiful woman in the world, who lays golden eggs, and whose tears heal the bloody sick."

Gerrod couldn't stave a laugh. Vince, who was busy wiping tables nearby, shivered in agreement. "Well, I dunno about 'most' beautiful, but she's the prettiest I've ever seen, 'cept for one, that is." Gerrod flushed around his freckles. "I 'spose I don't have much basis for comparin'."

"No, you do not. In Aes Sidhe, there are women so beautiful; a single glance could freeze a man in place for a whole year."

"That sounds nice."

Tam Lin pulled him close, giving Kaer Yin a pointed look. "Know the worst part of that? They're all in love with this ungrateful wretch. When he was banished, hundreds cut their hair in mourning."

"Did they, Ben?" Gerrod's eyes were very round.

"How would I know?" He answered, stepping aside for Rian to hobble by. As she passed, she gave Gerrod a small pat, and Tam Lin instantly recognized who Gerrod's 'one' had to be.

Ah, young fools, he thought.

"Have you eaten?" Kaer Yin asked Rian with a sigh. She held up an apple and sank onto the stool Dabney held for her. Kaer Yin grumbled something about 'real food' and 'idiot waifs.'

Tam Lin squinted at her. "Let's hear it from a woman then. *Oi*, Mistress Nursemaid. What makes this Una person worth so much trouble?"

She didn't turn around. "Ask your cousin."

"I did. Now I'm asking you."

"I imagine someone like you will never understand the answer to that question."

"What's that supposed to mean, then?"

Kaer Yin replied, "I think she's intimating that you have the emotional depth of a gnat, dearest cousin."

Gerrod's answering giggle earned him one of Tam Lin O'Ruiadh's finest scowls. The lad shrank into Rian's side. She sliced her apple into quarters with her belt knife and handed the scrawny boy half of them. Tam Lin couldn't halt a scowl. Kaer Yin noticed. He gave Tam Lin a smile that annoyed him very much. "Well, perhaps not? Anyway, Barb, my love, are we ready?"

"As ever, Ben."

"Good. Help us over to that stool, will ya, Dabs?"

Dabney's outrageous girth shook the glass behind the bar with every step. Tam Lin leaned against the corner of the bar with Robin, taking sips of a moderately decent first batch and glaring at the back of Rian's flaxen head. The cheeky wench. Never had a kind word for him. Not one. If Tam Lin had a mind to, he could make her life miserable. Perhaps, he should take her back to Croghan and force her to serve as his stewardess? He highly doubted she could maintain such priggishness when forced to help him bathe and dress daily.

It would serve her right.

Tam Lin dragged his eyes away from her hunched frame to watch Kaer Yin limp to his fate. He managed to stumble onto a chair before the fireplace, thanks to Dabney and his massive arms. Kaer Yin slapped his shoulder, but Tam Lin doubted the lug even felt it.

"Hello there, everyone. Thanks for coming."

Tam Lin's eyes rolled back so hard that he feared he might bruise his brain. A sea of dirty faces stared up at the Prince of Innisfail with mild disinterest and not a little humor. Already, tiny beads of sweat formed over Kaer Yin's brow, though he put a good grin on it. Tam Lin hoped this fiasco ended quickly; the moron had no business being out of bed so fast. Tam Lin swung his glare back to the bar, hoping this irritating faerie girl would acknowledge her lack of foresight, but her head lay against her arms, her fair hair pooled around her like a shawl. Mistress Dormer gave him a saucy wink, patted the girl's slender arm, and returned to her pipe and uishge. Gerrod hadn't seen a thing. He was too busy giggling with that stringy Vincent character. Tam Lin wasn't sure why the damned girl had to be drugged to sleep at night. There were more capable adults in Rosweal, weren't there? Why should she fantasize that the wide world needed her particular attention, every moment of every day?

There was something wrong with her. *That* was plain.

"Well," said Kaer Yin with a stupid smile. "Guess you've figured out my name isn't Ben Maeden?"

"Ye don't say, ye sneaky cunt!" shouted Barb, raising her tankard for the crowd's praise.

Kaer Yin took his jeers with an affable grin. "I suppose it takes one to know one, Barb."

Barb sketched a courtly bow, and the crowd roared.

Milesians, Tam Lin thought, shaking his head.

At least Kaer Yin understood them because he didn't.

"My name," boomed Kaer Yin. "Is Kaer Yin Mac Midhir Adair. First Prince of the Tuatha De Dannan; Lord Marshal of the Wild Hunt, High Commander of the Daoine Sidhe, and Champion of Bri Leith. I am Lord of Meath, Dowth, Knowth, Munster, and Mann, Crown Prince of Innisfail, and heir to the Ard Ri's throne. Any questions before we move on?"

Tam Lin scanned the suddenly silent room waiting for the outcry, or at the very least, a well-earned round of boos for that atrocious introduction. Nothing. It went so quiet; Tam Lin could hear the heartbeat of the fellow nearest him. After an uncomfortable eternity, a young man stepped away from the windows. "Does tha' mean the future High King owes me twenty coppers for booze and four hands o'stacked porter?"

The Hart filled with a deafening bevy of 'oohs.' Kaer Yin, casual as a tinker, scratched the scalp above his ear with a sky-high brow. "I think you'll find I cleared the debt with your wife, Dan."

The laughter shook the rafters overhead. Kaer Yin, mimicking Barb, raised his glass and shared a bow with the erstwhile Dan. Tam Lin couldn't believe what he was seeing.

Kaer Yin was one of them.

RoRosweal, a town of poachers, thieves, cutthroats, and whores of every stripe, had claimed the Crown Prince of Innisfail as one of their own. What's more, they bloody well loved him, too. Who could have guessed such a thing was possible after Dumnain? Then... most of these men and women weren't old enough to recall the events of that day, were they?

"All right!" shouted Kaer Yin over the din. "Now that's all cleared up, does anyone have anything they want to get off their chest?"

"Nah," said a faceless voice in the crowd. "Me mam's got stew on. Wrap it up, ye ponce."

"He's too bloody pretty to fight now. Be like breakin' fine porcelain," agreed an old woman at the back.

"In that case, so much for the fine speech, I didn't have. Anyway, who wants to come kill some more of the Duch's men with me...?"

Tʜᴀᴛ ɴɪɢʜᴛ, ᴡʜɪʟᴇ ᴛʜᴇ ʙᴏʏs ᴀɴᴅ Bᴀʀʙ ᴘᴏʀᴇᴅ ᴏᴠᴇʀ ᴍᴀᴘs ᴀɴᴅ sᴛʀᴏɴɢ uishge, Rian appeared at Tam Lin's elbow, yawning but alert. Tam Lin couldn't be sure, but she seemed to be building a particular tolerance for Barb's sleeping draughts. From the perplexed scowl he glimpsed on Barb's face, the old bawd seemed to think so, too. Tearing his attention away from the map he and Robin were perusing, Tam Lin scowled at her. "No."

The hollows under Rian's eyes made her look like a half-starved owl. "I haven't even said anything yet."

"I know what you would ask, and I'm telling you: don't waste your breath."

She bristled; a high-burnished rose bloomed on each cheek. "I'm *not* asking, though if I were, it wouldn't be your permission I'd be interested in," she retorted, sweet as pie.

Across the table, Kaer Yin looked up from a worn bit of parchment. "What's this, then?"

Rian raised her chin. "I'm going with you."

Kaer Yin laughed in her face. "Not a chance."

Her nostrils flared. Tam Lin thought he'd seen a similar look on a cat once or twice before. "Oh no? You owe me, Ben Maeden."

"That's not—" Shar attempted, but the glare she set on him stopped his statement cold.

"I prefer Ben, thank you very much."

Kaer Yin sighed and leaned back in his chair. "Why would you *want* to come, Rian? We're going to fight, not make pleasantries."

She tilted her chin at him. Tam Lin stifled a chuckle. "We just went through a fight, remember? You can barely climb the stairs alone, Ben. You're going to need me. Besides, I owe her my life, same as you lot."

Kaer Yin struggled with a response. After a few tense moments below her glare, he squirmed in his seat. "We can't take you with us. You'd be a liability. I'm sorry."

Twisting her mouth, her attention snapped back to Shar. Shar, always weak around women and horses, sat up straighter. "May I borrow your dagger?" With a moon-calf grin on his stupid face, Shar passed her his long dirk. Tam

Lin made sure there could be no mistaking the intensity of his scowl. Shar shifted in his seat.

A headstrong, impertinent faerie wench was this Rian Guinness.

Tucking the blade into the sash at her waistband, Rian smiled. "There, now I'm armed. Feel better?"

"Do ye even know how to use that thing?" asked Robin, whose legs were stretched across the chair in front of her.

She speared him with a bit of side-eye. "Funny, you didn't ask me that when I used one to cauterize wounds, remove splinters, or dig arrow tips out of dozens of your men. Did you?"

Robin sputtered, "No, I... Ben, yer gonna lose this one."

Kaer Yin groaned. "I'm aware. Fine. Have it your way, Rian."

Tam Lin's head swiveled around. "You can't be serious. She's a— well...." He didn't like to insult her, but a limping, sarcastic, lightweight female wasn't going to march into Bethany and take the Doma's heir back, and she wasn't going to swing a sword in anyone's defense either. The road south was undoubtedly not going to be a leisurely affair. They couldn't afford to worry about how it would affect her. Rian shook her head as if she expected his comment.

"What do you think is going to happen to your neat little plan if His Highness here," she jerked her thumb at Yin, "falls face-first into the dirt as soon as someone bumps into him, hm? I'm the least of your concerns right now." She turned back to Kaer Yin. "You shouldn't even be out of bed. You go, I go."

Tam Lin wagged a finger at her. "I warned you not to fall in love with him, didn't I? He's fine, woman. Leave him be."

She shot Tam Lin a withering stare that would have made him flush were he a weaker man. Instead, he found himself decidedly uncomfortable in his own seat. "Listen, Ben's my patient, and since I'm the single healer available to treat him— and since he's the Crown Prince of Innisfail— someone ought to be keeping him alive, don't you think?"

"'He' has already agreed to let you come," Kaer Yin added for posterity. "Truce, you two. You're giving me a bloody headache."

"Not sure why ye have so many fierce lasses circlin' round ye, Ben, but I can't say as I envy ye." Robin shivered. Barb reached over and slapped his boot.

She cackled. "Mind yer mouth. I like this one just fine."

"You would," Robin chuckled.

Tam Lin ignored them. He decided he liked this sharp-eyed faerie less and less. What Milesian woman in her right mind would *dare* to speak to him the way she often did? None, damn it all. He found himself grinding his molars to dust. "My idiot cousin will live, Mistress. He'll heal faster than your average patient, I think. I cannot spare the men to keep you safe, and I refuse to claim responsibility for you."

"*Responsibility for me*?" The air in the room chilled by half-a-thousand degrees. Without ado, Rian leaned over and lightly punched Kaer Yin in the chest. His face bleached white as herringbone and his head dropped onto the table with a resounding 'thwack.' His whimpering, pathetic attempts to suck air into his lungs made Tam Lin's fists clench. "I rest my case, *Your Highness*." She kicked Robin's feet out of the way and leaned over Kaer Yin with a gooey pellet of something that stank of willow bark and nettles. Kaer Yin gasped when she shoved the offensive little missile down his gullet.

His eyes burned with betrayal most foul.

Tam Lin cursed aloud.

You were outdone by this slip of a girl, again.

"Fine! You'll haul your own gear, ask no questions, and remain well out of my sight, Mistress Guinness. I'll not risk a single man for your comfort."

She patted Kaer Yin on the back. "I'm Eirean, remember? I don't need to beg your leave to travel where I will."

"I am the—"

"You've said. Welcome to Eire, Your Highness. I don't think you're going to like it much."

Barb eyed Rian with a new appreciation. Robin visibly repressed a guffaw, and Shar found something fascinating to ogle on the ceiling. Barb pushed a chair toward Rian with an ear-splitting grin. "That was well done, girl."

"I beg your pardon?" Tam Lin hissed from his defeated corner of the table. For the first time in his life, he felt there were too many bloody females in his presence. Barb shot him a bit of a sneer. He *did not* like Eire in the least now that he thought about it. A shame, for he was growing inordinately fond of Eirean uishge, if not her women.

"Take a seat and help me explain to these fools that Bethany ain't some backwater. The Prince o'Connaught and his two companions here haven't set eyes on the South for eons." Barb said around her pipe.

Rian took the proffered seat, mindful of the murderous glow rapidly coloring Kaer Yin's face. Sniffing, she tactfully folded her hands over her knees. "I've only been once or twice, but I'll never forget it. It's not as large as Tairngarc, but it's better built. Every building is made of stone and laid out in a grid, not smashed together around the palace, like the markets around the Citadel. Streets are paved with cobbles or flagstones, and even the stables have tiled rooftops. Tairngare might be grander to look at from a distance, but Bethany is cleaner and more orderly. I remember the guards on the walls. Hundreds of armed knights walked back and forth, day and night. I don't think you'll be able to march in."

"I thought Tairngare was the best-guarded city in Eire?" Asked Shar, who flushed for his question. "One never hears of Bethany boasting better fortifications."

"That isn't strictly true," wheezed Kaer Yin, rubbing his chest. "Tairngare is larger and more impressive for its wealth and population density, but if we compare the two based strictly upon their defenses, Bethany has always had the upper hand. Tairngare is huge but jumbled; buildings stacked one on top of the other to accommodate its populace. It's hard to say if the South boasts more soldiers or stone."

"Wonderful," grumbled Tam Lin to himself.

"Bethany's well-built and well-guarded, that's true," offered Robin. "But that ain't to say she don't have her soft spots. Getting in won't be the trouble; it'll be getting out."

Tam Lin raised his brows at Kaer Yin. "I told you. Two hundred Blood Eagles aren't going to fight their way in and out of a stone fortress, Kaer Yin. Meanwhile, Aes Sidhe will remain unguarded for far too long with the bulk of us down south. We should go home. I said I would help and will, but we need reinforcements."

Kaer Yin straightened. "No."

"Yin—"

"She's only in this position because of me. She traded herself for me, for all of us. I refuse to let her suffer for that choice."

"Perhaps, it's best if we wait it out, Ben? A shame about the girl, but I don't see what good a handful of men would be against the Duch's twenty-thousand retainers. D'ye?" said Robin.

"Who said anything about a fight?" Barb tsked at Robin and stole his map. "Here," she pointed at a cluster of boxes labeled the 'Pleasure District.' "Tunnels from the Lee lead straight into the sewers, and from there the cellars of several skin-shops down the posh end o'the city. My Da made his coin smugglin' spirits and furs 'neath Duch Michael's long nose."

"They might have closed up them tunnels, love." Robin scratched his chin.

She shook her head. "Nah. Got Gilcannon's contracts now, don't I? He had a special relationship with *The Butterfly*'s proprietor. Now seems as good a time as any to let them know they've got a new supplier."

"You're sure of this? I'd hate to get overly enthused about this plan just to have a Corpsman's spear shoved up my arse for the trouble." Kaer Yin said, visibly intrigued.

"Funny ye should mention it, but that's the sort o'play one might seek at *The Butterfly*. When I was a grand dame, once upon a time, they kept very the rarest sorts o'entertainment in Bethany. So rare, none but the gentry could afford them." Barb cleared her throat suggestively, tapping another block of scribbles a half-inch to her right. "Gentry never want anyone to know what they get up to at night. In Michael's time, there was a passage leadin' from the Northern Gatehouse to a stairwell below the Pleasure District. Since I'm no fool, I'd argue things ain't likely changed much. Ye've been runnin' our ale back and forth to Ten Bells all these years, Robin. Ye've never smuggled the odd cask into the Machine City?"

"Sure, but never dealt with any o'the bastards at *The Butterfly*."

"Why's that?" asked Rian.

Robin squirmed under her narrow eye. "Well, ah... same reason we didn't deal with Gilcannon's *Black Corset*. Don't approve of 'em, as it were."

Her nose wrinkled. "I see."

Tam Lin didn't. "What's this mean, then?"

His cousin let out a long sigh. "*The Butterfly* caters to pederasts."

"*Tá morghanna beithigh...*"[5] hissed Tam Lin.

"Indeed," agreed Kaer Yin. "Many are."

For the first time, Rian didn't look at him like his breath soured the air. He ignored her. "Are you implying we're to creep in and out of the city through this *Butterfly*'s cellars?"

---

5   'Mortals are beasts.'

"Smartest plan I can conceive. Lots o' nobles and wealthy merchers in there, keepin' their heads down. I daresay, if ye grease the proprietor's palm well enough, no one will bat an eye at any o'ye if yer careful."

"Anyone have a better plan?" Kaer Yin looked at each of them in turn.

"Aside from abandoning this scheme altogether," snarked Tam Lin, "no."

Kaer Yin spared him a warning glare. "All right then. Barb's plan seems the best we've come up with so far. Now, for the hard part. Provided we can smuggle ourselves into the city, how do we get inside the castle and get Una out again?"

"Disguises, definitely," noted Robin. Might scare up some Corpsmen's tunics or somethin' like that?"

Rian leaned forward. "Why disguise yourselves at all?"

Scowling, Tam Lin disregarded her entirely. They all did. "Well, sneaking in through sewers and cramped cellars will be one thing. Leaving the brothel as noblemen and sneaking into the keep will be another. I assume your girl will be locked up tight or under heavy guard. As Robin said, getting in won't be the problem."

"Aye, we need someone on the inside to—"

"I *asked*, why would you disguise yourselves at all?" Rian raised her voice.

"What are you on about now?" Tam Lin growled.

She inhaled. "Seems to me the Duch is going to wave Una under the nose of every Eirean lord he can in hopes of attracting men and fainne to his banner. I imagine he'll advertise a contest or some ridiculous patriarchal ritual for her hand. The Princess of Bethany *and* the Domina of the Moura Clan will be a handsome prospect for any ambitious nobles with fainne and influence."

Kaer Yin's smile was slow but beatific. "Rian, you're a bloody genius."

"Aye," grinned Barb. "She is that."

Tam Lin coughed. "Yin, I know you're not stupid enough to believe you can play suitor to the great-granddaughter of Kevin Donahugh, a man you're infamous for murdering. They'll shoot you on sight and declare war on Aes Sidhe for your gall."

Kaer Yin's grin got on Tam Lin's nerves. "You're right. *I'm* not that stupid."

"Oh," Robin threw back his head and laughed. "That's bloody brilliant, that is!"

"If you're not going to play the suitor, who should?"

"Ben's not the only Dannan noble in the room, is he?" said Rian.

It took a minute, but Tam Lin's neck flared hot. "*No*. No bloody *way* will I agree to this. It's daft."

"Think about it. Donahugh hasn't advertised that he means to go to war with Aes Sidhe. We are the only ones who know what he's got stuck up his sleeve. A tourney or series of feasts to promote his newly returned daughter's hand will surely attract a horde of suitors from all over Eire and points beyond. Why *wouldn't* a Sidhe noble answer that call? You're our liege lords, aren't you? No matter Patrick's true intentions, he'd be mad to reject your suit outright."

Every pair of eyes in the room rested on Tam Lin with renewed vigor. He didn't like it one bit. "No. You're all barking."

"It's a great idea," prodded Kaer Yin. "We'll be granted rooms within the interior keep, and you'll be feasted and fêted upon Donahugh's dais. He'll have no choice. Your father is a king. It'll gnaw his guts to splinters, but he wouldn't need Una if he were ready to declare war outright. Admit it, Lin. It's the perfect plan."

After several moments of fruitless, silent pleading, Tam Lin crossed his arms over his chest. "Fine. But since I'm to woo your girl publicly, you'll have yourself to blame when she decides she prefers me."

Kaer Yin gave a short bark of laughter. "Good luck with that."

Robin's laughter grated the last of Tam Lin's patience. "Oh aye, I wouldn't, were I you."

Rian, he noticed, smirked into her ale. "Hope you brought *lots* of fainne with you, Your Highness. Because a prince of the Tuatha De Dannan should court a princess in style, don't you agree?"

8

BETHANY

Una slid from her saddle into Damek's waiting, if covered, arms. His cool mask of indifference was once more firmly in place. He might have been a block of wood to her at that point, so little difference his presence made. So many days on horseback, with meager rations, terrible weather, and the constant ache of the Spark drag of a lifetime, had all taken their toll. If he meant to embrace her in full view of everyone in her father's Court, she was too bloody exhausted to mind. If his arms tightened the slightest touch too close or his breath dusted too near the damp hair at the crown of her head, no matter. She needed a bath, food, and weeks of sleep to approach anything resembling her former self again. More's the pity, these luxuries were not to be. Once she crossed the threshold into her father's Great Hall... she wouldn't be free to do anything she wished for the foreseeable future. Damek must have sensed the futility of her thoughts. Without asking, he tucked his arms beneath her knees to carry her through the portcullis. Vaguely, Una was aware that they received several shocked and curious stares as they passed. Martin followed behind, giving her a sympathetic but altogether helpless smile.

That was as well.

Nothing he could do would help her, either.

Damek carried her past the iron Gatehouse towards the Inner Bailey. As they approached the Keep and its yawning arch, his boots made hard, wet smacking sounds over the sodden flagstones. Una realized she was entering the heart of the spider's web now, no mistake. Greasy torches sputtered in the late autumn mist, lighting their way through the courtyard and up to Duch Kevin's four-hundred-foot Keep. Somber and silent, the massive granite edifice stared her down. Her grandfather had seen to it that every surface was as smooth as polished glass; only the hundreds of murder holes placed at every third level betrayed a hint of a handhold. On the opposite side, facing the sea, the Keep dominated a monstrous cliff face that plunged to a precipitous drop of nearly nine hundred feet into the churning Sea of Manannan. She could hear the relentless surf beating its ceaseless, eternal rhythm against the crags. She'd found the sound comforting when she lived here long ago.

Now, that steady tattoo might well have been her death knell.

As Damek brought her through the foyer and into the Great Hall, a blast of warm air sent pins and needles over her frozen skin. Goosebumps raised up and down her arms, and her cheeks caught flame. People poured out of every nook and cranny to ogle the Duch's prodigal daughter and her handsome, disobedient cousin. Damek ignored them with a clenched jaw. Courtiers, servants, and clerks dashed every which way, eager for a peek. Their whispers might have been trumpet calls.

"Ignore them," Damek said into her hair. "They're merely curious. You owe them nothing."

Marching toward the stairs, Damek tugged a chin at Martin to intercept, should any of their onlookers dare to impede his progress. Taking a turn beneath the stairs, he strode through a narrow series of corridors that led to a hidden staircase past the kitchens. This passage tunneled directly to the Duch's private apartments. Una had played on these steps as a child. However, Damek didn't seem in a hurry to whisk her upward; he took his time. The stairs wound upward, lined with fine glass windows overlooking the vast grey sea. Una's stomach churned with those waves. She wasn't sure she wanted to face what came next. It seemed too cruel a fate after all she'd accomplished in Tairngare. Damek pulled her nearer still, as he used to when she was young.

It wasn't a lascivious move, and for once, she didn't mind.

He'd been her dearest friend once upon a time. She hated his guts and always would, but he knew better than any what she faced here. "I won't let him use you, Una. No matter what he threatens... I won't allow it. Do you believe me?" his voice wasn't even strained, despite four floors of winding steps. How he wasn't as exhausted as she, she failed to guess.

"No. Don't pretend to be my ally now, Damek. It's too late for that." She wanted to cry, but she was a Moura. Moura women did *not* weep like weaklings. She would endure. She must.

His answering laugh was far too warm for her taste. "I'm the last ally you have, Una. Accept it. Accept me." He paused on the landing. She saw Martin hesitate a few steps down to give his lord room. Ahead of them, the fourth floor's sconces illuminated the cold, isolated stairwell. A gloved finger slid below her chin. "You know he can't harm you. You're too valuable, and his ambition is too great. Stop fighting. You'd do better to play his game and win."

"I will not be his broodmare, Damek. I'll kill any man who tries. *Every* man. He knows I'd rather die, and so do you."

"Any man? Una, think it over. Why let him choose for you?"

She stared up at him, her ears growing hotter by the second. "I mean it, Damek. *Any* man."

He groaned. "You misunderstand. You've always misunderstood me." His tone lacked any trace of sarcasm. "He means to use you, but he's an old man, and like or not, you're his sole direct heir. He has no sons. You are all he has. Why hasn't this occurred to you?"

Damek wanted to be Duch. That's what 'occurred' to Una... no different from before. This time, she wouldn't have free reign of the castle to escape him and his incessant plotting. "Damek, you don't have to use my womb to launch yourself into his position. Go ahead and take his throne. You have my full and free support. I couldn't care less."

Something crossed his face, then— disappointment, hurt, maybe? Indifference numbed her. She was fairly sure Damek Bishop didn't have feelings to dampen, nor would any stop her from speaking her mind, either way. "You have no idea what I want, Una. Don't presume to know me, and don't you dare equate me with the simpering, sycophantic effeminates in Tairngare, either."

She wished more than anything that she had use of her own damned legs. "Whatever you say, Lord Bishop."

"As you like, *Lady Donahugh*," he mocked through his nose and hefted her higher to resume his climb. "But remember this, if you honestly believe I'd let another man touch you or attempt to take my birthright from me, I won't settle with the man alone. I'll kill everyone in his sphere... women, children, parents. It won't matter to me in the slightest. Unless you wish for dozens of deaths on your conscience, I suggest you find a way to implore the Duch to be done with the whole business and choose me. Am I making myself clear?"

"Why sweet cousin, you make me blush. Why not seal your lovely proposal with a kiss?"

He didn't flinch away as she expected. Instead, he gave her an odd smile. An alarm rang somewhere deep within her gut. The air tingled with unspoken malice— and confidence.

What?

Damek's soft but insistent mouth locked over hers.

You arrogant son of a bitch!

In her blood, the remnants of her Spark surged to life. Spent though she was, she sent every bit of it into the crush of his heated skin.

Nothing happened.

The last of her strength fizzled out, useless. Her Spark retreated in hissing, unsatisfied hunger. She was merely a woman, lighter and smaller than him. His free hand pressed the back of her head, forcing her against him. She made a frustrated, furious mewling sound in her throat, and Damek took advantage. His tongue slipped between her lips with a heady, masculine groan. She did the only thing she had the strength left to do. She bit down hard on his lower lip. He came up bleeding but smiling, a triumphant sparkle in his hazel eyes.

"I think you'll find, dearest cousin," he licked the blood from the corner of his mouth. "As things change, the more they remain the same."

Her Spark had failed her.

How was that even possible?

It had never failed her before. Not *ever*.

The serving girls who bathed, dried, clothed, and braided her hair wore gloves and long, thick sleeves. As if she would harm any of them... yet, they had reason to fear. Didn't they? Why didn't Damek? How had he managed to foil her Spark in such a way? It didn't make an ounce of sense. Had she wholly depleted her reservoir? No. It couldn't be. Beneath her flesh, she could feel the definite current in her blood. She was far from bereft. Why hadn't it latched onto Damek and drained him dry as toast? It must be a random occurrence! Damek's mother wasn't Tairnganese, so there wasn't any way he'd been born with the Spark... right? How else could he manage such resistance? The triumph and sheer, perverse pleasure in his eyes when he deposited her here, in her new prison, was unmistakable. Somehow, he'd developed the ability to defy Siora's Grace. Whether by talent or potion, she couldn't say for sure. Perhaps he possessed some charm or other, which bolstered his resistance? She *must* discover the truth. If he were resistant... *no*, she wouldn't give that gloating beast the satisfaction of her.

"You've grown," rumbled a deep, distinct voice from somewhere behind her. She jumped. Distracted, she hadn't heard anyone enter her chamber. The maids bowed so low; their foreheads nearly brushed their knees as they backed away. Duch Patrick Donahugh stood in the doorway, arms tucked behind his back. His balding pate and stone-grey eyes gleamed in the well-lit antechamber. Her quarters were largely windowless, save for a single rectangular slit facing the wild sea on the far-right wall. Beneath the glass was a stone seat overflowing with vibrant cushions. Patrick was slightly shorter than he had been. Portly now, too. His midsection swelled beneath a loosely belted tunic. Perhaps her perception was skewed by years of trying to forget his malevolent presence.

He wasn't smiling.

Good.

She'd take imperious over smug. "I despise those witch-marks, you know. I'll have to summon a skin healer from Bretagne." His nose wrinkled at her tattoos.

She exhaled long and hard. "Sure you don't want to check my teeth first?"

He chuckled, moving to her bedside, and leaning against the massive chestnut bedpost. "Ah. It's to be bravado, then? Fine, daughter. We can pretend your opinion of these circumstances make the ghost of an appeal to me." He looked around appreciably. "Anyhow, I hope you earn this room. There are others that you would enjoy far less— so you're aware."

"I'm ready to move whenever it suits you."

"Defiance now? Capital! I'll doff pretense altogether and simply chain you to the wall. Failing that, certain men enjoy a bound and helpless woman, you know?"

Bile rose in her throat.

Fucking bastard!

"You malodorous piece of shite! I'll kill *any* and *all* comers. Don't doubt it for a second. Send in two dozen, and I'll drain them dry. Mark my words."

"Two dozen? Who do you take me for? In Bethany alone, I hold twenty thousand troops. You're sure you want to play this game?"

She felt the blood drain from her face.

"Oh yes," he went on. "You might be a witch, little queen, but you're still a woman, and we both know your strength isn't boundless. Perhaps you'll kill the first three? Maybe it'll be the fourth or the fifth... maybe the fifteenth... who'll sample your wares? What do I care? Maybe we'll make sport of the affair. Yes! That's it! The first rider to remain mounted wins!" His laugh was dry, cruel, and utterly humorless. There wasn't an ounce of levity in his expression. Not a bit. Could he watch a group of men attempt to gang-rape his own daughter?

She would never be sure.

Her bones felt hollow and empty as air.

That despair she'd been battling coiled deep in her heart; he saw it. "Now," he said finally, smug as a cat. "Will we be making a spectacle of our familial drama, or shall we retain our dignity? Hm? I mean to have my way, Una, whether you care for the details or not."

She watched him in silent fear for a long while. He never blinked once. Finally, she declared, "I'll kill myself. I will not breed more thuggish males for your line, Patrick. I am a Moura—"

"You are a *Donahugh*!" he bellowed, though his face betrayed no emotion whatsoever, not even anger. "Your Tairnganese witch-whoring family no longer exists. I am the last of your family. If I say you're going to fuck the chamber-boy to give me heirs, I bloody well mean every word. Decide now, here, how you will perform your duty. Shall it be your way or mine?"

Una's temper flared hot and ready, chasing all traces of fear from her blood. "Go to the Hells, old man. I *dare* you to feed me fifteen, twenty... *a thousand* men to drain. How sad and impotent their little corpses will look. Why should I fear? They're only males."

She expected another outburst, but he surprised her again. He threw back his head and guffawed until he had to grasp his sides to halt his fit. When he finished, his eyes were wet. He wiped at them with both thumbs. "Oh, how I've missed you, Sprout. You've a pair of bollocks on you that would shame any man."

Coloring, she clenched and unclenched her fists. "Whatever pleases you, My Lord Duch. My mind won't change."

He held up his palms in a placating manner. "Truce. If I thought for a moment you'd allow any man to take you against your will, I'd slit your throat myself. That fire is the spit of my grandfather, I tell you. He would burn with pride."

She sighed. "No need for the sales pitch. Get to the threats. They're more convincing."

He shook his head. "No threats. You're my daughter and my heir. You'll wed and produce a Donahugh child that I will designate the next ruler of Eire. It's that simple."

"I'll choose no one. I don't accept you, your title, or your imperialist fantasies. I'm a Moura Prima. My grandmother is the rightful Doma of the most powerful city-state in Innisfail."

"Aside from Aes Sidhe, of course. Our benevolent overlords...."

"Apart from Aes Sidhe, yes. I don't need you. Find yourself another 'kingmaker.'" She paused, watching him beam back at her as if she were describing the weather. "What do you even need me for? You have Damek. He'd be more than happy to take up the family standard."

She didn't like the grin that he gave her. A chill traced down her back. "Eventually, I intend to, little girl, but not yet. The boy reaches too far, too fast. That's always been his failing, as your arrogance is yours." She understood. He knew, then, whatever Damek could do to resist her Spark. Perhaps even engineered the marvel? *No.* That would undercut his power, and Patrick would *never.* It must be something Damek had managed on his own. "For the immediate future, you will entertain my barons. I don't expect you to mate with them. Never fear. Merely allow them to believe you might desire them. I expect these men to linger here and lavish you with coins and gifts, and I expect you to be a gracious, indecisive hostess. At the close, we'll perform a small drama in which the fair princess despairs of her impossible choice; then you'll choose Damek."

"I will *not*—"

"—You're to use these greedy fools for their bride price, then deprive them of both a bride and their gifts. Do you understand?"

"You'd abuse your men this way?"

He sat down with a chuckle. "Of course. You're a princess, my dear, and your father's the most powerful man in Eire. They'll fall all over themselves for the opportunity to win Bethany. I expect the gifts to be lavish, indeed."

"That's rather disingenuous of their liege lord, isn't it?"

"Bah. Men love competition."

"You expect me to flirt and play courtier? Are you out of your mind?"

"No. Is that what I said? Forgive me. I expect you to do this and show me respect as your father."

"What a dreamer you are."

"I think not. I know how you feel about the girls in this city, Una." He marked each servant trying to squeeze themselves through the walls to avoid his eye. "I can leave one in your bed with you each night. Try me—a new death for every act of insolence. You *will* come to heel if I must keep you in chains like a mongrel. Do you doubt my resolve? Don't take too long to answer. I need only snap my fingers, and you'll be sleeping with fresh corpses within the hour."

Una felt ill. "No."

"'No,' what?" he tucked two fingers behind his ear. "I don't hear you."

"I don't doubt you."

Good," he said, slapping a palm against his knee on his way off her bed. Stopping an inch shy of the doorway, he turned back. "Oh, one last thing. I expect an heir rather soon, and I think you know well whom I expect to father it. Perhaps you'll take the time to appreciate his affection for you before I give you to someone else for spite? The faster you warm to the idea, the better. I could always arrange a less attractive prospect. Might teach you both a bit of respect, no?"

He shut the door quietly behind him, but its gentle click might have been a cannon shot for its effect on her already taxed nerves.

"I refuse," Damek spat, stalking the length of Patrick's throne room with sheer pent-up rage. "The first hand that reaches out to touch her will be severed from its body. I'll have none of this ridiculous scheme!" He'd worked himself into quite a lather. Sweat dampened the dark hair at his brow, and his eyes flashed a particular shade of green wrath.

Martin, stalwart as always, stood between them. The gathered were aware there'd be little choice but to cut Damek down should his temper get the best of him. "Lord Bishop," he warned in a whisper. "Your best behavior now, as promised."

Most of Patrick's Court squirmed in discomfort in mute observance of this absurd family squabble. This wouldn't be the first time the Duch and his nephew had quarreled in a public venue, but it was the first time any worried it might come to blows. Damek was incensed. Dressed in his road-weary trousers and mud-stained boots, his black brows drew deep runnels in the muck on his face. The Lord of Clare had no doubt expected a warmer reception than this. Having returned less than an hour ago with the Duch's precious captive in hand, many of them visibly sympathized with his plight. Furious as he was, Damek marked them all. This was important information for later examination. Now, however, the foremost priority was his thrice-damned uncle and his absurdist schemes.

Patrick, never enamored of his ostentatious stone throne— brutal on his old bones, he would often remark— sat on the top step, rifling through Damek's hastily scratched reports with a raised brow. The tale they told was vivid as any fable and unlikely as a fire kindled beneath the sea. He should know. He'd lived through each one.

"Damek, you're behaving like a spoilt child. It's a harmless bit of competition, hardly an execution. It might be if you don't move your hand away from your pommel."

Nostrils flaring, Damek relented. Martin heaved an audible sigh of relief, and Patrick's guards backed up a step. The Court, too, relaxed. Damek cleared his throat of burning bile. The rage in his gut threatened to burst from him in flood. "I require no competition, Uncle. Una is mine by right and Reason."

Eyes roving a sloppy bit of vellum, Patrick blew a hearty scoff. "Indeed? I think you'll find Una is *mine*, boy. My child, my burden, and heir to *my* throne. Any claim you've ever imagined you have over her comes through me. What did you think you'd accomplish here? That you'd flout my express orders and return to make demands of me? You've been a malign boil on my arse, nephew. This is the price you pay."

Damek sent his eyes around the room. None of Patrick's courtiers seemed eager to meet his gaze. That was telling.

Interesting.

Patrick lost face today, though Damek was sure the pompous old rat was scarcely aware of it. Damek had marched North with only a few hundred men to save a woman each regarded as the rightful heir to Duch Kevin's legacy. They respected him for it, as he hoped they would. *Quite interesting, indeed.* He squared his shoulders. All he must do to prove himself the better man was keep his temper firmly in check. "Did I not bring her home to you? For over ten years, the Doma and her flock have kept our Lady Donahugh under lock and key in that zealous mortuary in Tairngare. How can you punish me for being the one man here whom you could count upon?"

Ignoring this rather poignant statement, Patrick set his scroll down and reached for another. He shook his head with a wry grin. "I will say, this is quite the yarn. If soldiery fails you, you might turn a pretty coin penning tinker's tales for simpletons. Dead men on the road. Betrayal and calamity. Murderous monsters and treacherous cutthroats." He smacked his lips. "Did you meet Finn Mac Cumhail on your travels, too?"

The Court gave a nervous, rumbling titter in response.

Damek's ears burned. "It's bloody true. Every *word*."

"If you say so, it must be true, mustn't it?"

Again, his courtiers laughed. Damek turned to give Martin a long, searching look. "Aye, Your Grace," Martin sighed. "Lord Bishop speaks true. Our men *were* ambushed by dead... things in the Greensward. Soon after, a host of stinking goblins descended upon them from the trees. I've interviewed each survivor at length. Not one uttered a single disparity. Besides, what few of our casualties we could reclaim were in a state I despair of describing."

Patrick nodded slowly. "Martin, you know I trust your word over any man here— but you were not there, were you? To escape my wroth, I mustn't put it past Damek's loyal honor guard to back this story."

"Uncle, ask Una. She was there. Many more would have died if it weren't for her and her... abilities."

"I intend to, in due course," droned Patrick. "For now, whatever might have befallen over forty of your troops does not mitigate your profound disobedience to me. I ought to have you scourged for such blatant disregard for my commands."

Careful, Damek thought.

Three of his barons are watching. "I stood in your company, Your Grace, and told you I had no intention of leaving my cousin in the barbarous North to die. I made a decision for which we are all better served, Una most of all. Forgive me, but what choice did you leave me?"

Patrick absorbed that performance with a tight, knowing smile. So the Duch did realize the game they played?

No matter.

He is too old to win, and he knows it.

Lord Wender, Damek noticed, smirked as he waited for Patrick's response. Patrick wasn't well-loved; he had never been. Men served him because he left them little choice, not for undo loyalty.

Damek counted on that.

"Very well. So, you've saved my ungrateful get from Otherworld beasties, walking dead men, and randy Sidhe lords risen from the dead. You have my thanks *and* my edict."

Damek laughed through an open mouth. "You can't be serious? Farm boys from Reason knows where— in competition with *me* for the throne?"

"Oh, I'm very serious, Damek. Better get used to it."

This time, it wasn't just Lord Wender who visibly soured on the Duch. "Fine. If my long-entombed uncle's sons mean to challenge me for Una's hand, by all means, let them meet me in the courtyard now."

"You'll leave them be, or I'll hang you from the walls by your bollocks."

Damek's filthy cloak swirled muck over his uncle's mosaic floor as he turned with a wry leer. "I don't believe you. Name a better soldier, aside from Martin here. A better statesman? Someone with a greater love for his home or its people? You can't, for that man does not exist. I refuse to compete with a pair of feral rabbits who can barely read or write their names."

Patrick stood up, crossing his arms behind his back. "I'm sorry if I gave you the impression that you'd be competing with Henry's sons— alone. Any man of means and property is free to present his suit for her dowry. Why so pale, nephew? Surely you didn't imagine you were the only worthy man in Eire?"

Damek's jaw flexed. He was suddenly even more acutely aware of how many powerful men were watching this exchange. "You would not *dare* to dangle *my wife* —"

"— Again, the union was annulled."

Martin's fingers dug into Damek's chest. Stout Lord Wender grabbed hold of his right elbow. Damek nearly dragged the pair forward in his urge to throttle his pernicious old uncle. Patrick, to his credit, did not flinch. "We were wed beneath the light of the Southernmost Star, Your Grace! By Reason, our union was *consummated*. She is not yours to give or take as you please!" If the other lords and nobles had any sympathy for the justice of this statement, Damek was beyond caring.

This age-old grievance boiled like venom from his pores.

Martin leaned in close to his ear. "If you press him any further, he'll be forced to make an example of you. You are wiser than this, lad. Let it go."

Patrick patted his belly, his grey eyes hard. "If this was meant to soften my stance, I daresay you've done better, Lord Bishop. By all means, dig your grave here today," he waved a hand. "We could do with a bit more entertainment."

Martin's firm hand moved to his opposite shoulder, squeezing hard, his expression pleading. After several calming breaths, Damek balled his fists and choked back his pride. He stepped back from Martin and shrugged his arm out of Lord Wender's grasp. He adjusted his blood-stained cuirass, his cheeks thin. "How long will your feasts and tourneys last, uncle?"

Patrick was never one to resist a smug smile, especially when he'd won an unfair argument. Taking a glass of wine from his terrorized steward, he resumed his seat on the steps. "Weeks, I expect. Maybe months, should it please me. So, what will you do? Shall you acknowledge your cousins' right to contend or be removed from Court altogether?"

Not having a choice didn't make Damek feel better about his obvious advantage. If he'd been paying attention, he'd have noticed the mutual look of revulsion each of the present Barons shared between them. Insulted and livid as he was, he must admit, deep down, Patrick's purpose was sound. He needed fainne, lumber, food, and troops to march on the North. How better to gain the men, promises, and supplies he needed than to charm it out of wealthy men and Merchers eager to woo a great heiress? Indeed, the added bitterness between them would spice the broth. Time was Damek's real punishment here. He must accept it if he wished to remain in the game a bit longer. With his grandmother's coup in Tairngare having pushed him so much further from her orbit, he had little recourse. "As you will it, your Grace," he said, his tongue sour in his mouth. "If it is your wish that I formally throw my cap in the race, so be it."

"It is."

"However, allow me to say this once and very clearly: *any* man with the gall to lay hands on my wife— including the sons of Henry FitzDonahugh— will taste my steel."

Patrick sipped his wine with a deep chuckle. "Well, there wouldn't be any sport without a strong contender, now would there?"

9

THITHER, BOUND

All necessary preparations having been made, Kaer Yin and his troupe of thirty-five men— Greenmakers and Sidhe alike— readied themselves to depart at first light. They'd gathered all the extra weapons, furs, uishge, and supplies Rosweal and its demolished environs could muster for the trip. Tam Lin had taken to sulking around the city, avoiding Kaer Yin and his retinue until the last excusable moment. That was as well for Kaer Yin. He'd had enough of his cousin and his ceaseless nagging for a while. Everyone was ready to move on, whether eager to return home over the border or trek into the inhospitable South with Kaer Yin. The Sidhe, Kaer Yin remembered, grew restless very easily. Though reserved and unfailingly polite in mixed company, they could be boisterous and quarrelsome in large groups. Already, the Roswellians shied away from the horde of towering, bored, blond giants. Several semi-serious fights broke out in Wanderer's Alley due to a copious amount of unaged uishge and general carousing. The Sidhe did not drink much uishge in Croghan or Bri Leith, a fact Kaer Yin grew more thankful for by the day.

As for Kaer Yin himself, he'd divested himself of his bandages and escaped Barb's stuffy office as soon as Rian's back was turned. Free of his swaddling, at last, he accepted Barb's invitation to take a turn around the walls. The sky threatened rain, but the weather wouldn't deter him. He wouldn't get back into that bloody bed, not for all the uishge in Barb's cellar. If he didn't move as swiftly or smoothly as usual, no one had the nerve to say so aloud. Shar, for one, followed him and Barb at a respectful distance, his mouth twisted in the slightest of half-smiles. The lad knew better than to gainsay his Crown Prince. Pent-up as Kaer Yin was, he could drag himself around the city with his teeth.

At a wide tumble-down gap in the South Wall, Barb pointed. "That there is what I'm talkin' about, Ben. The whole bloody wall might as well be made of snot and thistle."

Feeling the wound in his chest more than he'd like, Kaer Yin pretended not to sweat. "These walls were built long before the Transition. I'm amazed they've stood so long."

"It's a problem." She pursed her painted lips. "Ye and Robin are the only two fools who honestly believe we've seen the last o'Gilcannon."

"Matt's not coming back, Barb. You beat him fair and square."

She made a face, taking his arm to lead him onward. "Ain't no such thing, love. Ye'd bloody well know that too if yer head weren't crammed up that Siorai girl's—"

"Barb."

"Right. Well, aside from the Matts o'the world, if we aim to repel another invasion, we won't manage it with a farmer's pen for walls."

A chill breeze rustled the gold in Kaer Yin's right ear. Rian had done her level best to entomb him in shirts, jumpers, and scarves, but he felt the wind in his blood, regardless. Rian had been vehemently opposed to his walking around like this, but he would be damned if he'd heed her. It was well past time he was up on his own two feet. Fresh air was what he needed now, not the irritable prodding of a mean-spirited faerie. Gerrod, bless him, intercepted Rian in the tap so Kaer Yin and Barb could duck out the back. Gerrod seemed too happy to help. Kaer Yin wished the lad all the luck in the world.

He would need it.

Realizing Barb waited for a response, Kaer Yin sighed. "Not you too, Barb?"

"Course, me too! They're bound to return and bury Rosweal for good once you get that blasted... erm, yer *lovely* lass back. I was in the bloody room when you heard about Navan, wasn't I?"

Target struck.

Kaer Yin flinched. He was sorrier for Navan than he could say. The Tairnganeah, thwarted in their attempt to drag Una back to the Citadel in chains, had left quaint, pleasant Navan a smoking ruin. The Innkeeper of the unassuming *Bowman's Cross* and his son were killed in the onslaught. Kaer Yin had sent Niall and Ferdam to verify the Greenmakers' report. The village had been razed to the ground, and all that was left of the *Bowman's Cross* were two blackened walls and the charred remains of its former occupants. Kaer Yin might not be alive now were it not for the Innkeeper and his lad. He would never forget their kindness, and as soon as he set things straight with Bethany, he'd be back to deal with the Corsairs and their new mistress. He was certain Barb had poked that raw wound on purpose. "Tairnganeah were to blame for Navan, Barb. Not Una."

"Aye, all the same. They woulda done the same to us if we'd let 'em. Them Southers, a sight worse, yet. What d'ye believe is gonna happen, Ben? Ye'll have a grand caper, stealin' the Duch's get from under his nose... and no one will try to stop ye for your brass?"

"My father's troops—"

"Ain't here yet, and them that are, yer dividin' again to march South. Ye know Vanna Nema's taken the Doma's hat. Yer girl's family has fled or been imprisoned for heresy. Smartest place for the Domina now is her father's hall in Bethany."

Kaer Yin sucked at his gums while he considered her impertinent observations. A light rain began to fall as they walked. Though he felt stronger with each step, tripping over any tumbledown stones in their way would end this little foray on the lowest possible note. "What would you have me do? I cannot allow her to suffer for me."

"What about the rest o'us? We should be made to suffer for *her*. Don't be ridiculous, love. Her dear ole da won't live forever, ye know? Girl's his bloody heir, ain't she? She can wait him out. Meanwhile, we can get on with rebuildin' our lives under the protection of our restored Crown Prince. Ye belong here, guardin' the North, milord. We got plenty troubles o'our own."

He stopped midstride, drawing her up short. "Are you implying that I'm shirking my duty now?" He scoffed. "You realize that I'm technically still an exile, and none of you would have been the wiser about me if not for Una?"

"Would it make ye feel better if we pretended to be happy to know?"

Ben recoiled slightly. "Ouch, Barb..."

"Ben, I love ye, same as I do Robin, Gerry, and Dabs— I swear it. But the North can't bear the brunt for yer romance. Leave her be to make it up with her da. I'm beggin' ye."

Kaer Yin snuck a glance over his shoulder at Shar. Tam Lin's lieutenant affected the ghost of a smile. Kaer Yin's heart sank a bit to see it. No one seemed to know what they were up against, did they? Only those who'd been in the Greensward on Samhain had the first bloody clue of what they'd faced and lived to discuss due to the Duch's prodigal daughter. How could he make someone as self-centered as Barb understand? "You weren't there on Samhain. No, don't make that face. You've no idea what we survived that night or how much worse it could have been. Una put her life on the line for us. In so doing, she sacrificed the one thing she wanted above anything else: her freedom. This is not a romantic whim. We owe her a large debt. You may say she'll learn to live in Bethany and accept her fate. You may say she'd be better off, that we might all be better off. I beg to differ. Her father and his thuggish Barons mean to make war through her. You seem eager to ignore that fact. That war will come to Rosweal, whether you like it or not. For my part, I will not leave Una *anywhere*, ever again, unless I hear the demand from her lips."

"Ben, see reason—"

"No. As a friend, I appreciate your counsel," he said, gently gripping her elbow. "As your liege lord and the Crown Prince of Innisfail, I do not require it."

Barb trudged along in silence for a while, chewing at her cheek. Her sulk was fine by him. He didn't need her blessing or her permission. As long as Patrick Donahugh had Una in his custody, Bri Leith could never truly be safe. To Barb's—and perhaps most of Rosweal's— isolationist way of thinking, Una might serve the realm better dead. Kaer Yin did not share the sentiment. He'd scour the blackest depths of Tech Duinn for her if he must.

"Politics aside, she deserves a choice, Barb."

"So do we, damn ye."

"War will come, with Una or without. Wouldn't you rather serve your Ard Ri in this matter rather than hinder him?"

"Yer assumin' we'll have the option. If there's to be a war no matter what we do, why bother to conflate it by raidin' the lion's den? Ben, ye must see sense here. I know yer cousin has said as much many times, but one girl won't change the course o' things. Our Crown Prince and his Wild Hunt, now, might."

There was a thick ring of fairness to that statement.

Nonetheless...

"I won't abandon her, any more than I would Robin or Tam Lin. She saved my life, and I owe her. Robin, Rian, and Gerry owe her. *Rosweal* owes her. I'll have it from her what she wants to do and where she'd like to be, questions no one has ever bothered to ask her. Rosweal will not go undefended, Barb. I vow it."

"Between 'em, Tairngare and Bethany have the whole of Eire divided into opposin' camps. Sure as the sun sets in the west, we'll be someone's target. We need ye here to keep the peace, Yer Arseness, not off chasin' a skirt into enemy territory."

Kaer Yin rounded on her for a stinging retort, but Gerrod jogged up to them from the ramshackle Taran Gate. "Ben," he panted, jerking a thumb behind him. "A woman is askin' for ye."

Both Barb and Kaer Yin blinked back at Gerrod. "A woman?" asked Barb.

Gerrod fidgeted to a profound degree. "Yeah, um, Ben... she's—"

"A bloody *Moura*," Barb spat, peering around his scrawny back.

The woman in question calmly stepped past Shar without fear. Behind her, a small retinue of Tairnganese Merchers loitered beneath the Gate. She was tall and lean, with lustrous dark skin and bright, uishge-colored eyes. She spared Barb the slightest twitch of her nose.

"*Alvra*, actually. Eva is my name. My lord prince Kaer Yin, I've come to offer you my service."

EVA ALVRA WAS PERHAPS THE MOST IMPOSING WOMAN ANYONE, SAVE the Sidhe, had ever seen. Her fine, honey-dark skin, and bright amber eyes, caught and held the light in fascinating ways. Added to the stark beauty of her face, there was something *present* about her bearing that made her all the more substantial, despite her thin frame. The Greenmakers had no idea how to look at her, much less speak to her. Kaer Yin invited her and her man-at-arms to converse with him in the privacy of Barb's once-private office. Mel Carra struck an equally impressive figure, being nearly as broad through the shoulders as he was tall. Refusing a seat, he stood at Eva's right elbow, watchful and silent as a stone lion.

"Your Highness," said Eva, her voice rich as a wind flute. "My aunt, the true Doma of Tairngare, has sent me to bring her granddaughter home."

Barb sat beside the window, her brow cross as she could make it. "To execution? Yer families're outta power now, ain't they? The bloody girl *is* home. Ask anyone with a brain."

Eva's gaze raked Barb without mercy. Kaer Yin saw the hardened bawd flinch for the first time, ever. "Do you know to whom you speak, *novitiate*?"

"Y-yeah."

"Then I would mind that mouth, were I you."

The threat was enough to force Barb into a chair facing the hearth, her cheeks livid. Robin and Kaer Yin shared a look over Eva's head.

"Well," said Kaer Yin. "I'm pleased to make your acquaintance, My Lady. Though I don't wholly agree with Mistress Dormer, I do have to restate the obvious. Tairngare is hostile territory now. Surely you knew that before you approached me?"

"I do know it," she frowned. "My aunt has fled to Cymru, though I fear she'll find no harbor there. In the meantime, my mother has been executed, and my grandmother scourged and imprisoned. Thank you, my followers and I are well aware of the dilemma."

Sitting beside Kaer Yin, Rian covered her mouth, her brows drawn down hard. Tam Lin and Shar touched two fingers to their temple, then their hearts: Dannan mourning.

Barb scowled into the flames, sullen and unsympathetic.

"Siora," breathed Robin with a grimace. "I am so sorry, milady. Terrible luck that, but I'm not sure how we can help ye?"

"On the contrary, it is *we* who aim to help you. Your Highness, you mean to liberate my niece from Bethany, correct?"

"Yes," Kaer Yin answered, ignoring the tightened lips of two people in his company. "But I do not intend to return her to the Red City. It's my opinion, and my father would concur, that she'd be safest in Bri Leith. I intend to offer her the choice. I will respect her decision if she wishes to remain in Bethany." The intensity of Eva's stare made Kaer Yin slightly uncomfortable, but he would not bend. Not for anyone. "Forgive me, but the Doma's wishes are none of my concern."

Eva studied him so long that he struggled not to squirm. After an eternity, her mouth quirked. "I see your intent quite clearly, Your Highness. I approve."

He did squirm a bit then. Was that this one's power? To read the hearts of men. *Wonderful*, he thought. "Not everyone shares your sentiment."

She scanned the dissenters with a raised brow. *So, she* does *know a person's innermost thoughts? Herne, Una. Your family is terrifying.* "They fear for you, Your Highness, and for their homes. They have reason to. Many terrible things are happening in Eire."

"Exactly," grumbled Barb to the fireplace. Robin patted her leg.

"None of this is Una's fault," Rian said, crossing her arms at Barb's back. "How often do we have to explain it before it sinks in?"

Barb ignored her. Tam Lin's expression remained flat and disinterested as he could make it, but Kaer Yin knew he was dying to speak his piece. "Then we are after the same thing, Your Highness," smirked Eva. "My aunt wishes for Una's safety, above all considerations. You have my full and free support if this is your goal."

Tam Lin butted in, "What support can you offer for this absurd quest? A lone woman and a handful of barely armed men?"

Eva folded her hands. "I hear the fear of the unknown in your voice, Prince O'Ruiadh. Thus, I will forgive your insult."

"No slight intended, but honestly— I don't understand why we need another woman on this march. We've already got one, and she'll be about as useful as tits on a bull."

Rian's head swiveled around to Kaer Yin. "I can slap him *now*?"

Kaer Yin pinched the bridge of his nose. "My Lady Alvra, what my cousin means to say is—"

"He can speak for himself, *Ard Tiarne*," Tam Lin interjected. "We're leaving in the morning, counter to every argument. I fail to see why we require another damned woman to defend along the way. It's not as if we're headed to Ten Bells for a bloody fête, now is it? I'll not have—"

Tam Lin broke off as suddenly as he started. His eyes went slightly slack at the corners as Eva leaned forward to tug up the hem of her robe. Sinking to his knees with a mooncalf expression, Tam Lin pressed his lips against the toe of her boot. When he looked up, all adoration and innocence, Eva patted his cheek. The spell was broken. "Doubt any males in your company could do anything like *that*, could they, Your Highness?"

Acutely embarrassed, Tam Lin lurched to his feet and scrambled away from her as fast as he could. "You... *witch!*"

Rian threw back her head, laughing until her cheeks went scarlet.

Gerrod, Shar, and Niall backed as far into the wall as they could.

Kaer Yin wrenched Robin's flask out of his hand and took a long gulp.

Barb didn't move a muscle.

Mel Carra coughed into his fist while Eva grinned at the Prince of Connaught. "Domina Alvra is the finest practitioner of Mentis Imperium in Tairngare. She had many acolytes in the Cloister before she retired."

"I can see that," Kaer Yin set a steadying hand on Tam Lin's shoulder. "Ah. Forgive my cousin. He never met Una, you understand?"

"Of course." She dipped her head.

"Yin, you mean to say the girl you're after can... I knew it! I knew she must have cursed you in some way!"

"My niece's gifts differ greatly from mine, Your Highness. She does not practice Mentis Imperium at all. Rather, Corpus Imperium— a discipline so advanced that there are no precedents. In a thousand years, only Una was born with the aptitude for it."

"And that means... what?"

"'*Corpus*' means 'body,'" said Rian behind her hand, cutting her eyes at him. "Thousands of years to live and no time to read. How did your kind conquer Innisfail?"

Tam Lin curled his lip but refused to take her bait. "You're telling me this idiot's paramour can control a man's body? Why am I not surprised?"

Kaer Yin shoved him into the mantle with a dismissive snort. "She's not my paramour, erm, or whatever. And that isn't what Lady Alvra said, is it? Una can... well, maybe we should discuss that later?" A mutual chill ran through several of the gathered occupants.

They'd each seen what Corpus Imperium meant firsthand.

"I appreciate your offer, Lady Alvra, but I warn you, it may come to a terrible end. I'm taking those who fully grasp the danger. I can't promise you or anyone else will return unscathed."

"Oh," Eva winked at Mel Carra, who chuckled in return. "No need to worry about us, Your Highness. I ventured here for my niece. If I'd doubt you or your ability to retrieve her, no conversation would have been necessary between us."

Kaer Yin shivered. He didn't doubt it. "Right."

"We're with you, Prince Kaer Yin. Who knows? You may find your men are on their best behavior all the while."

THE BOAT, SLAPPED BY INCESSANT, FRIGID GREEN WAVES, SLID ONTO the pebbled shore. In the hard rain, the crewmen who dragged her up the beach could scarcely see the end of their noses. Between these eight half-frozen bodies sat a tiny woman huddled within the vessel. Despite a layer of furs capped by the finest sealskin cloak fainne could buy, Drem shuddered for the unrelenting cold. Almost a month of ceaseless travel in abysmal Dor Oras weather had taken its toll on her. She was disused to the outdoors, to put things mildly. Nearing her seventh decade on earth, she'd spent most of her life in the safety and warmth of the Cloister of the Eternal Flame, where she belonged. To her mind, she had no bloody business traipsing around the Continent like some crazed bard-seeking patrons.

Yet, what choice did she have? Her great enemy's long reach had all but chased her to the edge of the world. With most of her allies dead or imprisoned, Drem had grown desperate for more.

Driven from her rightful seat in the Cloister, she went first to Cymru to garner the aid of Merchers loyal to the Moura Clan. Nema's heretics had gotten there first. The Ruma Clan, who had been granted oversight of the Tairnganese Consulate in Swansea, had been wiped out to a woman, and one of Pors Yma's toadying relatives installed as Governess. Loyal Siorai were rounded up and defrocked en masse. Those who disavowed the Mouras and the Libella were granted lands, titles, and honors in the new Doma's name.

Drem had barely escaped the Swansea cesspit of Unionist vipers when she came upon another well-plotted coup in Kernow. Before reaching the Siorai rectory to gain her bearings, a mob descended upon her retinue, killing several handmaidens and a dozen of her loyal Cohort. This second escape proved more harrowing than the first. Sometime later, while she lay sick upon the freezing Sea of Mannanan, her chief of staff informed her that her niece Ana had been captured on the dock, then executed in Tairngare's dungeon a week after. Drem hadn't had time to mourn or lament her cousin Basa's lengthy internment.

Nothing much she could do about it now, was there? When Lord Gaelin fled his Hall in Bretagne, rather than meet with her, Drem realized there was one place left to sail.

Aes Sidhe.

The only Sidhe harbor friendly to Eirean transports was located on the peninsula of Man. Once she landed in Lomond, she was forced to hire ponies for the long trek around the Bay of Man, over the hills at Dalriada, then through the Argyll forest to Dale. The going had been quite hard on her old bones. From ice-choked waterways to long muddied roads snaking through impenetrable forests below snow-capped peaks, the wilds of Scotia were not for the faint of heart.

She had caught a cold in Dale and rested at an inn reserved for Merchers and visiting dignitaries for several days. Mortal men and women were not much welcome in Aes Sidhe, and her reception in each port and town had been as frosty as the weather. That was as well; she was too tired and ill to mind. Once her cold subsided enough to travel, she booked transport to Skye with the last of her ready funds. If Lord and Lady Bres would not have her, she had no one else to whom she might turn. She knew this was the end of the line for the once mighty Drem Moura.

Vanna Nema had done her work well.

So well, Drem despaired that things might never be set right again.

On the beach, some fifty paces ahead sat three silent figures atop smoke-grey mounts: Duskendales, Drem recalled from her studies, thoroughbreds of unequaled breeding, for which the Port of Dale was named. If the Sidhe felt the cold in their marrows as Drem did, they didn't show it. Motionless as statues, they waited while she was ushered from the inundated boat by two burly Eirean sailors and carried to dry sand. Her ladies followed, the hem of their robes dragging behind them in the surf. The middle rider— a female, Drem noted— nudged her mare forward. Huffing, shivering, and miserable, Drem held out a hand to keep the boatmen from leaving should this meeting fail. The rider had the white-blond locks of her Dannan ancestors. Her skin was pale and smooth as spun moonlight, and her full pink mouth drew into a sharp line as she neared. Her beauty was staggering. Drem flushed to the roots of her grey hair. She dreaded to know what she must look like to such an ethereal creature.

The pale lady circled Drem twice before spinning her mount to a halt. Silver eyes flashed. "Doma Drem Moura. What brings you to Skye?"

Finding her voice with some difficulty, Drem croaked, "I've come to beg the hospitality of the Lord and Lady Bres. I hope our near-forty years of friendship and fidelity will not be forsaken."

The lady considered her for some time, rain falling in sheets around her. "The new Doma has you on the run, it seems? Yet you come here last. Why is that, your eminence?"

"Had I known I'd be welcome, it should have been the first. Let's not pretend the Sidhe hold any great affection for my race."

The lady's mouth twitched. "True. Though I wonder that you'd venture here instead of Bri Leith or Croghan. The Ard Ri and his brother hold far more influence in Eire than the Lord and Lady of Skye. What did you hope to gain from Lord Jan Fir?"

Drem chuckled. She was not a fool; the lady's torc marked her out as no crier could have. "I didn't come to treat with Lord Jan Fir. I came to see Lady Eri, specifically. I have news that is sure to interest her personally."

"Oh," the lady's brow quirked. "What might you wish of the Ard Ri's daughter?"

"That her brother has emerged from his exile, and if I'm not mistaken, means to take my granddaughter to your father's court."

Eri Ap Midhir Bres, the Lady of Skye and Queen of Scotia, stared down at Drem as if she'd told her the sun was filled with cheese. "Kaer Yin would *never....*"

"He would. He *has*. You and I have much to discuss, it seems... Your Highness. If we might—" But here, Drem faltered. The world spun a bit on its axis. The heavy grey sky overhead swirled and frothed, riotous as the sea behind her. The Queen of Scotia had but a moment to stare at her in confused horror when the stony beach rushed into Drem's face.

10

POISONED WELL

Aoife hated Grainne more than she'd ever hated anyone in her life. She thought she'd already accumulated quite an impressive list of people she'd love to murder in a lovingly articulated order. Those at the bottom, she thought to kill in an offhand, incidental sort of way: casually, caustically. Those at the top, however, inspired half-a-thousand scenarios in which she'd exact revenge for every ounce of pain, humiliation, or derision they'd ever spared her. Vanna Nema, of course, had squatted at the very top for ages. Now, Grainne Mac Nemed dueled the imperious Nema for first place. Grainne was the new standard by which Aoife would gauge her deepest loathing. The woman was officious, vain, posturing, and indiscriminately cruel.

The Mac Nemed Clan were the most arrogant creatures to plague the Gods' green earth in Aoife's vaunted experience— but that was not to say some weren't worse than others. Much, much worse, in Grainne's case. The spoilt, selfish grandchild of Falan Mac Eochaid, the Elder; Grainne had been born to imagine herself superior to every living thing, including her relatives. Unlike their cousins among the Tuatha De Dannan, the Fir Bolg left their rule almost strictly to their women. Thus, she'd been the great Liadan Mac Nemed's only true heir for centuries. Insignificant half-breeds like Aoife were nothing to the immortal descendants of the Fomorian King, Balor.

Aoife forgot that for any length of time at her peril.

Having descended upon a nameless village twenty miles from Tara, Grainne's troupe of 'Dannan' warriors looted, pillaged, and burned at her command. Aoife, partially healed of her wounds, had watched the flames stretch high into the predawn sky while chained to the rear wagon. Two days later, their disguised Warhammers struck a pair of towns ten miles nearer the city.

None were left alive.

The broken bodies of women and children were strung from trees or displayed before their burning farms. Aoife, manacled and humbled before her compatriots, was tasked with many of the macabre decorations herself. On the fourth night, the Bolg rested. Ignored, starved, and humiliated, Aoife spent that eve and many after bound and gagged among the supply train. It took days for someone to remember to feed her and longer for Grainne to find a reason to strike her from her iron bracelets. Ten days into their clandestine mission, Aoife was ordered to take a branch of their force into Tara itself to sow discord, foster fears, and murder with impunity. Aoife was whipped again at Grainne's pleasure before she allowed her to roam unfettered. The purpose of this cruelty, Grainne told her over a glass of Cymrian wine, was to reaffirm Aoife's newfound humility.

If the unwitting citizens of Tara had any idea why their Dannan overlords were slaughtering Eireans in increasingly ingenious ways, they had Grainne Mac Nemed to thank for their terror. Aoife had thrown herself into her work with malicious fervor. Each child she had strangled in the dark, every man they gutted or woman they garroted, bore Grainne's mocking face. Each further whetted her appetite to add parricide to her list of sins. Aoife vowed to kill her cousin first. Even Vanna Nema, her oldest and most persistent torturer, could wait. When all of Eire was conquered for the Bolg, at least Grainne wouldn't live to see it.

Mighty Balor, Aoife prayed.

Bless this child of your bones with your patience, power, and vengeance. When the blood of your enemies soaks the soil of your forebears, I will ravage your bloodline, purge the Clan of Eochaid's filth… hear me, Balor. Grant me your blessing.

Bearing an ogham charm and the false silver hair of their greatest foes, Aoife and her kin crept through slums and back-alleys, spreading death and discord like a plague.

Gan wasn't sure why he was still alive. The slightest twitch sent hot waves of roiling pain throughout his body, yet he lived. How could one feel the anguish of a thousand wounds and not die? Each breath was agony. He could scarcely speak above a whisper for the raw ruin of his throat. What was left of his stomach grew thinner each day for lack of stable nourishment. He could not eat or drink save from a tube that was mercilessly shoved down his blistered gullet three times a day. He couldn't urinate on his own, either. Another tiny cylinder had to be inserted into the scarred remnants of his phallus, an organ that had been burned clear of skin and fat, leaving behind a nerveless muscle devoid of purpose. Nearly all of the skin on his body was cracked and sloughing off like charred pork. For days and days, tormented by hunger and terrible thirst, the smell of his cooked flesh had almost driven him mad. He might have wept had he any tear ducts left to cool his eyes. A few weeks ago, Fawa Gan had been a plump, well-dressed figure of some importance in the Cloister of the Eternal Flame. Now, he was a hairless, skinless monster from his own worst nightmares, a pitiful wretch, too odious to kill.

Fawa Gan would never know mercy again.

Nema would have it no other way.

After being dragged away from Aoife, however many days, weeks, or months ago—he had no idea how long—he was shut up in a minor ward on the Second Floor. The Secundas' medical wing, he knew instinctively. At least this new cell was not so dark as it had been underground, nor as filthy or endlessly damp. He had a dry cot to lay upon, a small window to wail through, and a steady stream of silent Secundas to care for him, bearing various implements of well-intended torture. Some brought soap and water. Some brought stinking medicinals. Others brought sharp things: needles, slim knives to cut away his dead flesh, or silver rollers to test his reflexology. Most, he could not feel enough to mind. The nerve endings that snaked through most parts of his body were dead. There were a few, however, which tore at his sanity to touch... and touch them, Nema's servants did. The pain was unreal, unimaginable, *mythic*.

A worse hell he could never dream possible.

Relentlessly, the Secundas came. They poked, prodded, abraded, squeezed, popped, tore, shredded, pounded, and cut at him like handmaidens of the Kneeler's Devil. Throughout, he was offered no sedatives, no pain relievers, and no sympathy. The Secundas Nema selected to treat him were chosen for their lack of squeamishness and, likely, their lack of empathy. As it wore on, Gan found himself rather used to the pain. Their needle-pricks didn't sting as they had at first, their tiny blades did not bite so deep, and their salves and unguents did not sear his exposed tissues like acid. The longer he lay there, he grew less and less interested in how much he hurt; and oh, he hurt.

His was an absolute symphony of suffering.

Though, it was also true that he minded *less*. He feared *less*. Hope had dwindled to the smallest particle in his heart. Its imminent loss pained him *less* every hour. In its place, a rich, beguiling apathy took hold. Nema had something more planned for him. A spectacular terror should have gnawed at what remained of his guts. He should have lain awake nights, feverish (if he could sweat, that is) with fear and dark anticipation. He did not. Indeed, he struggled to care at all. The pain became familiar, almost welcome. It might be all that he would ever feel again. Internally, his spirit was cold, flat, and heavy as lead.

At some point in the haze of silent grey days, Nema's head bootlicker came to inspect him. Pors Yma, reinstated to the Cloister and appointed to Alta Prima without undergoing the Ninth Ordeal, squinted down at him for quite some time. He turned his face away from the commingled horror and sadistic pleasure in her dark eyes. "How long before he'll be fit to move, Secundus?"

One of his stoic nurses dipped her head. "He might be moved now, My Lady. Though I doubt he'll walk on his own. His muscles are intact, though the outer flesh has been largely damaged beyond repair."

"I don't care that he's in pain. I care that he's able to attend the Doma. When will that be?"

"His fingers lost most of their nerve-endings, My Lady. I cannot say when—"

"You there," she addressed Gan directly. He ignored her. "The Doma has spared your worthless life for a reason, ingrate. I'm going to hand you this stylus," he almost felt a cold object pressing against his partially healed right hand. "You'd better grasp it, you pathetic, mewling worm."

He did not. To the Hells with them all.

He was a hollow, quivering tragedy of a man. What urge he'd ever had to please any of these arrogant, ungrateful witches had peeled off with his skin. He was a new man, ready and eager to die. Gan chose a dark spot beneath the windowpane to focus upon. Pors struck him. Blissfully, he didn't feel that either. She shouted unintelligible invectives into his ear, but he did not care. Instead, he imagined the stain was a tiny rabbit hopping through spotty bracken. Shapes emerged and coalesced all over that filthy rear wall. By the time Pors left in a huff, quite a menagerie of harmless woodland critters frolicked before his milky eyes. He slept for a time then, and when he woke, he immediately tumbled into a dreamless slumber.

Hours passed. Days, perhaps. He had no way to tell.

In one of these wakeful dazes, they came for him again. Rough arms hauled him upward. Burly hands hefted him from his cot. His rabbit hopped along the wall, unable to stall the inevitable. Dragged down the hall and up many flights of stairs, Gan wondered how Nema would do it. Would she have him gutted before her? Thrown from the Crown of the Citadel? Beaten to death, perhaps? Impaled, poisoned, or hacked to bits? He was unmoved. She'd already burned him alive; what else could she do to him that would hurt near as much?

In an unfamiliar room, with a particular rug that he'd purchased for her from Lady Devaschelle in Bretagne twenty years before, Gan was tossed to the floor. The pain was a bright sword in his mind, but that hardly mattered to anyone, least of all himself. Nema sat in her high-backed chair, smirking at him from her vanity mirror. "Ah," she said, her tone light and teasing. "There you are, my dear boy. We have important guests today, so I expect you'll have your work cut out for you."

He blinked back at her in dumbfounded silence.

She raised a brow. "Is his hearing affected?"

"No," said one of his manhandlers. "Secunda Marta was clear, he retains his faculties, if not the full range of motion."

A vivid green eye held Gan captive in its cold depths. "Gan, I will have the Cyrmian knot today, I think."

Wait... she *could not* mean...?

"Get him up."

He was jerked upright and held to his feet from either side. One of his captors shoved a comb and stylus into his hand, viciously closing his mauled fingers around each implement. Gan wavered in their arms, unsteady as a reed in the wind. His fingers shook. "What are you waiting for?" she asked, watching him through the glass. "I expect your best work, of course."

Gan dropped the tools and spat, thin spittle trailing down his peeling chin. His guards struck him until his breath came in thin whistles, though they did not allow him to crumple to the floor. They held him up and shoved the tools into his hands once more. He wheezed while Nema grinned from her chair. "Now, now, Gan. We mustn't be rude. If you'd rather, perhaps your sister Hela would take your place for you? Your mother, Nina, maybe? They are both here, of course. I'm surprised you did not see them in the dungeons on your way past?"

Another kind of pain gripped Gan's heart then, digging its sharp talons in. "Shall I send for one of them?"

A guard shoved Gan forward, keeping a forearm against his spine to steady him on his feet. A helpless gurgle escaped his chest. He could feel the stylus in his hand but struggled to grasp it. Had he imagined there was no worse pain? What a fool he was. He had always been such a pompous, greedy fool. Hadn't he?

"I give you no leave to exit my service, Fawa Gan. Where once you held the honor and privilege of being my most trusted steward, you are now my dog. Where I walk, so shall you crawl. Where I sit, you shall kneel. This is the *geis* I place upon you, treacherous Gan. I curse you to shadow my every move in perfect adoration for the rest of your miserable life. A simpering, loathsome toad you shall be. A disgusting wreck of mangled flesh and putrid obeisance. *That* is your punishment, my love. Is it not perfect? Are you not grateful?"

One of her guards punched him in the middle, hard. He doubled over but was not allowed to fall. He glared at Nema with all the defiance he could muster. She observed the display with dispassionate humor. He took a second blow to the belly, then dangled queerly from his captors' arms.

"Each time you flash me an independent eye, your family will bear the brunt. Every wound you have shall be replicated in your mother's hide. Your sister, I will pass through the Cohort's Hall for *any* disobedience. Do you understand?"

Inside, Gan bled. His heart's blood boiled anew.

He *did* understand.

He and Aoife shared the same fate, the same curse.

He didn't answer. Nema smiled. "Excellent. I hope I won't need to explain myself again for their sake. Now, pick up that comb, and come here."

THE CORPSE SWUNG, PURPLE AND BLOATED, FROM THE CLOTHESLINE, small face distended, head twisted at an unnatural angle. Beside him, his mother wailed, kicked, and thrashed at any who meant to pry her away from him. The child couldn't have been more than ten when he'd died. His neck had been broken. His scrawny little body posed like a scarecrow at the end of a line of sheets and petticoats. Dumbfounded and infuriated by the discovery, the citizens who should have been preparing for the day's market stopped to gape and rail at their neighbors. The outrage was palpable but not quite *perfect*.

Not yet.

The victim was too old. That had to be it. A wizened street urchin was hardly the picture of youthful purity.

Oh well, Aoife would catch a younger one next time.

Nothing motivated a mob quite so much as innocent blood.

A filthy farmer in high-patched coveralls careened around the corner, accompanied by half a dozen men. His roar rattled her teeth in their casings. From her place at the rear of the crowd, Aoife was careful not to smile.

Now we're getting somewhere.

The farmer threw himself at the woman as she cradled her murdered child: the father, no doubt. In slavering disbelief, the farmer's heartbreaking, pathetic cries echoed about the market. "*Who?* Who would do this to my Denn?" he bellowed, drooling into his sobbing wife's hair. "He were a good lad! A good lad!"

Aoife smothered a cough. She had caught the little bugger with his hand in her pocket. He'd picked the wrong person to rob, as it turned out. From the fading lash marks she spied peeking out of the neckline of his tunic; this wasn't the first time he'd been called to account, either. These two carried on like he'd been a Kneeler's saint. The way his mother's tits sagged out of her garish bodice told Aoife all she needed to know about the family. Should she weep for the lice-ridden child of an uneducated ruffian and an obvious whore?

Hardly. Who cared about one more dead pickpocket, anyway?

Yes, yes. Grab your pitchforks, Milesian scum, and be quick about it already. I'm starving.

A constable arrived on the scene to control the crowd and get to the bottom of this terrible affair. On his heels jogged an overweight lamplighter and two more officials, each bearing the appropriate bands over their upper arms. The lamplighter, perhaps the most important of these unimpressive personages, mounted the communal drying platform with slackened jaws and grey cheeks. He gawped at the dead boy and his hysterical parents as if he'd never seen such a thing. Aoife resisted the urge to scoff. Tara had been sacked by Bethany and retaken by Tairngare more times than she could count.

The loss of one boy would hardly tip the scale.

The lamplighter set a calming hand on the howling father's shoulder and whispered soothing, nonsensical gibberish to the mother. This was taking entirely too bloody long. Aoife cupped a hand over her mouth. "What's he got in his hand there, master?"

The lamplighter glanced at the crowd to locate the speaker, but Aoife had already moved along the far wall, near the exit. After several more minutes of shouting and carrying on, he finally knelt to pry open the boy's blue fingers.

Took you long enough, fool, she thought with palpable relief.

She was bored of Tara and more than ready to move on. Despite the noise, she heard his high gasp well over everyone's heads. In apparent disbelief, he mumbled over his discovery for an undue span. Aoife rolled her eyes. Just how thick were these people? Gods! He showed the wad in his palm, first to the boy's parents, who shook their bleary heads in confusion, then to his two companions in town governance. They scratched their heads and argued amongst themselves to an infernal degree.

The crowd grew more curious by the second but not fast enough for Aoife's taste. "Ain't those *Sidhe* colors?" she called, moving further away. The gasp that rippled through the onlookers was precisely what she wanted to hear.

"I was at Dumnain, Master Lilken! Them are Sidhe colors— the High King's guard!" bayed one fellow. "Leapin' stag, three stars. All done up white."

"Why would the Sidhe murder a young boy in Tara?" disagreed a matron behind him. "Yer barkin'."

"How would a lad like Denn have such a thing if it ain't true?"

"I seen them colors too. At Palsneath, two days ago. They found a pair o'girls dead by the riverside there. One o'em, lovely lass by all accounts, facedown over the white arrow what done her in," said another.

A bevy of 'nays' answered that accusation.

"What's he doin' with that sort of tunic in his hand then, eh?" asked someone else.

"Well," said a neighbor. "Denn *were* a bit fleet of finger, ye ask me. Maybe he—"

"... heard there's been loads o'these sorts o'attacks, younguns, mostly. Up and down the—"

"... Aye, they all say the High King's ailin'. Ain't left his hall in near on twenty years. Maybe he's losin' control o'his—"

"... Ain't the same no more since the Crown Prince died. I hear—"

Mission accomplished.

Aoife whirled away from the gathering. Creahal and Carn waited for her in the woods, a mile outside of town. They were twins. Aoife had known them since she was a girl. Their presence was the sole kindness Grainne thought to provide for her on this most odious of quests. They'd been her father Sionnavar's thrains and, technically, part of her inheritance. Blood-bonded men were hard to come by and equally challenging to keep from their masters. They could not serve her within the Cloister, but they were ever ready to ride to her aid. Once Grainne grew bored of punishing her, she'd given Aoife leave to choose her accomplices.

No choice could have been simpler.

She wouldn't call the brutal pair 'friends': Aoife did not understand what that word even meant, but she disliked them least. Besides, they came in handy. Usually, she was left to perform Nema's impossible tasks on her own. Creahal passed her a bone flask once she was properly seated on her mount.

"Any word from Her Whorish Majesty?" she asked.

Carn grinned at his brother. Their skin gleamed bronze in the cold morning sunlight. "Aye, Lady Sionnavar. She bid us tell you we're meant to march south this time, closer to Bethany."

"Whatever. Where will she be while we're doing all the work?"

The brothers were well used to Aoife's vitriol. If her grandmother couldn't break her of the habit, two low-born Bolgish warriors would be hard-pressed to try. "In Tairngare, lady. The Dowager is holding a banquet for visiting dignitaries."

Aoife whistled, tugging on her reins. Behind them, Tara's bells chimed furiously, and farmers trickled through the gates like their crops were after them. They would lock those gates now and stand watch on the walls while their officials sent messages to neighboring townships. A murdering band of Sidhe warriors was on the prowl. She expected the news would be all over Eire in a few days. "So soon? Well, she is in a hurry, isn't she?"

Creahal concurred, "Our time approaches."

Aoife half-laughed. "We'll see if it's an improvement. She can't repudiate Midhir this quickly. She must have some other game in mind."

"She intends to feast the lords and ladies of the Cymrian Merchers Guild, her most recent converts, and allow them to air their grievances over the High King. The Dowager is quite clever, Lady Sionnavar. You take after her," said Carn.

"I'll forgive you for that, once."

Carn ducked his head. "No offense intended."

She made a face. "While she and my worthless cousin Grainne are busily stuffing their holes with pie, we have work to do."

"Yes, My Lady," they said in unison.

Unrolling a worn map from the breast pocket of her tunic, she traced a forefinger around the mound of Tara to the South. "I suppose Malahide and its satellite townships are ripe for a raid? Let's hit the villages first, then round up in the city, as we've done here."

"Very good, My Lady."

Ahead, under the shade of crackling, winter-stripped trees, waited twenty well-armed Bolgish Warhammers. Each wore a lovely white Dannan cuirass, stained with blood and darker things. Giving them a slight nod, she reined in below the far-reaching boughs of an ancient oak. "We're headed south. Keep your ogham charms close, boys. We don't want these simpering Eireans to have the first idea what's coming for them, now do we?"

11
THIS GILDED CAGE

Una watched snowflakes gather and swirl outside her tiny window and longed for the courage to squeeze through and leap. If the seven-story fall didn't kill her, and the cold idn't finish her, perhaps she'd swim to safety on the far shore? Donahugh's Bay was not especially deep at its northern side. The muddy, dark Lee wound inland through spotty reeds and shallow tidal pools. Here, below Kevin's Keep, the dark green sea writhed and churned along its engineered cliff. Many centuries ago, before the waters receded and ice reclaimed the northernmost reaches of the continent, the ocean had nearly gobbled up all of the southeastern shoreline.

In a furious bid to salvage their coastland and protect their farms and homes from inundation, the ancient Eireans had hastily constructed huge cofferdams filled with limestone and shale from the Eirean interior. Massive granite girders and artificial cliffs of cultivated earth and stone were stacked one on top of the other until the Southeastern shore bore as many crags and cliffs as the Ring of Kerry in the west. None could ever deny that Bethany's builders had been a remarkable group of engineers.

Her ancestor, Duch Thomas Donahugh, had been more enamored of the Bethonair legacy than anyone before him. He spent decades adding to the founders' achievements. Substantial stone walls were stacked atop cliffs he'd heightened by another twenty feet. The old roads, leading through to the ancient city of Cork a few miles upriver, were repaved to stretch to the coast, where the foundations of his new fortress were laid. Naturally, the citizens followed the workers. A new city sprang up around his rudimentary Keep. By the time her grandfather Kevin had become Duch, Bethany was already a bustling seaside port, with some four hundred thousand families thriving under Donahugh rule. Duch Kevin was himself an avid builder. He spent twenty years rebuilding Thomas' fortress to its present might and grandeur. Hence, it now bore his name. For Una, the engineering marvels that produced such an imposing seaside citadel were equally infuriating. A sheer drop over steep cliffs into frigid waters choked with ice and sharp stones muddled any escape plan she might have— as Patrick had known it would. If she survived the fall, she'd be sucked out to sea by the current long before she made it to the shallows on the opposite side of the bay.

She was well and trapped.

Short of condoning the murder of her maids, she had little choice but to wait for a better opportunity. She couldn't fly, could she? What else was she supposed to do? Sighing, she watched the snow billet against the glass pane and buried her longing down deep. Moaning over her fate would do her no bloody good. She had time to *plan* if nothing else. That must be how she approached things from here on. Defying Patrick's wishes and remaining cooped up in her chambers for weeks might have satisfied some inner need to humiliate her father, but it did nothing to further her cause.

Indeed, the one person suffering from her sulk was herself.

Perhaps, Patrick's greatest weapon was boredom.

"Planning to leap into the wind, my dear?" inquired the man himself from the open door. His voice made her jump.

She hadn't seen him for some days. Chuckling, he turned to wave his guardsmen in. Each bore a heavy trunk, which they heaved onto the bearskin rug and took their leave. Una groaned. "What in the Hells is this?"

"Clothes, jewels, pretty things I expect you to wear. What else?" he said, patting his shrinking gut with a knowing smile. "Come, Una, a lovely frock is hardly torture."

She wrinkled her nose and turned away. "Leave them and go."

He looked around. "It's dull as a library in here, girl. Get up. We're going for a walk."

"*No*, thank you."

"You can walk on your own two feet or be dragged through the halls by my Corpsmen. Don't test me, Una. There are people I want you to meet."

Patrick crossed his arms. They glared at each other in silence for a long while. In the end, Una's acute boredom won out. What was a little humiliation to weeks of self-imposed solitary confinement? Sucking her teeth with exaggerated malice, she stood up and smoothed her gown, a cream and gold-colored bit of frippery that looked well with the pearls winding through her hair. "Fine. Where shall I pretend to be a simpering maiden first, father?"

Patrick cocked his head. "I believe that's the first time you've called me 'father' in years. I'm overcome with paternal pride, child."

Una smiled. "Finding a fact odious doesn't make it less true."

It was his turn to snort. He stuck out an arm, and Una took it without further comment. Steering her out into the hall, Patrick grinned from ear to ear. The walls had been recently washed and rehung with thick, colorful tapestries, Una noted as she was led toward the winding stair. When she'd been carted up here so many days before, there had been dirty rushes scattered everywhere, soot-stained walls, and endless leaves had blown in from a broken window. Now, the glass was refitted and sparkling, the walls were clean and brightly decorated, and the candles illuminating their path were scented beeswax. It seemed the servants had been quite busy while she'd been incarcerated in her mother's former apartments. She tried not to look too impressed.

"So," he said as they reached the third-floor hall. Workers rushed about, hanging textiles, cleaning, and making minor repairs. Undoubtedly, Patrick intended Kevin's Keep would be gleaming for the coming festivities. She chewed her cheek in silence. "Tell me of yourself. What do you enjoy most?"

They passed through an arch, then down the second flight of stairs to the Grand Hall. She caught sight of Martin O'Rearden barking orders at a group of Corpsmen in the far alcove. Raising his head, he grinned when he saw her.

The ghost of a smile flickered over her face as they strolled by. "Freedom," she answered.

Patrick patted her forearm, where it wound through his. She chewed her cheek in irritation. Courtiers crushed themselves into the rich wooden paneling before his throne room to make room for the Duch and his scowling daughter. "You are free, Una. Realize it before you ruin yourself... or someone else."

"What is *that* supposed to mean?" she hissed, trying to keep her voice down. There were far too many curious faces in here for her comfort. Every one of them stared, some with their mouths wide open. She felt like an insect under glass. "I am not here by choice if you recall?"

He led her past the throne and the huge stained-glass mosaic that depicted her great-grandfather's demise. She forced herself not to look up into Kaer Yin's face, emblazoned there in brilliant, multifaceted relief. She refused to weep in front of anyone. Patrick snapped his fingers. His guards opened the door to his private apartments, then shut them again on the whispering crowd. Inside her father's rustic office, two boys that had been seated leaped to their feet. Well, one was a boy— twelve or thirteen, at most. The other was taller and broader through the shoulder, blond, handsome, and nervous. He was perhaps twenty years old or less. Both squirmed when they saw her. The younger sulked while the elder's face flushed a vivid scarlet. Una raised her brows.

Patrick nudged her forward, ever so slightly. "Una Alis Donahugh, future Duchess of Bethany and heir to my throne, meet your cousins, Micah and Isaac Donahugh."

The boys ducked into the most awkward bows Una had ever seen. She bit her lip.

"Well, daughter. Say hello," urged Patrick, shuffling off to the fireplace and his armchair. His steward, Shanley, had a full tankard of spiced cider already waiting. Una fidgeted a little. This wasn't what she'd expected at all. She thought the old bastard wanted to parade her through his court and humiliate her to the nth degree. Meeting two twitchy boys who appeared to be as nervous and out of place as she was far from that.

"Ah, hello. Prima Una *Moura*, sirs. Pleased to make your acquaintance." She dipped into a half-remembered curtsy, ignoring the sharp flash of her father's eyes.

"It's your turn to say something, Micah," the Duch prodded.

Micah had a hard time glancing up from his shoes. "Ah, we... ah. That is... we're pleased to make yer... I mean *your* acquaintance too, milady." He elbowed his brother.

With his wild, dark eyes, Little Isaac glowered back at her. "Yeah, whatever."

Una failed to repress a smile. "Erm, thank you."

Patrick patted the chair in front of him. She tucked herself into the seat without complaint and accepted a tankard from Shanley. The boys took chairs opposite, backs ramrod straight. Micah turned an even brighter red. "Now, Una, Isaac here is going to be a knight. He's quite fierce. Try not to be frightened."

Isaac, she noticed, perked up at that.

"Oh, indeed?" she asked him. "Will it be quests and noble deeds, or will you be the bravest knight in the tourney?"

"Battles, o'course." His narrow chest puffed out. "I'll be more famous n'me da, one day. He were the best knight around. Everyone says so."

Una had yet to meet her wayward uncle and was somewhat surprised not to find him here with his sons. She tucked that tidbit away for further examination. She took a sip from her tankard, politely waiting for Micah to cease swallowing before she addressed him.

Not so good with girls, this one.

"I see. And you, Micah? To which discipline do you aspire?"

"Uh... s-statecraft, milady."

"Is that so?"

"Yeah... er, *yes.*"

"Una is quite studious herself, Micah," interrupted Patrick. "For twelve years, she studied Civic Law in Tairngare. Is that not so, daughter?"

How did he know that? "Yes."

Micah blinked at her. "Ye did? But yer so... so...."

"Una's mother hailed from the Red City. In Tairngare, noblewomen are expected to be highly educated. I think you'll find the two of you have many interests in common."

Una's head swiveled toward her father.

Pimping me out already, old man?

"The Duch is right. I studied Civic and Ecclesiastical Law, Particle Theory, Economics, History, and Bretagn. You?" The way Micah flushed anew told her all she needed to know. Poor boy. He, too, was another of Patrick's pawns, in way over his head.

"Law and History, milady. S'all."

"So far," amended Patrick. "Master one subject at a time or understand none, I always say. Now, in a little while, I'll be holding Court. I'd like it if the two elder children were there. What better way to learn? Isaac, my brave lad. You'll be sent to practice with Master Gremel." Isaac beamed. No politician would that one be. "After the proceedings, I think we should have supper in here. Doesn't that sound nice?"

Una shifted in her seat.

Micah echoed her sentiments. Neither answered.

"Excellent! Let's chat a bit longer, then—"

The door burst inward. Damek stalked inside, his expression thunderous. Martin followed as always, with his furrowed brow and apologetic demeanor. "What is the meaning of this?" Damek demanded, raking his eyes over those gathered. When he came to Una— her tankard paused midway between her lap and lip— he feigned a simper. "Having a family meeting without me, uncle? That's hardly sporting."

Patrick groaned, "Don't be so dramatic, Damek. The boys wanted to meet their cousin now that she's home, as is proper."

"*Did they*?" Even Isaac shrank beneath Damek's murderous glare.

Una twisted her lip at him. Unperturbed, he kicked over a chair and took a seat beside her. "In that case, let's *do* get to know one another. Shall we?"

Patrick struggled between laughter and rage. Una could tell. "Boys, this is Damek Bishop, Lord of Clare, Marshal of my Souther Legions, and High Commander of my Steel Corps. Damek, this is Micah and Isaac *Donahugh*."

Una nearly winced at the venom in that last dig. She watched a muscle tick low in Damek's cheek and hid her grin behind her tankard. Her uncle Henry's boys murmured scarcely decipherable greetings. Without warning or excuse, Damek snatched Una's tankard and glared at them over its rim. Patrick snapped his fingers again, and another was hastily placed in her hand. "Charming as ever, aren't you?"

Damek didn't turn. Wherever he'd been, he was filthy and reeked of sour ale. His raven hair was unkempt, his collar askew, and if she weren't mistaken, he bore a fair slathering of rouge at his neckline. Disgusted, she leaned away.

Observing her from the corner of his eye, he shrugged. "You can pretend you don't like it, and I'll pretend to be duly chastened."

"You're *nauseating,* you—"

"Was there a bloody point to this embarrassing interruption?" growled Patrick. Martin had the grace to flinch and back up toward the door.

Damek rolled a shoulder. "Part of the family, aren't I? Maybe I wanted to meet them, too? Besides, now they've seen *her, my* face should be the image burned into their eyelids forever afterward. That, my dear cousins, is the point of my being here." He took a long sip and made a face. "Reason. Don't we have anything better than this swill?"

Patrick's steward dashed off to find more robust fare. Patrick chuckled. "You burn through all the uishge you brought south?"

"Unfortunately. I'll say this for that cesspit of trees and backward fools, they know how to make a drink."

Micah sent Una a sympathetic half-smile. She was surprised. Was it so obvious how she felt about her brutish cousin? "F-forgive me, milord. What is 'wis-key'?"

Damek raised a brow. "You're kidding, right?"

Una answered for him. "A spirit made from smoke and peat. The old Eireans used to call it 'the water of life.' Currently, it's illegal, but that hardly stops it being made."

"Can I go to practice now, Uncle? This is borin,'" whinged Isaac, as a young lad would. Una, again, couldn't conceal her amusement.

Patrick waved a hand, and a guardsman escorted Isaac from the room. He didn't spare any of them the slightest interest, including his older brother. When he'd gone, Micah cleared his throat. "Apologies for my brother. He's young yet, and ah... as ye see."

"Quite all right. It does wax stuffy in here," laughed Patrick. "Now then. Damek, Micah is a great admirer of your career."

"Oh?"

Patrick opened his mouth to make further pleasantries when Micah finally found his voice. He sat up a bit straighter, his attention fixed. "Yes! I've wanted to meet ye, long as we been here, milord. They say yer the best swordsman in the South. How many battles have ye fought? I heard about the time ye were ambushed by that Bretagn Lord Gaelin and how ye—"

"Micah," Patrick chided.

Faced with such guileless flattery, Damek's ire deflated. "Ah, well, that's all right. Perhaps I'll give you a demonstration—"

"Damek!" Una snapped.

"As My Lady commands." He saluted her with his stolen tankard.

She turned to Patrick with an irritated huff. "I think that's enough for today, don't you? This idiot is dawdling here to mark territory that is neither his nor wants to be. I'd rather spend the day pondering the leap from my window if it's all the same to you?"

"I suppose you have a point, my dear," Patrick agreed. "Micah, would you care to escort your cousin to her rooms? My old knees, you understand. The climb is not so simple as it once was."

Una could hear the air whistle through Damek's nostrils.

"Of c-course, uncle." Micah blushed, getting to his feet.

Damek gripped Una's elbow first. She clawed at his arm, but he wouldn't be detached. "Nonsense. I'll see her back—"

"Lay a hand on me again, and I will make you eat your tongue," she warned, shoving him off. Before he could collect himself and lunge again, she strolled behind Patrick's chair. "Father, I'd prefer it if Lord Bishop were kept apart from me."

Damek snickered. "Oh, well *done*, Una."

"Martin?" Patrick called.

"My lord?" he replied.

"See that the Lord of Clare is scrubbed, chastened, and *sober* when next he's in my presence. If he refuses, remind him he may be denied the privilege of the Keep altogether. What a shame that would be, eh? With so many fine lords on the way?"

Una watched that muscle flex again in Damek's clenched jaw. "Una. Don't forget what I said. I'm all you have." He gave her a long, accusatory look, spun on his heel, and marched out as suddenly as he appeared. Una's fingers unfurled.

"Is he always like that, uncle?" asked Micah, with an anxious sag to his shoulders.

"Lad, you haven't seen anything yet," Patrick sighed.

IN THE FOLLOWING DAYS, UNA OPTED TO SIT WITH HER FATHER AND Micah at Court. As long as Damek was disinvited, she had nothing better to do. After a few tankards of cider, she could even imagine she was having a good time. Her cousin Micah, it turned out, was a sweet, biddable young man with an inquisitive mind and wholesome manners. He was a bit rough around the edges, having been raised in the less cosmopolitan Cymrian lowlands, but to Una's mind, his flaws were part of his charm. He sat beside her, asking questions and answering those directed his way. Despite herself, Una quite liked him. Their family squabble aside, she was glad to have at least one relative in the South she didn't despise. Two, actually. She couldn't help but enjoy savage little Isaac as well. Since their introduction, Patrick had a sideways smirk on his infuriating cheeks that she didn't care for at all. She endeavored to ignore him unless he spoke to either of them directly.

Thankfully, she and Micah sat upon the dais, slightly behind the throne. Patrick's courtiers buzzed like bees over their convivial appearance, but neither paid the least attention. Una felt she might have made her first friend in Bethany. After all, they were both hostages here, weren't they?

Why shouldn't they find some common ground?

The proceedings passed with uneventful adjudications and quiet conversation until a farmer stomped up to the dais with an armful of bloodied rags, which Una assumed had once been a girl's gown.

Bleary-eyed, he tossed the wad at the Duch's feet.

Patrick stiffened. "What's the meaning of this?"

His guards tugged the farmer upright by his grubby collar. "My girl," he sputtered. "Found her at the mouth o'the Lee, not a fortnight past. Ye've done nothin'!"

"Watch your tongue, peasant," the Duch spat. "We are doing everything—"

"No, yer not! *Three* so far, last I heard, been pulled from the river in bits and ye sit there protectin' that foul brother o'yers, what done this!"

Lord Wender put his hand on his sabre. "You'll be whipped for that!"

Perplexed, Micah got to his feet. Una stood with him. "You can't be speakin' o'my da? He can barely walk by himself!"

Struggling against the guards who held him, the farmer shook his daughter's bloodied clothing at him. "Ye don't know him, do ye? Many o'us are old enough to remember— oof!" The guard nearest the dais rammed his gauntleted fist into the farmer's hollow midsection. The farmer shrank in their grip, but his burning eyes met Micah's nonetheless. "Why don't ye ask him, eh? Ask anyone who don't fear the truth."

"That's enough," Patrick rumbled, slapping a hand against his knee. "The crimes you're alluding to were solved. My father strung the perpetrator from a crow's cage. Now, the Court mourns your loss but lobbing accusations at a man confined to quarters for his health most days will not bring your girl back. Sir Gaffigan? Please ensure this man is given a warm meal and enough coin to see him and his family through the winter." Patrick waved a hand, and the farmer was dragged out, spewing denial and curses. The blood-stained rags remained on the floor before the throne.

"Uncle?" asked Micah uncertainly.

Patrick smeared his palm over both eyes with a heavy sigh. "Court is convened for the day. Leave us."

Courtiers filed out, their footsteps against the flagstones half as loud as their whispers. Una absorbed every shocked, suspicious glare, every nervous giggle, or mocking comment. She watched the Duch shrivel in his chair. It seemed the notorious Henry of Bethany was not the only tired old man in residence.

"Uncle?" Micah repeated.

"You too, lad. Both of you, return to your quarters."

Micah flinched away. His expression proved a war between uncertainty and indignation. Dutiful lad he was, he bowed and awkwardly extended his arm to lead Una away. She shook her head. "I will stay a while."

He retracted his hand with a brief nod. "As you will, milady."

Patrick leaned back against his ancient, mahogany throne with a dry laugh. "Now she wants to stay behind. Surrender, is it?"

"Hardly. Tell me about these girls."

He attempted a caustic shrug. "The corpses of three servants were found near the river in the last month."

She sucked in a breath and took a seat on the stairs. Patrick gestured for his guards and servants to back away from the dais. "How were they found?"

"All done the same way: beaten, strangled, then stabbed."

"*Siora*," she whispered. "Were they... interfered with?"

"You mean raped?"

She flushed. "Yes."

"No. Killed merely for the sport of it, it seems."

Una was silent for a time. "Why would anyone believe your brother did this?"

He gave her a cruel sort of smile. "Why the sudden interest? Aren't we Donahughs all murderous brutes? I know I am... as are you, so I'm told." The blood rushed into Una's throat. Above her head, Kaer Yin glared down at her from the stained-glass window. She didn't look up, as if his eyes might bore a hole straight through her skull. Patrick noted her discomfiture. He pointed. "Some say your great-grandsire's murderer rescued you. Damek is drinking himself half to death, believing you cared for the Sidhe bastard. Is it true?"

"No," she lied through clenched teeth. "You're changing the subject."

Patrick fiddled with one of his rings. His father's, Una recalled, set with a great round emerald the size of her pinky nail. "Once upon a time, my brother was the most handsome man in Eire. He was a brave and brilliant knight, charming, intelligent, and well-loved by everyone, despite his bastardy. Much as Damek is now," he said, staring up at the mosaic she refused to acknowledge. "Then our father died, and I was crowned Duch. Henry considered himself better than me at everything, and I suppose he was. His temper grew worse by the day. My men often found him in the Pleasure District, drunk as a satyr. He vented his bitterness on the commoners, most. Women, especially.

"I wasn't forced to intervene until a few of their families made formal complaints. To expedite this tale, I will tell you Henry was sent away for a time, and when he returned, he'd found the Old Religion. He behaved himself for a great long time after, and I heard no more of any molested girls. That is, until our sister went missing from the High King's Council," Patrick's voice went cold as the sea outside. "We declared war to reclaim her. We lost. That pretty Sidhe princeling you purportedly admire smashed Henry's vanguard to bits on the first day of battle, then crept into the village where Henry's officers were encamped and murdered them to a man. Henry, himself, escaped the same fate because he and his honor guard had gone to spy on the Tairnganeah's camp, some five miles east. Without our officers, the troops were leaderless and divided. The next day, Fionn O'More, the High King's next champion, rode over our footsoldiers like insects in the road.

"Henry did not take defeat or the loss of Alis well. When he returned home, beaten and conflicted, many more girls were abused. So many, I was forced to confine him to chambers. He didn't like that one bit. Still raw at me for our losses up North and for the death of our sister (no doubt, for the air I breathed), he attempted to overthrow me. Again, he was defeated. He fled to Cymru, got those two boys on some washerwoman in the Wastes, and styled himself a wandering priest. When we found him years later, he and his followers were making a name for themselves as crusader bandits. They burned half a dozen small villages to convert the Ancestor's worshippers. I had him brought home in chains and thrown into the dungeon for a decade."

Una's brow wrinkled after this recitation. "Why would you release such a monster?"

"Henry has a part to play in my plans, Una. A critical one, at that. He's a sickly specter of a man now, but he has his uses."

"He's a rapist and a murderer."

"Rapist, yes. I won't argue that, but none were ever killed. I'm told that one died in childbirth, but otherwise, his victims lived. Cruelly used and discarded, yes. Never murdered."

"Then why?"

"Did that farmer lob the accusation? He was distraught, and Henry had lost his favor among the common folk long ago. His circle is limited to dithering old bigots and dry old women seeking validation from his backward religion."

Una mulled that over for a while. "That doesn't mean his... tastes have changed. Why would you assume that he isn't responsible this time?"

"Do you genuinely take an interest in this case?" he tested, tenting his fingers. "These are Souther girls, after all. Why would you care?"

He had her there. Her cheeks blazed. "Whatever we think of each other, and however much I despise this place, I take a *keen* interest in the suffering of my sex."

"Very well." With a curt nod, he reached into his doublet to retrieve a folded sheaf of vellum and handed it over. Una sifted through the hastily scratched report on each page, perplexed. "Coroner's reports."

Una skimmed through as quickly as she could. In the end, she gasped. "None?"

"None," he agreed and leaned forward to tap the conclusion on the last page. "Henry assaulted one of my serving girls this past month. I had to pay her off and move her family from the city. The girl is carrying my wizened elder brother's fifth illegitimate child."

"This is not conclusive evidence."

"The killer is impotent."

Una tsked. "You can't know that for sure. I'd say your brother is a very likely candidate. Some men are not, erm, always able to—"

"Look at the dates."

She did. The final entry was dated two days before. "What does this prove?"

"I confined Henry to his quarters a week ago. He's had neither the time nor the opportunity. It can't be him."

She set the sheaf down on the top step. "That means?"

"... Someone else is doing the killing."

12
BONE OF CONTENTION

Damek watched her from the southern parapet, drinking from a horn flask and grinding his molars to powder. A familiar dragging step behind him brought an even deeper scowl to his face. "For an ailing man, you do get around. What do you want?"

Wearing his prized white-bear cloak, Patrick slid beside his nephew and looked down. He made a sort of chuckle that heated Damek's blood to boiling. It had stopped snowing, but in true Innish fashion, a frigid rain dappled the white earth brown in the courtyard below. Una and Micah strolled together, arm in arm, guards following at a respectful distance. Their two golden heads dipped in mutual mirth.

"She is a beauty, I'll say, so much more than her mother ever was. Arrin quite stole my breath the first time I beheld her. A shame about all those ugly tattoos, though," Patrick mused. "Nevertheless, she'll be a formidable Duchess."

"You haven't answered my question."

Patrick ran his gloved fingers along the stone wall, clearing it of ice. "You'll never woo her this way, you know? Watching her from afar, goading her to fight each time you see her, or drinking yourself unconscious in the bloody *Butterfly* every night. She is angry with you, and you're making it worse."

"I ask again, whose fault is that? You played the game of matrimony with us to tease wealthy lords to jealousy. You ripped us apart."

"You broke into her chambers and assaulted her after the annulment."

Damek thought about pitching him over the wall. Patrick's guards—silent, ever-present sentinels—gripped their sabres at his expression. "I've had more than enough of that baseless accusation. She's furious with me because I told you of our child. That's the truth. Because of my mistake, you incarcerated her to keep it a secret from your Gods-damned barons. If you try that tack with me again, your guards will never stop me in time, *uncle*."

"Fine," Patrick conceded with a tight-lipped smirk. "I'm to blame for your unhappiness. I tried to save my daughter from an unseemly union."

Damek took another long pull from his flask, his guts stewing. "You stole her from me for amusement and spite. With an heir, female or no, *I* would have been too powerful for you to control. Our child might have pushed you from the throne. You couldn't have that. Could you?"

"No, I could not," Patrick admitted with a sidelong glance. "Had I known what a miscalculation that would have been in the end, I might have merely had you murdered. Nevertheless, the failings of yesteryear grow rotten on the vine. Here we are now, all this while later, and we must make do."

Damek's fists clenched and unclenched. "That's the first time I've heard you admit to folly, uncle. I hope you choke on it."

"I'm dying, Damek."

Everything stopped: the rain, the starved gulls circling overhead, the crash of relentless green waves beneath, and the hammer of his pulse. "*What*?"

"Weeks, maybe more. That's what I have left."

Damek drew a long stream of air through flaring nostrils. "Why tell *me*?"

Patrick quirked a lip. "You're my child, same as she. I raised you and need you now, as you need me."

Utterly floored, Damek took a step back. "I—"

"Don't bother. I require no sympathy or honeyed words. Instead, there are many things we must discuss. Obviously, I desire my daughter on the throne."

"Of... course."

"I've had papers drawn up. You *will* sign them or be expelled from my service. You'll be beholden to my barons, as I am, and make no premature bids for the throne. I will have your vow or your head."

"Are you... passing me the crown?"

Patrick made a face. "Of course not, you idiot boy. I'm passing *her* the bloody crown." He swiped a hand at where Una and Micah made for the Hall once more. "If you want her, you'll have to convince her yourself. I won't force her a second time."

"I could kill you now and take them both."

"You could. I've no doubt you'd best my guards, but for Una's sake, you won't. Why are you up here brooding, hm? You make so much noise about being the only man worthy of her, don't you? Here's your chance to prove it. I'm legitimizing you, Damek. You no longer need Una to achieve your goals. Hells, I imagine right now she'd even abdicate in your favor if you'd turn her loose, but I'm hoping she'll stay and rule of her own accord. My barons won't approve you as Duch unless she wills it. So, what will you do now? Is it Una you want or my throne? I believe you could have one without the other right now."

Ears buzzing and head gone hot, Damek crouched against the wall. He could be Duch. *In weeks*, if he wished. All he had to do was ask, and she would give it freely. Happily, even. He could be Duch and, eventually, King of Eire. He could do it.

He *would* do it.

This was the only thing Damek had ever wanted. The crown was in his grasp, at last! He could let her go; she was just another woman. He had dozens of women, heiresses, and whores, alike.

What did he need Una for, if not the throne?

Patrick saw the ambition clouding Damek's face. "If the crown is all that matters to you, set my daughter free when I pass. Keep Henry's boys busy but unharmed. It will be *that* simple for you. I'm giving you everything you've ever wanted, as you deserve."

Una laughed in the distance.

The sound whipped through Damek's middle like a scythe.

Patrick saw that too. "Remember, this offer is valid so long as my daughter is unharmed and happy. My barons will revolt the minute you press your luck and be warned, there's a reason why the High King has never tried to sack the South a second time."

Damek expelled a long breath. "Why the sudden concern for her happiness? It's never troubled you before now."

"It doesn't matter why. If you mean to be King of Eire, despite that old hag you call 'grandmama,' you will obey me. Let her go and be all that you ever wished to be."

He could do it. Live without her.

She hates you, anyway.

His mind raced.

"However, if you wish for both, you'll have to earn them on your own, boy. My tourney will provide all the wealth, troops, and suitor-gifts I require for my barons to reclaim Tara and the Midlands. My final wish as Duch Donahugh is a country of our own. I would very much like to imagine my daughter and her children will follow me as queens and kings of Eire... but I will not force her, and by Reason, neither shall you. I won't stand in your way if you can woo her during the fête. However, that is all the time you'll be given to decide."

A black grease spot settled in Damek's gut at the thought of another man taking his place. He'd already calculated the myriad ways he planned to murder his cousin Micah for his brass. Additional suitors were sure to drive him mad.

Forget her. You don't need her.

Look what he's offering you. Finally!

He stood up. Decision made. Una meant nothing to him.

Nothing. She could take herself back to Tairngare or the Kneeler's Hell for all he cared. He would be Duch. "I value the crown over a woman's whims, even hers."

Patrick observed him from under lowered lashes. "Good. Then you won't mind that the Prince of Connaught has bid for her hand and is on his way here with a 'mountain of gold and silks' for his prospective Milesian bride?"

"*What*?" he repeated darkly.

"I did warn you. She's the catch of the Continent, nephew. Lord Gaelin and his sons are travelling here to hail her, as well as Ladies Wendelin and Penwyth of Kernow and their broods. Let's see, there's Baron Grim, Lord Talbot, Earl Jasper of Cymru, Lady Rhiannon, and all our Courtiers here, of course. Why do you look so green? I hear the Prince of Connaught loves a challenge and is wealthy and stupid enough to venture here to bid for her hand. Must be pretty dull in unchanging Aes Sidhe, no?"

"The Prince of Connaught? Uncle, you can't be serious? That's *his* cousin! He's surely coming here to—"

"So what? If you aim to be Duch and rule over all of Eire one day, Una will have to go somewhere, won't she? I won't take that remiss if she taints the Adair Clan with my bloodline. You'll hear me laughing from Tech Duinn."

"I will *never*—"

"You're not Duch yet, boy. I repeat, if you'd have *both*, you must earn them. Now, I've said my piece. I'll give you two weeks to decide. If you eschew my offer and attempt to wait me out, I must warn you, you'll be wasting your time. I've had two wills drafted. One shall be fed to the flames the minute air ceases to pump through my lungs. One names you my heir and the other Una's enemy. My barons already have my instructions. Some are very eager to remove you altogether." With that, he patted Damek's shoulder and shuffled away.

Damek's voice caught him at the bottom step. "What of Henry, uncle? Why let him go if this was going to be your decision?"

A dark smirk crossed Patrick's mouth. "Why don't you think on it a while? It'll come to you."

HENRY WAS ESCORTED INTO THE HALL FOR SUPPER. WITH A TIGHT smile, he took in the shining tableau, his resplendent family, and their accouterment upon the dais. Patrick sat in the center, in state, their father's slim, iron coronet upon his balding head. He looked up at Henry's announcement and waved his brother over. Ignoring the knights and commoners gawping at him from the lower tables, Henry glided by. The Hall positively glittered as it hadn't in Henry's memory. Their father certainly hadn't prioritized a tidy Keep nor a grand reception space in which to feast. Patrick must have been keen to impress the incoming gentry. Behind the throne swung two massive banners emblazoned with the Southernmost Star, and the Donahugh colors flashed from every dust-free corner and bench throughout the room.

To Patrick's either side sat his heretic daughter and Henry's own son. Supper was a small, light meal of stew and bread for the courtiers seated below the nobles. Finer fare—pheasant and roasted boar— awaited him upon the dais.

Micah beamed down at Henry, his blond curls gleaming in the candlelight. Henry nodded, careful not to display too much pride, or else his brother would seize the chance to humiliate him further. The girl appeared even less enthused about her surroundings than Henry. She was pretty enough, he supposed, for a witch. She had that lovely Tairnganese complexion many Souther girls had envied in his youth. Her mother, Arrin, had been a gorgeous, refined lady. This one seemed a touch savage for the cutting amber gleam in her eyes. He could sense her disdain like a brand.

Wasn't that interesting? Patrick must have been telling tales. He stopped at the bottom stair while Patrick sucked at a chicken wing.

"Brother."

"Bilford? Get Sir Henry a chair, if you please, and a setting."

So, he was to be included in a 'family' meal?

Bilford dragged over a stool and situated him at the foot of the table, directly below Patrick's eye. Inclusive but unequal. He didn't mind, did he? He'd been through far worse indignities than this. While the soldiers and Courtiers tittered from the room's rear, he mocked them in his heart: *Laugh now, for I'm up here... and you're all down there.*

As if he'd been invited to take Patrick's seat, Henry folded his rough linen napkin like delicate lace and clutched his wooden utensils like the finest silver. They'd really get a show when he removed his dentures to gnaw at his meat. For now, he stuck to the potatoes and softest fare. "To what do I owe this rare honor? I hadn't thought I was meant to dine with other human beings in a civilized manner."

Patrick chuckled. "Stop whingeing, Henry. Our guests will be arriving for the fête next week. I'd like everyone in the family to know what is expected of them, yourself included." Patrick paused, dropping his bones onto his plate. He looked around. "Matter of fact, where is my irritating nephew? Hisk?"

"My lord?" said the Corpsman, rising from his place at the back. The local lords and ladies were gathered on cushioned benches arranged below the dais in four rows, though many seats were empty in expectation of incoming guests. Their tables were nearly as decked out as the Duch's, with roasted boar and geese awaiting carving at the center and many gleaming goblets of ale and mead held aloft in bejeweled hands. Beyond this collection of wealth and privilege lay the less-ostentatious tables and benches reserved for Damek's officers and elite Corpsmen. Of these, Martin, Douglas, Ridley, and Hisk sat nearest the front.

"Where is Damek? He'd better not be at that infernal tavern again, or I'll have someone's fingers. I vow it."

"I'm here, uncle," said Damek, revealing himself near the windows.

Henry nearly gasped at the sight. Aside from his Bolgish height and coloring, Damek was Alis' spit, through and through. Same narrow nose, wide mouth, and winged brows. The lad turned, tankard in hand, with a sardonic smile. He wore a cobalt doublet over a dusky scarlet tunic, the colors of Donahugh's house.

A bit on the nose, wasn't it?

Henry had to admit, though, that the boy did turn out. Damek's gaze skipped everyone in the room to rest directly on Henry's wild niece.

Bold too, Henry thought, slurping his ale.

"Lady Wendelin's troupe have begun to arrive. I can see her colors on the hill," said Damek.

"Excellent. Shanley, run out to the stables and make sure all is prepared for our guests. I don't imagine they'll be joining us until tomorrow morning," barked Patrick.

"My Lord." Shanley bowed awkwardly and dashed off.

Damek strolled over with surefooted grace and sank into a chair beside his favored cousin. Una stiffened slightly but made no comment. She kept her eyes firmly on her plate. "Her sons might join the men later for ale and songs. I assume Lord Gaelin will be here the day after tomorrow?" Damek inquired of his uncle, though he grinned at Una.

"Last report, yes. Micah," said Patrick, leaning over. "Lord Gaelin's youngest, Castor, is also quite studious of Civics, as you and Una are."

"Is that so, uncle?" Micah hummed. "Perhaps we shall be friends?"

Damek coughed behind his tankard. Una shot him a very dry glare. He spread his palms. "Let's not forget, we're all here to compete for my fair lady's hand. Gaelin's sons are great burly beasts, more interested in horseflesh than women. But do go on. I love a good fable."

Una set her fork down. "I wish to be excused."

"You may not. Eat your potatoes. You're too scrawny by half," Patrick chewed at her but pointed a greasy bone at his nephew. "Mind yourself, remember?"

Damek dipped his head. "Of course, uncle. I merely meant to encourage my cousin to direct his affability at more... appropriate targets."

Henry dipped his head at that. "Bravo, boy. One might urge a man in your position to heed his own advice, Lord *Bishop*."

Damek's teeth flashed white. "You're quite right. Una, my dear. Shall I take you riding tomorrow?"

"Drop dead."

He spread his hands dramatically, and the Hall burst into laughter. "I'd make a poor groom, I see. I'd best stick to what I'm good at, eh? Hisk? Would you care to remind everyone what that is?"

Hisk resumed his feet with a half-drunken leer. "Lord of Clare and the Isles, Lord Marshal of the Bethonair Legions, Commander of the Steel Corps, Victor of the Siege at Guernsey, Hero of the Kernian Campaign, nephew to the greatest lord of this or any other land... and finest swordsman in the South! Hail!" Hisk raised his pewter tankard, and the Steel Corps officers pounded their table with their fists, howling approval. Hisk curtsied like a dancing girl. Damek toasted him.

"Perhaps, it's not *all* in the name, is it, uncle?"

Down the table, Micah sat back, defeated.

Henry crossed his arms. "You lost *how* many men on your failed raid North, nephew?"

"Many," Damek didn't flinch. "My cousin's life was worth every man."

Una pushed her plate forward, visibly put off her meal. "My lord father, I respectfully request—"

"Oh, stop!" Patrick cooed jovially. "This is a celebration. Lady Una is home! I'll have no more of these backbiting jabs. Eat, everyone, and be merry!" When the observant crowd bent back to their conversations and ale, he spared Damek a stern glare. "I thought I bloody well warned you?"

"I *am* behaving myself, uncle. If the boy can't bear a bit of light-hearted ribbing without his father leaping to his rescue, perhaps he should take his supper with the children?"

Ignoring the jibe, Henry's smile deepened, despite his son's obvious embarrassment. "Lady Una. You have the look of your mother."

That sent Patrick back into his seat with a low grumble.

"You knew her?"

"I did. Quite lovely, as you are now."

Patrick struggled not to fidget. Damek drank quietly from his tankard, brows raised.

"Then, I assume you know how she died?" she asked dryly.

Henry delighted in his brother's discomfort. "Slipped in the Lee and drowned. The cliffs around high tide are never very stable. Especially in spring. All the rain, you see?"

"Hm," she answered, mirroring his pose. "That's odd. I heard she was thrown off."

"Now," Patrick cleared his throat. "Let us return to more pleasant topics. I would hate to have you dragged from the Hall in chains."

"You surround yourself with hostages and wonder why none love you?" She exhaled through her nose.

Henry held his cup up for more ale. "Well said. Though some could argue you've fashioned those chains. Disobedience is a sin, My Lady."

Damek interjected, "You would know, wouldn't you, My Lord Fitz-Donahugh?"

Una held out a hand, her spine very straight. "I can answer my own challenges, thank you. Disobedience, to *whom*?"

"Your father," Henry spat. "Your family, your people, and your honor. Had to be dragged home in burlap, last I heard. Covered everywhere in those vile witch marks. Aren't you ashamed of yourself?"

Someone behind them gasped.

Damek drummed his fingers against the tablecloth.

Patrick had to wave his guards off. Several Corpsmen had gotten to their feet.

"Funny you should mention 'shame,' uncle. I've been introduced to your exploits only recently, but I must say, you might reflect upon your deeds before mine."

"Da," begged Micah. "Please?"

Henry's attention clapped back to his mortified son. His tone softened. "I meant that your father mourned your loss for many years. *Honor thy father and thy mother*, child."

"Henry, if you speak to my daughter that way again, you'll be taking your meals in the kennels with the dogs. I've had enough of this." Patrick clapped his hands so the lutists in the music box above would dispel the tension. "We've all got our measure, eh? Planted our flags and taken the piss? Good. Bore me again at your peril."

Micah, good lad that he was broke in: "I've been told you've read Callaghan's '*Seasons of Transition,*' My Lady?"

Una severed eye contact with Henry and leaned over. "I have, cousin. You're reading it now?"

"I am! I'm a bit muddy with the language he uses; otherwise, it's an intriguing tale. Who could believe such a civilization once lined these shores?"

Henry had never been prouder of his son and gummed his bread rather than disturb Micah's excellent showing. Una's demeanor wasn't affected in the least.

Very good, boy! Very good. Henry smirked behind his bread.

"Some find it a dull read, but the details are fascinating. Did you know our forebears were said to have flown through the clouds on steel wings? I find that tidbit the most outlandish."

"Callaghan was a staunch literalist," Patrick added. "I doubt the old fart ever made a joke in his life. However, one need only visit the hill at Dubh-lin to see proof of his claims."

"In Drogheda, the remains of several iron-bellied ships were discovered below the marshes. My grandmother displayed them in the Citadel for a time before they were removed to the Libellum in Ten Bells."

"Did you see them?" Micah breathed.

"I did! They were in pieces, so some reassembly had been necessary, but as sights go, I've yet to see their equal. Judging from a single prow, one could put them at nearly two hundred feet in length."

Patrick grunted his approval. "Bloody brilliant, the old Eireans were. Great ships, carriages, and entire cities were built from steel. No substance ever aided man more, save maybe fire."

"I disagree," dissented Henry. "Nothing ever inspired a man more than faith."

Damek snorted into his cup. "How many cities did faith build?"

"Many. *All.*"

"I believe stone and steel hold the monopoly there, old man."

"I'm not speaking of base materials, son. The purpose... the *intention* for humans to gather has always been to ward off invaders and congregate in mutual worship. Most ancient cities were built to house soldiers or temples."

"Tairngare was not. Siora's Mysteries were scarcely contemplated when the markets sprang up in Drogheda. You're leaving basic geography out of your observation," remarked Una with a slim smile. "I see where you're directing this conversation, uncle. Far be it for me, a lowly woman, to argue."

Henry gripped his tankard. "Yes, there is something to be said for the Old Ways. Women have a place in God's Plan, but it isn't seated in dominion over men. Tairnganese men must be mad, allowing you females to dictate to them. An educated woman is an affront to God."

Damek's stare blew as cold as the North in winter. "My Lord Duch, I believe it is well past my uncle's bedtime. Don't you agree?"

Pinching the bridge of his nose, Patrick opened his mouth to speak, but Una beat him to it. "Which 'Old Ways' are you referring to? The more recent, in which men and their arrogant greed nearly drove our species to extinction, or the distant past, in which a woman could be bought and sold for the price of a goat? Enlighten me, *sir*. To which misguided past should I aspire?"

"You should respect your elders, especially the men in your family. If I were your father, you'd be allowed no opportunity to wag your heretic tongue until you were properly wed and under control."

"Henry," Patrick rumbled.

Una pushed her chair back. "I imagine a base rapist and murderer like yourself would have fairly strong feelings about a 'woman's place,' uncle. As always, *beneath* you. Let me tell you what we do to your kind in Tairngare since you're curious about our audacity." She rocked forward on her knuckles. "Men who dare to abuse and violate women, as you have and do, are dragged through the Drough Market and castrated before a howling crowd. You see, men and women in more civilized parts of the world find malicious worms like you unworthy of manhood."

Henry launched upright, his blood boiling.

"Do it, old man, and I'll take your arm," Damek warned.

Patrick gesticulated wildly to his guards, but not before Una's hand clasped down hard over Henry's, where it lay flat against the table. Shocked, he tried to lurch away, but she was stronger than he, and her nails made little half-moons in the skin of his wrist. "I do not require a man's advice nor his protection. You sad, hoary little beast."

Patrick struggled to wrench her behind him, but she shrugged him off. Micah watched the guards inch close, horrified and embarrassed. "Gods damn it, Una. Leave him!" Patrick cried.

The Hall erupted into whispers and outright arguments. Damek's Corpsmen got up, mouths full of meat and mead. Meanwhile, Henry strained to pull his hand back, but Una's strength was quite unequal to her size. What devilry could make a woman so absurdly strong? Her teeth were very white against her dark skin. "Perhaps you think I am cowed because I'm here against my will? That I must be susceptible because I'm simply a humiliated female? Well, you'd be wrong."

"Una, don't...." Damek protested halfheartedly.

"You're a *witch*," raged Henry. "You'll never be—"

"*Down!*" Una said, and the world spun white at the edges.

Henry's last glimpse of the Hall that eve was his niece's face leering down at him in vivid triumph.

PATRICK'S HAND SHOOK AS HE HANDED MARTIN A DRINK. HIS ELBOW propped against the mantle in his wood-paneled office, Patrick sucked down his own like a drowning man gulps air. Damek and Martin eyed each other from opposite ends of the room. "*Reason*, it's all true, isn't it?"

"We told you so," grumbled Damek from the stacks while he thumbed through a dusty old tome from the Reference section. "Still think you can parade her before the Lords of Innisfail like a prized heifer?"

"I... suppose not. Though, it's too late to disinvite anyone. Lady Wendelin is already here, and Gaelin is sharp on her heels. I can't exactly keep Una locked in her chambers until they leave, either."

"Don't bother," said Damek, tossing the book back on the shelf. "Saves me from murdering half a dozen overeager fools."

"My lord," ventured Martin. "Wouldn't you rather she was capable of defending herself?"

"Of course, but... *Reason*." Patrick drank. "Poor Micah is terrified of her now."

"Good," observed Damek. "To be fair, that boy flinches from his own shadow. I told you this wasn't going to go how you planned. If what we discussed on the parapet this morning holds, you must realize there's not a man in this world who'd want her now but me?"

Patrick turned a stern eye on his nephew. "You'd prod me again? Now? Why aren't *you* afraid of her, Damek? What protection do you imagine you have from power like hers?"

"She won't harm me."

"You don't know that."

"I supplied her with many chances. She never took one."

That gave Patrick serious pause. He shuffled to his desk and sat down on the polished wood. "Is this true, Martin?"

"It is, My Lord," said O'Rearden. "The lad dared her many times."

"Interesting. I knew she wielded some dread gift, but I'd no idea she could utterly drain one of life at a touch. My physician fears Henry's heart isn't strong enough to pull him through this coma. He scarcely breathes."

"He'll wake, though he might wish he hadn't when I'm through with him," Damek assured him. "Regardless, I'd urge you to take this as a lesson, uncle. Don't push her, or she'll push back."

"How did she learn of Henry's reputation?" asked Martin.

"I told her," Patrick bemoaned. "She was in Court with me when a farmer levied a formal complaint. His child was one of the murdered girls."

"What 'murdered girls?'" Damek asked, oblivious.

Patrick gave Martin a sour look. "A handful of servants have gone missing from this castle, only to turn up bloodied and broken in the Lee."

Damek laughed sourly. "No bloody wonder! What were you thinking?"

Patrick shrugged. "My daughter and I were having a conversation for the first time in nearly fifteen years. I didn't think she'd try to kill him."

"Oh, if she meant for him to die, he would have. Horribly."

Patrick noted Martin's silent agreement with a deep sigh. "So, what do I do now? I can't punish her, or it will cheapen her before My Lords. I can't allow her free reign, either."

"For one, Henry of Bethany should be kept well out of sight. If I see that poisonous old bastard once before this bloody tourney of yours is over, I'll gut him, I vow it. Secondly, Una should be given gloves to wear in public. Make it a suggestion for her dignity, not admonishment for an action that odious zealot richly deserved. Lastly, give her a purpose other than the role of 'rich demoiselle.' Now you know how much she values women's rights. Make use of that."

"How do you mean?"

Damek pursed his lips. "Show her the women of Bethany could benefit from such an educated lady's perspective. She hates this city for its 'patriarchy,' right? So, introduce her to the other half. Give her a reason to love the people here, one gender at a time."

Patrick pondered this for a while, stroking his beard. "Hm, you're on to something there, boy."

Damek's smile was dark and full of hidden wheels. "Of course I am, uncle. I'm sure I understand your daughter better than anyone else in the world."

THAT NIGHT, TWO MORE BODIES WERE DRAGGED FROM THE REEDS beneath the cliffs. This time, each woman had been brutally violated... by a blade.

13
THE DAMAGE DONE

N.E. 508
10, DOR CROMNA
THE TARAN HIGH ROAD

"*A mountain of gold and silks?*" asked Kaer Yin, incredulous. Looking around their homely little camp, he turned back to Tam Lin with a snort. "Bit of an overstatement, you think?" Kaer Yin did his best to ignore Rian's 'I told you so' glare.

Digging into the stew Gerrod ladled into his bowl, Tam Lin's lip twitched. "Do you think I oversold it?"

There were less than fifty of them, all told. The Sidhe, realizing the mortals in their company would fare poorly on the Shadow Path, opted to take Eva's suggestion and travel as common Merchers on their way to Market at Ten Bells. Once there, Tam Lin proposed an idea to use his father's credit at the Sidhe Consulate for appropriate gear and supplies. To woo a princess, a man was expected to arrive in style. Their current state, however, decried any notion of such an outlandish claim.

Gerrod busied himself, drying several pairs of holey socks over the fire. Having dressed the night's supper, Robin and Shar were occupied with stretching a buckskin over a broad branch. Niall and several other Croghenian warriors were engaged in a fierce archery competition: shooting at a target one-hundred yards away. Jeering onlookers pummeled those who failed to split the previous contender's arrow. The game grew steadily more serious, the drunker each contestant became. Horrified, Eva and her Tairnganese retinue remained close by Kaer Yin's side. He supposed they'd be even more appalled when he and Tam Lin joined the game after supper. As for Rian, she sat close to the fire, mending holes in a tattered homespun skirt. Her cheeks were filthy, her fingers soot-stained, but she didn't seem to mind.

Kaer Yin smirked to himself. At this point, she was nearly better suited for the wilds than some of his countrymen. What a difference a few months could make. "I think your name might have been advertisement enough. Not every day, a prince of the Sidhe rides south to hail the Duch in his own fortress."

"This was her brilliant plan." Tam Lin jerked a thumb at Rian.

Kaer Yin chuckled around his spoon. "You could be the prince of farmers, maybe."

"Whose fault is that? I told you we should wait for more men and supplies, but *no.*"

"My family holds an account with the Libellan Bank on Freal," said Eva. "I'm happy to contribute whatever is required. She is my niece, after all."

"Your offer is appreciated, Lady Alvra. We're owed obeisance (of sorts) from the Consulate. Their coffers essentially belong to my father." Kaer Yin gave an embarrassed cough.

Robin's knife paused over his strip of buckhide and wagged at Kaer Yin. "What the Hells are we doin' out here like a pack o'brigands, then? I could use a nice feather bed, me. A fire and a hot bath, too. Remind me why we're roughin' it?"

"It's safest to travel in disguise, Master Gramble," answered Eva. "Wealth is not something one wishes to advertise along the High Roads these days."

"We could have traveled through the Oiche Ar Fad, but you tender humans would be far too delicious a lure," said Tam Lin.

Kaer Yin pulled a face. "Again? I'm tired of arguing about this. We'll draw less attention traveling this way, either here or on the Shadow Path. Stop griping, Tam Lin. You'd be drinking yourself blind through border *raths* and taverns in Aes Sidhe right now and be bored to death. Don't tell me you aren't enjoying yourself, at least a bit."

Tam Lin humphed and dug a bone flask out of his cloak. The amber ogham charm around his neck jangled on its silver chain. Every Dannan was obligated to wear one. While Kaer Yin's shaggy blond hair and less brilliant eyes were recognizable to the Greenmakers who'd known him as 'Ben Maeden,' the rest took some getting used to.

Tam Lin's once fiery red and gold hair was now a dull, flat auburn. His teeth were too broad for his mouth, and his eyes, which burned a glittering violet, were transformed into a ruddy brown. Shar went from a barrel-chested youth with fern-green eyes and a fair complexion to a lanky young man with a cowlick and coarse brown hair. Niall, much the same. Even Eva, who lacked the talent for Sidhe glamor, managed to tame her dark, radiant beauty to an impressive degree. Her skin no longer held its luminescent sheen, and her hair had been painted white at the temples. She'd made herself look a great deal older and feebler.

In Rian's case, she had neither the need nor desire to humble herself further. As far as Kaer Yin could tell, she'd never owned a proper gown in her life. Like the Greenmakers, she was right at home on the road. Being in such 'illustrious' company hardly bothered her, either. Outwardly, she was the frailest person one could conceivably meet, but with regard to her personality, he'd met decorated generals with less grit. A ways away, Niall missed his mark and submitted to his lashing with a grinning grunt. "Do any of you know how to enjoy yourselves without making each other bleed?" sniffed Rian.

"I can think of *many* things I enjoy more," commented Tam Lin, with a pointed stare.

Sucking at her cheek, she elaborated, "Long as you idiots live, you'd think you'd have developed some class."

"Rian," Kaer Yin sighed. "What did we talk about?"

"I remember," she relented grumpily.

"I'm going to ignore your misguided judgment, Mistress Guinness," Tam Lin said. "Games with consequences are training. The Tuatha De Dannan are the finest warriors in Innisfail for a reason."

"If you say so," she dismissed him, holding her skirt up to the light to check her handiwork. "Ben, when we get to Ten Bells, you owe me two Royals. Don't think I forgot. I need a new dress, among other things."

"I am well aware, Rian. We have many things to buy, apparently." He spared Tam Lin a sour look.

Tam Lin pursed his lower lip, unaffected by his cousin's ire. "Who's the Ambassador these days, anyway? I've honestly no idea."

"Sioarse Cathal, last I heard."

Tam Lin's nose wrinkled. "That Bolg woman? Sionnavar's sibling? Gods. That's going to be loads of fun."

"Why?" Rian asked. "What does that matter?"

"Bri Leith and Armagh might be allies, but they're far from friendly. The Cathal Clan serves the Black Bull— the ruling family. They're descended from Eochaid Mac Nemed, the last Fir Bolg Ard Ri."

"But that was *ages* ago."

"In Aes Sidhe, bad blood festers with time. A commodity we have in abundance," explained Kaer Yin. "They can't move directly against my father, but that doesn't mean they don't try to be a thorn in his clan's arse whenever an opportunity arises."

"Wonderful," she cut her eyes away and dug another roll of thread from her bag. "I gather they're going to hand over any funds and weapons you need without a word of complaint?"

"Well..."

"Whatever. I hope you have a backup plan for your 'mountains of gold and silk,' then? We won't get more than one shot at this."

Robin patted his chest. "That's where we come in. Greenmakers are connected down in Ten Bells. Ye'd be surprised what we'll come up with."

"I want my Royals, damn it," repeated Rian more sternly. Her expression promised an intolerable amount of nagging. Kaer Yin scrubbed a palm over his eyes. He was going to throttle her one day. He was sure of it.

Heath and Dorcan both missed their marks, and the beating each earned sounded worse than Niall's. Eva's lip curled. Mel patted her shoulder on his way over to watch. Gerrod went too, after the briefest guilty smile at Rian. "All right," announced Tam Lin, tossing his bowl in the midden. "Time to show these ingrates how it's done. Yin, you're not invited."

Robin hooted with laughter.

Eva craned her head, askance. "Why not?"

"Ye ever seen His Arseness shoot?"

Kaer Yin stood up anyway, skirting around Tam Lin's groan. "He's just bitter because I *always* win. Look at it this way, Rian, you might get one Royal back tonight after I'm done embarrassing our fine Prince O'Ruiadh here."

COLD FLAMES LICKED THROUGH A CAVERNOUS DOORWAY CROWDED BY the dead. In the distance, a high bell peeled above a windblown hillside. Wet pine and ether thickened the air. It was Samhain, and he was dying. Then... she was there. Her amber eyes loomed large and bright in the filthy perfection of her face. Though brief, the weight of her in his arms left his palms quaking with need. Una's soft mouth poured warmth into his.

He gasped.

Kaer Yin came awake with a start.

The salt of her tears lingered on his tongue like heartbreak. He sat up, gripping his head. She was far away now and alone.

Soon, he vowed to the night sky.

Wait for me, Una.

The fire dwindled to embers outside his tent. Beside him, Tam Lin turned over in his bedroll. In the second tent, Rian and Eva slumbered fitfully. Kaer Yin could hear the young faerie whimpering in her sleep again. Eva's presence helped— her abilities being such as they were— but she could not cure all. Now, Rian called Una's name in fearful wonder.

So, he and Rian shared nightmares this eve?

The bell in his dream chimed from the corners of his mind.

Perhaps that terrible night would haunt them all the rest of their days? For Kaer Yin, Samhain had been both a terrible curse and a blessing. He'd gained and lost the only thing he'd ever cared for in the sweep of a single hour. Frowning, he rubbed at his sore temple.

I won't fail you again.

I swear it.

With a defeated sigh, he got up. Dawn would break soon; they should get back on the road. The horses were tethered together beside a mound of sleeping men and Sidhe, cradling packs and each other for added warmth. Robin had argued that a sea of Sidhe tents and furs would've drawn undue attention. Kaer Yin had attempted to eschew one altogether until Rian swore to gut him in his sleep if he dared try. He clutched his itchy but swiftly-healing chest wound and strolled from camp to relieve himself against a frozen tree. He was beyond nursing now, wasn't he? Cursing when the frost-ridden breeze bit into his bared flesh, he hurried through his natural duty. Then, replacing his stays with godlike speed, he jumped to discover Eva standing a few feet away, watching him with her eerie, Una-colored eyes. He fidgeted.

"Ah, good morning?"

"Not quite, Your Highness."

"Right, not for some while, I suppose. What can I do for you?" Nervously smoothing his tunic down and shrugging his cloak tight, he made to brush past her.

Slender fingers caught at his sleeve. Her eyes gleamed like polished jewels in the snow-bright darkness. "I know what you dreamed, Your Highness."

Kaer Yin was proud not to flush. "I can't say I love that about you, My Lady."

"I hear it too."

He cocked his head, confused. "What?"

"The bell," she said, gesturing. "Listen."

He heard nothing but icy leaves rattling together in the wind and the deep silence of newly fallen snow. "I don't—" but then he *did* hear something. Faint, crunching footsteps along the road and the jingle of a distant bell. No, not a bell... a bridle. His eyes flew wide. "Bandits?"

"They'll overwhelm you."

Kaer Yin muttered something foul in his mother's tongue. "Can you keep Rian safe?"

"Not for long. They're coming from the river. There are twenty in the first rush. Twelve more are waiting ahead. They're hungry, and—" she craned her neck as if listening to a voice he couldn't hear. "Many are wounded. It seems they ran afoul of your Lord Bishop earlier this month."

Kaer Yin's heart thumped to life in his chest. "Una?"

She smiled. "Unharmed."

Thank you, Brida. "Good."

Shar slid from the pre-dawn shadows, his expression alert and wary. "*Ard Tiarne*, you have heard them?"

"Yes. Go wake Tam Lin and Robin."

"No need," assured Tam Lin from his left side. He wasn't smiling. "Get the women to safety, Shar. Be quick."

Shar saluted both princes and melted into the trees. Kaer Yin signaled to Tam Lin and Eva and marched into camp to find Robin passing daggers and bows to his men. Of course, Gramble was already awake. He never could sleep after so much uishge. He and Robin shared a smile over Eva's head. Gods, but this had been a dull month. "Singles or doubles?"

Robin affected an offended snort, pulling his sabre. "I've a reputation, you know?"

Tam Lin warned, "By Herne, take any from me and regret it."

Kaer Yin tripped Tam Lin on his way past. "Then you'll have to catch up!"

Beneath the rising sun, the Greenmakers and their escort descended upon their would-be attackers like starved locusts. The Sidhe were used to hunting poachers like the Greenmakers this time of year and had taken to their Souther-bound mission with a collective groan. Days of drinking, riding and sedentary camping had made for poor sport. Sure, it would get exciting enough once they passed Ten Bells, but for now, they couldn't have been more excited for the distraction. The bandits had no clue what they were in for. That was pretty obvious from the outset. "No arrows!" Kaer Yin mouthed from his perch among the lower boughs of a fir tree. Shar slid his bow around to grasp his larks. Tam Lin grumbled something unintelligible but drew his dagger anyway. He preferred to shoot than engage hand-to-hand, though Kaer Yin knew he was aware of their predicament. Any arrows they left behind would prove a complication for the utter secrecy of their purpose.

Having lost their quarry nearly as quickly as they'd been spotted, the bandits crept around their abandoned camp, faces smeared with equal parts mud and frustration. Several passed very close to Rian and Eva's hiding spot but didn't so much as glance in their direction. That was interesting. Kaer Yin reminded himself to ask what else she could do.

High above the invaders in the canopy, the Sidhe waited. Not one to permit Kaer Yin a lead in any aspect, Robin had sent Gerrod and the boys to track the group around the river, then shimmied up with the Dannans. Reclining at height like any Sidhe, Robin impatiently flipped his daggers and pointed at the ground. A road-weary young man shuffled through the underbrush beneath Kaer Yin's tree. Tam Lin gestured to do something about him.

Lip curled, Kaer Yin shook his head.

"*Not enough*," he mimed.

Tam Lin shot him a mocking glare.

Three more bandits squirmed up behind the lad. With a wink for his cousin, Kaer Yin dropped from his perch, flashing a mouth full of white teeth. The landing hurt more than he'd like, but that hardly deterred him. He rolled upright, taking the first bandit through the middle with a quick, one-handed swipe. Before the lad could cry out, Kaer Yin slit his throat with the lark in his left hand. The boy crumpled to the ground in gurgling surprise. Kaer Yin didn't stop to watch him die. His lark sailed through the air ahead, pinning his next opponent through the ear to a tree. The loud 'thump' whipped several larcenous heads around to face him. Holding up two fingers for Robin to sneer at, he launched himself into the knot of thieves like a cannon shot. Whirling left and right with vicious accuracy, Kaer Yin dealt death with gleeful abandon. He scarcely noticed if the bandits he slaughtered brandished weapons little better than spades and cudgels.

If most of them seemed barely old enough to shave, he couldn't have cared less. Weeks of pent-up aggravation and stunted urgency took precedence over the gnawing ache in his chest and midsection. By his sixth victim, he leaned against a tree to catch his breath. His wounds were no longer urgent, but they were present, nonetheless.

He muttered a curse when Tam Lin vaunted past him, chasing one of the quicker bandits down. "Eight." Tam Lin blew both Robin and his cousin a kiss.

From behind him, Kaer Yin heard Robin growl, "No one invited ye to play, ye pretty bastard!"

The element of surprise was long gone. Realizing their mistake, the bandits dashed for the road with all the speed they could muster. Most were slain fairly quickly. A few pounded down the muddy thoroughfare as if the Kneeler's Devil snapped at their heels. From the southern edge near the river, a handful of Greenmakers burst from the hedges with ear-splitting grins. The whole affair was over in moments. Those bandits who didn't try to run for the frigid riverbank dropped their weapons and threw up their filthy hands. Colm kicked one fellow over, stripping him of a rusty sabre and a pair of daggers.

Sheathing his sword, Tam Lin waited for Niall to tie up the remaining prisoners. Kaer Yin and Robin arrived last, both scowling. "How many?" Kaer Yin asked him.

"Four," Robin sighed.

"Damn Tam Lin to the Hells."

The redhead shot him a raised brow. "Sore loser."

Grinding his molars, Kaer Yin nudged the nearest prisoner with his boot. "Well, look who chose their victims poorly. Which one's the leader?"

The fellow— a youth, really— glared back. "I don't have to tell ye nuthin.'"

"You're right. Niall? Cut his throat."

The boy squealed when Niall's gorgeous silver-handled dagger hefted his chin. Not even fourteen, if Kaer Yin were any judge. "Wait!" the boy begged. "We was hungry, sir. I swear it. Saw yer fire and thought ye'd have food and maybe better weapons."

"Horseshite," said Robin. "A gaggle o'girls like ye ain't out here lookin' for mutton. I know raiders when I see 'em."

"You might say he's a bit of an expert," Kaer Yin whispered behind his hand.

The boy squirmed. "The road's our meal ticket, sir. I swear it."

"That's as may be, but ye answer to someone, doncha?" Robin prodded.

Kaer Yin knelt, refusing to wince at the pain in his aching thigh. "Do you know who this is, boy? I bet you've heard of Robin Gramble, haven't you?"

The boy had. He paled by five shades. "I don't... I mean... we can't... *Siora*."

"Where do you hole up?" Robin pressed him.

"Cairnream, twenty miles southeast."

"Whole town, or just ye scamps in on it?"

"Not much of a town, sir. Was once, afore I was born maybe. Now, it's our camp."

"Young fella like ye could hardly be the leader. Who d'ye pay tribute to, boyo?"

The boy hung his head. "Wencel, sir. He's raisin' funds for some toff from the North. Bootlegger, I hear, though I never met him."

Kaer Yin perked up. "*Bootlegger*?"

Robin scooped the lad up by the collar. "What's this toff's name, then?"

Under Robin's fist, the boy shrugged as best as he could. "Dunno, sir. Never met him, like I said."

Robin dropped him to scratch at his grizzled cheek. "Who would know?"

The boy sent a nervous glance sideways, fat beads of sweat dribbling down his muddy cheeks. Another boy, some ways back, flashed his teeth. Shar hauled him up by his neck. "Matt, sirs. That's all any o'us knows."

"Shut yer gob, Ian!" another hissed.

"I din't come out with ye's to be murdered, Lance! Ye prats can die for him if ye like?"

Shar shook him silent. Robin advanced, eyes sparking like twin coals. "Matt *Gilcannon*, is that right?"

The boy shrugged as best as he was able, considering he fairly dangled from Shar's overlarge fist. "Gil-somewhat sounds about right. Yeah."

"He's gonna have yer tiny balls in a jar, Ian!" swore the first.

"*Shut up!*" answered four voices in unison, including Kaer Yin's.

"Well," Robin intoned, giving him a long look. "Do we have time for a slight detour, then?"

Kaer Yin shook his head. "I wish we did. I promised that fat pederast his comeuppance, didn't I?"

"Aye. No more than I or any Greenmaker, Ben."

Irritably, Tam Lin folded his arms. "Who's this now?"

"A nasty sort who deserves what's coming to him," Kaer Yin scowled. "We don't have time for him right now, Robin. You know we don't. When we get Una back safe, he'll have my full attention. I swear it."

"It ain't me yer gonna have to reassure. Once Gerrod hears about this, he'll—"

"I'll what?" asked Gerrod and the lads, emerging onto the road from a thorny knot of brambles toward the riverbank. They were all wet to the knees and none worse for wear than Gerrod himself. He had a bloody nose and a longish gash on his left cheek but seemed otherwise as hale and amiable as always.

Robin scratched at his scarred chin, silently pleading with Kaer Yin to change his mind. "Ah, well, ye see boyo... the thing is—"

"I don't see why some shiftless bootlegger would warrant the attention. Yin, we have more pressing issues at hand, yes? Let's strip these lads of anything useful and get a move on," interrupted Tam Lin irascibly. "This Matt character can't be more important than your girl?"

Robin threw his hands up in the air.

"*Dénann déithe dochar do bhéal mór, Tam Lin O'Ruiadh!*"[6] Kaer Yin barked. Tam Lin opened his mouth to retort, but Kaer Yin shouldered him out of the way to face Gerrod, whose face puckered nearly purple. "Now, Gerrod, we have to—"

Gerrod's ordinarily warm brown eyes darkened. "Aye? Were gonna keep it from me then? Why's that?"

"Well, lad. Ye know we want to finish the job we started all them weeks ago, same as ye but the lass—"

"Not me problem. Matt, on t'other hand, *is*."

"Gerry, you know I want his head as much as you do, but I have a promise to fulfill," Kaer Yin said, attempting to pat his arm. Gerrod jerked away.

"Ye made a promise to me and to Robin too. And to Barb, Colm, Dabs, and half of Rosweal, while ye was at it. Matt's *our* top priority, *milord*. Or does pretty quinny take top billin' over yer mates?"

"Gerrod!" Rian screeched from the side of the road. She and Eva had come down the track from the opposite end. Her face was livid with confused shock. "What would make you say such a thing? Una saved all of our lives. You know that!"

Moderately cowed by the outrage in Rian's blue eyes, he turned away. "Nothin' against her, Mistress Guinness. Just sayin,' if Matt's around, I got somewhere else to be."

"That's lovely, that is," Robin told him. "Gonna haul off on yer own and get yer fool self killed. For what?"

"Who's gonna stop me?"

"I bloody well will, Gerry," Kaer Yin rumbled, making sure Gerrod couldn't mistake the deadly-serious tone. Despite his bravado, Gerrod backed up a pace. Perplexed, Tam Lin spoke to Shar in rapid but inaudible *Ealig*. Shar zipped back into the trees. Meanwhile, Gerrod squared his shoulders under Kaer Yin's glare.

"If yer not gonna help me, ye don't have the right to stop me neither."

"Who in the Hells do you imagine you're speaking to?"

"Someone I thought was my friend."

Kaer Yin flinched like he'd been bitten.

Tam Lin made a rude sound at the back of his throat. "I don't understand what the fuss is about. Apologize to your Lord while I'm asking nicely."

---

6   'Gods damn your big mouth, Tam Lin O'Ruiadh!'

"Gerrod has his reasons, Prince O'Ruiadh," Robin spat over his shoulder. "Best stay out of it."

"Gerry," Kaer Yin held up his palms as if to soothe a wild colt. "Matt'll keep. I promise we'll see him soon. You have my word. I wouldn't give it if I didn't mean it."

Despising being the center of attention, Gerrod muttered a curse. A sharp glance at Robin told all. "Ye too then?"

"Aye. Ben's the boss here, Gerry. Not me. Besides, he's right."

Gerrod shrugged. "Fine. Let's go and save Ben's piece. Nevermind what Matt's done to Rosweal, or me family, Hells, to *loads* o'families in the North. That's not nearly as urgent as the weight of Ben's bollocks, is it?"

"Gerrod! What is the matter with you?" Rian cried, aghast. She'd never seen this side of the lad before. Ignoring her, Gerrod sheathed his dagger and spun on his heel. Kaer Yin moved to follow, but Robin's hand caught at his shoulder.

"Nah. Let him go. He'll have a stew for a bit and give us sass the next couple o' days, but he'll be right as rain in no time. Matt does it to him. Gnaws his guts we had to let that bastard go when we might have had him."

"Why does he hate Gilcannon?" Rian wondered aloud. "I mean, so much more than the rest of you?"

It was Eva who answered. "No hatred burns as bright as a son's for an abusive father." She paused to see her expression. "What? You didn't know?" Rian's owlish silence spoke the truth of that. Eva chuckled mirthlessly. "He seeks vengeance for his mother and two sisters."

"His *father*?" Tam Lin inhaled hard. "You're a dark bunch down here. You know that?"

"This isn't funny, Lin." Kaer Yin elbowed past him. "Gather these lads' weapons and anything useful. We should get back on the road as soon as possible."

"What do we do with this rabble?" Shar tipped his blade at one whimpering bandit.

"Set them loose. Matt won't have them again after failing him. Leave them for the winter roads."

"Ben, he didn't mean what he said. Ye know that," said Robin.

Kaer Yin lacked the oxygen to formulate a grand defense. "Of course he did, Robin. What's more, he might be right."

LATER, WHEN THEY'D PUT A SAFE DISTANCE BETWEEN THEMSELVES AND their previous camp, a lone rider kicked his mount onto the High Road, veering East. That this rider seemed to possess little knowledge of the animal he'd stolen was lost to the wind, the dispassionate gleam of a sky full of brilliant white stars, and the plodding of the mare's hooves against a frost-bitten road.

14
COMMON CAUSE

Una threw down her wad of vellum and sat up, scrubbing her eyes. She'd been at it for hours already. The library was as cold as a windswept moor, and she was pretty confident every chair in the room doubled as a torture device. Yawning, she stood up to crack her aching back. If only one could relieve a bruised tailbone as easily. From his seat in the opposite chair, Micah glanced at her from beneath his unruly blond fringe. What he lacked in age and couth he made up for in scholastic enthusiasm. She admired that about him. For one so intelligent to be reared in such an intellectually desolate environment as the Briton Wastes, he took to his newfound resources with a relish that nearly shamed her. How dreadful to be born inquisitive in a world of privation and drudgery! For all the injustices she might have suffered in her brief life, a lack of education and rearing was not among them. After Rosweal, she must accept that her understanding and empathy for the less-fortunate parts of the world was decidedly lacking.

Knowing an inequality exists from an intellectual perspective is not quite the same as bearing its experience. She was ashamed to admit that, on this subject, her education far exceeded her grasp.

Micah's bright eyes clinched in a warm smile. "Uncomfortable, milady?"

"'My Lady,' and yes," she sneezed, tugging her cloak tight. "It's too bloody cold by half in here. I forgot how drafty this old pile of rocks was."

The library was a grand but largely neglected space on the top floor of the Keep's west side. Una's great-grandfather had been a voracious reader and intellectual, but the rest of his family did not seem to share his enthusiasm for learning. Each of the library's four long, slate walls was draped with floor-to-ceiling mahogany bookshelves that had once graced the ancient library at Trinity in old Dubh-lin. While many of the college's once impressive books and scrolls had long since disintegrated, Duch Kevin had managed to salvage what treasures he could and add to the collection throughout his life. The result was this beautiful, stately room with its grand fireplace beneath the delicate glass and lattice windows on the western wall, crowded everywhere by books of every shade and binding. Tall ladders climbed stacks that were now dusty with disuse but somehow managed to emit the faintest hint of linseed and Bretagn lemon oils. Una was reminded to ask Shanley about a proper housekeeper for the library's precious contents. She could manage that much, she hoped.

Micah set his book aside with a flush. He was a rather attractive young man. She hoped he wouldn't be ruined by the political machine in her father's head. "What was it like, erm, *My Lady*? Growin' up here, I mean?"

"Tiresome as it is now, cousin. Though, in those days, I had free run of the place," she smirked at the impassive guards. "Not so much, now."

"How did you... you know?" whispered Micah conciliatorily.

"What do you mean?"

"How did you escape? Can't have been easy."

"It wasn't." Smile flickering, she turned to warm her numb fingers by the fire. Though he blissfully did not share his father's rigid adherence to Kneeler superstitions and Scripture, she doubted Micah was keen to learn more about her... talents. "Perhaps we'll discuss it some other time? For now, have you found anything?"

Micah groaned over his abandoned book. "Nothin'. Haven't seen Da's name in any of these court records so far. Ye?"

"No. Patrick did say he had the majority of the records expunged, but that doesn't mean the incident reports would be concealed as well. Maybe we're looking in the wrong place?"

"How so?"

"Well, if the Duch wanted to conceal the crimes, I thought he'd have them brought here with Duch Michael's accounts. We've been through these stacks eight times. They're not here."

"Do ye think they've been destroyed?"

She pursed her lips. "No. Blackmail is much more effective with ample documentation. I imagine he held onto them in case he need bribe or intimidate those involved."

"Would they be in his chambers, d'ye think?"

"Too obvious."

Micah's groan mirrored her mood perfectly. "Beggin' yer pardon, milady. I know Da's a rough touch, but he ain't no murderer. Maybe we should ask someone who was there? Why d'we need to dig up his old, erm, 'incidents?'"

She turned around with her arms crossed. "Because I'm not inclined to take Patrick's word. Once you learn how theatrically devious he is, you'll feel the same. If Henry is innocent, the records will add credence to his defense. If not..." she cleared her throat and gave the lad a long look. "You don't have to do this, Micah."

He squared his shoulders. "I swore to help ye."

"Well then, I can think of one other place they might be. Though, we'll have to be careful. I'm forbidden from that wing of the castle."

"Why? Surely you don't mean to run away again, do you?"

She flinched. She couldn't do anything but blink back at his perplexed expression for several moments. Did she not? Honestly, she hadn't thought about it in a while. After everything that had transpired in Rosweal, what good *would* it do to escape now? Hadn't she inflicted enough harm upon innocent (well, relatively, anyway) people already? How many lives were lost throughout the North in her attempt to shirk her responsibilities? Having nothing but time to think these past weeks, she realized many unpleasant truths about herself. While no amount of introspection could repair her relationship with her father, she had to admit there was much she could do for Bethany.

As Queen of Tairngare, she might have held power to effect change the Continent over— including the belabored and long-suffering women of the

South. She could have bridged the gap between both cultures have encouraged something of a social coup by example. Now, however, the likelihood of any of that happening was as feeble as a feather in a storm. All she'd ever wanted was to be free. To make that dream a reality, she had purposefully trod over that potential future on her way out of the Citadel. She'd been beaten, hunted, terrorized, and abjured by her people ever since. It seemed the only place she had left was the last place she'd ever wanted to be.

Bethany was not an ideal destination for her by any stretch of the imagination. She loathed every slab of stone in this castle, point in fact. However, no one in the South had plans to burn her for a heretic, did they? What little news she could wring from any of her guards or her father's courtiers about Tairngare was dire. Her grandmother had fled to Siora-knew-where. Her aunts, Ana and Basa, were dead or imprisoned. Commoners burned the Moura sigil in the streets and dragged any loyalist nobles or Merchers before the mob for censure or execution. Many lives had been lost, most undeserving. Una's grief over the affair had been a daily trial to conceal. That so many were suffering on her account, intentional or otherwise, was more than she could bear. At least, here in the South, she had a purpose. If she so chose, perhaps power enough to march North one day, herself? Returning to Tairngare for the foreseeable future would be foolish with her family in public disgrace. Resuming her plans to travel east into Alba seemed equally redundant... and Kaer Yin was gone.

She had nowhere else to go.

Her father was right, loathe as she was to admit it. She had a place here: a *purpose*. Her life needn't be spent fleeing from one fate to another. Bethany was a terrible place for women. Did it have to be? What might she achieve as Duchess for the women here and everywhere? Fresh guilt burbled in her throat at the thought but clung all the same.

Free yourself, Patrick had said.

Clenching her fist at the memory, she felt her power thrumming through her veins. Hadn't Diarmid Adair said the same?

Whatever she decided, her fate must be her own. "My plans are irrelevant. Girls are being slaughtered on our doorstep. I want to know why and by whom."

"My uncle said—"

"Again, irrelevant. Patrick is ill, Micah. I doubt he has the stomach for this, with the tourney and Cromnasa Feasts to oversee. This wolf requires a snare."

Micah's flush teetered between pretty and petulant. She frowned. He should learn to mind his expressions if he wished to survive the South. Though the political atmosphere here was far less labyrinthine than in Tairngare, it was perilous, nonetheless.

One should never broadcast one's thoughts.

Unaware of her scrutiny, he ruffled his hair. "Forgive me, cousin, but yer a lady, and I'm a nobody. Neither o'us is an expert in crime-solvin'."

She picked up his ledger and held it under his nose. "Here's your first lesson in statecraft, My Lord. Murder victims make terrible supper guests. If you mean to save your father from further accusation, help me find the court records which prove he's never slain a victim. Otherwise, any number of my father's Barons might ask for his head, and Patrick will have no choice but to imprison or execute him. Do you understand?"

He stared up at her for a moment, face white. "He wouldn't lock him up again?"

"He'll have no choice if more girls turn up dead."

"But why would ye want to help me Da? Ye didn't get on, last I saw," he understated.

"I don't," Una replied without hesitation. "I'm ruling him out."

Micah chewed his lower lip in silent debate with himself for a long while. Eventually, he took the tome back with a wry smile. "All right then."

Leaning against the arm of his chair, Una smiled. "Good."

AN AGING LIBERTINE WITH A PENCHANT FOR WINE AND CHEESE— THAT was what his uncle had said of Lord Gaelin. Damek was amused to find the statement comically accurate. Though he'd defeated him in battle once, he'd never actually met the man before. He was tall and thin through the back and shoulders, with an overlarge paunch and greasy fat fingers. His heavily tanned face bore sagging jowls, deep lines, and a plump lower lip. Damek supposed he must have been handsome once upon a time on account of the many tales he'd been told of the Marquis' many conquests. Now, the Duch's description rang all too true. A bejeweled hand patted the thinning brown hair at his crown as the Marquis Gaelin affected an effeminate bow. Damek inclined his head slightly; he was not in the habit of genuflection. Gaelin narrowed his dark eyes but made no comment. Martin saluted after Damek, and the Steel Corpsmen in the ranks hammered their breastplates.

"I see your men have manners, Lord Bishop," observed Gaelin.

Damek slung his leg over his saddlehorn to lean closer. His smirk was mirthless, as intended. "They know how to treat their betters in Bethany, My Lord Marquis."

Gaelin muttered something foul behind a strained smirk. His horse, a lovely white mare, pranced nervously beneath him. "Shall I grovel for you then, boy? Would that appease your arrogance?"

"Not at all, My Lord. Your sons will do it for you."

Gaelin's nostrils flared, but he did not rise to the bait. Damek had superior numbers, better mounts, and the right to stamp Gaelin and his brood into the mud if he so chose. By right of conquest, Damek now owned thirty-five percent of Gaelin's modest kingdom. The price of betrayal was steep in Bethany. All the same, Gaelin waved two riders forward. One was fatter than his father, with the same complexion and bearing. Vexos, no doubt: fond of the axe, a fight, and not much else, Damek had been told. The younger, on the other hand, was a good deal finer of frame. He sat his palfrey like a man born in the saddle. His eyes were blue and quite direct. Damek had heard of this one too. Castor Gaelin: a man with two mistresses— both male. Castor's interest in Damek was plain. Damek shared a long look with Martin.

"My sons, Lord Bishop. Vexos is my champion but of course. No finer man with a blade in all of Bretagne. The skinny spare is my youngest, Castor. He prefers books and poems to a skirmish, but the Gods made him clever at least. One of these two lumps should serve as a good bridegroom for your cousin, no?"

Damek filled his mouth with teeth. Every lord in the South knew Una was technically Damek's wife. He let the insult pass with a caustic shrug he did not feel. He'd better get used to the treatment, for not a single incoming noble would let him forget it. In Gaelin's sons' case, however, he was less worried than annoyed. "I'm sure she'll be charmed. We're here to escort you to the castle. Any men in your train who aren't in your immediate retinue should follow at a sedate pace. My uncle's steward has prepared the barracks in the West End for all incoming soldiers."

Without waiting for a reply, Damek spurred his mount around to march toward the city. Gaelin's mare settled in beside him. "So?"

"What?"

"Tell us of her! Is she as beautiful as they say? Dark, soft skin? Luscious tits? Vexos likes a woman with curves, as did I, when I was younger," he leered.

"She is the most beautiful woman in Innisfail, My Lord," responded Damek without flair.

Vexos' nasally giggle hardly matched his oxen frame. Gaelin said something else in Bretagn, but Damek refused to let on that he understood. The eldest and his father threw their heads back in a shared laugh. "Wonderful news! Tell me, since you're the expert, is she a screamer or a prude?"

"If you'd met her, I think you'd regret that comment."

"Oh, *oui*. We've heard of her powers. It's disappointing, no? That the women in Tairngare are bred to witchery? Some would be quite charming did they accept their place. Basa Alvra, for one. When we were young, I greatly enjoyed her wit. Her and that mouthy piece your uncle took to wife," Gaelin made a face. "Don't think Vexos will tolerate that. Will you, my boy?"

"*Non*," droned the ox. "I'd knock her teeth out if she tried, *mon père*."

Castor spoke up in a bored, flat tone. "I heard Lady Donahugh once melted a man's flesh from his bones for the attempt."

Vexos picked at his nose. "Then I'll keep her trussed like a sow. She doesn't need to be conscious to breed. Does she?"

"*Père, tu devrais lui mettre une laisse. Nous sommes des invités ici.*"[7]

"No need. I'm sure Lord Bishop has heard it all before," chuckled Gaelin.

"Indeed," Damek allowed, with his eyes on the woods ahead. "I have. Nevertheless, you've come to woo her anyway, haven't you? She will rule a kingdom ten times the size of your modest holdfast, My Lord."

"So grand, the lot of you. Bretagne was once the mightiest kingdom in all Europa, boy. You might recall that, were you not so arrogant."

"Once, perhaps. Now it is an overgrown string of rocks with soil suited for naught but grapes, where men are forced to pirate and raid to sustain their families. Any power you might have had fled with your black soil."

Gaelin bristled. "Bethany is not much better. You're hostage to a gaggle of elves and women simply for lack of timber. Timber *we* have in abundance. The few mighty Innish ships our sailors spy in the Straits of Manannan are Tairnganese or Cymrian. Bethany's sole boons are steel, tin, and cattle. Not much to brag about."

---

7   Father, you should put a leash on him. We're guests here.

"Oh, I dunno about that. Seems our soldiers more than make up for our lack of ships, wouldn't you agree, Marquis?"

"Humph," said Gaelin.

"If I'd been of age, you'd have died on the field that day, and *mon père* would be Lord of Clare, no? Yes," sniggered Vexos. "I'd have been fucking your wife from her first bleed, and she'd never have learned anything but the length of my cock."

"Lucky for me, you were yet a pimple-spotted lass, humping dead animals in your father's stables," Damek said. "I've heard of you too, as it happens."

"Once I win your woman, perhaps I'll fuck her over your corpse, *joli garçon?*"[8]

"Vexos!" susurrated Gaelin. "*Garde ta langue!*"[9]

Damek met Martin's eyes over Vexos' head. He held up three gloved fingers. Behind him, Ridley fell back a few horse lengths. Weak, mottled sunlight glinted from their armor. Gaelin's men seemed ill-equipped by comparison, being that they wore ancient, poorly oiled leather cuirasses and held spears and swords that bore touches of rust and wear. The woods inched closer, with them, yet more shade for an already frigid morning. "Perhaps."

Vexos glared back. "She threw you over, did she not, *mon ami?* I think I'll offer her your finger bones on a chain. What I hear, that'd make her wet as the *Aber.*"

He turned to his father, whose face had gone an ugly shade of green. "*Pourquoi ce subterfuge? Nous devrions le tuer et prendre le château! Nos hommes sont prêts, mon père.*"[10]

Bare treetops creaked overhead. Martin gnashed his teeth at Damek, who straightened in his saddle. "You'd allow your heir to insult your liege lord, Gaelin?"

Gaelin fidgeted at the stern faces gathered around him. "Ah, he is young, My Lord. Eager to meet your cousin, that is all."

"Do you believe threatening to murder My Lord and rape My Lady was a wise way to introduce yourself to the Duch's men?" demanded Martin, with a tick in his jaw.

While Gaelin fumbled for excuses, Vexos engaged his fellow Bretagn soldiers in an animated conversation in Bretagn, replete with vulgar gestures.

---

8   pretty boy?
9   Watch your tongue!
10   Why the subterfuge, father? We should kill him, then take the castle! Our men are ready.

None of his cavalry appeared comfortable in their seats. Several nervous sets of eyes shifted around for obvious offense. Given the Steel Corp's general readiness and reputation, the Bretagns would be the obvious underdogs in a tussle.

Castor's upper lip curled at his brother. *"Mon Père, est-ce que tu vois? Quelle bête stupide, il est."*[11]

"D'accord," answered Damek, earning two very surprised glares. *"Mais bien sûr, il n'aura jamais l'occasion.* Martin?"[12]

O'Rearden waved a mailed fist, and Damek allowed himself the satisfaction of watching Gaelin's face crumple. A cloud of arrows sailed out of the trees on their right. Fourteen Gauls fell under the first volley. Vexos' stallion reared, hurling him from his saddle. Hearing a nasty crunch as Vexos clutched his mangled shoulder, Damek smiled to watch the oaf roll around in the grass, keening like a whipped girl. Still seated, Gaelin went for his sword, but Damek got there first. Beneath the whistling arc of a second volley, his hand lashed out, ripping Gaelin's weapon away from him— a useless piece, really— too thin, too light, and too ornamental to be lethal. He scarcely had time to gasp before Damek's dagger plunged into the hollow beneath his clavicle. Surprised, Gaelin stared back at his murderer in silent contempt. A thin ribbon of bloody spittle dangled from his over plump lips. He cut his knuckles attempting to wrench the blade from his chest to no avail. Damek jerked it out again with a malicious grin. On the ground, Vexos' wail reached a particular pitch. With Gauls dying on either side of him, while countless hooves and booted feet threatened to trample him at any moment, he cried out, *"Père! Castor, sauve-le!"*[13]

But Castor was nowhere near the fracas. He and a handful of comparably well-attired retainers arranged themselves at the opposite end of the road. None made the slightest move forward, swords stuck fast in their scabbards, quivers pregnant with arrows. Vexos lurched to his feet, clutching his wounded shoulder.

"Espèce de salope! Je vais vous arracher les tripes pour ça."[14]

The loyalist Gauls around Vexos attempted to surround him with their heavy oaken shields, to no avail. Damek's archers were better. Vexos' defenders fell nearly one-by-one into the muck at his feet. Through it all and dying slowly,

---

11   You see? What a stupid beast, he is.
12   Agreed. But of course, he will never have the occasion.
13   Father! Save him, Castor!
14   You bitch! I'm going to rip out your balls for this.

Gaelin watched from his saddle, eyes furiously raking the tableau ahead. He grunted something unintelligible at his youngest, who merely shrugged.

"*Nous sommes comme vous nous l'avez fait, mon cher père,*"[15] Castor replied, with a venom that chilled even Damek's lukewarm blood. Taking one last look at his beloved eldest child, Gaelin slumped from his saddle into the mud. In its desperation to flee the scene, his charger smashed his brains in on its way out of the wood. Damek tossed a cheap, wood-handled dagger atop the Marquis' corpse.

Raising a fist, the arrows stopped. Roaring in rage, Vexos faced him. With his good arm, he ripped off his cloak and tunic, showing a swath of swirling red tattoos over his well-muscled chest and abdomen. A thin but vicious-looking sword sprang to hand. "I will kill you, half-breed."

Damek pursed his lips. "I'd be disappointed if you didn't try."

"Be careful, *mon ami*. He's not a noble fighter," advised Castor.

"Neither am I," Damek assured him, dismounting. He tossed his cloak to Hisk. His Corpsmen gathered close. The Gauls had been slain to a man, save for the several dozen pooled behind Castor.

Vexos didn't see them. He couldn't pry his eyes away from Damek. "You're a fool to trust a man who'd murder his father."

Striding over, Damek unsheathed his sabre. "Who said anything about trust?"

Vexos aimed the point of his blade at his indifferent brother. "When I'm done with this faerie scum, you're next, *mon frère*."

Castor said nothing.

Damek flipped his pommel into a low guard, his arms and feet perpendicular with his shoulders, back slightly hunched.

Vexos hefted his cumbersome two-hander with a wheeze. "What's this? You look like a frog."

Damek dashed forward rather than bandy words. Coming in too low for Vexos to block in time, he swung into his middle with two testing blows that rocked the Gaul back on his heels.

Vexos parried but clumsily, gritting his teeth. Damek spun around him, keeping his sabre level with the ground. Vexos took an audible slash to his rear-right knee and a second to his left calf. Grunting, he stumbled, forced to lean against one of his broadswords for support. "*Espèce de bâtard infidèle.*"

---

15   We are as you've made us, dearest father.

"I thought you'd be more of a challenge, mighty Vexos?" mocked Damek, reclaiming his ugly but efficient low guard. "A large man with a long arm, indeed."

With a hearty bellow, Vexos hacked wildly at him. The air whooshed in Damek's ears with each wild swing, though he effortlessly danced out of their way. Bloodied and breathing hard, Vexos staggered against a tree trunk. He faced the amused onlookers with an increasingly heavy brow. That Damek made sport of him was not lost on anyone— least of all, Vexos. The realization of an imminent and ignoble death dawned all at once. He threw down his sword and drew a dagger with his injured left hand. "Where did you learn to prance around like that? *Merde,* your father's people taught you, *n'est pas*?"

"Something like that."

Vexos glared over his head at his brother. "You think our ships and timber will be enough for him, *mon frère*? *Non.* When he's done with you, your bones will rot in the midden, same as mine and *papa*'s. To slay an ally under a flag of truce?" He shook his head once. "I'll await you in Tech Duinn, Castor after the High King finishes you both."

Damek cocked his head. "Which High King?"

"What?" Vexos blinked.

Too sluggish to parry, Vexos could not prevent Damek's next charge. His dagger skittered away from him as Damek's sabre sank deep into his midsection. The blade was finally halted by the girth of the oak behind him. Vexos' fingers flexed uselessly, dropping his broadsword. Damek backed up a pace to enjoy the fading light in his eyes, but Vexos, bloody spittle dribbling down his chin, reached out with the last of his strength and smashed his forehead into his. Damek backpedaled, cursing. Vivid stars flashed behind his eyes, his nostrils streaming. Vexos' grin was a macabre rictus as he died. "Not so pretty now, are you?"

Martin handed Damek a torn bit of tunic to hold below his nose. In the meantime, Hisk accepted his lord's sabre for cleaning. "Gods *damn* it," groaned Damek, tilting his head back to staunch the bleeding. "That whoreson had a massive blockhead."

"Not much of a fighter, though," noted Martin with a shrug.

Castor waved a hand. "Brute strength has its uses in a melée, not much in close combat with a swift opponent, *non*?"

"I suppose," Martin conceded, his steely grey eyes unabashedly suspicious. "No feelings for your departed family, then?"

"I knew them better than you, My Lord."

Damek tossed his bloodied rag into the muck, accepting Martin's waterskin. He spat out several mouthfuls of blood before turning to his newest ally. "I don't care about any of you. A swift death will not factor into your fate if you fail me. Am I clear, Marquis Gaelin?"

"*Oui*," Castor agreed with a half-bow. "As a mountain spring, My Lord. My men are ready for what comes next."

"Excellent." Damek allowed Hisk to refasten his cloak, then remounted his destrier with renewed purpose. "The bruise should help, don't you think, Martin?"

"Oh, aye," said Martin with a wince. "You're going to be beautiful for a day or two, I'd say."

Damek spared him a wink and bloody grin. "Maybe My Lady will kiss it better?"

"For the love of Reason, don't ask her to," sighed Martin.

Damek waved at his Corpsmen. "Remember, you're in pursuit. You know what to do. Wait for my summons."

Two dozen men saluted and kicked their mounts to a gallop, heading west.

Castor pulled up beside him, his expression impassive. Damek winked at him. "This should be fun."

In their wake, the sky opened up. Rain pattered against the steel-capped cuirasses of nearly fifty dead Gauls, left to rot where they lay.

15
UNMOORED

n.e. ʃ08
12, ÐOR CROMNA
bethany

The dark was stale and close, wet and sour as a whale's tongue. Swirling below, the Lee waited, frigid, black, and greedy. She shivered at the thought. The river lapped over a stack of tumbledown stones that held up a small dock at the end of this semi-cavernous chamber. Its walls were slick with moss and damp from unseen water trickling from within the bedrock. Above, huge stone arches were cut or engineered to bolster the castle from beneath. Bats and other chattering vermin tittered from the deepest shadows on the dripping, recessed ceiling. The floor was made up of enormous slate paving stones her grandfather had laid, which were warped from the years and slanted perilously steep toward the edge of the cliff. Una made sure to place her booted feet carefully, lest she slip. Gulls shrieked from the cavern opening at the bottom, though very little fresh marsh air made it inside the crack. A few wooden boats clacked together at the end of the manufactured jetty. Spying the one she sought, Una made her way to the dock, clutching her hissing torch like a shield.

According to Shanley's report, this is where both girls had been found. She crept up a short set of grimy wooden steps that had surely seen more years than she had and onto a creaking, dilapidated dock. Ancient wood groaned beneath her heels, and she sucked in a breath. She'd never thought to worry about plunging to her death in an icy river fraught with hidden currents, but the possibility increased with each halting step. This place had been used for decades, but she couldn't imagine how or why. This was hardly the safest or most cleanly space in Bethany to conduct trade. Though this cavern had been cut into the cliff for the safe and swift delivery of goods and men, any use nowadays must be clandestine or nefarious.

Why else would anyone seek out this moldy, dank little Hellscape?

A fat river rat squeaked across her toe. Una bit down on her tongue rather than cry out.

Disgusting.

She'd bet that if the river were drained, one would discover an entire city's worth of the nasty, gnawing beasts. She did not care for *that* thought either. A light sweat broke over her brow, thinking of each victim's wounds. While they'd been strangled and bludgeoned, the report she'd pilfered claimed neither had been raped nor 'cut' while living. Shanley's nervous, quivering penmanship seemed to show that he'd scribbled the following words out as fast as he could— '*extreme distress to the soft tissues of the throat, eyes, nose, and mouth. Wrists, ears, palms, and the under soles of their feet chewed away. We did not cut into the distension of each belly, for both girls were infested with rats and other vermin.*'

Meaning that rats went for the softest pieces they could get to, then crawled inside to help themselves to the girls' innards. Thank Siora, the girls were long dead before they went into the river— or so the report read. The bodies were so badly mutilated that no one could be sure of the order of events.

A sharp gust of wind found its way through the crack and into her face. Eyes watering, she gritted her teeth and knelt near a mainly discolored spot near the end of the dock. Reaching out with a gloved hand, she ran her finger over the stain. Dried blood. She was certain of it. Quite a lot of it, too. She waved her torch over the area. About a foot wide, and three feet long, was the ruddy black mark where one or both of the victims had met their end. The spot was now dried to a rusty void, but she felt wide nicks in the wood, where the murderer's weapon must have slammed into it.

There were dozens.

The assailant must have struck as hard as he could several times to make such indentions. Pity and anger commingled in her throat. What sort of creature did such things? How crazed did an individual need to be to beat and choke a woman to death, then leave her body for the rats? Having done the deed twice that she knew of, how long before he struck again? She got to her feet, raising her torch higher. The curious and insistent squeaking grew louder the longer she remained. She wrinkled her nose—little bastards. The killer's disease-ridden accomplices were likely eager for another meal.

Not today, you monsters.

As soon as I catch your horrible friend, I'll burn the lot of you together.

Someone really *did* need to do something about the Lee. It had never been the cleanest waterway in the South, nor did she imagine the loveliest— but the rats, flies, and refuse seemed to have worsened in her absence. Due, in no small part, to the Duch's obsessive war efforts, no doubt. Most of the fainne he collected from the populace had bought the Corpsmen's shiny cobalt armor, their brilliant, razor-edged sabres, and the obscenely expensive Bretagn warhorses they rode into battle... and battle they did. Whatever coin wasn't demanded from the populace was earned at the tip of Damek Bishop's blade. She sniffed. Bethany boasted the finest army in Innisfail, aside from the mythic Sidhe armies of the North, that most had never seen. Every inch of Bethany suffered for it too. Unclean waterways were choked with rubbish and vermin. Rundown streets were filthy and poorly lit— an invitation for larceny of every stripe. On her daily walks, Una could see many of these crumbling lanes from the northern parapet. Even Duch Kevin's once mighty fortress had fallen into a bit of disrepair. The bulk of the castle reeked of neglect, except for the halls that Patrick had scrubbed to impress their incoming guests. Her father had more lofty pursuits on his mind than the health and wellbeing of his citizens. He'd spent so much time and fainne building an army worthy of challenging the High King that he didn't have much left for anything else.

Una knew very well that was where she came in.

With a potential dowry of millions to look forward to, Patrick expected this year's *Cromnasa* to refill his much-beleaguered coffers. Of course, that her would-be suitor was sure to be fleeced of every coin, and she remarried to her oafish cousin, in the end, made no difference to the Duch. What was one more battle in pursuit of a crown? Well, the Duch may make his plans.

She'd be happy to disappoint the old meddler in the end.

Her eyes flicked to the hardiest of the little boats slapping time against its moorings. She could disappoint him *now* if she chose to. She stood, staring, for quite some time; she wasn't strictly sure why she didn't.

No one was here to stop her.

She could be well away, long before the watch was ever raised. She had enough ridiculous jewels draped around her neck to buy a team of horses, guards, and even weapons if she wanted them. So, why didn't she? The little curragh bobbed up and down at her.

Her feet wouldn't budge.

Why?

You have nowhere else to go, Damek's voice rang in her ears.

She looked away. The hatred that crept into her heart at the memory would not lessen its truth. He was right. Her father, too, damn his eyes, was equally succinct. She had no refuge to escape to. No Tairngare to return to. No silly adventure quests to look forward to.

Una was home now, for better or worse.

If she wished it to be the former, she resolved to do what she must. Someone had to see to the people; why shouldn't it be her? These murdered girls were the first of many wrongs she intended to right. They'd died in service to her family, such as they were. By rights— she would fight for *them*. No more women would be brutalized in her father's house if she had anything to say about it.

If she couldn't live the life she wanted to, then by Siora, she would make something of the one she had.

Sighing, she got to her feet. Wherever the murderer had gone, she was positive he'd return to this spot. Her father's questionably brilliant steward had assumed he'd merely dumped each body into the Lee from here, but the stain and nicks in the dock begged to differ. The river entrance was the darkest, least likely place for interruption in the Keep. Plenty of loose rocks, nails, dock chains, and other detritus with which to bash in a girl's brains... and a vast, obsidian pool with built-in disposal at the end of the dock. Hidden currents would rip anything not nailed to the cliff through the crevice in the wall and eventually out into the harbor. That is if they weren't caught in a fisherman's net as these two girls had been... or eaten by rats first.

There were no records of women having been found mutilated in the river until this year. While that didn't wholly rule out a practiced villain, it did lend credence to the argument against one. She'd wager Henry of Bethany was a lot fleeter of foot than he let on. He made much of being a knock-kneed cripple, but she'd spied him climbing the garden steps alone as late as the day before. He was stronger than he appeared at first glance. She remembered the way the table shook under his fists the night she'd taunted him, the fury and cold hatred in his eyes, notwithstanding. Her uncle was fully capable of such violence against a woman, no matter what her sweet, foolish cousin might have to say. Indeed, she aimed to prove it and rid the city of the fiend as soon as possible.

Be careful that you don't fix your conclusions before you've ascertained the facts. Una frowned again, sick of other people's voices fleshing out her conscience. She was quite capable of rationalizing on her bloody own, thank you. Having seen what she came to, she carefully retraced her steps up the rickety steps to the shale level. A heap of fallen stones blocked a good portion of the path, so she had to duck around them toward the wall. A good thing. Someone appeared at the top of the far stair, his face obscured by a deep hood. She shrank back with a hiss, allowing her torch to tumble into the Lee. When her eyes adjusted, she stole a peek at her visitor from around her stack of stones. If he hadn't seen her, he *had* spied the light from her torch, hadn't he? Straining to be as quiet as possible, she leaned over a tad farther. The figure stared into the shadows that concealed her, lifting his torch high. Her heart leaped into her nose. He said nothing. Pulse pounding, Una flattened herself against her stone. Had he seen her, or was he merely being cautious?

You don't even know if this is the killer.

He could be a custodian or a servant meeting someone for a tryst.

But the figure grew more menacing by the moment in his perfect silence. If he weren't the individual in question... wouldn't he call out or announce himself somehow? Holding her breath, Una traced around the stone to the far edge to get a look from the other side. The figure was no longer there; only his torch remained, stuck fast against the rotted iron railing. The air caught in her chest. She backed away, tucking her body into the darkest crevice she could. Now in near-total darkness, she waited. Sure enough, a vague shape limped by. His footfalls were clumsy but largely silent. *So, it is you,* she thought with a rueful grin. *And how very sneaky you are, my dear.* Had he followed her down here, perhaps? Maybe raced her steps through the armory and then below the dungeons?

She took off her gloves with a tight smile.

Come closer, friend.

Her ears pricked at a small skittering of pebbles on her right. Una lunged at the sound and was immediately slammed into the wet, hard stones below. He caught her wrists in one hand, dropping a sharp elbow into her temple. Her body slackened, and he struck her in the eye. Ears ringing, she felt something warm trickle down her jaw from both nostrils. The noise had been a ruse to draw her out, obviously. She might have kicked herself if she could manage the task before he killed her. Only an overeager fool with something to prove would have shown her hand so quickly.

Rats squeaked excitedly near her head, and her stomach swam.

His breathing labored; he leaned over her, gloved fingers pawing at her breasts and abdomen. She didn't have long to experience the intense revulsion that surged through her blood at the action. The figure soon groaned in frustration and struck her anywhere he could with balled fists. Una gathered every ounce of sense she had left and kicked out with her left heel. Her boot mercilessly plowed into his groin. With a mewling whimper, he crumpled to the slate floor. Knowing she had bare seconds to escape before he smashed her skull like an egg, she doused her blood with every dollop of Spark she could and scrabbled to her knees. The killer roared in a fury, snatching at her cloak. She stumbled before she could make it much farther than the dock. Desperate fingers dug into her ankle with bone-breaking force, dragging her backward. Thankfully, her Spark revived her enough to get moving. Again, she struck out with her heel, connecting with his unseen jaw.

Once his grip loosened, she slithered for the dock on her belly.

Una slipped into the freezing, malodorous Lee with scarcely a splash. She heard his furious bellow, despite the rushing whir of the current tugging her down, down... then out through the crack toward the sea.

SHANLEY, RED-FACED AND HUFFING, DASHED FROM ONE CORNER OF THE Duch's antechamber to the other. Patrick was in a lather. His cup spewed

wine in every conceivable direction while he cursed and ranted at his nephew. Shanley was beside himself as he attempted to keep the vessel full. Sweating and bleary-eyed, Patrick threw a sheaf of half-written warrants at his mud-spattered nephew. Lord Bishop took the abuse with an irritable sigh.

"Uncle, I have men combing the forests and hills as we speak. They'll ride halfway to the Kneeler's Hell to get to the bottom of this, I assure you."

"Who would *dare* lift a hand against one of *my* guests but you, boy?" screeched Patrick, with vein-bursting volume.

Damek spread his hands wide. "Don't be absurd. Ask the Bretagns yourself, damn you. They were all there."

Rumbling, Patrick speared Martin with a glare. "Explain, Commander. *Not you, boy*! I've heard all I mean to from you. Sit down and shut your bloody mouth before I fill it with iron. I want to hear Martin's version." Damek refused the chair. Instead, he bowed and took up space beside the larder. Shanley raced to fill his cup too. The poor fellow looked no less harried than a whipped dog.

Martin cleared his throat. "It is as My Lord says, Your Grace. We discovered the party on the road. They were already engaged. Honorless shits couldn't resist the lure of so many wagons in Lord Gaelin's train, no doubt. We saved who and what we could, but much was lost, I'm afraid."

"And Gaelin?"

Martin shook his head. "Died in the first rush, or so his surviving son, Castor, tells us. Bandits were waiting for them in the Brough Trace, Your Grace. Not a large wood, but deep enough to hide a decent-sized force. A clever trap."

"Mm," jeered Patrick, narrowing his eyes at Damek. "Practiced this together, did you?"

"Your Grace, we did no such thing. You have my—"

Patrick waved him away. "That's enough! I don't know why either of you thought I'd be foolish enough to believe this tripe. I'm ill, not mad. Shanley, for the love of bloody Reason… why is this cup empty?" Shanley did his duty with a shaking arm. Once finished, Patrick shoved him to the door. "Don't show your face in here again until you've retrieved the whole barrel!" When his nervous steward had gone, Patrick sank into a high-backed chair beside the window. It was snowing again, though this time heavy enough that it might stick. Damek sipped his wine, thinking of all those dead faces buried in fresh white snow. He broke off a laugh. "Dismiss them all, now," said the Duch, his haggard face pinched in visible suspicion. Martin bobbed his head in answer. His officers saluted before filing out and closing the door behind them. Only Damek, Martin, and the Duch of Bethany were privy to any further conversation. "Tell me the truth."

"We have, Your Grace." Martin didn't blink. "It happened just as we said. We were attacked ourselves a few weeks ago. The bandits are getting bolder, with so many visiting nobles on the roads for Cromnasa. It happens every year, but not on such a scale."

"Damek?"

He turned his face a mask of perfect indignance. "I've said repeatedly that Cairnream should be purged once a season, Uncle. You never want to waste the arrows; now, look what they've done."

Patrick blew air over his lower lip. "Oh, *very* good, nephew. You've got the Donahugh bollocks. I'll give you that. Very well, 'murdered by bandits for his gold' will play before my more foolish Barons, but not all. I suppose you and this Castor have struck some sort of arrangement, no? It had better be worth it for the trouble this will rouse between the remaining nobles at feast."

"Uncle—" protested Damek again.

Patrick enunciated: "Not another word. I warned you not to press your luck, didn't I?"

The threat crackled in the air between them. "You did," relented Damek. "Anything I do benefits this family. On *that*, you may depend."

Patrick's lips puckered around the rim of his cup. "It had better, or I will live long enough to ensure you regret the lie."

Martin opened his mouth to say more, but a sharp and frenzied pounding preceded Shanley's tumbling inside. Apoplectic, he shook himself to his full height. "Y-Your Grace! I bear grave news!"

Patrick rolled his eyes. "Haven't we already discussed 'getting to the point,' Shanley?"

Shanley flushed puce. "Y-yes, My Lord. T-the Lady Una. She's not in the Keep, Your Grace!"

Damek's head whipped around at that. "*What?*"

Shanley shriveled under the attention. "She was in her chambers for breakfast but hasn't been seen since, Your Honors. One of the armory attendants saw her in the Low Hall sometime before noon."

Patrick buried his face in his hands. "She's escaped again! I *knew* I shouldn't have trusted her to honor her word any more than yours, idiot nephew of mine."

"You don't know that, Uncle. There may be more to this than you realize."

"How so?"

Damek pointed at Shanley, who flinched. "This fool has been very irresponsible with his reports, it seems."

Ignoring Shanley's sputtered amazement, Patrick scratched at his chin. "Indeed?"

"My man found four hastily penned missives in her valise two days ago. Taken from your desk, I would imagine, Uncle."

"The murdered girls?"

Damek rubbed his temple. "The Low Hall leads to only two places."

Patrick visibly brightened, then noticing his nephew's smug smirk, immediately darkened. "How do you know what she's been reading and where she stole it from, boy?"

With an odd smile for Martin, Damek said, "We are as you've made us, Uncle."

"D'you think she would take it upon herself to escape once down there? It wouldn't be hard. There are almost always boats waiting at the dock. She could be halfway to Kinsale by now!"

"Send riders out in both directions, My Lord," said Martin, in his sure, deep voice. "Just to be sure. No matter how hard she rows, she'll never outpace my Corpsmen."

"I'll head to the Moorings, myself. Martin, when you send outriders, have men comb the riverbank from here to the Bay," Damek agreed. "Even if she hasn't taken it into her head to run, I doubt she's gone far."

"No need for such a fuss," replied a weak voice from the far door. Una, soaked and dripping blood from at least three points on her face, had come in through the hidden door from Patrick's bedroom. One of her maids and two pageboys held her upright by the elbows. She looked half-drowned at best, nearly frozen at worst, aside from the marks on her face and neck. "I'm too damned cold to run anywhere right now."

Martin recovered himself first. He ripped off his cloak and threw it around her shoulders before tucking her into a chair beside the fireplace. Shanley was fast on his heels with a tall goblet of wine. Damek stared like a man possessed. "What in the *Hells* happened to you?"

Martin handed her a kerchief with which to wipe her blackened nose. "Someone tried to murder me."

"*Who would dare*?" repeated the Duch, with thrice the venom. He came around his desk, eyes full of brimstone. "Please tell me today's events are not some hair-brained scheme hatched between the two of you to vex me?"

Una glanced up at Damek. "You nearly get beaten to death, too?"

"Something like that."

She tugged a shoulder up. "No, father. I ran afoul of our mysterious villain, I'm afraid. As I suspected, he's been murdering his victims in the caverns, then dumping them in the river. Rats do the rest."

"You went after him? Are you mad?" thundered the Duch. "Shanley, get the remainder of her maids down here, *now*, and I want every available guard in this hall for the night, d'you hear?"

Una snuggled deeper into Martin's cloak while her maid dabbed a cloth at her seeping temple. Though he kept his expression mild as a summer breeze, inside, Damek's rage boiled hot as any tempest. He couldn't stop staring, as if the bruises and gashes on her cheek were happening before his eyes.

"Who did this?" he managed to ask evenly.

"The man who's been murdering our serving girls. I assume he followed me downstairs hoping to catch finer fare, as it were."

"Did you get a look at him?" asked Martin softly.

She tried to shake her head and winced. "No. I went down to have a look at the site. I didn't expect him to turn up so soon or brazenly. He must know I'm looking for him."

"What? How could he know you're looking for him?" her father piped in, taking the opposite seat.

"He knows about me. About my, erm, gifts. He went for my hands first. Everything else, after."

"Everything else?" Damek's voice finally found its edge.

She waved a hand at her father. "You were right. He can't... perform. I think the murders are a form of vengeance for his lack of ability. Almost an afterthought."

Patrick paled by four shades. Martin looked as if he couldn't decide if he wanted to embrace or throttle her. Damek went cold as a mountain peak. "That is to say, he tried and failed?"

She ignored him. "Anyway, he'll find somewhere new to take his victims now. We have to catch him before he strikes again."

"Una." Patrick patted her hand. She swiftly concealed her disgust. Damek saw. "You're remanded to quarters until further notice. No more walks on the parapet, no more trips to the library, and no more bloody detective work from you! Stupid girl. You could've been killed!"

"If I were anyone but me, I daresay I would have been," she scowled at the fireplace. "My Spark, as usual, saved my life. He's quite quick despite that limp and very clever."

"A limp, you say?" Patrick asked.

"Yes." Her eyes came up hard. "Like a certain someone we both know and revile. I told you, father. It's him."

"It can't be. You've said so, yourself. He tried and failed."

"Perhaps the serving girl you sent away *did* lie, after all? Even you can be wrong from time to time."

"Excuse me," interrupted Damek in his flattest, most dispassionate voice. "You're bleeding all over your father's rug, and the two of you are arguing over facile details? Tessa? Will you please escort the lady into her father's bedchamber for the evening? See that her wounds receive the attention they require and allow no one but myself or the Duch entry into these apartments. Am I clear?"

Tessa nodded, flushing.

"Issuing orders already, are we?" chided Patrick.

"This blackguard isn't likely to let her escape without a peep, is he? With all the incoming guests, as I've said, this place is an open invitation for villainy of every stripe. Or, if you'd prefer, I'll take her to my chambers?"

"Not on your life, you cur," Patrick got through his teeth. "I will sleep in the next apartment. Shanley will see to the arrangements," he frowned. "What'll we do about your face, my dear?"

"It will heal," Una said sourly. "We won't disappoint your guests, Duch Patrick."

Patrick bristled for a fight, but Martin quickly handed him a goblet and steered him toward his chair. In the meantime, Una sagged a bit in hers. She caught Damek's stare with a tight-lipped smile. "Go ahead. I know you're dying to scold me to the moors and back."

"I'm not. What you did was attempt to help someone else. Who am I to scold you for that?"

She seemed surprised to hear him say so; that probably hurt him worse than the deep welts in her skin. "This man must be found, Damek. He's not going to stop."

"I know, and you're right. We will find him."

She was quiet until Tessa came to help her to her feet. Una stumbled against the girl. Damek gently shoved the maid away and hoisted his cousin into his arms. Una didn't protest, for once. Her skin was hot to the touch, which he knew firsthand meant she was healing already. Most people with so many head injuries should be kept awake at all costs, but in Una's case, her Spark worked best with rest. She would sleep for a day or two and be right as rain in no time.

Patrick eyed the two of them with something nearly akin to human sadness in his steel grey eyes. "Una, do you think you'll know this man if you see him again?"

"She's already asleep, Uncle." Damek carried her to Patrick's bedchamber door but paused a breath shy of the eave. "I'll stay with her tonight."

"Not likely, boy. I will sit with her and Shanley after me. *You'll* hie off and entertain our guests in my absence. I'm interested in how your intrigue with the new Marquis of Bretagne will play out."

"Uncle, I've told you—"

"Pish and posh, Damek. Worth less than nothing to an old schemer like me. Just be sure to play the bystander to the hilt, or it'll be war with men you had better not cross yet. Am I understood?"

"Perfectly."

"Good. Now, you may set my daughter down and get to work. Martin, while my nephew sees to the guests, I want you to raise every able-bodied man in my guard to the castle grounds. This murderous ruffian will have to hunt for victims elsewhere until he is found and eliminated."

"Yes, Your Grace," saluted Martin.

"Also, I want my brother removed to the lower cells in the East Tower. He'll have no ink, vellum, books, or company until I am sure my daughter is wrong about his guilt."

"Forgive me, Your Grace, but I doubt she is. I never liked your brother much, even before he found this odious religion."

Patrick's expression was inscrutable. "We'll know, sooner rather than later, I expect."

Damek tuned them out on his way through Patrick's spacious but spartan chamber. He shook with an unquantifiable fury as he lay Una on his Uncle's bed. She looked so tiny, like a drowned songbird. His lips touched hers before he could stop himself, and he heard Tessa gasp from the doorway.

"My lord, ye mustn't! She's got an ailment, ye see, and—"

"Get her out of these wet things, immediately," he cut her off and stomped past without a backward glance.

16
CAIRNREAM

Kaer Yin hadn't felt the urge to limp in days. That was something. Even though Rian made a lot of noise about 'overeager idiots' every chance she got, he no longer gasped when walking, and the hole in his chest had nearly healed. Perhaps he wouldn't win any races for a while yet, but at last, he was no longer an invalid. That he had the opportunity to be simultaneously elated at his newfound strength and livid over the actions of a trusted member of his inner circle was equally of note. The climb up to this promontory cost him less than the gnawing anger in his gut for the scene below. There, in the distance, was a tiny Gerrod stripped to the waist and dangling from a crow's cage. In the five days since he'd seen the lad, Gerrod seemed to have lost ten pounds he could scarcely afford. His ribs jutted from his flesh like the carcass of a gutted fish. He was left to dangle from a sturdy tree some distance from the rudimentary walls of tiny, insignificant Cairnream.

If Kaer Yin weren't currently gulping brimstone at Matt Gilcannon's gall, he might be impressed by the genuine cruelty of the scene. He passed Robin's glass back.

Robin spat witchroot into the dirt, shaking his head. He'd looked long before Kaer Yin and refused to do so again. "I say we kill that piece of shite today, Ben. Be done with it."

"After I'm done stripping Gerrod's hide to ribbons for the trouble, of course."

"Think his dear ol' da's already done for him."

Kaer Yin's mouth tasted of metal and bile. "Shar?"

"*Mo Flaith*?"

"I want you and Niall to track up that ridge there. I want to know exactly how many people are in there, where they sit, where they sleep, and most importantly, where Matt fucking Gilcannon stains the earth with his arse."

Shar gave a nervous sort of chuckle. "Erm, we don't... I mean."

Robin stuck his chin out at him. "He means where the bastard lives and works. I swear, ye lot are meant to have spawned our bloody language, and none of ye seems to speak it."

Shar saluted and sped away with an odd grin. Robin watched him go, scratching at his scar. "Strange one, ain't he? Finds everything funny."

"Not everything, just Yin," offered Tam Lin from down the trail a pace. He wasn't even slightly winded. Kaer Yin decided they should have a fistfight at the first opportunity. He was tired of Tam Lin's pretty, bored face. "What are we waiting for, *Ard Tiarne*? My Blood Eagles could sweep that pathetic compound in minutes."

Marking Kaer Yin's scowl, Robin answered for him. "He's a slippery one, Gilcannon is. The last time we rushed in, he got off scot-free. Won't be happenin' again, ye ask me. I owe that cunt the closest shave he'll ever get."

"Fine, fine," sighed Tam Lin. "Have your fun, then. I'll dawdle here, and someone can wake me when this nonsense is finished."

"Tam Lin," said Kaer Yin through his teeth. "You're being a boor, again."

Tam Lin threw up his hands. "What do you expect, cousin? None of us came here to chase after headstrong teenagers, nor 'rescue' questionable damsels from their own father's house! We *should* be on our way home to Croghan for Cromnasa, not traipsing through the South dressed like flea-ridden Merchers on the stupidest mission in history!"

"Is that *all* you'd like to say, Lin?"

Tam Lin gestured to Gerrod's cage, downhill. "That young man is hanging from a tree right now, Yin. Let's get the boy and get out of here. Or aren't you worried for your lady any longer?"

"Of course, I'm worried about her!"

"Well, she's fifty miles in the opposite bloody direction. I swear. This is ridiculous, and you know it."

"Everything is ridiculous to you, Tam Lin. Unless it's got teats, a horn of ale, or a *rath* to rob, you're never interested, are you?"

"What was that?" Tam Lin crossed his arms.

"You heard me. I'm calling you boorish, predictable, and dull. Do something about it."

"That's fine talk from a mooncalf cripple."

"Why don't you step up here and see how crippled I am, Lin." Kaer Yin had already dropped his bow and was busy unstrapping his belt. He shrugged Robin off as easily as swatting a fly. He was near twice the woodsman's size, after all.

Tam Lin tossed his daggers into the dirt, removing his cloak. "Love to. Your stupid face is looking far too lovely these days." He pulled his arm back to swipe at his cousin, but Rian got in between them. Tam Lin staggered a bit. "Brida's teeth, woman! That could have been your head."

"No one has time for you two idiots to dry hump each other into the dirt right now. Knock it off, or I swear to Siora, I'll poison the pair of you." Her fists balled at either hip. "I believe Gerrod is more important than either of your gripes at the moment."

Tam Lin reared back as if she'd slapped him. "*You dare—*"

"She's right," added Eva. "The boy hasn't had water for two days. He needs to come out of there."

Instantly sobered, Kaer Yin cursed. "Gods damn it. His own son."

"Now ye see why that perfumed pederast has to go? He's a real gem, he is," reminded Robin. "We let him leave again, who's to say he don't have more half-starved brats waitin' on the road home? Not to mention them lot what serve him. Know what he's doin' to them?"

"I do," Eva assured them. "He's... abominable."

Kaer Yin turned to her with renewed interest. "Can you see him?"

"After a fashion, yes. He's in the second-largest building, on the right there. Do you see it?"

He did. Rian came up beside him, squinting. "I don't."

"Red paint on the shutters."

"Oh," she said, wrinkling her nose. "Hideous."

"That's Matt for ye," tsked Robin. "Gauche till the end."

Kaer Yin studied Eva's fine-boned features, again dismissing the pang summoned by the resemblance to her niece. How was Una now? What was she doing? Was she being mistreated or locked away? He shoved those thoughts down deep, lest they plague him to distraction. Gerrod first, Gilcannon next, then Una. One thing at a time, like he constantly preached. "Can you tell if he's in there at all times?"

She peered into the distance, craning her neck a bit. "No. There are so many voices down there that it's hard to drown them all out. I can hear the echo of his thoughts but not the full litany. I'm sorry."

"Not at all. If you were down there, could you do it?"

"Yes."

"Looks like you're about to get your wish, Robin."

Tam Lin made a rude sound. "If I end up bleeding by the end of the day, Yin, I'm breaking your nose."

"If you don't stop whingeing, Tam Lin, I'll be happy to test that vow."

THE GREENMAKERS, INCLUDING KAER YIN, APPROACHED THE CRUDE hamlet from the South, while the Sidhe crept in from the Northeast, effectively blocking any mass exit. The town was situated on a broad plain tucked between two youngish woods, and it would appear to anyone on lookout that their group had materialized out of thin air. The walk toward the roughly hewn gate wasn't a long one. Kaer Yin didn't feel the familiar and irritating catch in his side, which made this predicament far less annoying than it should have been— he was thankful for the Sidhe blood in his veins.

A horned owl screeched from the opposite end of the field, behind Gerrod's cage: Shar, checking in. Kaer Yin nodded. Bru called back. Shar and Niall would free Gerrod before Kaer Yin and Robin scaled the squat southern wall. Rushing through frozen, waist-high weeds and bracken, they made the dash in under a minute. Robin set his hand to his mouth and whistled into it: a marsh swallow... common as nettles in the Midlands. They waited for half a dozen heartbeats, then heard back. The deed was done. Gerrod had been removed from the scene; now, all that remained was vengeance.

Tam Lin had volunteered to accompany Kaer Yin's party if only to catch a scratch that would earn him the right to take it out of his cousin's hide later.

They really did need to have that fight, never mind what the bloody women had to say about it. Animosity would fester so long as the wound wasn't properly lanced. Tam Lin was raw at Kaer Yin for many things, but chiefly for choosing the company of Milesians over the notion of traveling home to Aes Sidhe. He couldn't understand it yet, and that bitterness seeped further into him each day.

Well, it would have to wait. Gilcannon was the priority.

An ugly, pitch-stained inner gate had been hastily erected at the center of the village, where mismatched logs of varying heights and girths had been driven into the hardening soil at all angles—several youngish men filtered in and out of the haphazard structure. One or two reclined on top as if the need for guards were perfunctory rather than necessity. Kaer Yin's mouth quirked a bit at the corner. If only they knew what was about to happen to them. The tallest guard noticed Kaer Yin first as if he'd materialized from thin air. Matt's hideouts and outbuildings lay beyond the rusty length of this boy's spear. Eyes agog, the lad yipped a curt command, "Ye! Stop right there."

Kaer Yin raised his hands as Robin came up beside him. Tam Lin, Bru, and Carn Gor hung back a pace. Kaer Yin gave the guard his most affable grin. "Well met there, friend."

The other teenage guards stumbled together in an awkward, ill-practiced knot. "Who the feck are ye, and where'd ye come from?" demanded the first lad. The others were so shocked by Kaer Yin's sudden appearance they couldn't seem to move fast enough.

"Oh," hummed Kaer Yin, craning his neck around to see through the gap to the house beyond. "An old friend of Matt's. I wonder if you'd mind announcing us?"

One of the junior guards got a good look at the sword strapped at Kaer Yin's waist. "Shoot 'em, Billy. He's trouble." Billy was the lone archer. He struggled to nock his poorly strung bow.

Kaer Yin kept his face impassive. "How about you do as I asked, and we'll leave you well out of it? If not..." He raised a hand, and a silver-fletched arrow kicked the bow out of Billy's fumbling hands. Billy skittered backward with a cry. The first guard gripped his spear with renewed menace. The others filtered behind him as if he were taller than the wall around them. Bedraggled people in the courtyard stopped in their tracks to see what all the fuss was about. Robin gave them his best wink and a wave. Someone dropped the water pail they were hauling and trudged up to the big house in a hurry. Another belted an alert to anyone within earshot. Much good it would do them. Kaer Yin set his hand on his pommel. "For your own sake, boys, get out of the way. Matt's not worth one drop of your blood. This, I promise you."

Alarmed bellows rang within the inner courtyard, causing ruckus inside the house. A single shutter was thrown open, and a familiar head popped out and back in again with lightning speed. Robin glanced his way. "Ben?"

"Saw him," said Kaer Yin. He gestured to Bru, who cupped a hand over his mouth for yet another birdcall, a loon, this time. "Get ready. They're going to rush us. It's all they can do. Try not to kill them."

Robin made a rude sound. "If any o'em gets too close, their own damned fault."

"Try, all the same. It isn't hard to manipulate the desperate."

"Bloody do-gooder," Robin groaned.

The first rush was comical at best. The lead guardsman tilted forward with his half-broken spear, only to trip over the heel of Kaer Yin's boot. Face-first in the mud, the boy, sputtered and lashed about beneath the weight of his heel. Kaer Yin drew his sword and let the rest of the ragtag get a good look at the length of Nemain's pure, sylvan steel. "Now, I did ask nicely the first time. Won't happen again."

Despite his obvious lack of skill with a bow, Billy had a pair of daggers on him that might make Robin proud. He rolled past Kaer Yin's reach toward Bru, brandishing his little blades with a sloppy but deadly serious fury. Bru had no choice but to draw his blade in defense. Meanwhile, the others spilled from the gate like oversized ants fleeing a hill. That none of them carried a weapon better than an old farmer's spade didn't lessen their ferocity a whit.

Robin grabbed the next boy who attempted to rush him by the scruff and tossed him aside to fend off another. "Ben," he said, sweating already. "Move yer arse before I change me mind."

Kaer Yin ducked under a wide spear thrust, grasped the wielder by the shoulder, and cracked his forearm in half. The young man screeched like a hungry eaglet and collapsed into the muck beside his fallen friend. Kaer Yin leapt over both inert figures and into the thickening crowd without pause. Bodies flew this way and that as he spun into the courtyard proper. Many went down with nasty wounds, though he was proud to say most would bear a painful lesson rather than a fatal mistake.

Two boys darted for him from the first outbuilding. One swung a wide cudgel with a howl. Flipping his blade upside down, Kaer Yin hammered the lad with the flat, forcing all the air from the boy's lungs and breaking several ribs. This youth didn't have the wind to wail as his fellows did. The other attempted to wedge a spade under Kaer Yin's sword arm, but he pulled the fool in by his elbow and smashed his forehead into his nose. This one squealed like a ten-year-old girl. Six more questionably able individuals attempted to stay Kaer Yin from the side door of Matt's buzzing household to no avail. Each was merely a minor impediment for Robin to step over as he followed a half-pace behind. Kaer Yin grabbed one boy by the scruff and threw him head-over-arse into the wide door. It shattered inward in a spray of garish red splinters. The house's interior didn't appear to be finished, with its low ceilings, bare timber stairs, and plain wooden walls. It also seemed quite empty save for a plush violet couch, a lovely pin-back walnut table and chairs, and the odd Bretagn silk cushion. Kaer Yin frowned, eyes tracing upstairs.

"Matt, love. I suggest you come down before I come up."

His answer was silence, save for the weeping of an unknown child.

"He's hidin,'" scoffed Robin, tracking around the stairs. The kitchen was unfinished, and the back door remained locked from the inside.

The one place Matt might have gone was up.

Tam Lin, who had yet to lift a finger to help in this endeavor, crossed his arms. "Well, after you, cousin."

Kaer Yin glared back for a moment, then took the steps two at a time. He was obliged to leap aside on the landing as a heavy oak bureau came clattering down the stairs. Hearing Robin's colorful curse, he imagined his friend had taken the brunt for him. Next, a pair of boys, no older than seven years each, took turns whacking Kaer Yin's shins with broken broom handles. Grunting, he shunted one away with his knee and the other with his stick. Growling for his smarting shins, he turned to find Matt Gilcannon at the window. His former paunch was a shadow of its old girth. His once fine, if greasy, black hair had withered from his freckled scalp like ink from a pitcher. He held up one scarred but bejeweled hand.

"Ben Maeden, Robin? What're ye doin' here?"

Kaer Yin's grin was easily a thousand watts. "Matt! Delighted to see you." A third small boy dashed for his ankles as he strode forward, but a swift kick sent the kid rolling. "I'm sorry we missed each other last time."

Matt backed himself into the newly painted window frame, his cheeks white as spoiled milk. He was clean-shaven and smartly dressed, though the scars around his neck and collarbone were telling. Had he been tortured by Lord Bishop's men before or after he betrayed Rosweal? Did it matter, either way? How many people had died for this man's greed? Matt wagged a finger with a weak, terrified smirk. "Too right! We should've been introduced properly. There're so many opportunities we might yet—"

Robin cut him off with a snarl. "Shut yer mouth. Thought ye could hide from me, did ye?"

Matt gulped loud enough for the whole room to hear. Whatever defense his thugs could manage seemed to be waning. The piercing shouts and metallic clatter had stopped almost as abruptly as they'd begun. "A man has a right to rebuild when his life's work has been destroyed, no?"

"Whose fault was that I wonder? Whom was it invited that Tenma by-blow and his soldiers into Rosweal? Whose plotting with Souther mercenaries brought that Bishop cunt to our door? Hm?"

Kaer Yin filled the space on Matt's left side, leaning over his sword. "Who strung his *own son* from a cage like a common criminal? After a lifetime of rape, larceny, and murder?"

"Gentlemen, please. Be reasonable," begged Matt, shrinking into the wall. "He came to kill me. No one did him any harm."

Tam Lin grunted, "My men tell me he'll lose two fingers to frostbite. Is that not harm?"

Confused, Matt's black eyes flicked around at all the new faces. "Who're ye, sir?"

Tam Lin ignored Kaer Yin's warning glare. "Tam Lin O'Ruaidh, at your service." He bowed an unimposing figure in his disguise. "Peer of the realm, as it happens."

Matt gave a nervous laugh. No one else moved a muscle. After several rapid breaths, he giggled, "I too love a good jape, now and again."

Tam Lin scratched at his newfound stubble. "Not particularly fond of jokes, myself. Yin, kill him, and let's be done with this. I do believe he's wet himself."

On a heavy exhale, Kaer Yin shrugged. "Robin?"

"Wait! Wait, I'll give ye anythin' ye want! I have fainne, a few gems from Scotia, wine from Cymru... women, boys, whatever ye want!"

Robin's nose twisted about ninety degrees the wrong way. He drew his favorite dagger from the inner pocket of his vest. "Ye shoulda thought that bribe through."

"Please, Robin! We was mates once!" Matt squished himself so far into the window that the pane cracked at the far edge. "Yer woman wants my recipes, don't she? They're hers! Anythin', *anythin'* ye want! Don't kill me, Robin. Ye don't have to."

Robin covered Matt's quivering mouth with his left hand, but before he could ram the point of his dagger through his eye, a familiar horn sounded in the distance. All the blood in Kaer Yin's veins ran cold. Robin's wide eyes met his when the horn came again, closer.

"Your Highness!" Eva called from the rear yard, "Steel Corps!"

Tam Lin's head whipped around. "What does that mean?"

Matt whimpered behind Robin's hand. His face purpled. Robin dropped his arm by a breath. "Friends o'yers?"

Matt swept his head side to side, apoplectic. "No! The Lord Marshal said he'd gut me if he ever saw me again. I don't know—" The horn blared beyond the southern wall. Matt looked like he would faint. Screams from the southern edge of town told Kaer Yin everything he needed to know.

"We have to get out of here, *now*."

Tam Lin wasn't convinced. "Why? My *Iolair Fola* can handle this rabble and—"

Kaer Yin jerked him close by the collar. "These are Bethany's shock troops — armored cavalry— and they're good, Tam Lin. Very, very good. It's not worth the risk." He released his cousin and slapped Robin's shoulder. "Make it quick or leave him. Dunno what Matt did to take the piss out of the Lord of Clare, but they can't be here for us. We have to go."

Matt blubbered, "Please! *Please...*"

Sneering at the fat glob of snot that slid down Matt's chin, Robin shook himself and stood, resheathing his dagger. "Not feckin' worth it, are ya? Snivelin' gobshite."

An eagle called from somewhere outside, and Kaer Yin cursed.

"What?" Robin bashed Matt's head against the wall with a crack. Matt sank like a soft-bellied stone into a stinking puddle of piss.

"Retreat," Tam Lin clarified, stepping over him. "My men know better than to let themselves be surrounded."

"That means *we're* bloody surrounded then, don't it?"

"Seems so." Tam Lin developed a dangerous tilt to his jaw. His brows knit together over a glare that should have boiled his cousin's guts to broth. "Yin, I swear to Danu, when this is all over, I will bash your worthless brains in."

"Duly noted." Kaer Yin peered through the window at the stream of horsemen in their flashy blue and silver armor. He was partially disappointed that the Lord of Clare himself was not apparent among them. "Not that many. Twenty or so."

"Twenty knights, Yer Arseness. Not twenty farmers' boys." Robin took up space beside him, his expression dour.

"Oh good," Tam Lin carped. "I was already having so much fun."

Matt's boys ran for the trees when the horsemen galloped through the gate. One of them, a squat fellow in a cobalt blue cloak trimmed with ermine, looked a bit familiar to Kaer Yin. The knight drew his sword. "Round them up."

His men rode down whoever had been slow or stupid enough to be caught. Quite a knot of old men, young boys, and lasses were corralled in the central courtyard beyond Matt's gate before Kaer Yin was forced to look away. "What are they doing?"

"Their job looks to me." Tam Lin pursed his lips over his head. "These are criminals, are they not? Good riddance."

"Be quiet."

"What more do you need to see?"

"I know that man," Kaer Yin said, indicating one of the officers.

The fellow, probably their commander, danced his horse around his easily won prisoners. "You stand accused of the brutal robbery and murder of the Lord Gaelin and his son—visitors to our shores and the good Duch's Court. How do you plea?"

A general outcry was met with several vicious kicks and horse lashings. One lad, who was perhaps no more than twelve, took the lash for a younger boy. "We didn't do nothin' o'the sort, sir! We was here, mindin' our harvest. Ye can ask anyone!" Yet more stragglers were shoved into the boy's ranks, and he stumbled.

"Is that so?" The officer was unimpressed. "Kerns?"

"Sergeant Douglas?" called a second, less decorated knight.

"Bring the archers up, and have the bodies loaded within the hour."

The second knight saluted with a fist to the chest. He waved an arm. A squad of longbowmen was brought up from the rear before a pair of emptied carts. The young boy who'd been brave enough to speak was the first to take an arrow through the throat. Two volleys and the deed was done. Fifteen men, women, and children crumpled to the dirt together, dead. Kaer Yin paled. Tam Lin recoiled.

"*Siora*," breathed Robin. "They was just bairns."

The commander turned toward Matt's house. "Bring Gilcannon to me, alive. He will answer to our lord for this."

"Time to go, lads," Robin urged, racing for the rear window.

"What about him?" Tam Lin motioned to Matt's unconscious body. "Thought you wanted to kill him?"

"I do." Robin kicked the bootlegger's pudgy form for good measure. "Looks like our fancy Lord of Clare intends to do it for me, in any case. C'mon, Ben. Let's shove off before we have to fight our way out, huh?"

Kaer Yin stared at Matt's piss-stained rump for several moments. Booted feet stomped through the house downstairs.

"Let's go!" Robin whisper-roared, waving his hands for emphasis.

"I agree," Tam Lin reminded him. "There's no point otherwise."

But Kaer Yin ignored them both, contemplating Gilcannon's fate. He couldn't leave Matt to the Southers when there was a chance the wily bastard would get away again. Decision reaffirmed. Kaer Yin hauled Matt's wide arse over his shoulder while Tam Lin made short of the two soldiers climbing the stairs.

"What in the Hells are you doin?" Robin looked like he swallowed a wasp whole.

"If Bishop isn't done with Matt here, then I'm not done with him either." Without further explanation, Kaer Yin shoved them both out of the window.

17
REFLECTIONS

n.e. 508
17, Dor cromna
bethany

The dead swirled past her eyes. Their flesh churned in the current, loose and torn, shredded and distended. Gnarled fingers caught in the tangle of her hair, caressing, reverent. Bulbous, waxy eyes stared up at her with gratitude and affection.

Thank you, their whispers comforted her.

Thank you, Lady.

Her foot caught in a bed of river moss, and she floated for a while in their embrace, timeless, ageless, *free.*

Thank you, Lady, they sang.

Come home to us now.

A child's lovely white skull drifted before her, its skeletal arms reaching to hold either side of her face. She sighed, releasing all the air left in her lungs. How she loved them, loved them *all.*

Una... crooned another voice, a deeper voice. It spoke of endless summer skies and the cool trickle of a starlit fountain. His eyes were green as the depths of the Lee.

Come home, Una, the voice sighed.

Content, she held the child close as any mother, rocking it against her convulsing ribcage. Then, a splash broke her reverie into a thousand, thousand pieces. She was ripped from the comfort of her frigid peace and into the searing light of day. Someone strong dragged her ashore, where she was lain against the reeking bank, and breathed into like a deflated waterskin.

Una's eyes snapped open.

She jerked upright in her mile-wide bed, clutching her throat.

"Una," said Damek, leaning over her. "I'm here. Tell me."

Her eyes welled with tears. "You wouldn't understand."

"Try me."

She drew her knees up. The moon was high in the sky outside her tall windowpanes. She had no idea how long she'd been asleep nor how long he'd been by her side. Did she care anymore? The harder she fought him, the less immediate her hatred of him felt. What did she imagine she had to hold over him any longer? He'd betrayed her, true, but so too had she betrayed him. They'd hurt each other many, many times. Yet, here he sat, despite every effort to be rid of him. Sighing, she leaned into the headboard. She could feel the unease seeping from him like a mottled breath.

He didn't believe she would answer, nor did she. *Yet...*

"You remember that night in the Greensward?"

"How could anyone who'd been there forget?"

She looked away from his shadow to the massive, iron-hinged door. "The Sluagh. There were so many of them, and I took his power. I took *them*, Damek."

"Took whose power?"

She whimpered, "The King of Tech Duinn. I didn't mean to. It just... happened."

Damek was quiet for a long time. His warm fingers threaded through hers in such a familiar, comforting way that she nearly wept anew. "Perchance, he had enough to share?"

She blinked into the dark where his face would be. "What?"

"The King of Tech Duinn is no vessel to be drained dry at the first sip."

Ice cold sweat broke over her brow. She attempted to unwind her fingers from his, but he held her fast. "I see, now." Damek's voice dropped to a new, impossible timbre that sent shivers down her spine. "A woman of conflicting desires. You don't know what you want at all, do you? Poor thing. Such power, and no idea what to do with it."

She fumbled backward, tugging him into the light. His hair was not black but purest silver. Eyes not violet, but a burning emerald so rich, there was no gem anywhere like it in the world of men. His smile was beautiful and cold, warm and cruel, all at once.

"We are bound, child. For good or ill, forever."

"No!"

The fingers holding hers became claws, black and dripping with malfeasance. His teeth elongated to obsidian fangs as he leered.

Such delights I will ssshow youuu...

Una woke screaming, the sharp chill of his claws had tunneled into the veins of her right hand. She snatched the wounded appendage to her, but there was nothing there save a slightly clammy palm. It was broad daylight outside. The sun shone from a cloudless sky. Her maids rushed to her side.

Damek got there first.

"Una, calm down!" She leaped from him, racing to the corner of her bedchamber, eyes wild. For once, Damek looked truly afraid. He set down the goblet he'd meant to hand her and held his hands palms up. The world spun a bit around him. "Una, you had a fever. It's passed now, but you need to eat and drink, then rest. Do you understand?"

She swiped at her streaming nose. "How long have I been asleep?"

"Two days. Your fever broke last night, finally."

"Where is he?"

Damek looked around slowly, spreading his hands. "Who? The Duch?"

"No, the King of Tech Duinn."

His mouth compressed into a thin line. "There hasn't been anyone here but me all this while. Come sit down. Drink something, for Reason's sake."

"I'm not mad, Damek! He was here. He wants revenge."

As if approaching a skittish pony, Damek moved to her side. She flinched. "There now. I'm not he, I swear it. Let's have some broth, shall we?"

Seeing her maids' panicked faces brought the truth crashing in. Una's ears burned at the sight. She *was* mad! She allowed herself to be led back to bed like a recalcitrant child. "A fever, you say?"

"Una, the Lee is barely above fifty degrees in the summertime. Now, it's damn near frozen. You're lucky to be alive."

She'd never had a fever before. In fact, had never been sick aside from the occasional Spark drag. Maybe her Spark had exhausted itself keeping her alive? If that fisherman and his wife hadn't pulled her from the river, she would have drowned. There were slight scratches on her wrists and ankles that she sucked in a breath to see. Rats had been testing her flesh, it seemed. She gagged as Damek sat her down.

"Drink your broth," he prodded gently.

"I can't."

"I'll have these girls hold you down if I must."

She made a face but took the cup he proffered, gulping down its greasy contents without pleasure. Setting her fingers to her mouth to stall herself from vomiting, she handed the cup back. "There were rats in the river, Damek."

He pulled up a chair and waved a girl with a shawl over. She draped the velveteen garment over Una's hollow shoulders. "Of course there were. Patrick's physician has already treated you for the scratches. Good thing the current was up that day, or it would be a damn sight worse." He pointed to her wrists.

She chose to stare at the lovely flat wall rather than imagine those disease-ridden beasts digging their teeth into... "*Siora.*"

He dismissed her maids, then regarded her in silence for a while. When he spoke, he did so with measured confidence. "I don't want you chasing this man again, Una. He could have killed you."

"He tried."

She heard his teeth grind together. "My point, exactly. You have no bloody business traipsing around the castle, anyway, let alone in pursuit of a man who's murdered two girls already. Enough. Let me handle it."

"Like you've *been* handling it?" She squeezed her quivering hands together. "I'm well aware that the Duch is mildly put-out about these crimes, being that he has so many esteemed guests arriving this week. I, however, can and will make this murderer stop."

"No, you won't. You'll be in bed for another day or two until the doctor says otherwise. Then, you'll be very busy with your... admirers. You won't have time to hunt criminals and get half-killed in the process."

"Admirers." She huffed, "Pretense is everything at Patrick's court. How banal."

He leaned forward, steepling his fingertips. "It is, and simple enough too. This is about fainne, Una. Give him what he wants this one last time, then you'll be free to do as you please. We both shall be."

That gave her pause. "What does that mean?"

"Play your part, as I must play mine."

She didn't like the sound of that at all. She studied him for a moment, nose twisted. "What have you done, Damek?"

"Why should I have done anything?"

"Because. I know you."

He opened his mouth to say more, but Shanley opened the door for Patrick, bowing as the Duch shuffled inside. Patrick's grey cheeks brightened at the sight of her sitting upright. "Ah! Wonderful news! Wonderful. You look much improved, my dear."

She repressed a groan. "I wish I felt that way too."

Patrick waved her comment away, patting her knee as he sat beside her on the bed. "In no time, child. No time at all. Food and rest, you'll see."

Nodding, she chewed at her chapped lower lip. "You're anxious. How many have arrived for your charade?"

His smile flickered. "Never mind that now. Despite what you think, I have a care for your well-being."

"Right," she said, drawing up and hugging her knees. "What's been done about Henry, father?"

"It isn't Henry. I've told you."

"I'm not sure," her voice trailed off as she tried to recall her assailant's features. He was stronger than she and taller— though this was not a remarkable feat. She couldn't remember if his chest was broad with youth or wider for shoulder span. He'd been clever, whoever he was, and nearly got the best of her overconfidence. "It could be someone else, but I doubt it. Who else has a reason to murder me?"

She ignored Damek's answering scoff. Patrick eyed her sidelong. "You're not going to let this go, are you?"

"No."

He smoothed his fur robe over a bony thigh. "Fine. You'll rest for two more days, then make yourself available for Court, beside me, twice daily."

"I don't see—"

"If your villain is a member of our number, you'll have the opportunity to observe the Court and its servitors daily, will you not?"

"Y-yes."

"Besides, there's trouble in the North."

"What trouble?"

Patrick stared at the wall ahead, a calculated gleam in his eye. "Word is, the Sidhe have been raiding in the Midlands. Four towns and two farmsteads have been attacked, Hells, even Tara."

Una's gut dropped out. "*What*?"

"Nema has applied to the High King for an investigation, but we all know he will never answer. The matter has been relayed to the Consulate in Ten Bells, though that will not dissuade her from further extreme measures."

"The Sidhe would not raid in Eire," said Una evenly.

Patrick looked long and hard at her. "Wouldn't they? They've done so in the past, many times. I imagine eternal life gets rather monotonous."

"I wouldn't put it past that ingratiating snake to have invented this crisis as a means to consolidate her power," Una replied matter-of-factly. "Nema has the same goal you do, Patrick— absolute rule. Why else would she work so hard to strip the nobility from Tairngare?" She caught Damek's swiftly concealed smirk and narrowed her eyes at him. He said nothing.

What was he up to?

"That may be. Whatever the cause, I smell opportunity." Patrick stood, using the bedpost as a crutch. Una noticed how white his knuckles went. "Strife in the North aids our cause. My Barons will gobble this tidbit right up."

"The Sidhe would not raid over the Boyne, Patrick," Una persisted. "This is a ploy. Nothing more."

"Oh? An expert, are we? Let's say you're right, and Nema has a plan. Her power base weakens by the day, and her revolution flounders. She may make allies of the unwashed and powerless, may even bind the masses to her through brutality and avarice, but she has no real army. Half the Tairnganeah have fled with their mothers. The other half lack the skills or education to lead. While she might point the finger at Aes Sidhe for a power boost, she's busy making sure enemies surround her. Do you want your mother's city set to rights, or not?"

She bit her tongue. There was a plot here. She could smell it. "Of course, I do."

"Then, take it back, *Duchess*. Learn from me and unify Eire."

Ah. "You mean to sack Tairngare soon."

"Your mother's people are being ground beneath the bootheel of a tyrant. Or do they mean nothing to you?"

Damek rocked back in his chair. She'd nearly forgotten he was there. "I told you, it's a matter of *fainne*, didn't I?" He didn't wait to hear her response. He got to his feet and adjusted his swordbelt. "She won't see sense right away, uncle, and anyway, I have other business. I'll tell her women to bring more broth and tea." He spared Una a last, meaningful glance. Her brow came together. "If you'll excuse me?"

Patrick's voice caught him at the door. "You and I are not finished, boy."

Damek winked at him on the way out. "Never are, uncle."

By morning, Una decided she'd had enough convalescence for a lifetime. If she never saw a bowl of porridge or a cup of broth again in her life, it would be too soon. When the sun's first rays threatened the heavy clouds outside, she slipped past her sleeping guards on bare feet, carrying her boots under one arm. Most of the castle was abed at this hour, and she highly doubted she'd run into much trouble on her way. The stone in the corridor was so cold that she might have been tiptoeing over ice. Partway down the stairs, she leaned against the fine glass window to shrug her winter cloak tight and step into her fur-lined boots. A few maids and washerwomen were getting an early start to their labors when she made it to the landing below the South Tower, but they scarcely glanced her way as she passed. Una hung a right at the bottom of the stairs, striding past the kitchens with its kindling twin hearths and bustling servitors.

The cook and her minions would inform Shanley of her whereabouts if she were seen. Thankfully, no one batted an eye at her. She remembered having her fingers swatted raw by that behemoth for a stolen oat cake as a child. After passing through several nondescript stone passages with very few doors, she emerged into the sweeping Grand Hall under its gabled timber ceiling and an army of smoldering braziers.

There were people asleep *everywhere*.

Soldiers entwined with castle girls on or beneath tables, in various stages of undress. Men and women snored away on benches at each long table, clutching their ale or mead. The husks of several boars and pheasants were left to spoil in the artificial heat—so many people. More than half must have been guests, yet, Patrick expected more. No wonder the Duch was desperate for funds. Imagine trying to feed and entertain half a thousand people for ten straight days, once a year. The cost must have been unfathomable. She wrinkled her nose. The absurdity and hubris of the feast probably annoyed her more than the subject, the lure of her bride price, as it were.

She picked her way over and around the room, careful not to step too close to any snoring inebriate. Martin O'Rearden snored away in the rear-left corner of the room nearest the dais, hugging a pitcher of mead and mumbling into his beard. If he cracked an eye, she'd be back in her room in a trice. Tugging her skirts up, she hurried past as quietly as she could. In moments, she pushed open a side door to the inner bailey and sucked in a hard breath for the bite in the air. Dor Cromna was already at full gallop in the South, it seemed. The Boyne mouth at Drogheda must have been four inches thick with ice by now. Una exhaled slowly.

There was no point dwelling on things she couldn't change.

She filed those feelings away for later with the rest.

Coming through the armory from the opposite side of the Hall, she skirted the door leading to the dungeons and the subterranean Moorings she'd nearly died in a few nights before. With a shudder, she straightened her spine and marched onward. No one seemed the least concerned about this person wandering the castle, with all the guests and bootlickers arriving for Cromnasa. Well, she bloody well did. As long as she drew breath, that bastard's days were numbered. She wasn't quite sure where the inspiration had come from. Perhaps, this feeling was inspired by the strength of his arms, the confident clap of his well-made boots against the stone floor, or maybe the clean, white flash of his gnashing teeth. She couldn't say for sure, but she had a distinct opinion that this person wasn't feeble or old enough to be her uncle. She winced to think that she'd been so very wrong all this while but couldn't deny the obvious, all the same. She'd gone over the incident in her mind, from the moment he struck in the dark to the clamor of his roar as she escaped.

The murderer was a robust, healthy *young* man. Too muscular to be a feeble old meddler like Henry of Bethany. Certainly, too fleet of foot. Indeed, her assailant had to be both well-fed and given to martial practice. Una would bet all of her fingernails that the murderer was a soldier or a noble. Likely, both. While castle servants might be healthy and strong, which dockworker or builder had she ever met, could afford peppermint toothpowder?

There'd been a moment when his hands clawed for her neck that she'd caught a dose of his surprisingly fresh breath and a flash of white teeth her uncle no longer possessed. The Duch was right. It wasn't his errant brother at all. As infuriating as that fact was, it led to a new string of possibilities. She had a wealth of information to work with once she sat down and thought about it hard enough. She knew his general weight, height, and strength. She knew he bathed in bergamot and used peppermint toothpowder. She knew he'd been free to explore the dungeons during the day, below the central keep, and that it wouldn't be odd to see him in the escort of castle maids. She also knew that the few men who fit these descriptions were officers or lower-level courtiers with community postings in the keep. It so happened, there was a list of every soldier and courtier in Bethany at the Guardhouse ahead, as well as definitive timestamps for their comings and goings.

Una entered the Guardhouse from the Armory Hall, pouring some speed into her gait so she wouldn't be stopped before reaching her destination. What few guardsmen she spied leaning upright in their posts, or stumbling bleary-eyed into the hall, seemed less interested in her than the prospect of meat and eggs beckoning from the Mess back the way she came. The clerk, however, was a fastidious fellow. At his post before the break of dawn, he was busy stacking vellum and arranging logs when Una strolled into his office. He started when he saw her, dropping a quill to straighten his robes.

"My Lady! What are you... what can I *do* for you at this hour?"

Una gave him her most disarming smile. "Good morning. I'm here to review your register for the past two months, sir. Specifically, those relating to male courtiers and officers among the Steel Corps."

The clerk paled from the flap of his overfull chin to the crown of his balding pate. "Ah, My Lady, we don't grant access to—"

She pushed back her hood so that he might see the fading bruise at her temple. "I am asking as a courtesy." She took off her gloves.

He licked his lips, eyes wild.

Sometimes, her reputation came in handy.

"The Duch, My Lady—"

"Is not going to live forever. Whom do you suppose *I* am?"

She could hear the cogs turn in his head. After a while, he cleared his throat and pushed a heavy volume forward. "Of course, *Your Grace*. These are the registers for this month, and," he gulped, reaching below his desk for another heavy tome, "this is Dor Oras' log. I'm afraid we do not maintain separate files for varied titles." He pointed to a symbol resembling a star, beside some Corpsman's name. "Though we do maintain a shorthand for rank and file. The Asterisk denotes the Corps, the circle, stewards and servitors, and this," he tapped the page at a cross-shaped squiggle, "the nobility. We also do not delineate by sex, though the names should be obvious."

She gave him a look.

His eyes darted sideways. "Ah, yes. Sometimes they do not, I suppose."

"This is a rather inefficient way to manage this Gate, you realize?"

"We are understaffed here, My Lady. It would be impossible to organize every visitor and servant as you expect."

"Do you imagine Bethany is larger or more complex than Tairngare?"

He flushed. "No, I erm... no."

She scooped the proffered registers into her arms. They were pretty heavy. "Nevertheless, I expect you'll staff appropriately from now on. Won't you?"

"... The Duch has expressly—"

"You realize women have been murdered beneath my father's roof?"

"Y- yes."

"Perhaps you'll have also heard that this same villain attacked me?"

"No, I had not—" his face belied a horror of realization that assured her *no one* in Bethany had the slightest idea, as she suspected.

Shanley had done his work well.

She kept her features neutral as if the confirmation weren't infuriating. "These logs, such as they are, contain the name and rank of a criminal. I might have arrested him this afternoon if they were sorted properly as they should have been. Do we understand each other, erm... what is your name?"

"Finney, My Lady."

"Right. I will take them with me and any other documents pertaining to the castle's residents before the remaining Cromnasa guests arrive. When I return them, I expect a much more efficient system will be in place. Have I made myself clear?"

Finney bowed so low his chin scraped his collarbone. "You have. I'm terribly sorry, Your Grace."

"No need for all that, but you'd best get busy."

"Yes, Your Grace."

Una slowly put her gloves back on, making sure he watched her do it. His shoulders sagged a bit as if in relief. She drew her hood back up and turned to leave. But there was a sudden commotion at the Gatehouse, outside. Several shouts filled the frigid air from both sides of the heavy iron edifice. Una craned her neck at the window to see a group of formerly sluggish guardsmen rushing toward the portcullis. Finney scrambled to retrieve an empty ledger from the shelf behind him and pocketed his keys.

"What is happening?" she demanded.

"Corpsmen returning, Your Grace." He dropped his keys twice.

"Returning from where?"

"Patrol." He almost tripped, rushing for the door. "They've brought prisoners, it seems." He hesitated in the open doorway, allowing a fresh gust of icy wind inside. "Forgive me, My Lady, but I must—"

She waved him ahead, tucking the logs under the crook of her arm. "No, by all means." He bustled out, and she followed at a sedate pace, curious. Several of Damek's men, whom she recognized from their journey south, galloped into the courtyard before a pair of covered wagons. Breaking dawn light flashed from their frost-ridden breastplates and illuminated the dark stains which dappled their cobalt cloaks and the soft kid of their breeches. Her teeth clenched, eyes darting to the wagons. These mud-spattered Corpsmen were led by Damek's foremost Sergeant, Cillian Douglas. He did not glance her way at first.

Douglas clapped the Gate clerk on the back hard. The poor fellow fumbled his ledgers to remain upright. "Wake the Duch's steward at once. The men responsible have been dealt with, as ordered."

Finney held a hand out at two lower guardsmen, who rushed for the inner bailey. Slapping his notes down on the guard dock, he hastily dipped his quill and began to scribble. "I'm sorry, milord, but I must have the name and rank of each man in your company."

Damek's newly minted Sergeant dismounted with a sour glance at Finney. "Are you mad, man? We're half-frozen and starved for sleep."

"All the same, milord," Finney gawked, tugging his chin at Una. "As My Lady requires, so must I answer."

Douglas' sharp eyes snapped to Una's with a snarl. She didn't flinch. As recognition dawned, he blinked a few times before the blood drained from his unshaven cheeks. His bow was clumsy. "I... forgive me, My Lady. I did not see you."

"Well, I certainly see *you*, Corpsman. What is going on here?"

He fidgeted like a much smaller man, glancing back at the wagons. His companions dismounted with wide eyes. "Prisoners. Nothing to concern yourself with."

"Is that so?"

He fumbled to catch up as she made for the wagons. He threw his arms wide. "Erm, this is not for a gentlewoman's eyes, My Lady!"

She moved around him. "Prisoners of whom?"

"The Duch and Lord Bishop."

"I don't see what—" but she did, all at once. Blood seeped from the rear of the front wagon in a steady stream. Piled atop one another in a sickening lump of tangled limbs and blue flesh were the bodies of a half-dozen men and boys. Looking on in horror, she saw the corpses of one or two girls in there, as well. A heavy knot formed in her throat. "I assume the second wagon is the same?"

Douglas moved to close the rear flap, blocking the macabre spectacle. "It is. I tried to warn you. This was not intended for—"

"What crime would urge you to slaughter old men and children, Corpsman?" She struggled to maintain the even timbre of her voice.

Shanley, in a state of half dress, stumbled into the courtyard. He exclaimed to see Una standing so near the Gatehouse. "Lady Donahugh! What are you—"

Una held out a hand to silence him. Nostrils flaring, she turned to Douglas. "Answer the bloody question."

He wouldn't meet her eyes. "They ambushed Lord Gaelin and his retinue on the road to Bethany. The lord and his eldest son were murdered."

Even if she didn't already suspect Damek's duplicity on that score, she would have heard the lie in Douglas' rasping voice. "Is that *so*?"

"My Lady!" shrieked Shanley, his vocal cords cracking, cheeks purpling. "The Duch has expressly ordered that you remain in your rooms until you're well. I really must insist that you return!"

"Where is Damek now, Corpsman?"

"Escorting minor Barons south from the Midlands."

Another lie. Douglas at least had the grace to flush with shame at the derision in her expression. Shanley caught up to them, huffing. He squeaked a bit at the sight of those in the wagon but knew where his first urgency lay. "My Lady, *please*! Folk will rise soon, and—"

Ignoring him, she spun on her heel and marched back through the inner Bailey, utterly unconcerned about who might be watching or why.

18

SUBTLE DIPLOMACY

N.E. 508
17, Dor Cromna
Bethany

The Cymrian Trade Ambassador ogled Gan like a particularly ripe species of pond scum. She gaped shamelessly; her pasty face pinched back in a sneer for the ages. Gan stared over her head. It wouldn't do any good to show offense. Not one of the people gathered would spare a tinker's fart for the Fawa Gans of the world. These were wealthy Merchers from all points of the Continent. They had wealth, position, and influence Gan could never have aspired to. Aside from this, many of them were veterans of the previous war and had seen worse than him in their time... much worse. Though, never in civilized Tairngare. Nonetheless, the novelty of his head-to-toe burns wore off after a few moments in his company. Once it had been established that he existed merely for the amusement of his mistress, the shock lost some of its luster.

Only Melba, the wan Cymrian bitch in question, could not look away. She was one of about a half-dozen dignitaries who'd arrived to attend Nema's open

Trade Negotiations. Melba's province in Cymru was world-renowned for their carbon-rich peat and not much else. Though the soil in Tairngare's province of Meath was rife with the stuff, it proved much more complicated to harvest than in the wide boglands east of the mighty Danned Y Llew range.

Backwoods trash, Gan thought without a shred of irony.

No class whatsoever.

He caught Nema's disapproving frown from the corner of his eye and promptly looked down. The floor was a much safer place to devote his attention. Beside him, one of this Cymrian Tradesman's guards stepped a pace back. That was fine by Gan. Among the few senses the flames hadn't robbed him of was his sense of smell. This awkward Cymrian reeked of cheap uishge and sour fruit. Gan's haggard reflection winked up at him from the polished onyx floor.

He opted to close his eyes rather than share Melba's morbid fascination.

Breaking with hundreds of years of tradition, these dignitaries were invited to a feast in the Doma's ceremonial throne room on the Tenth Floor. Nema had promised an 'open government,' and thus far, she had been faithful to her word. The people, as usual, loved her the more for it. The pronouncement had been applauded in the Markets when announced, despite the ever-present soldiery which lurked around every corner. Of course, Gan had not been allowed to stray from the Citadel, but that didn't stop the chattering in every hall. The streets were heavily patrolled by the Cohort, day and night. Every gate, road, and warehouse leading to and from the Red City boasted cadres of watchful Corsairs. After the recent unrest in the wake of her coup, Nema would brook no further checks on her power.

Gan thought it excessive.

Anyone with influence or wealth enough to challenge her authority had been murdered or imprisoned weeks ago... and the commoners *adored* her for it. What additional security did she require? He braved the briefest glance at the dais. There she sat, on that great, glossy black throne. Her brilliant gold robes spilled around her like a lustrous golden river in flood. A surge of pure, unadulterated hatred pierced his heart.

Tamp it down, his subconscious warned.

She sees all.

He stood not six paces behind the throne. Close enough to be used but far enough to remain well outside her majestic tableau. Before the dais, where

Nema reclined with a goblet of Lord Rhiannon's finest vintage, sat her many illustrious guests. She'd had their tables situated in a semicircle around the throne, clearly as a means to impress a feeling of 'conversational inclusion' upon their ranks. None sat higher than any other, as each was invited to worship her 'Holiness' on equal footing. Everyone seemed to be having a marvelous time in Nema's vaunted presence, and if Gan were a betting man, he'd assume the evening's purpose to be a success, save for one or two more speculative people in the bunch. Melba, for one. She simply wouldn't take her eyes from him. Nema noticed. She half-turned in her seat to raise an eyebrow at the ambassador.

"Mistress Melba, we are honored to list your delegation amongst our guests."

Melba affected a half-bow from her seat. "We are pleased to be included, Your Eminence." Her gaze flicked to Gan once more as if she couldn't stop herself.

"Did you find your quarters satisfactory?"

"Yes, quite comfortable, Eminence. We thank you."

Nema raised her goblet in a brief toast before summoning another round. The servitor, in this case, turned out to be Gan. He shuffled forward on his crutch, as gnarled and knock-kneed as a man thrice his age. With shaking, partially bandaged hands, he refilled Nema's cup and shambled back to his place by the wall. Having regained every ounce of attention he'd previously lost, he faced away from his audience, sucking at his cheeks for shame. If only Melba knew her bloody place, Nema might have forgotten he was there.

You must not weep, Gan old boy.

You'd make a further spectacle of yourself.

"Have we piqued your interest, then?" inquired Nema, with a cruel grin.

Melba tactfully cleared her throat. "You have, Eminence. Though, I'd be remiss in my duty to my shareholders if I didn't consider the matter for a while first. Haste and finance are not happy bedfellows."

"I find it intriguing you would say so, Mistress. I've been told your Guild elected you to office just this year," wheezed Lord Rhiannon. "What wisdom could you have possibly gained in your position since?"

Melba dried her mouth and returned Rhiannon's smirk. "Well, I'm a peat farmer. Own several thousand acres, as it happens. My father left me the family business, along with his Guild's dues. Way things work in the East, you see?"

The far wealthier, far more refined Lord Rhiannon of Swansea, Head of the Vintners' Guild and owner of *ten thousand acres* of the richest soil in Western Cymru, hummed, "Hm. Quite."

"Not everyone can buy a lordship selling fruit, Rhiannon."

Coloring, Rhiannon gave a slight cough. "I beg your pardon?"

"You heard me." Melba's expression hardened, and Gan could see why she led her particular territory. "Without my Guild, you fancy Southers would have frozen to death years ago, your grapes long withered. Be careful whom you insult, sir."

Lord Rhiannon muttered into his goblet but looked away.

Nema flashed her perfect white teeth. "Now, now. Let's all behave in a manner that reflects our stations."

Melba laughed wryly. "Funny you should expect such a thing in *this* court, Eminence."

Nema's mouth drew into a line. "Whatever do you mean, Ambassador?"

Melba gestured to Gan. "We can see the lengths you'll go to attain power."

A collective hush descended over those gathered, save for Lord Rhiannon's shrill gasp. He had expected his Northern colleague to share his fiscal interests with the new regime in Tairngare. Nema's guards shifted closer; Melba's mirrored the action.

"I believe you mistake us, Ambassador. What was meted here was a much-desired justice. The people are grateful to be free of Libellan yoke. I wonder that you, who represent such humble origins, would not be sympathetic to our cause?"

With a sneer for her fellow Ambassadors, Melba dipped her head. "No one who works for a living can argue that the rich get far above themselves, far too often. Though, it's not your argument I find fault with, rather, your methods."

"You think us harsh?" asked Nema softly.

Melba stood. She wasn't incredibly imposing but there managed to be something sizeable about her. "These fools may grovel at your feet because you now control the port at Drogheda, but Cymru has long since outgrown the need for Tairnganese tariffs."

Rhiannon shot to his feet. "Your Eminence! May I assure you that Melba *does not* speak for all Cymrian Merchers. The rest of us are well pleased by your terms."

Melba stared a hole in him. "You'll find that claim proves false. If you haven't noticed, you're missing the Kernian Trade Ambassador, the Bretagn Assemblage, the Alban Agricultural Chief, and the Sidhe Delegation from Scotia."

"Your point being?"

"All save the Sidhe are headed to Bethany to treat with Donahugh," Melba replied. "The Duch may be many things, but he does not burn his opponents and dissenters alive, nor display his disfigured victims as a subtle reminder of his power."

Gan shrank away. He knew he would likely suffer for this later on.

"Well," Nema spoke up after a thunderous silence. "Is that all you wish to say?"

One of Melba's lackeys helped her shrug into her traveling cloak. "It is. Cymru— that is, the Energy and Agricultural Guild— shall not accept your terms. We cannot support a tyrannical regime responsible for class warfare and nominal genocide. I would bid you farewell, Eminence, but what would the point be?" She turned to waddle off, but several of Nema's silent Fir Bolg guardians slunk in with their weapons drawn. Before anyone could flutter an eye, a brief skirmish ensued, pitting the far stronger Fir Bolg against Melba's unprepared guards. The surprised Albans were overcome with embarrassing swiftness. Who could have imagined that the Doma of Tairngare would have such creatures in her employ? In the midst, Melba attempted to intercede and took a shallow wound to the temple. She backpedaled into the arms of her nearest defender: eyes wide to the pearls. Her colleagues below the dais leapt to their feet to retreat. Holding their easily defeated opponents with little effort, the Bolg guardsmen waited for Nema's order. Staring at the blood on her hand as if it were a serpent coiled to bite, Melba shrieked, "You'd harm an Ambassador under a sacred treaty? Are you *mad*?"

"Clearly," Nema agreed from her monstrous black throne. "As you've implied, my ruthless dedication to power is tantamount to my purpose here." She lifted a single finger. Her Sidhe mercenaries answered, drawing long, bone-handled blades across their captives' quivering throats. Too quickly, Melba's retinue sank en masse to the floor, dead. The rest of the ambassadors quietly retreated to a far corner, holding their hands out to show they had no interest in dissent. Melba's furious scream didn't stop her from being snatched up in the guards' merciless grip. "Ambassador Melba," respired Nema. "We find your actions as grievous as they are slanderous. The people of Tairngare no longer recognize the Libellan Court nor its pandering policies toward foreign Merchers. You have lobbed a grave accusation at the Doma today. As such, the Union of Commons must investigate your claims. You shall be held in contempt until proceedings. Do you have any further comments before you are taken to your cell to await trial?"

Melba looked around frantically. "She commits murder before your eyes, and none of you will gainsay this?"

Her colleagues looked anywhere but at her, obviously terrified.

Nema's smile was warm and light as a summer sky. "We will speak again soon, Ambassador. May Siora's mercy shine upon you."

Melba's cries reached a terrible pitch as she was dragged from the room.

Fading embers simmered in the gaudy silver braziers of Nema's amber antechamber, casting eerie shadows over gleaming walls. The grand golden dragon chandelier roared at Gan from her place in the heart of the chamber; ivory claws and fangs dripped garish garnets and rubies, like heart's blood. If there'd ever been a testament to the excesses of the noble class in Tairngare, this ridiculous centerpiece was in desperate contention. As if the gems and precious metals decking each over appointed room on the Tenth Floor weren't extravagant enough, the half-ton monstrosity hanging from the ceiling tipped the scales to the floor. No bloody wonder the Mouras were so officious. It appeared the former Doma couldn't relax in her apartments unless her every glance was accosted by one obscene display of wealth or another. Gan side-eyed the lot. He might be a nerveless, scabrous villain, but at least he had some fucking taste. Nema didn't seem affronted by the absurd décor, but she wouldn't, would she?

Appropriation was also one of Nema's numerous vices.

Gan should know; he'd served the witch for nearly forty years.

Nema's chambermaid had shaken Gan awake at the third bell to order him to attend his lady in her antechambers at the fourth. Ever since, he'd been hugging the wall beside Nema's bedchamber door, waiting for Her Eminence to make an appearance, and watching this strange figure pretend he wasn't in the room. No matter how hard Gan stared, the visitor wouldn't spare him a single glance.

Beneath his notice, Gan surmised.

That's interesting.

This guest waited patiently by the windows, hooded and stoic as a statue. His entourage waited in the Obsidian Hall beyond, a gangly, surreptitious group, mercurial and solemn as their leader. They wore indigo cloaks of costly sealskin with deep cowls. So far, all Gan could discern was that the fellow wore his black hair long and loose over his collarbone and that his hands were long-fingered and well-manicured when he removed his gloves. Gan had never met a man so tall who wasn't feeble at the shoulders, like a poorly cinched taper. This person didn't seem to share the unhappy trait of so many. Gan wondered where he came from. The longer Nema's guest stared out over the city, the more curiosity nibbled at Gan. Who on earth would come to pay court to Vanna Nema in the wee hours of the morning without invitation? More puzzling, who would she accept into her apartments at such an hour, uninvited?

In his many years of playing her lap dog, Gan had yet to see *anyone* make such a bold presumption. Who was this man? He'd never seen Vanna take a lover or make assignations of any sort. Indeed, she had always been asexual, so far as he could tell. If anyone would have been apprised of a lover, surely Gan would have?

Finally, the door to Nema's bedchamber swung open, and the malicious witch herself swept into the room. Nema had taken care with her appearance. Her hair swept back into a wide opal clasp that left the grey-speckled mass to pool down her back. She wore a vibrant chartreuse robe that billowed when she moved and knocked off at least a dozen years for its waist-cinching daring. Her maids had even applied rouge to her lips and cheeks, which Gan might have raised a brow at, did he have eyebrows to raise. Striding past Gan, she held out both hands for her guest to clasp. The fellow took them, if with some hesitation.

"Darling Falan," she lilted. "So good of you to call."

Gan felt, rather than saw, his eyes flick toward him. "Do you think an audience is wise?"

Nema snapped her fingers at Gan, who knew what she wanted without a word more. He limped to her larder to fill two goblets with Bretagn sherry. He served Nema first, who smirked over the rim. "Gan is my creature, through and through. Aren't you, my love?"

"I am, Eminence," lied Gan, atonally.

He passed a glass to her guest, who sighed, "If you say so, Lady." Gan felt that cold gaze rake him once more. "What have you done to him?"

She sipped from her goblet. "What he deserved. Now, enough about my servants. What news have you for me?"

Nema's guest took the farthest seat he might without appearing rude. Gan empathized; no one wanted to sit too near a grinning she-wolf. The stranger removed his hood, and a great hole opened below Gan's feet. If ever there had been a man to match this Falan, Gan had never seen him: skin like burnished copper, hair like the blackest depths of a twilight sea, his eyes cut the light like polished amethysts glinting in the sun. Indeed, no one this beautiful had ever existed before— no one human? He was Sidhe. *Fir Bolg*. Gan pressed his hands together so neither individual would see them shake.

Falan, the Elder?

No, it couldn't be... the patriarch is ancient... and why would he travel to speak with the Doma of Tairngare in the middle of the night? This makes no sense.

Falan leaned back, stretching his long legs below the warmest brazier. "Perhaps your newfound power has clouded your reason? Do you take me for a servant?"

Nema made a face. "There's no need to take offense to a simple question."

"I require answers rather than questions."

Nema straightened, setting her goblet down. "Do try to recall to whom you are speaking, boy."

Watching the two of them stare each other down, Gan was riveted. *What in the nine Hells is happening here?*

Who in the Hells is this Falan?

"Liadan, what do you believe you're accomplishing here?"

Liadan? Who...? Gan's thoughts reeled. He had no idea where he'd heard that name before or why it should relate to Vanna Nema, whom he'd served most of his life.

"I'm remaking Eire for you, my love. As has ever been the goal."

Falan's smile was sharp. "Is that so? You burned a group of nobles and loyalist Merchers alive, I hear. Aoife too."

"A necessary measure."

"Was it?"

"A demonstration of strength was required. Pity is a weakness to be exploited in Eire. Don't presume to know these people, Falan. You've never lived amongst them. Like cattle, they must learn their place."

Falan's brow raised. "Tell me, by that logic, how shall I answer your overreach? You were not meant to rule here, *seanmáthair*."

Gan's heart pounded against his ribs. He'd grown up in the Cloister. Education was an essential demand from each individual within its walls, servants or acolytes. Why would this Falan call Vanna Nema 'grandmother?' He forced his features to utter stillness rather than let on he was in the least surprised or interested in this conversation. The ideas swirling between his ears ran through a microcosm of infinite possibilities. How could this be? That Falan was Fir Bolg was plain as the nose missing from Gan's face. That Nema was not... was equally notable, and hadn't Gan known her for ages? Since when did she have children, Fir Bolg or otherwise? He felt Nema's attention slide his way and triple-enforced his 'no matter' mask. It had saved his life more times than he could count.

"You dare speak to me this way?"

Falan sat up, smiling. "I am no supplicant, and you are no queen. It's rather the opposite, or have you deluded yourself otherwise?"

The muscles in Nema's jaw flexed. "Any title you aspire to has been a gift of my blood. You forget yourself."

The room chilled by twenty degrees or more. Gan found himself shivering.

"I am heir to a seven-thousand-year legacy, and *I* rule Armagh now. That is my blood right, whether you will it or no. My grandfather was slain in prehistory, and your throne with him. You *will* obey me."

This... was...? But how? Falan the Elder was merely a client-king at best, and everything Gan had ever heard of him suggested he hadn't left the Sidhe Underworld in so long that he might immediately die if he set foot in Innisfail. A man some three thousand years old or more, by all accounts. Would he be so young, so *fresh* as this Falan seemed to be? Gan had little experience with the Sidhe. He had no idea. How Nema knew him was the greater mystery. His grandmother?

Surely not?

Nema drew a deep breath. Gan rushed to refill her goblet, then melted back into the wall. Falan frowned at him but made no further comment. "How good of you to visit. Perhaps you'd prefer to leave before another unkind word is spoken?"

"You do me no honor by persecuting and torturing my future subjects."

"How dare you pontificate to me? I *am* Armagh, you ungrateful, spoilt child. Without me—"

"Eochaid would have wed another, and his grandson would *still* be king. You overvalue yourself, as always."

Nema purpled. "I was Queen of Armagh when—"

"Ages ago. Now, you are a pampered dowager with more time on her hands than common sense. You seek vengeance for ills wrought in another life, another world, sowing chaos and misery wherever you are left unchecked. My father might subsist on dreams and fantasies in the Oiche Ar Fad, but you are the one living in the past."

Nema got up, tossing her goblet to the floor. "Leave. I will see you regret this."

"You'll do nothing," said Falan, flexing his beautiful fingers. Something electric and frigid swept through the room, dousing the braziers in a wisp of smoke and wrapping itself around Nema like a vice. She gasped, clutching at her neck and staggering to the floor. Falan rose slowly, hand shaking with an unknowable power. "These intrigues of yours have a limit, Liadan. Your purpose here was to prepare the Eireans for my arrival, not drive them beneath your boot. I am meant to appear before a grateful lot of Milesians who seek the justice and mercy of their *true* Ard Ri— not a whipped mob with no willingness to conform to Fir Bolg rule and nothing left to lose. In your vanity and greed, you attempt to supplant me. I will not allow it."

Choking, Nema threw up a hand. A gust of wind opened a gash on Falan's cheek. He gnashed his teeth, and she cried out. Gan shuffled out of the way as a window broke across the room, spraying shards in every direction. Falan was unphased. "You and Grainne may convince yourselves that you should be worshipped in Eire all you like; it will never happen. Do you know why the Dannans maintain their grip over Innisfail? Because their women have no power, no imaginary pedestals to place themselves upon. I have no queen and will take none... for obvious reasons, *grandmother*."

His fingers twitched, and Nema screamed, writhing on the floor. "Stop!" she pleaded breathlessly. "We are *clann*."

He knelt so she might get a good look at his passionless expression. "More's the pity. What of Damek, Liadan? Aoife? Hells, your own *son*? All forgotten or used in your pursuit of godhood." His expression spelled disgust. "Well, I'll tell you this— Damek is mine, as Grainne, Aoife, and *you* are mine. Each of you serves at my pleasure or not at all. Do I make myself clear?"

"Y-yes," she croaked. Gan was beside himself. He'd never seen anything like this, nor had he ever imagined anyone might get the better of the mighty Vanna Nema.

Liadan... where have I heard that name?

"Morcan?" Falan said.

One of his men came through the door. "*Mo ri?*"

"My gifts for the Dowager, if you please."

His lieutenant bowed and ducked out. A heartbeat later, he and two others returned bearing the grisly remains of two women. Gan couldn't help the moan that escaped his mouth. He crammed his scarred fingers between his teeth to prevent any further outbursts. Pors Yma had her head twisted all the way round, the whites of her eyes bulging from their sockets like a fish. Her tongue wagged loose from her broken teeth. Kalen Hamma had been split entirely in half, as if from the sharp edge of a giant axe. Each half was tossed casually at opposite ends of the room; organs and sinew that stubbornly clung to the severed halves dribbled gore onto Nema's precious carpets. Gan scrambled backward, drawing Falan's notice.

"Should I kill this one too, I wonder? Perhaps, in this case, it would be a kindness?" Falan's servants turned toward him, and Gan knew equal parts fear and the thrill of relief. Falan cocked his head at him. "Shall I free you from her menace, or would you endure more?"

Gan's partially missing lips flapped open and closed in soundless elation and terror.

Finally, the mysterious Sidhe pursed his lips. "I suppose I should leave her someone to vent her anger upon since she must cease torturing my subjects. Mustn't she?"

Nema whimpered, and Falan spread his fingers again, letting the spell go. She coughed into the plush layer of carpets beneath her, weeping. He knelt by her side to comb the hair away from her face. "Now, you will stick to your place, won't you? These Milesians will come to love me, through you, through our good works. Once Grainne has played her part, I shall be their savior. This is your purpose here, Liadan. If I learn otherwise again, it will be the end of you. Do you hear me?"

"I do." She shoved herself up to her elbow to glare back, huffing. "But I warn *you*, arrogant child, I am not so easily cowed."

Unaffected by her bravado, he gestured to the bodies splayed behind him. "If you say so." Then, he stood, sliding his hood back over his glistening hair. "Damek gets ahead of himself, but I'll allow it for now. His goal is also mine, as my son. You will not impede him again." He turned to leave but paused at the exit to smirk at Gan. "I should kill you for all you've heard tonight, Milesian. I can smell the hatred in your heart; it's blacker even than hers if such were possible."

Gan summoned all the courage he had left. "If that is your wish, *Your Majesty*."

Falan threw his head back on a laugh. "Clever too. What a shame."

His last comment drifted away on the frigid breeze screaming through the broken window. Snow swirled past the curtains, dusting both of Nema's fallen favorites white.

19
THE FERRYMAN

Ten Bells was by far the loveliest place Rian had ever seen. Though she had spent some time here as a child, she'd never experienced it like this. Coming through the Eastern Gate from the Burren High Road, one couldn't help but gasp at the whimsical picture Ten Bells presented. The town sloped toward a deep cerulean harbor from the coastal hills dotting the Central Innish Plain. Two- and three-story houses and shops, built in the old style with latticed windows and gabled arches, rode that descending wave in tidy, colorful rows. From each of their brilliantly colored rooftops in varying midsummer hues, little tufts of green and white peat smoke puffed into apricot and lemon skies. Through each twisting lane, the sunset over the Sea of Aenghus warmed the elegant paving tiles a rich, dark red. Tall glass lanterns were lit throughout every visible street, enhancing this otherworldly glow. Recent snow had dappled each rooftop and lane with the barest hint of white, which sparkled like scattered diamonds in the blazing sunset above. Her eyes trailed through the center of town to the mighty Shannon. Glowing green and gold, the river undulated through the city on her way to the harbor. Rian held her breath. Maybe once all was said and done, she'd move here after all?

The view alone might be worth all the derision in the world.

Following her eye, Kaer Yin pointed. "There, near the harbor, is our destination, though tomorrow, first thing. Tonight, I need a bath, warm food, and all the ale in town."

"Too bloody right there," huffed Robin. "Me flask's been empty for two days now."

Rian was too enraptured by the panorama to scold them for their alcoholism. "Can't we take a moment to enjoy this?" She gestured to the burning sky above.

"Not unless you mean to drag this wagon to *The Ferryman*, all by yerself," grumbled Gerrod, whose turn it was at the wheel. His filthy face and hands were scabbed over, and the nasty bruise over his eye had long since ceased to swell, but his attitude had steadily soured. In the wagon sat his errant father, the infamous Matt Gilcannon. Everyone, save Kaer Yin, thought it would be wiser to kill the old swindler than cart him around like an invalid, Gerrod, especially. "I'm tired of the road and the company."

Rian twisted her chin at him. "Well, I'm tired of *you* and the awful snit you're in since we're being honest. You have no one but yourself to blame, you realize?"

Gerrod flinched. "Ouch, Rian."

Kaer Yin spared him a growl over his shoulder. "Talk to her like that again, and I'll blacken your other eye. You ungrateful git."

Gerrod ground his molars and started pulling again. "I said I was sorry. Besides, no one asked ye to come after me, did they?"

"Gerry, ye best shut that insolent trap o'yers, 'fore it talks ye out of a nice warm bed and a spot o'ale. Ye hear me?" said Robin, taking the other wheel. They had no pony with which to pull the cart, and as they couldn't exactly march their injured captive through such a charming town as Ten Bells without raising eyebrows, the wagon was their best option. Since they'd left Cairnream, wagon duty had been Gerrod's punishment. Rian couldn't say this was wholly fair, but she understood the logic. Rather hard for him to get into more trouble if he was dead tired every night.

His quest to murder his father had put everyone in jeopardy, costing them precious time and supplies and nearly getting several of their group killed. To Rian's mind, Kaer Yin might be a bit of a bastard, but he was always fair. Gerrod grumbled under his breath rather than argue. When Rian had finally thawed the boy out and treated the worst of his injuries, Robin had been the one to blacken Gerrod's eye.

Again, harsh, but perhaps well-deserved.

Robin poked the lad with the end of his bone pipe. "That's right, ye hot-headed ingrate. Pull the bloody wagon and keep yer grousin' to yerself." Everyone was exhausted, even Eva, who Rian was quite sure ran on clockwork and gears. Her companion, Mel Carra, looked worse for wear than she. Even the Sidhe in their company had taken on a bit of a sag at the jowls. Walking for so many days in freezing weather, up and down hills over rugged terrain and sleeping outside in the elements had taken its toll on them all. Rian's foremost fantasy involved a bowl of cockle stew and a tub overflowing with scalding hot water.

The sunset faded to a dusty violet as they wound through well-lit lanes toward the Harbor. If anything, it made the walk toward the massive *Ferryman*, with its huge glass windows and the rosy lanterns hanging from its well-maintained façade, all the more charming. Several black carriages waited on the side of the behemoth structure, each replete with a handsome pony and a waiting driver. Rian assumed they were to escort guests and visiting dignitaries about town. Ten Bells boasted a half-dozen theaters, two large opera houses, porterhouses for cards, dicing and gambling, restaurants and publicans by the score, and of course, houses of ill-repute to suit every taste. While Ten Bells lacked Tairngare's gleaming red Citadel and bustling markets, or Bethany's high stone walls and stoic edifices, it made up for all that in culture, class, and charm.

Approaching *The Ferryman*'s wide yellow veranda, Kaer Yin waved Gerrod and the majority of their band toward the stables. "Don't hand the reins over, nor speak to anyone until Robin comes to get you."

Shar took over for Robin at the wheel. "Will there be trouble, *Ard Tiarne*?"

"No," Kaer Yin assured him. "But there will be a fuss."

"Why? They should throw their doors wide for the two greatest lords in Aes Sidhe."

"Because I'm supposed to be dead, remember?"

Shar's smile flickered. "I hadn't thought of that."

Rian used Kaer Yin's extended arm to hobble up the icy stone steps. "If you think it might be a problem, maybe let your cousin handle it?"

"Like everything else." Tam Lin pretended to examine his nails.

Kaer Yin spared him an unfriendly smile. "No need. I outrank him, don't I?"

Tam Lin bristled. Rian groaned aloud, dragging Kaer Yin toward the entrance by the elbow. "Oh, for Siora's sake! I'm bloody sick of this posturing. Ben, I'm cold, hungry, and tired. Now get in there and use your da's name to get me somewhere warm, damn it." She half-flung him through the door. He stumbled a bit and opened his mouth to say something rude, but a thin fellow with an unassuming face met them in the foyer. He bowed from the waist. Rian thought his fuzzy grey eyebrows looked wolfish in the lantern light.

"Good evening, masters and mistresses. How might *The Ferryman* serve?" His voice held a soft but gruff quality that reminded Rian of her father.

Kaer Yin, chafing against his disguise, straightened to his full height. He reached into his tunic to produce his *ogham* charm.

"*Lorgaimid Coiriocht.*"[16]

"Ah. *Conas is féidir linn freastal ort?*"[17]

Kaer Yin held up a hand, fingers splayed. "*Cúig leaba laistigh, trí chliabhán i ngach seomra. Dosaen cruinneachán taobh amuigh sa bheairic, móide bia agus deoch do chách.*"[18]

The majordomo pressed his hands together in supplication. In the common tongue, he said, "We cannot accommodate so many at this time, sir. With Cromnasa on the horizon, we are nearly at capacity."

Kaer Yin exhaled through his nostrils, raking a hand through his shaggy Ben-like hair. "You will make room for our party."

"Apologies, sir, but we cannot—"

Tam Lin strode forward, removing his *ogham* stone and shoving it in the man's wan face. His features shifted almost immediately, red hair glinting beneath the wall sconces. "Apparently, you didn't hear my cousin the first time. We need five rooms, three beds apiece, and all the bloody ale and food for twenty or more individuals."

---

16 "We seek accommodation."
17 "How may we serve?"
18 "Five beds inside, three cots to each room. A dozen cots outside in the barracks, plus food and drink for all."

The majordomo gawped at Tam Lin, then blinked again at Kaer Yin. "F-forgive me, milords, but we cannot shove paying customers out the door for you, gentry or no. Many of our guests are nobles. Our reputation—"

"Will mean exactly nothing if our needs are not met at once," articulated Kaer Yin, snapping the charm from his throat. "*Thiocfá mac an Ard-Rí ar shiúl?*"[19]

Rian felt for the majordomo as he backpedaled into the most awkward bow she'd ever seen. He stammered, "My lord, the Adair died long ago. Everyone knows that."

"Or the son of *Bov Dearg*, the King of Connaught, and his men? You mean to tell me you don't recognize *my* seal?" Tam Lin shook his bit of amber at the majordomo. "You have the honor of serving your Crown Prince this evening. Snap to your business, man."

Two assistants came around the corner with a pair of rods in either hand, ready to defend their boss, but they stopped dead in their tracks to see the two Sidhe males towering over the majordomo. As if in total shock, the hotelier squinted at Tam Lin's stone, hands shaking. "This... of— of course, *mo flaith*. If you say he is the Adair, who am I to gainsay you?"

"I am no liar, Milesian," cautioned Kaer Yin. "I don't need my cousin's word to press my point." He unraveled his sleeve, showing the mark at the base of his wrist. The poor man shriveled at the sight, gesticulating wildly for his inferiors to follow suit. "*Is mise Kaer Yin Adair, Prionsa coróin in Innisfail. Gach rud a theastaíonn uaibh, soláthróidh tú ... agus níos mó.*[20] Have I made myself clear?"

"Of course, *Ard Tiarne*," the majordomo finally whimpered. "If you would please wait a short while, I will personally see to it that you have the finest rooms in *The Ferryman* and all the meals and ale you require. James? Please clear the private dining room for our most honored guests. Offer any within a free supper on any evening of their choice, once Cromnasa has passed."

"Excellent." Kaer Yin cleared his throat and smoothed his tunic. "Two issues more. In our company, we hold a prisoner of the Crown. We expect to detain him in your stables with our supplies and horses for the night; will this present a problem?"

Bushy eyebrows came together over a flaming brow. "No, *Ard Tiarne*."

---

19   "You'd turn the son of the High King away?"

20   "I am Kaer Yin Adair, crown of Prince of Innisfail. Everything I require, you will provide ... and more."

"Good. Furthermore, we are here to visit the Sidhe Consulate. Under pain of death, we advise you and your servants not to bandy my presence about. Do you understand?" His cold silver gaze flicked over each mortal face with hard-eyed sincerity. Rian heard an audible gulp. Kaer Yin replaced his charm, lest anyone else see his face prematurely.

"Yes, *Ard Tiarne*. No one shall breathe a word of this. I swear it."

Kaer Yin craned his neck so the majordomo couldn't escape his irritation. "I think we're all aware of my reputation for mercy, aren't we?"

Rian scowled over the majordomo's trembling back. Kaer Yin lifted a single shoulder in return.

"We are, Your Highness. I'm... that is, we are overjoyed that you have returned. Please avail yourself of every comfort."

"That's bloody grand news, that," chuckled Robin. "Now that's all sorted, point me to the bar, if ye'd be so kind?"

AFTER A NIGHT SPENT DRINKING FAR MORE ALE THAN SHE'D EVER consumed, Rian awoke in the same room as Eva, her head pounding like a hammered anvil. Making her way through their private floor to the cream and gold decorated parlor, she stumbled over half a dozen prone bodies to get to the larder, which bore a healthy portion of ice-cold tea and half-eaten biscuits. Gerrod, who somehow escaped his fate in the barracks next door or as guard-dog for Matt in the stables, lay upside-down in a plush green armchair before the fire, snoring against an empty bottle of Bretagn brandy. She stepped gingerly around Niall, Bru, and Dorcan, who seemed to have collapsed mid-scuffle, and were now facedown in the floorboards. Parched, Rian poured herself a healthy dollop of strong black tea, not minding its frigid temperature.

Eva, who never drank spirits, followed her in. "Have they returned yet?" she asked, wincing at her first sip.

"Who?"

"The princes and their most faithful guardians."

Ah, Rian thought, working the ice-cold tea down her parched throat. *They must have gone ahead to the Consulate.*

She exhaled into her teacup. "I've no idea how they can stand this morning, let alone make themselves presentable for the Ambassador."

Eva's mien told her it had likely been a near thing. Rian felt a bit better about her own state. "Since they've gone for the day, I wonder if you wouldn't accompany me for a few hours, Mistress Guinness?"

Rian set her cup down for a refill, cocking her head. "Where to, My Lady?"

Eva's long fingers tapped against her cup. "It wouldn't be fair for only the men in our company to leave here in finery, now would it?"

Rian exhaled a short laugh, "Well, I'd love that, but unfortunately, Ben has all my coin. I'm quite the pauper until he returns."

"Pish and posh, my dear," said Eva. "I told you, my family holds great wealth in Ten Bells. What are a few gowns and baubles to an Alvra? Besides, I see the questions nibbling between your ears. You'll want to share them with someone before they gobble you up, no?"

"I..." There was no point in attempting to bluff. Eva *would* see right through her. She wondered how Una had felt about her every thought being interpreted by her aunt.

Eva patted her hand. "She hated it, of course, but we can't change our stars so easily, can we?"

Of course, Lady Alvra had read that thought too.

Rian considered her for a moment. "No, I suppose not."

"Then, it's decided, yes?"

Rian looked around. It *would* be nice to get rid of this lot of fools for a while. She assumed that once Gerrod woke up, he'd be begging her for some remedy or another to ease his hangover. Once that was done, she'd be charged with Gilcannon's care. And when Ben and his idiot cousin returned, she had no doubt there'd be yet more chores for her to perform while they dove headfirst into the nearest bottle. Why in the *Hells* would she say no to a day off?

"Lady Alvra, I would be honored to accompany you today."

By noon, Rian, Eva, Mel Carra, and two others in her retinue had nearly plundered the spice markets along the harbor, the haberdasheries and dressers in the Linen District, and finally, the apothecaries at the North End. Not only was Rian dressed in a lovely winter frock, with a thick wool underskirt and high collar, but she boasted a new trunk with additional cloaks, hats, boots, gloves, and underthings as well. While she'd been busy trying on second-hand but excellent quality dresses and shoes, Eva had taken it upon herself to furnish her with additional accouterment: a beautiful leather satchel to keep her medicinals in, a surgeon's set of sharps and tools, a box of needles in every shape and size with catgut thread and steel clasps, enough pungent herbs and salves to fill her new bag, and a new sealskin cloak, dyed a gorgeous indigo to flatter Rian's fair complexion. Rian protested vehemently, but Lady Alvra would not be swayed. Eva explained that, in Tairngare, 'twas the height of ill manners to reject a heartfelt gift. Immensely touched, Rian accepted them all as graciously as she could. When they stopped for tea, Eva paid a hansom to send the items ahead to their rooms at *The Ferryman*.

Feeling rich for the first time, Rian sipped her tea and tried hard not to cry. Aside from Una and her aunt, no one had ever treated her with such kindness.

Across their small round table, Eva reached over to pat her hands. Mel Carra took one look at Eva's thoughtful expression and excused himself. "Rian, my dear, it pains me that you should have such feelings. You are as deserving of love and respect as anyone, perhaps more than most."

Rian let out a long breath, blinking away tears. "That hasn't been my experience, My Lady. I'm sorry."

Eva's new kid gloves were soft against her knuckles. "It is easy to confuse outward perception with personal worth, but they are not the same thing. Perception is a lie we must counsel ourselves against at all cost."

"I don't understand."

Eva took Rian's hands and lay them flat against the table. They were scarred, rough at the joints, and quite small. Rian tried not to be ashamed of them. "You think these marks make you less lovely, less worthy, but scar tissue is strong. The flesh here," she tapped a healed gash Rian got from building the back paddock with her father, "is stronger than what surrounds it. It can't be cut as easily again. The same can be said for your foot, your poverty, and your parentage. None of these things make you *less* than anyone else, but they do make you twice as tough to wound."

"I appreciate what you're trying to say, My Lady. Truly." And she did. The call of gulls over the white-speckled harbor caught her attention for a moment. Though the sky today was a flat grey, the beauty of that cerulean expanse of water was undimmed. Indeed, it seemed bluer even than yesterday for the contrast. "I know I have worth, and I'm sorry to appear ungrateful and melancholy. Sometimes, I must remind myself that I'm here. Do you know what I mean?"

Eva's warmth was so like Una's; Rian felt a pang. "I do. I believe there is someone else who wishes to remind you of that fact, frequently, once it dawns on him."

"Ah, I don't... that is..." muttered Rian, flushing to the roots of her hair.

"You don't believe you're worthy of him?"

Rian squirmed in her seat. She wished with all her heart to be one of those gulls floating over the harbor: free and oblivious. "I... ah, well, he's so..."

"Wealthy? Imperious? Nonchalant?"

Rian's head popped up. That didn't sound like Shar at all. "Wait, Master Lianor isn't wealthy, as far as I know. Not to *our* standards of wealth, that is. I don't believe he can even attain a holdfast until he's served his lord for two hundred years."

Suddenly, Eva's smile faltered. She looked as if she had a great deal more to say, but just then, a rock burst through a nearby window. The lady seated there crashed to the floor with a scream, doused head-to-toe in shattered glass. Without thinking, Rian rushed to her side. Her right cheek suffered two deep lacerations and her ungloved hands dozens more. Thinking fast, Rian bound the woman's hands with two tea-stained napkins, then pressed her fingers against the seeping wound along her cheekbone. Someone handed her a third set of napkins, and she made swift use of them.

Outside, men shouted in the street. Several dark shapes swept past the windows, bearing signs, pamphlets, or things they could throw. Rocks and bricks struck windows on either side of the lane. "Imperialist scum!" they bellowed. Some took up a chant, "Purge the land. God's reckoning is at hand."

Rian looked at Eva askance. She shook her head. "Kneelers, or members of a new order. They seek... reformation."

"Reformation? Of what?" Rian cried.

"The church, as it had been in ancient times. Death to all heretics."

Rian had a pretty good idea to whom they referred. Eva straightened her spine as straight as an arrowhead. She opened the door. "No, Eva— don't!" screeched Rian, but Lady Alvra paid her no mind. Rian got up to chase her; even reached out to snatch at her sleeve, but Eva moved to stand alone in the middle of the street. She mumbled something unintelligible under her breath.

One brazen fellow in a black cloak and oiled boots sidled up to her with his hand raised. Eva's eyes met his, and he fell to his knees, clutching his throat. Another, after witnessing what had befallen his friend, made a dash for her arm. Eva glanced over her shoulder; he stopped mid-run, falling flat on his face and squealing like a cornered pig. She raised her right fist, and a third man mirrored the motion. Eyes wide with shock, the protester shoved that fist into a friend's head who stood beside him. Rian was utterly amazed. She had thought Una was incredible in a fight, but Eva was astonishing. The crowd mimicked every gesture and motion she made, one person at a time, or often all at once. No one made it near enough to stop her.

Sharp on these men's heels, the second round of protesters ran to catch up with the first. Rian made to run to her side, but Mel Carra beat her to it. He drew his weapon and raced headfirst into the knot of black-clothed miscreants. They went flying in every conceivable direction. His Tairnganeah followed suit, chasing the rioters downhill. Everyone on the street who wasn't a member of their number gave a little cheer. Rian, however, saw the sag in Eva's shoulders. She caught her in an awkward grip the moment she began to fall.

Breathing hard and sweating, Eva's lips twitched at her. "You're a sharp one. Let no one forget it."

"I'm friends with your niece, remember? I've seen Spark drag before. Let's get you inside for something hot to drink."

Eva allowed herself to be lifted like a child. Her expression wasn't one of pain or fatigue, however. Anger and fear burned bright in the amber of her irises. Mel Carra returned with a bloodied lip but otherwise no worse for wear. He knelt beside them, focused on Eva's stricken expression. He'd apparently seen this before. "Tell me."

"The Southernmost Star is fading," she said, gripping his arm.

"What does that mean, My Lady?"

"When Kevin's Heir dies, those men will rule the South. Reason fades as a Black Knight rides."

All the hair on Rian's neck stood on end. "What are you saying?"

Eva paled; her pupils dilated. "The South will bleed, and Innisfail will fracture. The Raven King marks the tide. All shall be consumed. All shall..." she drifted off into a stone faint. Gently as he was able, Mel Carra hefted her into his arms.

Rian didn't have the first clue what was happening. "Will she be all right?"

Using his free hand, he helped Rian hobble upright. People were staring but without hostility. Rian knew the difference. The shopkeeper from the teahouse bustled over, frantic. "Is the lady well?"

Mel Carra gave her a reassuring nod. "She will be. This happens when she wears herself out, you see?"

"Oh," she cooed, covering her mouth. "Please, bring her inside. I've hot tea and cakes aplenty, and after what she did for us, it's the least I can do. She's Siorai, isn't she?"

Mel Carra shrugged. "Yes."

The shopkeeper fanned her face. "My word. My sister won't believe a word of this!" She shuffled off, patting her frazzled hair.

Rian worried her nails as he sat Eva down in her abandoned chair. "That wasn't the Spark drag, was it?"

"No. It wasn't."

"Premonition is one of her gifts?"

He inhaled slowly. "Yes."

"Has she ever been wrong?"

His worried eyes met hers squarely. "Never."

20
A DEAD MAN'S NAME

N.E. 508

18, Dor Cromna
Ten Bells

In the wee hours of the morning, Kaer Yin, Tam Lin, Robin, and Shar had made their way down to the River District. The walk was a long, blustery one, punctuated by severe wind gusts and icy rain that fell in knife-slashing sheets. Each man drew his cloak tight, grumbling over the misfortunate decision to leave the coach behind at *The Ferryman*. The air dug into Kaer Yin's scalp like needlepoints, and his gloveless hands had gone numb less than five minutes into their stroll. Though the air was a good deal warmer here than in the wilds of Northern Eire, it was bloody cold enough to make his eyes and nose water at the slightest breeze.

None of their group had been to sleep the night before, and each was still stinking drunk. Kaer Yin had always preferred a late night to an early morning, especially when that morning's duties would include a healthy dollop of bureaucratic arse-kissing.

Having spent the majority of a lovely evening bootless before a roaring fire and tucked into a bottomless tankard of rich, dark ale, he almost wished they'd opted to spend the rest of Dor Cromna in similar vein. Yet, duty called, and they were out of fainne. Coin in the amount they needed wouldn't retrieve itself. Kaer Yin and Tam Lin's long-distant uncle Dian could supposedly rub two coppers together to make one solid royal, but neither of them had learned the trick. They were flat broke, and expeditions like this cost. Bellies cinched into their airways; they trudged on. A yard before the docks, the Sidhe Consulate emerged from the fog like a mountaintop from a curtain of clouds. This ungainly monstrosity squatted over a whole city block, pressing its imposing back to the rising sun. The massive, four-story stone edifice clashed with its surroundings. The charming, whitewashed plaster walls and elegantly tiled rooftops twisted up and down each lane.

The Consulate was situated near the docks at the far end of town, which certainly diminished the number of tourists and potential gawkers. Six dour-faced Sidhe guards standing at each entrance added to this ominous impression. In order to pass through the first of two enormous brass gates without being run through, Kaer Yin and the lads were obliged to remove their *ogham* charms entirely. The expressionless guardsman led them through the entrance with the barest salutation. The chains in their ears marked them as nobility, after all.

Inside was an even less-opulent stone hall, which wound up to a second-floor reception area with twenty-foot ceilings and no adornments whatsoever. Scratching his scarred chin with a dubious scowl, Robin looked around, unimpressed. "Figured ye lot would have fancier digs than these?"

Tam Lin jerked a thumb at Kaer Yin. "This boor's idea, actually. It used to be a fortress in the old Duch's time. He thought we'd have less trouble with the Southers if they felt a strong Sidhe presence here but weren't insulted by its grandeur."

Robin fathomed a guess, "I 'spose Ten Bells wasn't always so fancy."

"They were starved once," Kaer Yin confirmed. "This place used to be the seat of the Donahugh family, back before they declared themselves Gods of the South. Duch Kevin was no miser. The people of Ten Bells were taxed to the stars to provide funds for various rebellions and his new fortress at the mouth of the Lee." He squinted at torches lining the far walls, remembering. "I took this fortress from Kevin's brother in N.E. 397. Some would argue that was when the war truly started."

Shar, who hadn't been born when Kaer Yin marched through the South the first time, ogled the plain interior with something akin to awe. "I wish I'd been with you, *Ard Tiarne*."

"I was," complained Tam Lin. "A hot, fly-infested, shite-stinking mess, if you ask me. You'd much prefer the place now, trust me."

Robin shook his head with a wry snort. "Boggles me mind. Walkin' through history with ye lot. My mate, the hero in every tall tale."

Kaer Yin opened his mouth, but Tam Lin declared for him, "Far from a hero to these Southers. They hate him more than the pox. The way they get after him, you'd think he stomped down here and flattened their cities all by himself. Yin took this fortress, true... but it had been Falan the Younger who set the city ablaze and I who led the first sallies against Bethany. Won every battle too, I might add."

"But 'twas Ben who cut Duch Kevin in half, wasn't it?"

Tam Lin pursed his lips. "Yes."

"Well, there ye have it then. Ben's a hero to us *Northers* then, ain't he?"

Kaer Yin winked at his cousin, slapping Robin's shoulder. "Lin, you'll always be *my* hero. Never forget that."

Tam Lin rolled his eyes as they approached the chamber's far end. "Sod yourself."

The clerks behind the flat stone desk appeared less impressed by their motley group than the majordomo at *The Ferryman* had been. A lovely young Sidhe girl with hair the color of coal and eyes like the pre-dawn sky sighed at the group, "Your business, My Lords?"

Tam Lin sucked in a grin. "Withdrawal."

Not a single emotion crossed her brow. "From which account, lord?"

"Croghan."

She shuffled vellum around. Her pretty eyes flicked to Kaer Yin. "And you, Lord... erm?"

"Bri Leith."

She went very still. "I beg your pardon?"

Kaer Yin leaned over her desk so that she might get a better look at him. "Name's Adair. Should be right at the top of your list there." He tugged his brow at her chart.

"That is impossible." She looked around as if seeking the joke.

"Is it?" Kaer Yin tucked the hair behind his ears, displaying the nine gold chains in his right. After a long silence, the girl's face went white as milk. The clerks behind her cried out— one dropped an entire bottle of ink all over the dreary stone floor. "That's Kaer Yin Adair, mistress. Shall I spell it?"

She launched out of her chair, wringing her hands. "F-forgive me, *Ard Tiarne*!" She managed an awkward half-bow. "But you, you're...."

"Dead, I know. *Surprise*." He splayed his hands.

Tam Lin elbowed between them. "That would be Kaer Yin Adair *and* Tam Lin O'Ruiadh, mistress. We require access to our accounts if you would be so kind?"

Blubbering slightly, the girl looked around her in complete mystification. Her coworkers had little to offer but wide-eyed shrugs.

"I'm afraid," she gulped. "The ambassador herself must approve your requests, My Lords."

"Fine, fine," whinged Tam Lin. "Make it quick, though, I'm starving."

Fidgeting, she wilted under his gaze. "Ah, well. The ambassador is in residence, but she does not descend for some hours yet, My Lord. We are forbidden to disturb—"

"I believe she'll make the exception this time, don't you?" Kaer Yin's smile was hardly pleasant.

With another pained bow, the girl set off. He could hear her slippers slapping time against the polished stone floors as she bolted for the stairs. Tam Lin grinned at the two spare clerks.

"Got anything to drink back there while we wait?"

EVENTUALLY, THEY WERE ESCORTED INTO A WINDOWLESS CHAMBER AT the rear of the mammoth building, well away from prying eyes. With tepid water to drink and nothing to eat, Kaer Yin braced himself for his oncoming hangover and seethed. How dare these sycophantic pissants refuse them the basic hospitality the Sidhe must show to a common Mercher? Two princes of the Tuatha De Dannan— one of them the son of the Ard Ri— hurried through the back door like a pair of criminals! Between the hammering in his skull and the fury rising in his chest, Kaer Yin was nearly ready to murder everyone in the Consulate when the door finally swung open for the ambassador. Robin snored from his corner chair, while Tam Lin and Shar dozed across the table with their heads cradled over their arms. A lone buoy in this dull, grey sea of stone: Kaer Yin stubbornly remained awake to scowl at the tiny, officious woman and her two silent attendants. With her greying black hair tied back in a complicated knot that was once popular in Armagh, Sioarse Cathal gave a slight start when she set her dark eyes on him.

"*Macha*!" she burst out but immediately cleared her throat to resume a dignified indifference. She snapped her fingers, and two additional chairs were brought in. Kaer Yin noted that absolutely none of the Sidhe he'd seen so far were Dannan. He wondered how that had come to pass. "Forgive me, *Ard Tiarne*, but this is quite momentous for us. We'd long believed you deceased." She sat in one of the proffered chairs, lifting a hand to invite Kaer Yin to do the same. He did not.

"Tell me, is it customary to show the Prince of Connaught to an interrogation chamber when he makes an appearance? ...Whether you knew I lived or not," he said coolly. "Tam Lin O'Ruiadh should command better respect."

He had the pleasure of watching her pinched face flex. "Ah, we apologize to Lord O'Ruaidh, but we must be sure he isn't escorting an imposter. Dead men do not often materialize out of thin air to demand an audience with the Consulate."

Kaer Yin crossed his arms. "My apologies for the inconvenience of my existence, Ambassador. I'm afraid I didn't consider your delicate sensibilities when I decided to call upon you for funds that belong to *me*."

Here, she returned his glare. "The collective wealth and privilege of Aes Sidhe is not now, nor will it ever be, *yours*, Highness. Furthermore, though I may now agree that you are alive and hale, many others must also agree to the validity of your claim before we may process any funds or aid. Kaer Yin Adair is dead, as far as Aes Sidhe and the cities of Eire are concerned. To prove otherwise, legally, should be your first step."

Inhaling deeply through his nose, he leaned against the wall rather than wobble on his feet. "You dare?"

The Ambassador plucked lint from her sleeve. "I wonder why you haven't returned to Bri Leith for your father's direct approval? Surely, if the Ard Ri is aware that you live and approves of your purpose, you wouldn't need to access the Consulate's funds in Southern Eire?"

He was quiet for a moment, feeling every last trace of the uishge leech from his bloodstream. Undaunted, the Ambassador glared back. Kaer Yin did not doubt that as soon as he exited this chamber, messengers would be sent in every direction boasting that he was alive and begging for coin from the Consulate. That he was *not* yet in favor in Bri Leith would be devoured by every Sidhe and ally in Innisfail by week's end. This visit was a mistake. Tam Lin had been right.

They should've found another way.

"My business is my own, Ambassador Cathal. When I return to Bri Leith, I will remember this slight."

"All the same, the Consulate rejects your claim. You may apply through the appropriate channels. Once the Court has formally acknowledged your identity, we will review your case again." She made a big show of getting to her feet. "While we are most pleased to discover our Crown Prince of Innisfail is alive and hale, we must bid you a good day, Highness." She curtsied and turned to leave.

Tam Lin's voice caught her at the door. "Not so fast, Ambassador. Does *my* good name not warrant access to Croghan's funds?"

She turned her mask of imperious disdain firmly in place. "Of course it does, Your Highness. But you must await the review period, like any applicant."

"Horseshite." Tam Lin slapped the table with the flat of his palm. "You will march your narrow arse back to the Exchequer and produce those funds, or I will have your badge, your lands, and possibly your neck."

She squirmed beneath his glare. "Your Highness, this is most irregular—"

"Shall I replace you as Ambassador now, or do I appear to be an imposter too?" He held out his *ogham* stone. "Shar. Return to our Inn and retrieve our men. I want the Ambassador and all of her Bolgish pets in this Consulate imprisoned within the hour. If any resist, you have my full and free permission to execute them."

"*Mo Flaith*," Shar answered, rising. He pressed his fist against his heart and pried the door open to pass the Ambassador. Her guards grabbed his elbow, but Shar's lark slipped out, splashing dull red blood in the hall. Cathal screamed, careening away from the two falling bodies. Kaer Yin caught her before she could call for more guards. Shar had already disappeared whence they came. She trembled against Kaer Yin's hand.

"Now, madam Ambassador, I believe you owe my cousin— your liege lord and Crown Prince of this realm— an apology. You will have plenty of time to reflect upon your error here whilst you await trial for treason and usury," Tam Lin said ominously. Robin, who'd woken up in the clamor of Shar's brief scuffle, swore under his breath.

"Lead us to your office, My Lady," growled Kaer Yin, jerking her into the hall. Robin darted after him while Tam Lin clasped his arms behind him to follow at a leisurely pace.

"No need to be rough, Yin. I think my men will arrive in no time, and our point will be made. Don't you?"

IN THE END, CATHAL'S OFFICE WAS HAPPY TO GREET AND GENUFLECT before both princes. Tam Lin's Blood Eagles and a smattering of Robin's Greenmakers waited on the Consulate steps, ready to slaughter everyone if need be. Cathal's officers glanced at Kaer Yin's face and instantly recognized him. There were few from Aes Sidhe who'd struggle to identify the infamous Crown Prince, even if he was supposed to be long dead. Not many Sidhe bore Kaer Yin's famous silver eyes, height, and build— save perhaps for the Ard Ri himself, of whom Kaer Yin was the spitting image. An hour into the exchange, Cathal was forced behind her desk to stamp the notes and documents her clerks hastily prepared with a sneer that should have peeled Kaer Yin's eyelids back.

He raised a haughty brow at her. "What? Should you be locked away until your Deputy can be sworn in as Ambassador, after all? Where is he, anyway?"

"Armagh," she sniffed, her hand poised over the official seal. "Then on to Bri Leith to remand taxes from Lord Bearn's Treasury. We are but servants of the Ard Ri, Your Highness. What you are doing here is illegal, and you know it. I cannot approve your claim, whether you wrongfully incarcerate me or not."

Tam Lin pinched the bridge of his nose. "You won your argument about the Crown Prince's revenue, madam Ambassador... though you are not approving *his* claim. You're granting legal access to *mine*. Now get on with it. I have many things I'd rather be doing now than arguing with a lowly diplomat over funds she has no power to withhold. Press the damned seal to that sheaf of vellum already, will you?"

Her gums pulled back over her white teeth. "I am hardly a personage for you to belittle, Dannan. My blood is as old and noble as yours."

"Perhaps." Kaer Yin's expression was leaden. "Although he's still your liege lord... and *I* am his. Now, do you wish to be replaced or not? That power, the Prince of Connaught *does* have, I'm afraid. See? We're all familiar with the law."

All the color drained from her burnished cheeks. She must have been in Eire for a very long time to have aged to this degree. While such was not common knowledge in Eire, the Sidhe could maintain their immortality so long as they regularly passed back and forth through the Oiche Ar Fad.

It would take decades to age as many years as Cathal had, far too many to be noticed by the Milesians in Ten Bells but plenty to mark her out as someone of little political clout. She might restore much of her youth and vigor by returning to the Otherworld, though after today's debacle, Kaer Yin doubted she'd ever be granted leave.

"I keep your father's laws here, *Ard Tiarne*. Not yours."

"One day, you may... or not." Kaer Yin's eyes went hard.

She failed to repress a shudder.

Tam Lin jabbed a thumb into his chest. "Forget him and this ridiculous display. My funds, madam. I have places to be, damn you."

She hesitated again. With a groan, he reached over to press her hand down. The first note stamped; he pried her hand up to poise over the second. She looked like someone who'd been ordered to swallow her tongue.

"Good. Now this one. Just three left."

She allowed him to use her hand to direct the seal, like a child learning to hold a quill. Her derision was plain. "You do your father and uncle a disservice this day, Your Highness. If you believe yourselves unanswerable to the Ard Ri's laws now, I shudder to imagine that either of you may ever inherit our kingdom."

Tam Lin met her frown with one of his own. "Who do you imagine you're speaking to, *seirbhiseach*? In Aes Sidhe, you know you'd lose a hand for that comment, not to mention the vitriol you've spewed at your future king."

Without another word of complaint, she stamped the remaining documents herself. Refusing to look at either of them again, she carefully gathered each sheaf in an elegant roll and passed them over.

"Your funds, as ordered, Your Highness. As is my duty, I shall write a full accounting of each coin to Bri Leith and Croghan."

...and Armagh, thought Kaer Yin with a tight jaw.

"Good day to you both, *mo thiarna*." Her bow was purely perfunctory.

Tam Lin gathered the documents, stashing them in a handsome leather valise a clerk handed up to him. "Make sure you tell my father what words you used to gainsay me in detail, madam. I'm sure he'll be impressed by your humility."

She sank into her chair to fold her quaking hands. The Red King did not take an insult lightly. Even one lobbed at his likely deserving heir. "I shall, Your Highness. Be sure you don't regret them yourself."

Kaer Yin's mouth pulled down at the corners. "What is that supposed to mean?"

"A fool is the man who believes his name a shield. You spoilt Dannans aren't the sole *Clann* in Innisfail, are you?"

STROLLING THROUGH THE MARKETS OF TEN BELLS, LEADING A NEW team of lovely Eirean thoroughbreds packed down with half a hundred parcels swinging from their spanking new saddles... Kaer Yin fumed over their unpleasant encounter at the Consulate. They were corralled in the center of every street they moved through, wedged between the stalls on either side and their men's protective, watchful swords. The Dannans had resumed their disguises, leaving the perplexed populace who stumbled out of their way at a loss to explain why so many seemingly poor, bedraggled individuals could afford such mounts, let alone so many packages. If they had but an inkling of how much worse it would be when the tailors and haberdashers completed their orders by noon the following day. *The Ferryman* would be flooded with the best-dressed army Ten Bells never knew it had been hosting. The company of Tam Lin O'Ruaidh would exit the city in style.

The sun dipped low over the harbor by the time they rounded the hill toward their Inn. Robin stole a peak at Kaer Yin's sour expression. "What then? Should we turn back?"

"No."

"Then stop mewlin' over it. It's done. Ye'll have yer respect again soon enough, Yer Arseness. What're ye worried about?"

"She didn't seem all that surprised to see me, those mysterious parting words notwithstanding."

"Aye, well. She didn't strike me as the sort to be surprised about much."

"I think she knew I was alive before we arrived."

Robin lost a step to stare after him. Catching back up, he said, "How d'ye figure?"

"I don't know. It's just a feeling."

"D'ye suppose she knew ye'd come to Ten Bells for funds, then?"

Kaer Yin shrugged. "If a Sidhe is stranded in Eire for whatever reason, we have this one place to turn to for aid. If rumors about me are circling through Aes Sidhe already, it would stand to reason the Consulate would be a logical first stop."

"Hm," Robin hummed. "Maybe that's why she showed ye two through the back way? To control the tongue-waggin' before it got outta hand?"

"Possibly."

"Can't be every day two high lords come in, demandin' coin."

"We have a claim to our stipend at each Consulate in Innisfail. We don't truck with banks as you Eireans do, though each of the Great Clans may have access to their funds, permits, and power of warrant through the Consulate. It is also the single office in Innisfail with the power to veto any local laws that run contrary to the High King's commands and is responsible for collecting and distributing taxes. In other words, every Consulate is an extension of the High King's power," explained Tam Lin in a bored tone. "In this idiot's case, he flounced in there and expected to have his arse kissed by the most powerful Sidhe official in Eire."

"As did you." Kaer Yin's jaw flexed.

Tam Lin stopped, patting his skittish horse's neck. "Yet, I have an active stipend, a powerful father with whom I'm not out of favor, no *geis* to speak of, and the bloody right to anything I request. You, my dear cousin, cannot say the same."

Standing at the intersection between two less-busy lanes, Kaer Yin and Tam Lin squared off. Robin attempted to squeeze between them, knowing where this was headed but was promptly shoved aside. Shar called a halt to their group, who immediately began to pass coins around.

"I have every damned right," disagreed Kaer Yin.

"Maybe." Tam Lin conceded. "Though, not until you've made it up with your father and are officially reinstated in Bri Leith. Until then, you're just a grubby vagabond with a famous name."

"Midhir reinstated me. I'm in command unless you forgot?"

Tam Lin blew wet air through his lips. "Yeah, *in Rosweal*, to protect the North. Not down here in shite stinking Ten Bells, demanding coin and obeisance to chase a Godsdamned skirt to Bethany!"

Kaer Yin's face darkened. "Take it back, or I will take it out of you."

Dropping his reins, Tam Lin slammed his fist into Kaer Yin's nose. Kaer Yin staggered backward, smashing a hand over his streaming nostrils. Robin covered his eyes with a groan. Shar gathered up Tam Lin's abandoned reins and led his horse back to greet the others with a sigh. Shopkeepers ducked through their doorways to peer from open shutters. Citizens and fellow shoppers who hadn't already veered away from their group did so now, with a bit more urgency. Tam Lin dropped his swordbelt to the cobbles. Shar, again, waited for him to kick the item out of the way so he could pick it up.

"I'm done dipping my head for your arrogance, *mac soith!*"

Kaer Yin didn't bother to disarm. Roaring, he ran at Tam Lin full tilt, taking the redhead down by his midsection. Tam Lin hissed in pain as his back slammed against the cobbles, but Kaer Yin jammed a knee into his ribs to hold his cousin in place while he showered him with merciless blows. A woman screamed from an awning somewhere ahead, but neither noticed. Tam Lin twisted, dislodging Kaer Yin long enough to ram the crown of his head into his chin. Cursing, Kaer Yin scrabbled backward, hastily coming up to his knees. Tam Lin grasped him by the collar, throwing him bodily against a nearby lamppost. Kaer Yin's breath rushed out of him as his still-healing shoulder bore the impact. Face as bloodied as his cousin's, Tam Lin pummeled his waist with audible, organ-damaging blows. Hooking an arm around his shoulder, Kaer Yin jerked him upright to slam his forehead into his nose, taking them both to the ground.

More coins passed between their men while the two disguised princes bowled around in the mud and snow like a pair of snarling dogs. A great smear of bright blood trailed in their wake. Just when Kaer Yin had the upper hand, Tam Lin would wrench them both over and begin his thrashing anew.

Robin looked around them nervously. The Lamplighter, on his stilts, thunked down the cobbles in the opposite direction. People who weren't cowering in doorways began to duck around them to escape. "Eh, lads? We're drawin' a frightful mess of attention now. D'ye think ye'd better save this for later, maybe?"

Oblivious to Robin's voice, the two combatants were too busy making each other bleed. Kaer Yin held the high ground now, busily wrenching Tam Lin's arm aside so he could press his face into the gutter. "You petty, self-absorbed piece of shite!"

Tam Lin kicked out with his left boot, catching Kaer Yin in the ribs to dislodge him. Rolling him over again, he pressed his knee into Kaer Yin's back while he jabbed his fist into his liver.

"*I'm* self-absorbed? *I*? You commandeer *my* men, *my* title, *my* time, and *my* bloody fainne... and *I'm* self-absorbed? Remember we're all here because of some Gods-damned cunny you're mad for? *Not by choice!*" His knuckles came down with each word. "*This. Was. All. Your. Fucking. Idea.*"

As if the spell of competition had lost its appeal, Kaer Yin grabbed Tam Lin by the throat and flung him sideways. He followed close behind, skidding to a stop in the snow and mud, and delivered a blow to Tam Lin's solar plexus that had his cousin retching on all fours.

"That is the last time you speak of her that way, Tam Lin. By Brida, I swear it." Exhausted but determined, Kaer Yin pushed him over onto his back with the flat of his shin and dropped an elbow into his navel on the way down. They both lay in the filthy street, breathing hard up at the sky.

In the distance, faint whistles and raised voices flitted into the air. Wringing his hands, Robin prodded, "Yer makin' us popular."

Huffing, Tam Lin tuned over to spit blood. He narrowed a swollen eye on Kaer Yin, who was in similar straits. "Why are we here, Yin? Really?"

After a long silence, Kaer Yin's eyes met his. "You know."

Clutching his ribs with a pained laugh, Tam Lin sat up. "So, it isn't merely a skirt we're chasing to Bethany, then?"

"No."

"A *Milesian* woman." Tam Look shook his head. "I'll never understand it, no matter what you say. My apologies, I suppose."

"Accepted."

"Does she know how you feel?"

Kaer Yin looked away. "No."

Tam Lin and Robin shared a wince. "*Danu.* All this, and she may reject you?"

Kaer Yin didn't answer.

Tam Lin chuckled, "Well, let's hope she has equally terrible taste, then." With a grunt, he got up, extending a hand to help his cousin do the same. "Pray these scratches fade before we get there, cousin. You look like hammered shite."

RIAN BURST THROUGH KAER YIN'S DOOR WITH A SLIGHTLY MORE harried expression than usual. She took in the tableau with a deep inhale. Amidst a room full of packets and brightly wrapped packaging, Robin stopped wiping Kaer Yin's nose mid-stroke. Her eye slid to Shar and Niall, who busied themselves with Tam Lin. He gave her a sloppy half-grin. Her mouth dropped open and reclosed. She shook her head and crossed her arms. "Right," she said. "I don't care enough to ask. I'll assume it went well enough, given the horses Gerry can't shut up about and the state of things here."

"Hello to you too," replied Tam Lin, without warmth.

As always, she ignored him. She raised her brows at Kaer Yin. "We have trouble."

"We heard. Mel told us what happened."

Mel smiled at her from his place beside the fireplace. "Is Lady Alvra resting?"

Rian waved his comment away. "Yes, and she's better now. But that isn't what I've come to—"

"Are you all right?" Kaer Yin interrupted.

Agitated, she took a deep breath. "Yes. I'm fine. But—"

"What in the Hells were these Kneelers after?" Robin wondered aloud while jabbing a scrap of linen up one of Kaer Yin's nostrils.

"Converts, obviously," ruminated Tam Lin. "Christers have always tried to force people into their faith. You should read about what they did to our people in the old days."

Rian opened her mouth, but Kaer Yin, again, interrupted her. "They're harmless in small groups, but once they gather, it can quickly become a problem. They call their gospel the 'good word.'" He scoffed. "Since when have violence and bigotry been 'good?'"

"Do you think it'll be a problem?" Tam Lin winced when Niall pressed too hard near his eye.

Kaer Yin lifted a shoulder. "Not that we have time to worry over the matter. We'll be gone before—"

"Siora *damn you*," shouted Rian, having gone a bright shade of red. "Will you bloody well listen to the words coming out of my mouth?"

Every male in the room flinched.

She crossed her arms. "Your prisoner is gone. While we were out, he escaped."

Kaer Yin launched upright. "*What?*"

"How?" seethed Robin, throwing his uishge into the fire.

Without waiting for an answer, Gerrod leaped to his feet with a curse. Before Rian knew what they were doing, everyone had followed him into the hall and through the massive building to the stables. Fergal waited outside in the courtyard with a smattering of Greenmakers and Blood Eagles and the majordomo, who wrung his hands.

"*Ard Tiarne*," the majordomo bowed so low his head could scrape the snow-blown cobbles. "Forgive us, but there has been a murder."

Rian watched Kaer Yin shove through to the well-lit stable. She drifted in after him. In the farthest, windowless stall, a young boy sprawled over the remnants of a modest meal of meat and turnips. His head was twisted about ninety degrees the wrong way. Already, the flesh of his face leeched grey and blue. Rian covered her mouth.

He couldn't have been more than nine or ten.

"Lionel." The majordomo came up behind them. "A good lad. Another stableboy found him like this nigh thirty minutes ago."

"He's been strangled," observed Rian, trying not to weep. Shar's fingers brushed her shoulder, and she accepted them without comment.

Kaer Yin shared a long look with Robin. "He can't have gone far."

"No," agreed Robin. "But if we don't leave tomorrow, we'll never make it in time."

Kaer Yin cursed as Rian covered the lad's staring corpse with her shawl. "Matt Gilcannon deserves to die."

"Ye'll get no argument there, but we came all this way, and it's now or never," Robin went on, with an eye on Gerrod. "Ye hear me, Gerry?"

The boy laughed wryly. The sound was lighter than the occasion demanded. "I've waited me entire bloody life to kill that bastard. What're a few more weeks?"

Tam Lin patted him on the back. "There's a lad."

Kaer Yin set a hand over his heart, holding Gerrod's gaze. "I vow, Matt Gilcannon lives on borrowed time. Whether by a blade or the hangman's knot, his guts will swing for this... and every offense. I, Kaer Yin Adair, *Ard Tiarne* of Innisfail, swear it."

After several tense breaths, with Gerrod's emotions tracing across his face, his head bobbed at last. "Aye. I suppose a man can't get more fucked than to cross a future king. Let's do what we came here to do. Ben, I'm with ye."

Robin pulled the lad into a bear hug and led him outside, uncorking his bone flask as he whispered encouragement in the boy's ear. Tam Lin helped Rian to her feet and handed her a handkerchief, which she accepted without question. The majordomo's sigh sounded ancient. "My lords, I must respectfully request—"

"Yes." Kaer Yin knew what he would say. "We're leaving at dawn. I'll see that the boy's family is cared for through the winter. Of course, we will pay double the rates, with my deepest apologies."

"*Ard Tiarne*, I hope you'll inform us when this man is brought to justice. It has been a pleasure to serve you," the majordomo said tactfully, bowing out of the stable.

Rian couldn't blame him. She doubted murders were widespread in Ten Bells, especially not at an establishment as fine as *The Ferryman*. Beside her, Tam Lin straightened.

"Well, Yin? What now?"

Staring at the covered shape of the dead child in the hay, Kaer Yin clenched his fists. "As Gerry said. What we came here to do."

21
FIDELITY

Cromnasa was but two days away, and Una was no closer to unmasking her villain than she had been the week before. Long hours spent in the library, in the Hall of Records, or trolling the Courtyard Market for details, all… fruitless. If not for the bodies continually cropping up around her father's Keep, the killer might have been a ghost. Two more girls were discovered in the old kirkyard west of the inner bailey. Both had been brutalized with a blade after having been bludgeoned and strangled. The dead girls lay tangled together in a snowbank, half-frozen and unseen for some time. Try as she might, Una had been unable to examine the remains directly. Instead, she'd taken a cue from her father and bribed the coroner for his report, the details of which kept her awake all that night, seething with fear and rage. That a mere mortal man was capable of such bestial acts was not in question to her mind. That she might know him, walk the same halls each day, and sup in his presence each night drove her to distraction. Having given up the Moorings as a dumping ground, the killer seemed to be searching for a suitable replacement. The kirkyard's victims might have lain there from the night Una herself was attacked, for he'd left behind no clues other than the very bodies themselves. She had yet to wrestle a full accounting from the coroner, and just yesterday, another body was found wedged into the sewer exit near the gatehouse.

Bethany's resident monster had claimed the lives of seven women.

So far.

Una resolved to investigate the newest find as soon as she could extricate herself from her father's ridiculous fête. All the major and minor lords and ladies of Innisfail seemed to have materialized within Bethany's walls overnight. The castle was stuffed to the brim with overdressed nobility, their myriad servitors, guardsmen, and soldiers garbed in a hundred different heraldic colors, and the Duch's household stewards racing up and down every hall to accommodate the lot. With so many strangers to house, feed, and entertain, who could afford the time to search for the killer now?

She made a face at herself in the mirror.

No one, she thought.

As soon as the feast was over, she would extricate the coroner's Godsdamned report if it meant following the fellow into his bedchamber, herself— hang propriety.

Until then... the charade.

She caught sight of a familiar blond head at the foot of her private staircase. He wore a handsome cobalt tunic and silver waistcoat. Micah startled when he glanced upward, face rifling through several shades of scarlet. She took his quivering arm with a rue smile.

"Into the breach, shall we?"

Getting where they were headed was adventure enough.

The corridors were choked with people coming and going, loitering, lollygagging, and ogling. She'd never seen so many bodies crammed into such close quarters before— the Cloister included. How in Siora's name Patrick had managed to accommodate so many, she might never grasp. Her guards led them into the bulk of the staring crowds, through tightly packed hallways, down two flights of occupied stairs, to the holly and mistletoe bedecked doors of the Great Hall. Painfully aware of the stares she received, Una poured every ounce of Moura dignity into her bearing and glided toward the dais with the grace of an empress.

She felt eyes slide over her, some in envy, some in avarice.

So be it.

These dandies were nothing to her, and she would have them know it. She'd selected a gown of bright, gleaming gold cloth, a color only Tairnganese women owned the complexion to do any justice; backless so that gossips wouldn't mistake the coiling blue dragons riding high over her bare shoulders. Her hair had been arranged in Red City fashion. Long braids were roped together with golden beads and chiming bells, then tied into intricate knots at the nape of her long neck. She was a Moura noblewoman— Queen of Tairngare, or close enough as made no difference.

She would display no weakness.

The tableau was something to behold. The Hall sparkled like the interior of a forest hollow in winter. There were about thirty tables and long benches stacked in tidy rows. Between them ran several carpets lined with twisting arches of holly bracken and birch interwoven with silver streamers, flickering candles under glass, white-dipped vines, and snow-painted pinecones. The effort to construct these free-standing trellises must have been absurd. They ran the breadth and length of each junction, radiating with multifaceted candlelight and crisp-smelling herbs. The wooden timbers on the ceiling hadn't been spared either. Donahugh colors streamed nearly forty feet from the joists behind the dais. Huge red velvet tapestries, bearing the Southernmost Star in blue, swung twenty feet overhead, the largest of which spilled behind the Duch's throne like a crimson waterfall.

Below the dais, each long table was piled high with ridiculous mounds of food: braised duck with thyme, stuffed peacock with apple glazing, roast boar and venison, and in the center of each beckoned full hanks of smoked beef. There were also baked fish in cream sauce, freshly steamed vegetables, lovely fruits, cakes dusted in powdered sugar, and countless candies and biscuits generously sprinkled throughout.

Down a carpet littered with mulberry and cranberry leaves, Una and Micah strode toward the ungodly stone dais her father already occupied. Wearing an absurdly expensive white-bear fur cloak and a cobalt tunic belted with silver and gold, Patrick toasted the pair as they moved toward their seats beside him.

"Daughter!" he cried to the crowd at large. She suspected he concealed a charm about his person that allowed him to achieve that effortless boom. On his opposite side, Damek was resplendent but subdued, in plum velvet. He didn't look her way once. Instead, he sipped his wine and dipped his head to listen to what Martin said. Doubtless, Douglas had already filled his ears about what she'd witnessed the other day. Noting her blatant stare, Martin glanced up. Her narrowed eyes wiped the smirk from his face. She thought she caught the barest nervous tick in Damek's jaw.

They were going to have words soon enough.

Patrick took her hand to present her to the Hall. "Good people of Innisfail! I give you Una Alis Margaret Donahugh, Princess of Bethany, Countess of Kildare, and future Duchess of the House Donahugh." The Court, as one, bowed as low as they were able. Above the throng, Patrick and Damek remained motionless. When everyone rose, Una curtsied back as expected. She'd vowed to play her part, hadn't she? Pleased, Patrick lowered her into her seat before resuming his own. Micah, Damek, and anyone else on the dais followed suit. A servant brought over a delicious-smelling mead. She eagerly extended her cup. Patrick squinted at her. "Now then, you know the rules, girl. You're to smile, charm, and flutter your lashes at as many men as brave this dais to meet you. Are we in accord on that score?"

"I do love a good puppet show," she sang tonelessly.

Patrick grunted at her but lifted his goblet to the gathered. The golden fillet at his temple glinted in heady candlelight from the four iron chandeliers overhead. Dozens of blazing braziers near every floor-to-ceiling window added warmth to the festive atmosphere.

"Good families of Eire! What father could be more pleased to have his child home and safe with him at last?" A cheer traveled the length and breadth of the chamber. Una drank rather than allow her face to disagree. Patrick was a fine orator. His beaming, jovial expression seemed to leech the years from him. When he spoke, his voice rang clear as if he believed every word. His audience shared his fervor. "I bid you, come and greet your new lady. Show her your support. Let's give my precious child the homecoming of her dreams!" After the last round of cheers, Patrick sank into his seat once more, chuckling.

"Precious?" she quipped from over the rim of her cup.

Patrick shifted in his seat. "Wars are expensive, Una. All told, merely getting you here cost me more than I'd like to tally. So, *smile*. You're sitting in a place of honor at a feast, wearing a gown a woman from anywhere else would sell her tits to touch— and enjoying the adoration of hundreds of the richest men on the Continent. I daresay it could be a lot worse. You might enjoy yourself a little if you'd pull your head out of your arse."

Una took another sip. The mead was Cymrian, of course. Only the finest honey made it into the Swansea press. Hints of Bretagnic cinnamon and Alban pear went into each brew. Strong stuff, too, if she were any judge. She drained her cup and held it out for a refill. Her cheeks heated in appreciation. Damek frowned at her from Patrick's opposite side. She sat back, so she wouldn't have to look at him.

"I'll be a grand show horse, as promised, father *dear*."

Patrick made a sound with his nose. "You may be a tiresome nag like your mother, but you'll never hear me complain of your decorum. You're a Donahugh. That makes a thoroughbred of you, same as me." He cast a sharp sneer her way. "We are all on display, my love. Always. Artifice is everything from the lowest whore on the cobbles to the highest lord in any tower. We may be more or less in private, but to the world at large, the masks we choose set our place in the game."

"What game?"

"Life. Right now, you wish to wear a victim's mask and cloak yourself in its bitterness… oh, great Queen of Tairngare." He grinned sidelong at her. "You want to be a queen so badly? Take the crown I'm offering you and prove you deserve it."

Una said nothing; it would do no good to argue with him. Not here. Instead, she filled her mouth with teeth and bobbed her chin at anyone who meant to catch her eye. Silently seething, she pretended amazement at the first of three surprise courses (dueling swans stuffed with mint and blackberry confit). She picked at her food and made nice with Micah, those seated to her right, and any who dared present their sons to the dais.

AFTER THREE HOURS, UNA COULD ADMIT TO BEING SLIGHTLY DRUNK. Her stone-walled liver had always been a source of pride, but Cymrian mead was no laughing matter. Her head swam. Her eyes glazed over in the hum of conversation, warm firelight, and incessant pageantry. Micah had moved on to speak to a pair of Kernian boys, whom she vaguely recalled as Lady Penwyth's sons. As far as Una could tell, they were having an animated debate about something inane. The Duch had taken himself down to the next table, reminiscing quite loudly with another portly man she couldn't remember. Lord Whoever was a Souther Baron and had a son who stared at Una like she might leap from her chair and eat him any second. Poor thing. The lad had to be at least six years her junior if he was a day. Feeling bad for him, she gave him a genuine smile.

He flushed red as a beacon and looked away.

Keeping her eye on him while she drank, she was amused to find him stealing glances at her whenever he thought she wasn't looking.

One conquest down, three hundred to go, she congratulated herself.

"I'll kill him, you know?" said Damek, sliding into his uncle's vacant chair. "And his fat papa. Would that please you?"

"Don't you have anything else to do?"

She felt his stare glide over her back, making her wish she'd worn the black shroud she'd initially planned to. "I can think of several things I'd rather be doing. Did you wear that dress just for me?"

"You're drunk." She wrinkled her nose.

He stuck out his lower lip. "I am, no lie. You're far from sober, yourself."

"True," she admitted, with a tilt of her goblet.

"Did you know your cheeks turn the loveliest shade of orchid when you're in your cups?"

"I'll knock one of your perfect teeth down your throat."

"You'd better get used to the flattery if you've agreed to play Patrick's game. I shouldn't be surprised if I have to sleep outside your door tonight myself— it's going so bloody well." He drained his goblet. "You should be happy I'm here, cousin. As long as I sit beside you, none will dare approach."

"No such threat. Most've avoided me like a bad smell. Half of these lads are barely out of swaddling, and the other half is far more interested in fighting Patrick's war. Only your new friend Castor had the bollocks to touch my hand."

Damek's mirth flickered. "Leave it be, Una."

"Considering where we are, I'll do so. For now."

"Thank you," he exhaled slowly as if he'd worried they would have this out in public. "Let's set unpleasant things aside for a while, shall we?"

"Fine." She handed him her goblet for a refill. "We'll drink rather than speak."

Sketching a seated bow, he tugged the wine flagon from the servant's arms and overfilled Una's cup. She couldn't say she minded a whit. Her cheeks burned under her eyelashes. "Now," said he, conspiratorially. "About this dress. Does it clasp somewhere in the front? Because it looks poured on. I find myself dying to know."

"Why don't you lean closer, and I'll whisper the truth in your ear." Her voice came out a lot harsher than she'd meant it to. A few sets of eyes drifted their way, momentarily. She winced and hid behind her cup.

"Next time, I'd wear something demure if you don't want men to flirt."

She choked a bit on her mead. "Flirt? You Bethonair dandies wouldn't know how to talk to a woman if she penned instructions. Anyway, if you're going to sit there and breathe booze and bullshite down my back, you could at least fill the time by marking out those I should take notice of."

He sat up. "Quite right. How thoughtless of me. Martin there at the end, you've met." The Commander at Arms and Damek's faithful dog winked from a pillar opposite. "His brother, Lord O'Rearden of Fennel, is the fellow in the orange doublet. His wife is the Lady Janet, beside him." He looked around. "Baron Chatwick and his prepubescent son are at the end of that table there. Squire Mayhew, you've met already, and his son, Jacob. They hail from 'Who gives a Fuck,' round Malahide. Ah, and Lady Dana Cooley— she's just there in the gauche red mantle. She has three sons and a massive fortune: those lugs at the end there, with the brass to stare straight at you."

She grimaced. "Wonderful. Is there anyone you don't think ill of?"

"That hopes to take my place? Not a one."

"If you're going to be like that for the rest of the night, I'll have my keepers take me back up to my rooms." Her neck grew hot; alcohol made conversation with those she despised less and less a chore.

He gave her an odd look as he filled her cup once more. "Dare I hope you're properly soused enough to find me a little less loathsome?"

She giggled, pulled a face, then laughed again. "I think I've had too much."

"I haven't seen you smile in a lifetime. Here, let's have some more."

"Wait," she protested atonally. "You've already refilled it!"

He pushed her cup toward her and laid his head against his elbow to watch her drink. His eyes roved everywhere at once, but she lacked the sober breath to stop him. A young man and his lady mother— had Damek pointed them out already?— approached.

"Greetings, princess. My name is Talia Mayhew. This is my son, Rory."
The lad managed a shaky bow.

Una grinned back. "My lord, My Lady. It is a pleasure to make your acquaintance."

Damek waved them away with the back of his hand. "Get gone, little man, now." Flinching, Lady Mayhew grasped her son by the shoulders to lead him off the dais. Una apologized profusely with her eyes while her heel smashed into Damek's shin beneath the table. "Ouch!"

"Don't do that! You don't know what he'll do if he isn't happy about tonight."

"He's not going to kill your maids, Una."

"He's done it more than once."

"No, he hasn't. They were reassigned. You give him entirely too much credit as a villain."

Una sat with her mouth open, blinking at the vague shape a few tables away that might have been the Duch. "*What*?"

"It's mostly your fault for wishing to believe every ill of him in the first place. Besides, he couldn't be more pleased by the turnout tonight— never fear. My being here whets the stone of competition. Purses will empty to outshine me. So, as I said, relax."

She shot a glare at Patrick's back, where he sat drinking with his retainers. *Could it be true?* Had Patrick gone to so much trouble to make her believe the worst of him?

She mulled that over in silence for a while, pursing her lips.

Damek drained his cup and poured another. She removed her gloves and felt the tip of one raven-black curl brush her knuckle. It had worked itself free of his torc— a heavy silver piece featuring two hounds locked in a match. She couldn't repress a sigh. She'd given it to him when they were children. Before she could stop herself, her fingers stretched out to touch the cold metal. He drew in a deep breath, eyes growing more lavender by the moment. She used to think he had the most beautiful eyes she'd ever seen.

"I didn't think you'd still have this silly thing," she said.

"I have everything you've ever given me: a pair of the most hideous mittens ever knitted, that bundle of braid you gave me from your first haircut, the locket from Imbolg— do you remember?"

The clock seemed to speed through the evening the longer she sat beside him. After an indeterminable span, she realized she was enjoying herself. He moved closer. His hand curled around hers. Though his fingers were long and scarred, they managed to be elegant. That was who he was, after all: Damek of the Contradictions. Fascinated, she watched his pupils swallow his irises. "I love to see you like this, Una."

"Shut up." She took another drink to silence her fuzzy thoughts.

"I'd make faces at you for hours, trying to get you to smile as you are now."

Her mouth tugged up at the corners now for the memory.

"The sight of you tonight... it's almost... like I have you back."

That did it.

She jerked away, shocked into momentary sobriety. She stood so fast that her guard was forced to grasp her elbow for support. All conversation halted. Patrick's brow clouded over. "What's this?" A murmur circled the room.

"No, oh no. Una. I'm sorry, that's not—" Damek attempted.

"The mead, father. I fear it's quite got the better of me." She forced a blasé smile.

Patrick condescended. "Of course, child. You may go to your rest."

Her guards saluted and reached for her shoulders, but Damek got there first. "*I'll* escort her." Locking his arm around her waist, he swung her through the crowds before she could wrench herself free. Many unkind or curious glances followed them to the door.

"GET YOUR HANDS OFF ME!" UNA SHRIEKED AS HE DRAGGED HER UP THE stairs to her apartments. Unsure how they should respond, her guards trailed behind.

"No. You're going to listen to me, Godsdamnit. For once." Her main bodyguard, Belloch, set a hand against his pommel, but Damek paused to spare him a warning glare, and he thought better of it. The guards saluted, then backed off at least two flights downstairs. Una and Damek were alone on the third-floor landing. He pressed her into the wall, but she lashed out. Her right fist glanced the side of his cheek with a satisfying crunch. With a grunt, he caught and held her other arm against the flagstones. "Are you done?" he spat, leaving her stinging free hand to press into the meat of his chest as he inched closer. Baring her teeth, she dug her fingers into the exposed flesh at his collar. "Go ahead," he dared her. "Do it. I'm not going to stop."

Nostrils flaring, her nails carved half-moons into the skin below his Adam's apple. She could kill him now. She should. They stood there for some time, partially entangled, while she debated her next move. After several moments that beat like an eternity, her fingertips fell away. Pinpricks of blood welled from his throat.

Una swallowed hard. "I will kill you one day, I think."

"No, you won't. You love me."

"I do *not*."

"We are bonded, Una. Forever."

She cursed, low in her throat. "You're a delusional cudgel my father wields to keep his hands clean. You're a murderer and a liar." She tried to slap him again, but this time he squeezed the bulk of his body against hers, preventing room to draw back for another strike. His nose was centimeters away.

"I'll never forgive myself for hurting you."

"Right. You're so sorry, you'd force yourself on me to prove you can."

"Am I touching you in any way but to stop you from hitting me? Have I laid a hand on you that wasn't welcome *once* since you've been here?"

"Then take your hands off of me, right now."

"You'll hear this, whether you want to or not. Then, I'll let you go."

Her right hand was crushed between them, useless. He pinned her knees with his heavier thighs. Unless she wanted to fight for real, what choice did she have?

"We were too young, Una. At fifteen, the Duch had given me such a great responsibility. I didn't know how to behave." His voice wavered a fraction. "Here I was, this lowly, loveless boy. Related to this great, overbearing man... but never equal, never worthy. I wasn't raised like you. I grew up in Martin's holdfast, where I was taught to fear your father and heed his word as law. When he sent for me, I was so eager to prove myself that I would do anything he asked of me. Then, he gave me to *you*. This... this ethereal creature, both shy and sad. You were ten years old when he made me your personal guard. I never thought I'd be anything better than a guard and playmate at the time. Then one day, you were sent to Ten Bells, and I didn't see you again for three years."

"Schooling, my first. At the Libella."

"Yes."

"I was curious about my mother's people."

"Patrick didn't know what a fool choice he made when he let you study there, did he?" Damek laughed without mirth. "Your absence opened a hole inside me. You were my one friend, my sole family. The single person who didn't treat me as 'other.' I starved for need of you, and your father poured all his deceit, malice, and purpose into that chasm. By the time you returned, I was his tool, through and through. I was perhaps more changed than you, who left my heart a child and returned this glorious, otherworldly girl. By your fourteenth birthday, I was already so in love that I could barely look at you. When you finally reached for me at fifteen, I thought I would die of happiness." Feeling her warmth, he leaned closer.

She went still as the stone at her back. "Yet, you betrayed me."

Damek growled into her shoulder. "I had already been through three large battles, sacked two castles, put down one rebellion, and had been granted the title of 'Lord Marshal.' I was barely twenty years old but a man on the rise. When he gave you to me at last, I thought I'd earned my right to call myself a Donahugh. I was no longer a bastard-born half-breed, I was *Lord* Damek Bishop: a seasoned warrior, an accomplished statesman, and now I had the most beautiful wife in Innisfail. We had one perfect week before Patrick took you back. I was given seventy lashes for taking liberties, did you know?"

"No," she said, brows mixing. "I didn't."

"Our marriage was devised to alleviate pressure to wed you to one of his barons' sons. If you were married to one of his family members, he wasn't obligated to solidify allegiance with any of his lesser houses. Once it served his purpose— and Lord Gaelin's tawdry insurrection had been stamped out— I wasn't needed. He could hold your bride price open for further bait." His breath came hot against her skin. She felt herself relax slightly in his grip, despite her reticence. "He had no idea we were intimate until it was too late."

"Yet, you *betrayed* me," she repeated.

"What could I do? He's the most powerful lord in the South, Una. Everything I am or have originated with him. Where would we go? Where *could* we go? I told him the truth because I must. To save you."

"I lost a child because of your duplicity, Damek. I can never forgive—"

He gave a strangled sort of moan. "I didn't know!"

"You betrayed me, our future together— *everything*, to secure your position. Power is all you care about. All you've ever cared about."

"No. I never had the chance to crawl on my knees to you for your forgiveness. I never knew of our child until years later. I never knew what a fool I was until now. Forgive me, Una. Everything I did was for love of you. Misguided though I was."

"I left because you forced me to."

He fought tears. "If my life were enough to take it back, I'd gladly give it." She didn't need the Spark to sense his sincerity. It confused her. His eyes bored into hers, bleeding raw emotion that was very real. Somewhere deep down, something inside of her unlocked. She relaxed slightly in his arms, enough to slide her fingers up his swollen cheekbone. His skin was damp. He leaned into her palm until his lips caressed the pad of her thumb. *"Forgive me,"* he whispered. "I will love you forever, no matter how the world burns."

A small, helpless whimper escaped her lips. She wanted to believe him, or did she? She couldn't think anymore! Weeks of pent-up frustration, confusion, and mourning struck her all at once. Here was her most hated enemy, but also her oldest love. This man had wounded her far worse than any injury had ever done, yet... something within her *yearned* for him, all the same. Was it the same as her feelings for Kaer Yin? No. Never, but real, nonetheless. This was the part of herself that she'd buried so deeply that she'd almost forgotten it existed. She had loved him... once. Could she again? She didn't know.

As if sensing her internal dilemma, Damek's mouth moved over hers with a masculine sigh. Her heart racing, she felt suspended in disbelief and uncertainty. She raised a hand to shove him away but found it winding through his hair instead. He sucked in a breath at her caress and lifted her into his arms. So many doubts swirled through her mind, so many accusations— she shoved them aside. Her legs came to rest on either side of his thighs while he kissed her. Her hands slid over his shoulders and back, winding their bodies together. He whimpered something unintelligible into the soft skin of her nape, and she exhaled against his earlobe.

"Una... Una... Una..." he chanted along her skin, against her lips, like a mantra. She felt herself sink into the warmth of his embrace, but another voice entered her thoughts.

Someone else had called her name that way, hadn't he?

With a cry, she shoved against Damek's chest, dislodging him.

He broke off, breathing hard. "No, please, no."

Slipping down the wall, she covered her eyes in shame. "Leave, Damek. Now." Behind her eyelids, Kaer Yin's face was all she could see. "I'm begging you."

Damek knelt before her, prying her hands wide. "I love you. You love me. What complication can't we weather? I will wait for you, as long as it takes. I swear it."

Gingerly, he wound his fingers through hers. He was so near.

She need only lean into him.

Kaer Yin would be lost.

Her pain and grief would leech away like water from a sieve. "I…"

At that very moment, a single horn blew outside.

She blinked at Damek, who twisted his head toward the sound with a curse.

"I thought everyone had arrived?" she asked, alarmed by his expression.

The horn came again and was answered by the Gatehouse guard. Shouts rang through the courtyard. Una got up to peer through the North-facing windowpane. Damek came up beside her, clutching at her fingers.

"Don't look, Una. *Please*."

She ignored him, pushing his shoulder aside to see what the commotion was. It took a moment for her eyes to adjust, but when they did, she gasped. A team of white and silver horses swirled into the courtyard below. Those who rode them were taller than the average man and unmistakably blond. Beneath their heavy cloaks, Una could discern the white cuirass of Aes Sidhe. Snapping in the stiff, southerly wind, the heraldic device on the flags was a blood-red eagle on a white field. *Croghan*, her studies reminded her. The blood eagle was the animus of House O'Ruaidh— the Ard Ri's brother, Bov Dearg.

Kaer Yin's uncle.

Una's heart crawled into her throat. Without a concern aside from discovering what in the Hells was going on, Una staggered down the stairs whence she came.

22
DECLARATIONS

Kaer Yin followed Tam Lin's train toward a raised dais overflowing with food and pomp. Behind the few staring people seated there swung two massive silver and cobalt banners with the Donahugh device: a shining blue star blazing through a scarlet field. Deeper into that cavernous nave behind the throne, he'd been told Duch Michael had commissioned a stained-glass relief of some renown. That he'd heard it bore his likeness in the act of slaying Kevin Donahugh intrigued him all the more. He hoped he'd get to see it himself before all was said and done.

The Sidhe, of course, entered in style. There were twenty in their group, each taller than the average Milesian by quite a bit and broader through the shoulder. Their fair hair and flashing green eyes gleamed by candlelight. A collective inhalation spread through the crowd, followed by excited whispers and nervous feminine laughter.

Tam Lin strutted forward with pure regal grace, head high, wrapped in his house's snow-white and blood-red colors. Around his head, he wore a crown of copper leaves. Down his back draped a cloak of white wolfskin. His red-gold hair hung loosely around his shoulders, save for the Dannan braids at either temple. Eight gold chains chimed from his right ear. Shar and Niall took up space at his right and left flanks, bearing leather chests with massive brass locks. Kaer Yin and Rian carried the O'Ruiadh pennants a ways back in their line. Rian looked lovely tonight in a white velvet gown and burgundy cloak. Even Robin and Gerrod were turned out—both clean-shaven and uncharacteristically groomed. They were each meant to look their very best, except Kaer Yin, who wore Ben Maeden's ogham charm and moderately clean façade.

When one sought to make an impression, veneer was everything.

Around their party, people struggled to their feet, mouths agape. Several wine vessels were upended. Dishes and crockery clattered to the floor. Musicians in the gallery above stopped playing. The murmur was deafening. Try as he might, Kaer Yin couldn't pinpoint which of them was Patrick. Several lords and ladies of greater Innisfail were gathered for this fête, each dressed in their best. Hard to identify one amongst the multitude. Then again, Kaer Yin had never actually met Patrick, had he? Tam Lin nodded to Shar, who stepped forward.

"Now comes the son of Bov Dearg: Tam Lin O'Ruaidh of Croghan, Second Prince of the Tuatha De Dannan, and future King of Connaught."

More flushed faces and wide-eyed stares. A portly man with a worn golden fillet half-stumbled to the center of the dais. His heavy fur mantle slipped awkwardly from one shoulder. Red-cheeked, he cleared his throat. "Ah, well met, Prince Tam Lin." His bow was half mockery, half drunken arrogance. "The Donahugh Clan welcomes you to Bethany."

Tam Lin slipped a grin over his shoulder at Kaer Yin.

The Duch.

Kaer Yin could admit to being underwhelmed. A man of Patrick Donahugh's reputation should be a giant. Instead, this short, relatively ugly, middle-aged Milesian ogled Tam Lin like *he* was the butt of some joke. Still smiling, Tam Lin swept forward, hands on either hip.

"I've come bearing gifts for the lady of the house, My Lord. To whom may I direct my admiration?"

With a belch, Patrick patted his gut. "Forgive me, Your Highness, but my daughter—"

"— is here!" cried a familiar voice from the rear of the Hall. All eyes turned to the sound with rapacious curiosity. Kaer Yin's skin prickled. His breath hitched when Una raced onto the dais from the opposite side. "I'm here," she panted, holding her side. Her cheeks bloomed scarlet, and her amber eyes sparked like gems in the light. For a moment, he couldn't see anything else. In her gold and black gown that clung to every curve, with silken curls pulled back into a complicated network of braids that accentuated the sharp incline of her perfect cheekbones, and wearing a full, eager smile— Una wasn't simply beautiful; she was like the dawn after a terrible storm. Raking their faces one by one till she came to his, Kaer Yin's heart burned at the inaudible sob that escaped her throat. So much that was unsaid passed between them in that moment; his mouth dried up. The moment did not last, however. Behind her, equally flushed and obviously furious, Damek Bishop strode onto the dais, fingers clutching for hers. As if jolted to reality, Una shook him free and quickly swiped at her cheeks.

"I am Una Moura Donahugh, Prince Tam Lin, delighted to make your acquaintance." Her elegant curtsy did nothing to detract from her regal bearing, but it did allow her another peek at Kaer Yin. He read the warning there, loud and clear. Meanwhile, Lord Bishop glared into Tam Lin's party with open hatred. When Una sidestepped him again, his hand went to his pommel. A larger fellow with a terrible scar reached out and clutched his arm in support, staying his sword hand.

Noting the exchange, but ever the statesman, Tam Lin gave Una his most flattering bow. "My Lady Donahugh, I am your servant." The genuine interest in Tam Lin's tone irked Kaer Yin moderately less than the hint of swelling around Una's lower lip and the general state of Lord Bishop's rumpled tunic. Nostrils flaring, Damek shrugged the larger man off to stomp around to the Duch's right hand. His violet eyes scanned each of the Sidhe's faces with unrestrained loathing. When they settled on Kaer Yin, they paused long enough to make Rian squeeze Kaer Yin's fingers.

"Steady," Rian whispered. He doesn't know it's you, for sure."

Kaer Yin pledged, "He will, soon enough."

Jaw set, Damek smoothed his tunic and readjusted his belt. Holding Kaer Yin's eyes with a sly grin, he wiped his mouth with exaggerated hesitation.

Rian's nails dug into Kaer Yin's palm. "If you keep staring like that, he will know *now*."

Kaer Yin forced himself to glare at the back of Tam Lin's head and nowhere else, willing his blood to cool. "He forced himself on her."

"No one can force himself on Una, Ben."

That was *worse*. Kaer Yin cursed beneath his breath.

Tam Lin held out a hand. Shar and Niall moved forward to lay their trunks at Una's feet. Once opened, the crowd burst into excited titters and murmurs. They pressed forward to see the bounty. One chest overflowing with gold, silver, and myriad gems from Aes Sidhe. The other, bolts of brilliantly hued silks, satin, and gossamer. Bethany's ladies made appreciable, envious noises. As expected, Una gave another deep curtsy.

"I thank you, Your Highness. Never have I been so honored." Her eyes flicked to and held Rian's, welling with tears. She set a hand against her heart. Rian made a little sound that told Kaer Yin the sentiment was shared and squeezed his fingers anew.

"Steady on," Rian repeated. "There'll be time later."

Patrick seemed to rediscover his voice. Rubbing his hands together, he waved guards over to remove each trunk. "We are all honored to have you here, Your Highness. We accept these tokens and invite you to feast with us." Damek growled an inaudible rebuke, but Patrick shouldered him aside. "Please, avail yourselves of my Hall."

Tam Lin set his fingers to his temple in respect. "We thank you, Your Grace."

Patrick motioned for Tam Lin to follow him to the dais, offering the seat beside him. From the look on Damek's face as he watched them, he guessed that one had recently been his. Una took the next chair over, on Tam Lin's right. She poured a healthy dollop of mead into her cup and passed it to him— a sure indication of a lady's favor. Her other suitors would gnaw their tongues in envy. Lord Bishop certainly did.

Kaer Yin wanted to rip Damek's spine from his throat.

Tam Lin's entourage was shown to a table near the front of the Hall by the large, scarred man. Someone referred to him as 'Commander,' Tam Lin assumed the fellow to be Martin O'Rearden, Damek Bishop's first lieutenant. The fellow's crisscrossed brow spoke volumes. Rian relaxed a bit when she sank onto the bench beside Kaer Yin.

"Okay. The hard part's over. Keep your eyes down and look disinterested."

"I think ye've mucked that already, Ben," Robin coughed, glancing at the dais. "If looks could kill, ye'd melt on the spot." He indicated Damek, who hadn't stopped glaring Kaer Yin's way. "Not such a great fool as we'd like, I think."

"Doesn't matter," Rian said. "He can't prove it this second, can he? He won't risk making a scene in front of all the fine guests here tonight. The Duch needs their support. If all goes according to plan, we'll be long gone before he can make his move."

Robin twisted his lip at her. "Ye'd make a fine Greenmaker, girl. Ye know that?"

She grimaced. "Thanks, I guess."

"He means that as a compliment, Rian," grumbled Kaer Yin, trying not to look up into Damek's accusatory stare. Instead, he stole a furtive glance at Una and Tam Lin. Though she leaned close as if to listen to his conversation with the Duch, her eyes met his more than once. Relief and so much more radiated from her with each breath. He couldn't help but smile her way. *Soon*, his eyes told her.

With a snarl, Damek got up, knocking his chair backward. He held his goblet up. "My Lords and Ladies of Innisfail, may I propose a toast?"

Patrick's displeasure was plain. "You may not."

Damek ignored him. "To our grand overlords, in their fancy white armor... may you all rot." He drank deep, then threw the empty vessel at Kaer Yin's table.

"Martin," Patrick warned through his teeth. "Get him out of here."

Martin moved to haul him away, but Damek wrestled out of his bear-like grip. "You all might sit here in awe of the Adair's bloody kin, but I won't. Bootlickers, the lot of you."

Tam Lin threw back his head on a laugh and patted his chest. He got to his feet, Una's cup in hand. "Perhaps I've usurped someone's place at table? My apologies, *isasáeligh*." Damek sucked in a breath for the insult, which none but the Sidhe would grasp. "But I assumed we were welcome here?"

"You are," Patrick reaffirmed. "My nephew is merely drunk. My apologies."

"Good. I would hate to lose the favor of such a fine lady for such a paltry offense."

"You could never," flirted Una with gut-piercing sincerity.

Damek shrugged Martin off for a second time. He didn't linger any longer, save to point at Kaer Yin once. Kaer Yin's chin came up.

Anytime, his expression replied.

Without further ado, Damek Bishop stomped from the dais, trailing a horde of whispers in his wake.

HEAD AND HEART SPINNING, UNA CLIMBED THE STAIRS TOWARD HER chamber again, both weeping and laughing to herself. Belloch averted his eyes, no doubt believing she was either inebriated, or stark raving mad. Perhaps she was both? She cared less about what these people thought of her now than ever.

He's alive! screamed her heart, over and over.

Alive, all this time!

Her blood pounded the litany in her veins: *alive, alive, alive...* until she thought she might run wild. As usual, Damek had lied to her, and she foolishly believed him. Of course, he would tell her Kaer Yin died that horrible night. Knowing her as he did, Damek knew nothing would wound her more. She was too happy to waste one more thought on her cousin's duplicity. Absently, she scrubbed her mouth with the back of her hand.

NOT another bloody thought!

She heard Belloch apply the lock behind her when she slipped through her door. Patrick's orders. He'd say men are likely to be inspired by foolish notions. That was as well tonight— Kaer Yin was alive... nothing else mattered a whit to her, not even internment.

She leaned against the door, burying her smile in her hands.

The blow came out of nowhere.

She staggered forward, colliding with the nearest chair and taking it to the ground. Clutching her ringing ear, she struggled to push herself upright. Her assailant struck her again, spinning the world round her eyes.

"Whore!' accused a disembodied voice, buffeted by a strong hint of peppermint. Una gagged. Gloved hands tore her head back and down. She felt the press of a blade at her throat. "Disgusting, devil-fucking whore!" The edge bit down, but just enough to make her bleed. Belloch was a step outside the door. If she could suck in enough air, he would come crashing through with his sabre ready. A wet tear slid over her overheated cheek. It wasn't hers. "You choose *them* over your own kind?"

She knew that voice, that accent.

No, she wept inwardly.

It can't be.

"Micah?" she managed to squeeze out. Her attacker flinched; his knife hesitated. "Not you. Please, not you."

He snarled in her face, spittle dripping into her eyes. "Don't you dare attempt to beguile me now, you slut. I will make you pay for this."

His blade had yet to plunge through her flesh. His hands shook. Shoving her shock and revulsion aside, she slid her hand over his leather-encased fingers where they struggled with his blade. "Micah, this is not you. It can't be you."

He stifled a laugh, a dark, hideous sound. "Who else would it be? My deranged but feeble da? He can scarcely hobble through these halls, yet ye were so eager to accuse him. All he cares about is his Lord these days, or his grand mission to make me Duch. I don't care what that old fool does. He's nothin' to me."

"You... you tried to kill me, Micah. Why?"

His shadow shook its head. "No, not at first. Ye surprised me down there, s'all. Ye weren't 'sposed to be there, were ye?"

That was true. She struggled to swallow, drawing a trickle of blood down her throat. "Why do you want to hurt me now? We're friends, aren't we?"

"You want to fuck that unholy spirit, don't you," he gurgled through tears. The knife pressed deeper. "Battin' yer lashes for him like a bitch in heat. Ye was meant to be mine but thank god I'm stronger than me Da. Who would want a witch who fucks monsters, anyway?"

The knife began to separate the flesh at her throat. She had to keep him talking. "I am no whore, Micah. I have lain with one man, and he was my husband then. My father ordered me to entertain his guests. I had no choice but to smile."

He hesitated again, trembling. "Ye lie! I saw your face. Everyone in the Hall saw yer tears of joy. Watched as ye fawned over yer ex-husband first, then panted for the next comer with renewed vigor. Yer a vain, spoilt slattern!"

His blade slipped into her throat, just enough to tear a gasp from her chest. "Micah, no! I've asked my father for you! I want you too— don't you know that?"

He paused again. She reached for his damp cheek, but he jerked away. "Lying witch!" His knife bit into her soft flesh, slicing clean through to the floor. Not immediately fatal, perhaps, but immensely painful and likely bleed her like a sow in minutes. She cried out, drew one knee up, and jerked, forcing him to fumble sideways with a guttural shriek.

Her hand slammed over his brow before he could right himself. "*Burn,*" she hissed, though he broke contact too quickly for her Spark to take hold. He knocked her backward, slashing his knife against her wrist. The gash would be four inches wide if she weren't mistaken— it, too, would bleed her dry if unstaunched.

Wiggling sideways, she fumbled in the dark for something she might use as a weapon. Once her fingers came into contact with the leg of the upended chair, she attempted to drag it over. Unfortunately, she couldn't push herself upright far enough for the slick puddle of blood beneath her. She hit the tiles with a thud that knocked the wind from her chest.

"My Lady?" called Belloch from the other side of the door.

She opened her mouth to cry out, but a gloved hand slammed over the lower half of her face. "It's locked from the inside, cousin. He'll never break that door down in time." The banging and shouts outside didn't assuage her rising panic. Bleeding profusely as she was, without her Spark, and without a weapon... Micah was stronger than her, and they both knew it. She felt his free hand fumble with her skirts, tearing the fabric. Summoning all the tactile strength she could, she slammed the crown of her head into his nose. With a mewling screech, he broke contact, knife clattering to the flagstones.

Her hand closed over it, blade first.

Roaring, he rushed at her, half-impaling himself on his own knife. With a grunt, he shoved her off, leaving the weapon's tip in the meat of his shoulder. His fist crashed into her chin, cracking her head against the wall. She slipped downward, and he followed, dragging the knife out of his skin... readying to plunge it into her heart.

The blow never came.

A white hand snapped out of the shadows, catching Micah's wrist mid-strike. A pair of ruthless silver eyes flashed in the sliver of moonlight from the open window. "Not so vicious now, are we?" A sharp twist and Micah's scream rattled the casings. His wrist bent back about 90 degrees the wrong way. Kaer

Yin lifted him by the collar; the toes of Micah's boots barely dragged the floor. "Perhaps you should see your way out?"

Micah had a fleeting moment to gape at Una in surprise before Kaer Yin threw him through the open window one-handed. Her cousin's terrified shrieks could be heard for a long while, and then they abruptly stopped altogether.

Kaer Yin was at her side in a trice. One hand clamped over her throat while he tore off a piece of his tunic with the other. "Why are you *always* bleeding, Una? You're going to stop my heart one of these days." The banging at her door intensified. Shouts and screams flitted through her window with the cold ocean air. She held out her wrist while he wound shredded fabric around it. "You'll have to help me, quick. Press here. Good. Now, let's get you up." He set her gently against the wall, tearing and wrapping the second piece of cloth around her seeping throat. His face blurred a bit around the edges.

"Y-you're here," she croaked.

"You shouldn't talk."

"How?"

"Climbed through the window. Lucky too."

She winced when he pulled the fabric taught for a knot. "No, how are you... *here*?"

Through a haze of tears, she thought she saw him swallow. "I came for you, stupid. Who was that anyway?"

"My cousin."

He made a rude sound. "I just *love* your family, Una."

"He was going to kill me."

"Might have succeeded too, from the look of things."

She couldn't hear much over the pounding at the door. "You have to go. They can't find you here."

More guards clattered noisily up the stairs. The banging and clamor intensified.

Kaer Yin took a deep breath, moving closer. "I have to talk to you, ask you—"

"Yes," she responded without hesitation.

He blinked back. "I haven't even said— "

With more steam than she thought she had left, she pulled him to her by the hem of his tunic. Her mouth met his with a force she might be embarrassed by later. He had a heartbeat to sigh against her lips before she shoved him away.

"Whatever it is, my answer is yes. But you have to go, *right now*, before they kill you. You can't be seen with me... or anywhere." The door cracked and splintered while Kaer Yin's eyes devoured hers. Even bleeding and bruised, she'd never been happier in her life. He was alive, and he'd come for her. What more could she ask for? "Go."

"Una, I need to tell you—"

An axe blade burst through the center of the door. "My Lady!" roared Belloch.

"Tell me later... now get out of here, or you'll watch me puke."

He got to his feet, looking back at her from the open window. "Are you sure?"

She really *was* going to throw up. "Do you want me to say no?"

His answering smirk was infuriating as it was endearing. "I dare you to try now."

23
PRODIGAL SON

Henry watched them sew his firstborn into his shroud, boiling with a rage he could not quantify. There hadn't been enough fabric for the task at first, considering that Micah's body had been smashed and mangled so severely that his muscles and intestines had to be removed to make room. It took nearly three hours to gather Micah's remains from the crags below the South End. His son had been smashed against the rocks below the witch's tower as if he'd been a melon casually flung from the window—discarded like refuse.

Murdered, Henry wept internally.

Slain by a foreign whore on the eve of his ascension.

The coroner had yet to sew the heavy tarpaulin over Micah's remaining eye, which was still beautiful and clear as a spring sky. A knotted wad of formerly golden hair clung to the two inches of skull left above. The rest was a red and white waste: a mass of scrambled tissue, organ, and bone. The fall had removed

Micah's head from his spine, along with an arm and leg. Both now presumably lay at the bottom of the sea, washed away by relentless waves before the body could be recovered. All that remained was a broken husk of fluid and gristle. The coroner drew the tarpaulin tight over Micah's sightless eye, blotting it from view forever. Henry's hands shook. His gums ached around their dentures from clenching his jaw. He longed to wrap his fingers around his niece's throat and press his thumbs into her eyes. He craved revenge, as a starving man craves bread. He watched the needle wind in and out of the flat, white fabric and vowed an end to his brother's bloodline.

"Henry," came Patrick's voice from the open door. Henry didn't turn, though the fresh fury that traced through his heart burned the brighter for his presence. "You shouldn't be here."

"My son is here, so must I be."

Patrick shuffled inside, breathing labored. He came to a stop at Henry's side.

Henry spared him a single glance. "You look like shite, Patrick."

Patrick's gnarled, sweating fingers seized Henry's forearm. "Leave the coroner to his task, brother. Come away."

"Take your hand from me, or I swear to God, you'll lose it," rumbled Henry, facing resolutely forward. He refused to sully his eyes with this lying, manipulative bastard. "My son is dead. Slain by your whorish daughter. I do not heed the demands of the damned."

The chamber rang with drawing steel, but not from Patrick's guards. Tonight, Henry had his own. Lords Harrington, Coltrap, and Murphy drew their weapons. The Duch's guardsmen responded, but Patrick raised his hands. "Stop. This is not necessary. My Lords, I respect the sentiments that urge you to defend my brother in this tragedy, but I implore you to reconsider before it kills you and your men and strips your families of their livelihood."

Each man hesitated, as Patrick surely knew they would. Henry perceived all of this humorlessly. "Even now, you'd haggle for power?"

"If they draw against their Duch, that is treason."

Henry held up a hand, and they sheathed their sabres. "Why have you come here?"

Patrick exhaled long and hard. "Micah was killed in an attempt on Una's life. Please don't make this worse in misunderstanding, Henry."

"You say *my son*, a boy who wouldn't harm an insect for biting, attempted to harm your worthless daughter? *Lies.* You're a bloody liar, Patrick, and you'll pay for it." Patrick's guards raised their weapons, though more of Henry's followers filtered into the gatehouse, bearing candles in one hand and the pommels of their daggers or sabres in the other. Henry was pleased to note Patrick's surprise. Did he take the smallest step backward? "How dare you come here, slinging accusations while my boy lays here in pieces. In *pieces*, Patrick!"

The examination chamber sat at the far edge of the gatehouse, near the inner portcullis, a much more public venue than Patrick would have preferred. Passersby from various clans and states paused in the courtyard outside or in the hall at the Keep's entrance. Patrick licked his dried, flaking lips. "If we may speak in private?"

"No. Our people saw what your precious daughter did to me in full view of everyone. She is a vicious bitch, unfit to bear my father's name. God will grant me justice."

"That son broke into my daughter's chamber and tried to cut her throat. He very nearly succeeded. She bears the wounds now. You're telling me she did that to herself?" he raised his voice. "Your sweet, golden-haired boy butchered seven girls beneath my roof, Henry. We've already been through his chamber. He kept mementos from each of his victims and made drawings I will see in my sleep. Everywhere in his room, the signs were there if we had thought to look. I would've strung him from the walls tomorrow if he hadn't fallen from an open window tonight. How do you feel *now*, brother? Knowing that you raised a monster?"

As if he'd been physically cut, Henry staggered forward. "Lying dog! You dare—"

"It is no lie," Patrick raised his voice so onlookers could not mistake his words. "Micah *Fitz* Donahugh was a rapist and murderer. The proof was recorded in his own hand, even if he hadn't perished in an attempt on my child. Your son, your shame, Henry."

The gatehouse tilted on its axis, and Henry felt himself tumble into its vortex.

Could it be true?

Snippets of memory flashed through his mind at once. Micah running through a field, chasing a pup. Micah in the barn, holding a dead hen. Did he smile? Micah giggling as his father hefted him high. Micah drawing the tip of a dagger across his finger, fascinated. Micah reading his bible— such a clear, calm voice. Micah kissing his mother's gaunt cheek. Micah whipping his pony with the blade of his father's rusted sword.

Henry choked.

Could it be true?

Patrick's sigh was less resigned than pained. "Take him into custody."

Henry fought, gripping the edge of Micah's slab to stall the inevitable. Micah's remaining shoulder was bared to all and sundry in the tussle. Significant scratches— fingernails, no doubt— appeared, half-healed over this exposed flesh. Henry wailed and tried to wrap his hands over the spot. Patrick tore his fingers away.

"There, you see. These have faded, Henry, but there are more yet unhealed below. Every one of the girls he killed had fought for her life and fought hard, it seems."

"No," blubbered Henry. "Not Micah. Not my son. My perfect son."

Patrick waved him away. "I will hear no more of this."

As he was hauled back into the Keep, Henry's shrieks reverberated through the courtyard. His followers backed away at Patrick's advance. "Arrest any who don't disperse immediately," he ordered his guards. Though they retreated, Henry's congregation did so with eyes full of hate and self-righteous judgment.

The last through the portcullis gave him a cold smile.

Despite the men at his back, Patrick was unsettled.

He looked around at the gathering onlookers and realized the impressions he elicited were far from sympathetic. The whispers came next.

Heretic, he caught more than once.

Kinslayer was loudest.

Ignoring them, Patrick turned to the coroner as he resumed his work. "When shall he be ready for burial?"

"This morning, My Lord."

"Excellent. See to it. No fuss or pomp. He's already done enough damage."

"Yes, milord," the coroner agreed.

Patrick turned and strode toward the Keep with Shanley and his guards trailing in his wake. Courtiers and visitors moved aside for the Duch, but many expressions bore silent reproach. Patrick's guts knotted. Holding his breath, he strode through the hall toward his private apartments, with his spine as straight as it could reasonably go. By the time they crossed the inner arch, he doubled over, huffing and groaning. The pain was unimaginable.

"Your Grace!" cried Shanley, rushing to his side.

Patrick leaned against the balustrade and retched into the dark hollow beneath the staircase. White stars clawed at his vision as he vomited, his throat molten hot. When it was over, he slouched against the railing, held upright by Shanley and a nameless guard. He couldn't help but notice that the pile of fluid that he had expelled was naught but blood and foam. Though the dragon in his guts had settled down, the ice in his veins soon took its place. He shook, feeling empty and heavy at once.

"Help me get him to his chambers!" Shanley demanded from his guards, but Patrick's hand squeezed his elbow hard.

"*No*," he struggled to say. "Take me to my daughter."

"But My Lord—"

"Shanley... remember when I asked you how martyrs were made?"

Realization crossed the haggard fellow's beady eyes. "Yes, Your Grace. I do."

"Unless you want to empower my brother, I suggest you do as I say."

As Shanley helped him up, the lightheadedness struck. Patrick took a deep breath and willed it down.

So soon?

He clamped down on his jaw rather than give in.

Not now, damn you.

Not bloody now!

"Sprout," came her father's voice from the dark.

Una opened her eyes. The room was poorly lit, but she could see him smiling ruefully down at her. He looked... "What's wrong?"

She tried to sit up, but he gently pushed her back against her pillow with a shaking palm. "You're the one who's nearly been murdered for a second time, and you'd worry about an old meddler like me? I'm touched, daughter."

He did look terrible. Was that blood around his mouth?

"What's happening?"

"Micah's dead."

"I know," she rasped. It hurt like the Hells to talk.

"Did you kill him?"

She gave him a long look. "No, though I wish I had."

"Me too." He pinched the bridge of his nose with quivering fingers. "He's here, isn't he?"

"Who?"

"Una, don't play with me now. You have to know what a terrible mess this will become. Henry is an influential man. His followers plot revenge as we speak. If I hadn't had my Corpsmen around me minutes ago, you might already be strapped to a pyre."

"Me?" she inhaled and did sit up, though it pained her to do so. "Micah was a murderer, father. He killed all those women... he... did *all* of that." Her voice cracked a bit.

She had liked her fair cousin a great deal.

Patrick's sigh sounded wet and tired. "I realize that I've outsmarted myself. I've made a terrible mistake that I will regret for this time that I have left."

She'd never heard him say such things. Never heard him admit to being wrong, either. "What do you mean?"

"I thought to leave a parting gift before I shed this mortal coil, something that would remind our overlords that even immortals may bleed."

Unsure exactly what he was talking about, she *did* have an inkling of what his 'parting gift' would be. "The Kneelers?"

"Sharp one, you are." He beamed; his cheeks were chalk white. "I'm dying. I won't last the week if my surgeons speak truly."

A bottomless well of contradictory emotions opened at her center, rushing into her eyes, mouth, and nose. Patrick made a face, patting her hand. "There now. We weren't always enemies, eh, Sprout? Somewhere in there is that little girl who used to weave my beard with flowers and charge *papier maché* knights with her old man. You were the one thing I ever loved in this world, Una."

She couldn't see anything anymore. She swiped at her eyes with her unbandaged hand. "Nonsense. You can't die. Everyone knows Souther physicians are little better than barbers. Get a second opinion."

The whimsical, earnest expression on his face burrowed into her ribs. *He's joking, right? Dying... it's a ruse of some sort.*

Yet, his cheeks were gaunt, and the flesh beneath his eyes was all but black. There was a rattle to his breath she couldn't recall hearing before. What would the world look like without Patrick Donahugh?

She began to cry.

Patrick took a seat beside her and wound an arm around her shoulders. "There now. I haven't been the best father, I admit freely."

Angrily, she scrubbed the tears from her face. "That's an understatement."

"I should never have given you to each other, so young. I had never been in love, you understand. I had no idea the damage it could do."

She absorbed that in silence for a while. She supposed that was as close to an apology as she might ever get. "Your granddaughter would have been about twelve now."

Patrick's chest shook a bit against her back.

"She would have been an empress, wouldn't she?"

Was he *weeping*?

So... Patrick Donahugh has a heart, after all?

She choked back a fountain of anguish. "She might have been."

"You were too young," he heaved a clumsy sob. "I did what I must to protect you."

"You poisoned me. You robbed me of my child. Who could forgive such a bestial act?"

He went quiet for a while, with his nose at her brow. To the touch, his skin felt like a thin scrap of parchment stretched over ice. "I've made many blunders in my time, Una. That wasn't even the worst, though it's the one I regret most."

She took her time to respond. The oily knot of grief at her core unwound itself ever so slightly. "We have all made mistakes, father. I am no exception."

Patrick wiped his face and gave a dry laugh. "Old rivers, ruined bridges."

"Something like that," she settled.

He squeezed her shoulder a bit. "He's come for you, hasn't he?"

She said nothing.

"Damek loves you, you know?"

"I know."

"He'll never stop fighting for you, no matter whom you choose."

"I know," her voice broke. "I can't... not after...."

"I understand, but... give it time. As they say, it heals all wounds."

"Not this wound."

He chortled. It was a frail sound. "Perhaps. I think we have more immediate fires to douse."

"Henry?"

He nodded.

"Where do you think Micah learned—"

"I know."

She studied his profile in silence. "You fear his following is too great? That he'll stage a coup?"

"I imagine it has already begun. I never expected to hand him such fuel as a dead son. If I'd known, I never—"

"How many men does he have?"

"Hundreds, maybe. Micah's death won many more to his side."

"Powerful men, too?"

"Some of them, very powerful."

Her heart pounded against her ribs. "He'll try to overthrow you because of me?"

"He planned to overthrow me from birth, girl. Now, he'll use the death of his worthless spawn as an excuse. You have little to do with it save to serve as his scapegoat."

Hadn't this been the story of her life?

Would she ever be free of the burdens she placed upon others?

Free yourself, Una, whispered a rich, beautiful voice in her memory.

She shivered.

"When will it happen?"

"Tomorrow, I expect. He'll strike while the iron is hot."

"Damek won't let it happen."

Patrick made a face. "Damek isn't here. I have men out searching, but there's no telling where he might have gone to drown his sorrows."

My fault, she knew.

What wasn't, anymore?

"I'll ask you again, is he here, now?" Patrick persisted.

Una met his eyes. "I don't know."

He scoffed at the lie. "For your sake, I hope he is." With a feeble hand, he slapped his knee. "How embarrassing I might lose my throne in front of such illustrious company." He rose, reaching for and buoying himself against Shanley's arm. "But we won't make it easy for them, will we? Shanley will see to it that your guards are doubled for the night. In the morning, may I ask you for one last farce, daughter?"

Her chest felt raked from the inside.

She remembered a time when she loved this ruin of a man.

"Of course."

"That's my girl," he said. Shanley got him partway to the door when he paused and turned back. In the candlelight, the grooves of his face seemed skeletal. "Do you choose him?"

Una weighed the urge for pretense and found it wanting. "Yes."

The coughing fit he entered into held laughter. "Good. Then you have my blessing, such as it is. If we survive tomorrow, maybe I'll get to meet him?" He tilted his head. "Kaer Yin Adair. Of all the men in the world, you choose the most infamous. I suppose it's fitting, isn't it?"

He limped through the door.

Her voice caught him in the hall.

"Did you kill my mother, Patrick?"

He stood there in Shanley's grip so long that she thought he might have fallen asleep. When he spoke again, his tone held genuine regret. "She plotted with Henry to overthrow me."

"Is that an answer?"

"I wish I knew," he replied sadly.

24
MARTYRS

Gods, he felt like hammered shite. The new girl did her best to keep his bollocks dry as Alba, but no amount of fleeting pleasure could calm the rage, emptiness, and mourning that surged through his veins at each reprieve. Even now, with her wide hips swinging over his, he couldn't summon the least enthusiasm for anything. His body responded, sure; when had it ever failed him in that respect?

Never.

His mind was the poison, armed with carnivorous thoughts that couldn't be satiated, no matter the device. The girl, her brown skin shining like polished ochre in the lantern light, her spine curving like a taut bowstring, was not enough. Her hair was the right texture, if not the right glorious shade. Her mouth was too large, breasts too full. If he closed his eyes just so and consumed enough uishge straight from the bottle— almost there. He'd been furious, bleary-eyed, sodding drunk for nearly twelve hours, and he could not catch his fill. For the dozenth time in as many hours, he ground her rump into his sex in a ruthless, near painful rhythm. When her lips met his with a contented purr, he tried and failed to imagine they were the ones he craved. She gripped him internally, throwing her head back on a series of raucous moans. When he could no longer contain himself, she dismounted, then leaned down and allowed him to grip her hair as he finished deep in her throat. After, he lay back against the headboard while she opened another bottle. He took a drink, then another, before wedging the bottle against the curve of her sinuous thigh.

She smiled against his chest, and he stirred anew. "You're insatiable, My Lord," she giggled, running her fingertips over his crown. The offending organ was quite sore after such rough use, but uishge had only ever seemed to make him want more. "Do I look a lot like her, your lady?"

His eyes drifted closed as her palms plied their trade. "Not really."

"Shame. She must be quite something to inspire such desire."

Her fingers closed into a fist over his length, and he grunted. "She is."

"What do you want to do to her, My Lord?" She moved his hand to her hip, dislodging the bottle, which spilled between her thighs. His fingers followed. "Do you want to fuck her, My Lord... or taste her?"

He made a low sound.

When Martin burst through the door a few moments later, Damek had to frown at him from between the lady's legs. "Martin? The fuck you doing—"

The girl, ever the professional, slipped from the bed with a ladylike sniff, taking the coverlet with her into the dressing room. Damek groaned, lying face-down on the mattress, his bare arse in the air. "You're not invited, damn you. Get out."

Shaking his head, Martin kicked the mattress once, hard. Damek spilled onto the carpet below, sputtering. "The *fuck* you do that for?"

"You are shite-stinking drunk, your lordship... and you've got business at the palace. Get up, or I'll drag you home like this." Martin was a large man. Much larger than most men. Sober, Damek might have had the better of him— in his present state, not in the least. Martin had his tunic over his head and was already jerking on his breeches before Damek could figure out which way his arse was even pointed. "Been here for most of a damned day, My Lord! Had half the palace guard out looking for you, your uncle in a lather even the Gods have not seen."

"So what? I want to stay here."

Martin snorted as he fumbled to buckle Damek's swordbelt. "Aye, I'll bet. Playing pretend like a little boy while your lady endures at home. Some noble gent, you are."

Damek pinched the bridge of his nose, willing the floor to stop rolling beneath his heels. He was developing quite a spectacular headache. Martin smacked him upright, then leaned down to help Damek into his boots. "She hates me, Martin. It's no use."

Martin glanced up. "If you fucking cry right now, I'll spare her the trouble and slit your throat myself! Now, push down here." He moved to the next boot. "Of course, she hates you. You're an ambitious, womanizing, manipulative little shit, Lord Bishop. You deserve every ounce of her ire."

"I know. I *do*."

"I mean it, boy, if you shed a tear in my presence, I'll rip off your jaw. Man up, damn you."

"Martin, remember who you're talkin' to." Damek shrugged away from the wall and toppled straight into Martin's barrel chest.

"That's the spirit, My Lord," sighed Martin, shaking his head.

Broad daylight greeted them when they emerged from the tunnel below the inner bailey and into the courtyard. Soldiers milled about in every direction, not all of them Bethonair Corpsmen. Servants darted to and fro like small missiles seeking various targets at once.

One nearly ran Damek down on his way past.

"The hell is happenin' here?" he slurred. Martin gave him an uncomfortable look but said nothing. Instead, he led him through the courtyard and Great Hall, all the way to the rear stairwell that wound toward the royal family's apartments. Una would be on the top floor. She was probably dressing for another day of flirtation with the bloody prince of Connaught. Damek's stomach churned.

"There was an incident here last night. I've been looking for you since midnight." They were up the stairs before Damek could properly absorb this statement.

Martin cursed to discover a flurry of activity on the second floor. Damek dangled from his arm like a loose sack of turnips, reeking of stale uishge, dried vomit, and sex. Shanley paced at the top of the stairs, wringing his already chapped hands. He nearly wept aloud when he caught sight of them. "Thank Reason, you found him!"

"My lord was... ah, dicing," lied Martin, badly.

Shanley seemed too preoccupied to notice. "His grace will be relieved."

"Where is he?" demanded Martin.

"In his quarters. He's due to hold Court in an hour. Were your men able to locate our quarry?"

Damek shook himself semi-straight, suddenly curious. "Who else are you searching for?" Watching the shadow cross Martin's face, Damek croaked, "What happened?"

"He doesn't know?" Shanley wheezed incredulously, clenching his hands together so tightly that his knuckles bleached white. He opened his mouth to speak again, but Martin dragged Damek aside, waving a dismissive hand.

"I'll explain. Inform His Grace that we'll be ready in fifteen minutes. My Corpsmen have already taken position by the Northern Gate."

Shanley bowed once and dashed off. His slip-shod gait echoed through the hall for some time. Meanwhile, Martin dragged Damek toward his chamber door.

"Martin, what's going on?"

"Henry's escaped. He and about three dozen of his more powerful converts, I might add. Those men have soldiers and resources. Not to mention the people outside in the city." He gave a rough laugh. "It's Cromnasa. The streets are packed with revelers, aren't they?"

Confused, Damek clapped a hand over Martin's shoulder once the door closed. Inside, the fires had already been lit by some dutiful servant. His waiting armor glinted from its stand, oiled and ready. Hisk stood beside it. Cortram, the squire, waited by the larder with a bowl full of water, black tea, and a clean tunic.

So, he'd missed quite a bit. "Tell me."

Martin inhaled slowly. "Micah's dead. He tried to murder Una last night, after the feast. He was waiting for her in her bedchamber. Damek, he cut her throat."

The hand Damek draped over Martin's shoulder became a fist. The world spun ruby-red at the edges.

"*What*? Is she... you said, '*tried to*?'"

Martin backed into the door so Damek couldn't tear it from its hinges. "She's alive, fought him off, and somehow, Micah fell from her window."

Damek backed away, rubbing his face. "Where is she now?"

"She's fine. I vow it."

Godsdamnit... while he'd been fucking and drinking himself into a self-pitying stupor, Una had nearly been killed. There wasn't a hole deep or dark enough to crawl into from which he could hide from such guilt. Instead, he let fury take up the charge. It seeped through his blood with slow-simmering heat.

"Micah?"

The disgust on Martin's face was palpable. "Had the blood of a half-dozen women on his hands already. I hope the Gods see he's arse-raped every night in Tech Duinn," he spat. "It's Henry we must worry about now."

"Cortram, water," Damek demanded. While he availed himself of the cup that was passed over, his mind raced through half a dozen scenarios at once. "How many followers does Henry have?"

"Enough to be a problem. Worse, we have no idea where they are or how many are already within these walls. It's going to get ugly, Damek. There could be fighting in the halls."

"With so many guests, it'll be impossible to search everywhere." Damek removed his soiled tunic and scrubbed his face in the basin Cortram guarded. Once done, he dried himself and reached for a clean shirt. "Why is Patrick holding Court rather than dealing with this as he should be?"

"Appearances. As you said, many powerful people are here for your uncle's fête. The fewer that know his nephew was a murdering brute, the better. Yet, Henry will take it upon himself to martyr the boy anyway. Without a trial, it would appear Una is a kinslayer. This will bolster Henry's argument."

"We have the Corps. Henry has a few old men, women, and peasants. What can he do but make noise?" interjected Hisk, a clever man to be sure but not clever enough.

"If I were Henry, I would accuse her in open Court. Demand a trial. In front of so many of his barons, Patrick could never refuse. Where is his son? The other one?" responded Damek.

"Also missing, My Lord."

"Then we must find Isaac before Henry can make his move." Damek shrugged his breastplate on. He met Martin's eyes over Cortram's head. "Move Una somewhere else. Somewhere no one knows about and do it fast. The

Prince of Croghan is a ruse; the bastard's come for her. You know whom I'm talking about." Martin shifted uncomfortably. Damek growled, "What?"

"Against my advice, the Duch wanted Una close... in case. She sits in Court with him today. To maintain appearances."

The room shrank around Damek's ears. "Nevermind searching. I know exactly where Henry will turn up. Get our infantry to every gate, our Corpsmen at every exit in the Keep, and our officers to the Great Hall. Hisk? Gather Castor and the Bretagn contingency. I would have them meet me in the throne room."

"My lord," Hisk saluted as he took his leave.

Damek strapped on his vambraces. Martin waited with his sword. "How many men do we have, Martin?"

"Inside the walls? Two hundred."

"That should be plenty if we're quick."

Taking and sliding his sabre into his scabbard, Damek looked up, eyes wild. "Where are the Sidhe?"

"One problem at a time, My Lord."

UNA HAD FELT BETTER, THAT WAS SURE. WEARING A HIGH COLLAR AND long sleeves so no one would detect her wounds, she sat beside Patrick on the dais, trying not to sweat. Truth be told, she wasn't doing that great a job. Her Spark was a versatile tool, but even Siora's blessings took time to recharge. She hadn't slept, eaten, or taken anything for the pain, of which there was plenty. Micah had sliced through nearly two inches of flesh midway between her collarbone and jugular. Though she no longer bled like a gutted fish, the broken capillaries and lacerated tissues wouldn't heal so easily.

She *should* have been abed for a while yet, but Patrick had insisted.

The façade would make or break them now.

She stole a glance at him from the corner of her eye. At least she wasn't suffering alone. Her father looked grey round the edges, himself. Had he somehow managed to lose more weight in one night? The hollows under his eyes looked carved in, and his skin bore an unhealthy, limpid pallor. Indeed, she couldn't be sure which of them was in worse straits. Without disturbing the land dispute being argued before the Court, she leaned over to whisper, "Are you all right?"

Patrick gave her a tight smile. "Of course, I am."

"You don't seem to be."

He scanned the crowd to be sure no one overheard them. "We must keep order. The fewer people know what happened here last night, the better."

Una worried her nails, feeling weak and helpless. Across the room, Rian's blue eyes met hers in nervous fear. Tam Lin, behind her, chatted amiably with several women. His closest attendant stood beside him, with one or two others—no sign of Kaer Yin.

Though the Great Hall had been cleared of benches and tables, many of last night's Cromnasa decorations remained in advance of the anticipated final feast. Una certainly didn't feel up to more festivities, and from the looks of everyone else, her reticence was shared. Most of the courtiers gathered to either side of the large scarlet, and cobalt carpet that divided the room appeared as sober and fearful as she.

The day's grim reality was not lost on anyone.

"This is foolish. Micah was a murderer. He died trying to do the same to me for the second time. Declare it. Who cares about my reputation?"

"I couldn't toss a fig for your reputation right now, girl. This is bigger than you or I. Henry has support from among my barons, much more than I ever intended that he should. Until he and Isaac are found, he's a threat. It's better to maintain the appearance of order."

"How many men could he muster in so little time?"

"How many are here with us in this room now, child? Every one of my barons has soldiers within and without these walls. Given the opportune chaos Cromnasa affords, even one could be critical."

"What about *our* men? Aren't we armed and ready too?"

Patrick's head swiveled toward her. "Did you say, 'our men?'"

She flushed. "The Corps is in here with us, hundreds more than any of your barons could summon in time. Henry has no chance."

"He wouldn't have fled his cell if he didn't believe he had one. I know my brother, and I know his tactics. He'll be here soon."

"Here?" she asked, a little too loudly. She gave the crowd a nervous smile and settled back into her seat. "Why here?"

"To plead his case before those in power."

"*You're* in power, Patrick."

He shook his head. "Power like mine is an illusion. I need others to believe in my right to rule for it to hold. Accusing me publicly will earn the division he needs to cull my support. I expect he'll demand your life in return for his son's. I will refuse, and my barons will decide my fate."

A slow, creeping panic inched along her skin.

"Then we should leave, now!"

Suddenly sweating and shaking like a leaf, Patrick reached over and clasped her hand. "*We*," he placed intense emphasis upon the word, "have something he doesn't. *You*, and Damek."

She absorbed this, brows knitting together. "Why did you set him free in the first place, father? He's brought nothing but trouble."

He coughed and clutched at his gut. "For the Sidhe, of course. If my plans should falter, if the worst should happen… they will pay for it. Faith will exact my vengeance if strength of arms should fail." His attention drifted in Tam Lin O'Ruiadh's direction, though his eyes glazed over. Alarmed, Una touched his shoulder. Even through his clothing, his skin was burning hot to the touch. She inhaled sharply.

"You're ill!"

He patted her hand. "I'll be fine. Wait for Damek, Una. He knows my mind." But his pallor grew worse by the moment, his breathing more labored. While the two farmers made their case before the Court clerks, Una looked around for help. She didn't see a single friendly face, save for Rian's. A wordless plea passed between them. One of the Sidhe Una had never met, a fellow with bright green eyes and six silver chains, helped her through the crowd toward the dais. They were right on cue. Suddenly, Patrick doubled over with a violent groan, vomiting blood down the steps. The Court fell silent, save for Patrick's uncontrollable retching. Una dropped to her knees beside her father while he writhed against the carpet.

A guard stepped forward to block Rian's ascent, but Una cried, "Let her through, damn you!" He stepped aside. Watching Patrick convulse, tears sprang to Una's eyes. "Do something!" she begged Rian.

The faerie took command immediately. "You there," she demanded of a guardsman. "Help me get him out of here!"

Una, Rian, and three guards had him halfway lifted when the door burst open upon the Court. Henry and a dozen armed men stalked inside. He wore a habit black as pitch and a scowl that could carve stone. He moved forward with purpose, his eyes blazing. None could miss Patrick and Una on the dais steps amid a growing pool of blood and bile. Henry's finger came up like a spear aiming for Una's heart.

"*Witch*!" he exclaimed.

Around him, the courtiers were taken aback. People moved out of his way, aghast and outnumbered. Una met the inferno of his gaze with a raised but trembling chin. "Guards. That man is not to take another step forward." The guards answered by drawing their sabres and taking defensive positions around their fallen lord and his daughter.

Henry raised his hands. His men fanned out behind him, weapons ready. "You murdered my son! I'll see you burn for this, whore of Babylon!"

Coughing, Patrick slapped his hand against the stair to push himself upward. Blood and other things stained his mouth and nose. His eyes were nearly black.

Surprised, Henry took a faltering step back.

"Y-you!" struggled Patrick. "Your son was the mu-murderer. He tried to slay my daughter in her bed. He was rightfully killed for his treachery."

Rian dug her nails into Una's arm. "I can't treat him here, Una. We have to move him. Now!"

At first, Henry gawped at his younger brother, bleeding all over his dais... but that didn't last. Una watched a slow, smug smile drag his wormy mouth wide. "She's attempting to slay her father too! *Poisoner*! Stop her!"

A courtier moved forward to grab her arm, but one of her guards slammed the butt of his pommel into his temple, and he crumpled to the floor. That seemed to inspire Henry. He turned, raising his empty hands to the gathered noblemen. "Quick! Someone stop her and her faerie accomplice before we lose the Duch!"

"Liar!" Una hissed. "Your precious son slaughtered seven girls under my father's roof. *You* made that happen. Your example."

Her guards shoved people backward. The situation plummeted from there. Something heavy grazed her chest, and she grunted in pain. Rian tried to raise her voice to be heard, but Henry's drowned her out. "Murderess! Stop her, STOP HER!"

For a brief moment, no longer than the span of a wingbeat, Patrick set his hand against her cheek. "Too late. I f-failed. *Go*... and *forgive* me."

She gritted her teeth. "Get him up! Help me!"

The Court had devolved into chaos. Her guards made an admirable show of strength, but the crowd was so busy tearing into one another what they were pitted against mattered very little in the end. Someone's booted foot nearly connected with Una's jaw, but a large shape grabbed the fellow mid-leap and threw him bodily over the dais: Tam Lin O'Ruiadh, prince of Connaught, no less. His Sidhe warriors spread out at the base of the infamous relief of Kaer Yin Adair, striking her ancestor down. He held out a hand for her.

"My Lady. It's time to leave, I think."

"Not without him!" She gripped Patrick's gore-painted tunic. But where his skin had been warm, now it was cold. She looked down. His empty grey eyes were fixed on the ceiling, clouded and sightless.

A long, low scream built in her throat.

Rian's fingers found her shaking shoulder. "Una. There's nothing we can do."

A bone-rattling sob escaped Una's lips. She shook her head. "No! No. He's fine. He'll be fine. We need to get him—"

Henry howled into the sea of writhing, angry people. A chair struck the wall above them and shattered the stained glass. Thousands of shards rained down upon them. Tam Lin held his cloak over the girls while another series of screams pierced the air.

"Rian!" he shouted. "Drag her if you have to! More are coming."

But it wasn't Rian's hands that pried her away from her father. Kicking and screaming, Una was carried up and away from the violence. She fought with everything she had left, but he was stronger.

He was always stronger.

"Hush now, love," Kaer Yin whispered into her hair. "It's over now. We're going home."

25
BLACK KNIGHT RISING

Damek heard Henry's shrill, contemptuous voice long before he saw him. The halls bore signs of a sudden, violent skirmish. Large, gilded frames bearing important faces from Bethany's past lay torn or smashed in limp heaps at either stone wall. Sconces and candelabra had been upended or smashed, some leaving great smoke stains over the fine Bretagn carpets below. Bedraggled courtiers with stricken features and shredded clothing gripped each other in fear as they shuffled past Damek's men. The two mahogany doors Duch Kevin had carved for the Keep hung askew from their hinges like flags at half-mast. A stalemate of sorts had been brokered through the breach, though the shouting and general discord had not. Not yet. As Douglas and Hisk pushed through the doors, shoving people and debris aside like so much dross, Damek followed Martin into Patrick's courtroom, sword in hand. The room was a disaster. Broken glass was everywhere; blood coalesced beneath victims forgotten and trampled on the floor by dozens of feet that had now pulled into either corner to rail abuse at one another. Henry and his black-clothed followers had taken the dais and the door to Patrick's apartments, Damek noticed. The others, Patrick's loyal barons and friends, occupied a much smaller space near the exit. Damek scanned the room furiously, searching for the one sight that would condemn the man who stood before the throne. Finally, he found him.

Patrick lay on the steps in a bloodied heap.

He did not move, not even when Henry's booted foot trod over him.

Dead, Damek's blood sang with rage.

Dead and discarded, like a forgotten toy.

He felt a surge of pity commingled with loathing and disappointed hope.

Even a pillar must someday fall, lad, Patrick had said once. *Only our ideas live on.*

Nostrils flaring, Damek glanced at Martin, whose face was hardly dry.

"Kill any man that dares lay a hand, or foot, on your Duch."

"With pleasure," choked Martin.

Henry looked down, his mad red face full of unblinking black eyes. "*YOU!*" His followers— and there were many— turned to greet the newcomers with weapons high. Some filtered out of Patrick's private apartments, three here, four there, until the dais nearly swarmed with black-cloaked zealots. Henry's victorious smirk set fire to Damek's throat. "Come late, it seems! Your lord has been murdered, and your wife fled with Norther devils! Where were *you* when she mixed the brew that slew your uncle?"

Damek waved a hand, and his armored corpsmen took flanking positions around him. The light of whatever righteous horseshite they believed shone from Henry's supporters' eyes. Nevertheless, the gleam of all that steel surely began to sink in. Some visibly hesitated, and some backed away in cowardice. Others, well, their zeal burned bright as bloodlust. So be it. Damek vowed they would be first to feel his wrath.

"That's how you intend to spin this? Una is supposed to have murdered her father?" Damek gave a short, barking laugh. "For what possible reason?"

"Witches need no reason to do evil. They are Satan's playthings."

"So too, are old men chewed up by envy, greed, and ambition, like yourself."

Henry gave him a grin full of wooden teeth. "Have you come to plead her case before the Court, nephew? This slut who spurns you, even now?"

Damek glanced around. "*Whose* Court? The man who rules this land is dead. I would advise you to remove yourself and your grievances from this chamber while I am asking nicely."

Damek's great-uncle, Lord Bishop, cackled from the rear doorway. "Who do you imagine you are to speak to a son of Duch Michael that way, boy?"

From nine paces away, Martin drew his dagger and flung it into the scabrous old fool's throat. As the old traitor sagged to the floor, the crowd gasped as one. Martin swept his sabre in a wide arc, encompassing the room at large. His blue eyes were wild with grief and anger. "The next man that *dares* insult my Duch will die by my hand. Patrick Donahugh is dead... long live Duch Damek *Donahugh*!"

Damek's Corpsmen took up the chant.

Henry threw back his head and laughed until his eyes misted over. "Oh, that's rich! *You*, a faerie bastard, Duch? Never. Not one baron here will support you."

Martin took a threatening step forward, but Damek's hand caught his elbow. He looked behind him at Patrick's loyal retainers. Many visibly supported him. Some looked away. *No matter.* "I think you'll find, uncle dear, he who controls the army controls the nation. Una is the rightful ruler here, and until she is found, *I am* your liege lord."

"Una murdered her father in cold blood and fled this hall to escape justice. We stood here while she took his life! We saw her do it! None would see a murderous foreign whore take up Patrick's throne." Here, he sneered. "Neither would we seek to vaunt her faithful cuckold. There is a sole, trueborn choice to take the throne. Isaac Donahugh will be Duch!"

His supporters cheered so loud that Damek's ears popped. Were there more of them now, filing through Patrick's apartments and over Lord Bishop's corpse to drown the few loyalists in a sea of black? Martin shot a nervous glance over his shoulder. The courtiers began ducking out. Less than a handful stood to watch the proceedings.

"Damek," Martin warned. "We're outnumbered."

Damek shrugged him off and stalked forward until the vambraces at his shins brushed the bloodied furs at Patrick's collar. In death, he was so much smaller than he had been in life. "Do you think this rabble is a match for my men, Henry?"

"Your worthless wife murdered my firstborn before murdering my brother. None of us will *ever* bow to her."

"Murdered Micah, you say?" Damek cocked his head.

"*Yes*," Henry slavered, gone puce.

"That would be rather virtuous of her if she had. Considering your son was the creature responsible for the brutal deaths of several girls within this very Keep."

"You lie! Micah would never—"

"Oh, I'm sorry. Did you think I, like the simpletons behind you, would take your word on the matter? Douglas?" While Henry struggled for an appropriate insult, Douglas stepped forward to upend a box of items at the bottom stair. A journal flapped open with crude drawings of the female anatomy as it would appear if sawed into with a broad blade. Hanks of bloodied hair tied off with red ribbons fluttered to join several sexually explicit instruments and figurines. Henry lurched away like the pile had slithered forward to touch him. Damek stooped to pick up two separate bits of paper. One was a poorly rewritten verse from Callaghan's *Seasons of Transition*, bearing Micah's name and writing. The other was a journal page detailing the names of several women, Una's included. The text was hastily scribbled and repetitive in furious knife-slashing relief. "This is your son's handwriting, is it not?"

Henry said nothing.

Damek passed the pages to the battered loyalists in the room's rear. When he returned, Henry seemed to have collected himself. "This proves nothing. My son did not write any of this."

"No? Douglas, where were these found?"

"In Micah Fitz Donahugh's quarters, My Lord," rejoined Douglas.

"By whom?"

"The Duch's steward, Shanley, My Lord."

Damek beamed up at Henry. "Is he here?"

Shanley was led up to the dais, shivering in fear. When he saw the Duch crumpled up on the second-to-last stair, he wailed. Damek patted his back, turning him toward the loyal barons he was pleased to note seemed less inclined to leave by the moment.

Good.

"Shanley, please tell the Court where you found this rubbish?" Damek indicated the pile.

Shanley gulped. "In young Lord Fitz Donahugh's quarters, the night he attacked my mistress."

A collected gasp swept through the gathering.

"He did attack her then?" asked Damek, with a pointed glare for Henry.

"Yes, My Lord. He was found clutching the knife he used to slash her neck and arm. The coroner wrote a report detailing the type and make of the knife, concerning her ladyship's wounds."

"Do you have that report?"

"Y-yes." Shanley dug around in his valise until he produced the documents. Damek held them aloft for the whole room to see, his eye on his uncle, before passing those too to Patrick's barons. "Is the coroner present?"

"I am, milord," said an unassuming voice from the far corner. A balding fellow of middling years stepped forward.

"Do you attest to the validity of your report?"

"I do, milord. The girl was brutally attacked by a fellow matching your cousin's approximate height and weight. His hands and fingers bore sure signs of their struggle and the practiced use of a bladed weapon of the description listed in my report. The very same weapon was used on each victim. Furthermore, her ladyship was in a state of exsanguination and acute shock the night of the attack and therefore could not have 'thrown' or 'pushed' the Duch's nephew from her window. She would have been far too weak. The only explanations that make sense are that he either leapt from the window himself, was heaved through by an unknown third party, or fell by accident. Given his cruel proclivities, I believe suicide can be ruled out."

Henry went white as a shroud.

Damek pressed on. In the doorway and hall, some courtiers returned to see what was happening since the fighting had stopped. "So, he either fell or was thrown by someone not bleeding from several serious wounds?"

"Yes," said the balding fellow, shoving his spectacles up the bridge of his sweating nose. "More than this, the individual must have been quite strong to shove the window and latticing with Fitz Donahugh to the cliff below."

"And if Micah fell?"

"If he hit the window with some force, say after tripping over an unseen object— he might have struck the casing with the full force of his back, but really, I doubt this explanation. It's far-fetched."

Damek paused to gauge the shock and anger brewing around him. "Then you believe someone else was in the room with them?"

The coroner coughed. "Yes, milord. The window was already ajar when the young lord went through. He did not have shards of any size lodged in his back, which he would have, were the accidental death an explanation."

"Lies," Henry whispered, trembling.

"You're sure of this? Please answer the Court," Damek ordered.

The coroner turned. "Given the lady's state that night, there is no way she could have murdered Lord Fitz Donahugh's son. I examined her wounds myself. In my hearing, her father instructed her to conceal her wounds and put on a brave face for the fête, but by rights, she should have been abed for a week or more."

"She *did* look quite pale today," said someone.

"Aye, and what a high collar she wore," whispered another.

"I never liked that milksop lad. Had his father's temper."

Henry snarled at them all. "*Lies*. We're to believe my mild-mannered son was a vicious murderer *and* that he was thrown from the South Tower by a mysterious savior? You're reaching, the lot of you." At the coroner, he levelled a righteous finger. "This man is a known drunk and lickspittle. For enough coin, he'll swear to anything you wish to tell. If Una did not murder my boy.... *who am I to believe did*?"

Damek shrugged. "Me, obviously."

Henry's scoff spurred his supporters on. "Was that before or after she was seen fawning over that Sidhe devil at table?"

"After. Everyone saw *us* at the feast, didn't they? I entered her chamber about a quarter past midnight— I have a key, you see— and discovered Micah hunched over her with a knife. He'd bashed her skull against the floor and the door panel then opened several wounds in her arm, hands, and throat. I picked him up and tossed him through the window. I can't recall if the shutters were open or not, as I was far too enraged to notice. *I* killed your wretched spawn, uncle, and good riddance."

The murmur ran up and down the breadth of the chamber and did not end, even with Henry's rasp. "You're a bloody liar, boy. My men saw you leave for *The Butterfly* before midnight."

"A ruse cooked up by my uncle," he gestured to Patrick. "Who never intended that anyone should have Una but me. Shanley?"

"Ah, yes," the steward blanched. He pulled several more documents from his valise. These bore the Duch's infamous hand, as well as his seal.

Lord Wender read in silent fury for several moments before marching forward. "This stipulates that the Lady Una and Lord Bishop are the Duch's sole heirs."

Henry collected himself in the face of their indignation. "Whatever this charlatan sells you is false. Una Moura murdered my boy— and her father— for the throne. Once I appeared to accuse her directly, she fled with her Sidhe cohorts. We were *here*. We saw her with our own eyes. Where were *you*, Lord Bishop, hm? If you and she were together last night, why weren't you here to support her before the Court?" Henry's men caught their bearings from this impassioned display; weapons raised once more.

That was fine by Damek.

He'd been hoping there'd be a fight.

"I was detained, uncle. My cousin Isaac was loath to leave his games and toys behind, but in the end, the promise of a proper squireship was enough to tempt him from the Keep."

Henry stopped. Every muscle in his face froze.

"*What* was that?"

Martin answered for him. "Did you believe we'd allow you to usurp *My Lord's* rightful place without a proper accounting? You've no right to stand upon that dais, Henry Fitz Donahugh, and even less to slander My Lady's good name in favor of the murderous beast you spawned." Martin would not be restrained. "If you don't remove yourself, I will do the honors myself."

"Where have you taken my son, Damek?" asked Henry, ignoring Martin entirely.

"Where he'll cause little trouble, I assure you. The lad will not be victim to your ambition while I live, uncle. Now please, do as Martin has asked and desist. You may retire to whichever country estate you favor, with all due rights and tithes. Do it not, and I will have your head on a spike at the gate. Choose now."

Henry visibly counted the growing number of Courtiers at Damek's back. Many had returned with better weapons and more of their household guard. His was now the losing hand. "If I refuse, I suppose Isaac will suffer for it?"

"Not at all," disagreed Damek. "I am not a man who condones the senseless slaughter of innocents for power. That is *your* forte, uncle. Isaac will grow up to be whatever he wishes, far out of harm's way... whether I am forced to kill his rabid hypocrite of a father or no." Several minutes passed while Henry stared between Damek, his brother's cooling body, and the throne he'd been after his entire life. Damek watched the emotions trace across the old boar's face. He even empathized a bit. He knew all too well what it meant to want something you will likely never have. Douglas, Hisk, and Gordin advanced upon the dais. "I have places to be. Make your decision."

Henry held up his gnarled and fingerless left hand in the face of bloodshed that he could not direct. "I have your word that my son is unharmed."

"Yes," Damek vowed through his teeth.

"I will leave if you allow me to collect him."

Damek drew in a dramatic breath. "Not now, certainly, as you'd no doubt use him to further your agenda. No, I think I will hang on to him if you attempt to betray me in the near future. Perhaps one day, he will seek you out himself?"

Henry took a step back. He met the eyes of his staunchest supporters with as guilty a look as he could manage. "I'm sorry, brothers. God has called upon me to make this sacrifice for an innocent child. I have no recourse. Forgive me in your prayers." He limped down the steps toward a Corpsman with open manacles. Willingly, he placed his twig-thin wrists in the restraints. "Brothers, I now urge you to surrender your weapons and leave the scene with dignity."

Damek's laugh caught him short. "We made no agreement for your followers." He tugged his chin at the black-clothed throng. The result was a swift and bloody affair, over in mere moments. The Steel Corps moved through the zealots like scythes through wheat. Their sabres came away red, again and again.

As he was dragged from the room and down the hall, Henry's apoplectic screams echoed through the walls for quite a while. "This is not over!" he roared to no one and everyone at once.

Unperturbed, Damek knelt beside his uncle's body. Patrick had died with blood on his lips. Damek did his best to scrub the offal away. Martin's hand slid over his shoulder. "He was a good man."

Several courtiers took a knee, vowing fealty to their new Duch. Damek scarcely heard or saw them. His eyes were all for the man who'd raised him, taught him, loathed, and loved him. "No, he wasn't. Though, that hardly diminished him. Whatever one thought of him, he was a force to be reckoned with."

Martin wiped at his eyes with the back of his hand. "What's to be done with the boy?"

"Which boy?"

"Isaac. What will you do with him?"

Damek stood, hands on hips as he accepted the oaths of the shocked and bleeding nobles of Patrick's Court. "It's done."

Martin blinked several times. "In what way?"

"The only way, Martin." He gave his old friend a long, meaningful stare. "Who do you think raised me?" Martin didn't so much recoil as shrink into his own body. The deflation was subtle, but Damek noticed. O'Rearden nearly flinched when Damek patted his arm. "Now, how about we go and find my wife before she gets away, hm?"

As it happened, Henry was not incarcerated for long. Indeed, his captors had scarcely skirted the bottom stair in the Great Hall before his followers caught up with them. The Steel Corpsmen were fine fighters, it was true. Several men died in the fracas at the sharp end of both sabres, but two swords were not enough to quell the dozen men who poured down the stairs with clubs and knives held high. Henry was sharply shoved aside, whereupon he took a slight tumble that knocked the breath from his lungs. Lord Tendrick's son helped him to his feet after several bloody moments, bearing the key to his manacles. "My Lord, you are liberated."

Using Tendrick's hand to steady himself, Henry leaned against the wall to observe the carnage his men had wrought. Passerby had all but fled from the chamber, except for Lady Penwyth and one of her young sons. At any other time, he might have been impressed by her lack of fear. Now was not that time.

"Declare yourself, My Lady. Duch Isaac or the faerie pretender?"

Her nose twitched. "Surely you realize your son is dead, Lord Fitz-Donahugh?"

A dull ache in his gut attested to the truth of this statement. Though he longed to refute her claim, he'd known from the moment Damek had uttered his youngest child's name that there was very little likelihood he'd have been spared. Giving voice to that fear, however, was its own torture. Henry choked down the cauldron of rage and grief at his center. There'd be time enough for vengeance later. Now, he had a city to wrest from an idolater. He pulled his bony shoulder back. His followers fanned out behind him, wielding their clubs menacingly.

"We shall see. I'd loathe to learn you and your men have thrown support behind my brother's evil children?"

She noted the dangerous enthusiasm each of Henry's followers bore in their eyes. She half-smirked. "Not I. The pair of them snubbed my excellent sons for lesser creatures. I've no cause to align my house with theirs."

Henry dipped his head once, gesturing for his men to lower their weapons. "I have your support, then?"

"Depends." She crossed her fleshy arms. "Who shall follow you as Duch, now that your sons are both dead?"

He would see her scalp peeled away from her skull before a roaring crowd for such a flippant, calculating comment. He smiled. "I may yet make more sons, Lady Penwyth."

The dubious glint in her eyes sealed her future fate, as far as Henry was concerned. "I have a daughter, as it happens, My Lord. A worthless girl, to be sure. Far too old and ugly to be a prize, but wide of hip and meek as a mule. She'll make a grand broodmare, I'll wager."

Henry wiped the blood from his cheek. So that was to be the way of things, was it? His sons were scarcely cold in their shrouds, and this officious whore would peddle her daughter to him for a chance at power. Well. "How many men are at your disposal, My Lady?"

"Two hundred, My Lord. And you may rest assured, Lords Kendall and Pough share my table. I can add three hundred soldiers to your rabble. Enough, do you think?"

Henry did the sums in his head. Damek had many more men in his company, though they were even now in pursuit of Henry's slattern of a niece. The city guard could be bought with little action and coin, and the traitorous lords of Patrick's court could be dealt with... if he moved quickly. Now was the moment, he knew without much deliberation. Now or never. He muttered a silent prayer for strength of purpose; vengeance would be his, by God. "I would require assurances."

The lady's son gave a bark of surprise as she shoved him forward. "Take this one. He's quite stupid, but he's my firstborn, nonetheless."

"Mother," breathed the young man, wide-eyed.

"Shut your mouth, Kai. You'll serve as the Duch's squire, won't he, My Lord?"

"Indeed," Henry prevaricated. He waved a follower over with the manacles removed from his own wrist. "Though, I'm afraid one lad will not be sufficient."

"Take them both, then. Ned is out whoring, last I checked. Once you find him, do with him as you see fit."

"Agreed," assented Henry. "In exchange?"

"My daughter as Duchess, and Malahide for the Clan, of course."

"Done. Liam, will you?"

Tendrick's son led the Kernian lad away, protesting the while. Henry limped toward her. He held out his hand. She took it with the barest hint of hesitation. "We have an accord, Lady Penwyth. Now, let's go and greet your men, shall we?" As he led her away, he paused to ask, "Why me, and not Damek?"

Her shrug was ruthlessly casual. "One bastard Donahugh's as good as another."

26
FROM BELOW

They'd made it to the lowest point in the Keep without much incident. Patrols were primarily restricted to the walls and the lanes outside the palace. Any soldiers rushing to Patrick's Court beyond the Great Hall would never have spied them making their way down to the Moorings. The chill, damp air that greeted them from within the cavern made Una's flesh prickle. How many foul deeds had been performed in this place, she wondered? How many women dead, girls and boys taken, goods and wealth stolen, stealthy attacks mounted? She'd been nearly murdered here recently, hadn't she? Evil oozed from the walls, dripping into the filthy black water below like a drumbeat.

I have ssssuuuch delighhtsss to ssshow youuu… whispered her memory.

She shuddered.

Having been attached to each other's side since the throne room, Rian's arms tightened around her shoulders. "Are you all right?" They hadn't had much time to talk, but some things didn't need to be spoken aloud. Her friend's sure and steady presence was already more than Una could ask for.

Una patted her hand. "This place reminds me of Samhain, is all."

Her friend hadn't been conscious through much of that nightmare but had witnessed enough to empathize. She frowned. "You're right."

"Which way?" demanded the Prince of Connaught with an impatient growl.

Una pointed. "Down that set of second stairs, to the right there. I know that much, but then there are three forks. I've no idea where the other two lead."

"I do," promised Robin. "We veer left, then hook right. Leads us up under *The Butterfly* and into her cellars. That'll be the easy part, though. The second tunnel separated. We'll hafta access it from the first floor."

"Wonderful," Una sighed. She was so tired. Someone passed her a flask; she took it without glancing down. They hadn't spoken much, but Kaer Yin's quiet, steady presence at her back was her sole warmth. "This door bears a heavy lock. I have no key."

"No need," Robin grinned. "Ye have me, princess." He tugged a thin but sharp sliver of iron from his sleeve. It slid into the lock with a clang. Two twists of his wrist, and the bulky lock popped open and clattered to the wet stone floor. Opening the door sent a blast of dry, stale air into her face. "*Siora*," sneezed Robin with a curled lip. "Somethin' died in there, sure."

"It'll be us if we don't get moving," said Kaer Yin, glancing behind him. He and his Sidhe companions could hear things she, Rian, and Robin would never hear. "They're gathering at the gates, and I hear boots in the halls above. They're looking for us now. Whatever happened after the attack in chambers must be over now."

"Then we should leave," Tam Lin urged, sparing Una a curious twist of his brow. "Unless you're having second thoughts?"

Una didn't care for his tone. She narrowed her eyes. "Charming, aren't you?"

Kaer Yin jerked the torch out of his cousin's hand while Tam Lin appraised Una in silent judgment. "Come on. We're wasting time here." Kaer Yin's voice was slightly gruffer than usual.

Ah, Una thought.

I suppose every family is complicated, then? "After you, Your Highness," she ground out. "Unless you'd prefer to wait here?"

Tam Lin shared a small laugh with Robin. "This makes more sense by the moment."

"I told you. A pair," agreed Robin.

"I told *you* to hurry up!" barked Kaer Yin from somewhere in the dark ahead.

Rian didn't mind the dark as much as Una seemed to, but the smell... *Siora*. More than one thing had perished in here, surely? The high-pitched squeaks of various rodents chased them through the tunnel, and though she didn't want to think about it, she felt her boots smash several thousand similar skeletons along the way. She ran straight into every damned cobweb in their path, or maybe just the ones too low for the idiot Sidhe in their company to reach. Whatever the case, by the time they came to the fork in the passage Robin spoke of— she was thoroughly put out. Even wounded, Una fared better, though barely. Her delicate black gown was far worse for wear. Her amber eyes seemed hollow and dark in the torchlight. Every step she took amplified her silence. Rian gripped her fingers. "I'm here, Una."

Una gave the slightest squeeze back. "I'm grateful."

"Do you want to talk about it?"

Una shook her head. "Not now."

They rounded the right-hand corner. Kaer Yin, Rian noted, stared straight ahead with a fixed jaw. She didn't need to read his mind to know what he was feeling. Una's physical and emotional pain radiated from her, despite her visible efforts to choke it down. Her father was dead. No matter how she'd felt about the man in life, the finality of his demise was inescapable. No reconciliation, no reprieve. Rian understood this, perhaps better than anyone else; her own father had died suddenly, with much left unsaid between them.

In Una's case, the Duch had died in her arms.

Rian had no doubt the event would haunt her for a long time. She wanted to take a break and wrap her arms around her friend, whose shoulders shook ever so slightly from the effort to repress her emotions. However, the quiver in Una's shoulders convinced her to leave it be for now.

Tam Lin exhaled through his nose. "Thank Danu for that. We have more pressing matters to see to, don't we?"

Rian stopped short so that she might stare Tam Lin down. After bumping into her, Robin held his hands up and moved on, navigating by the bobbing glow of Kaer Yin's light. Though she struggled to see his face in the quickening dark, she could make out Tam Lin's haughtily raised brow.

"Yes, My Lady?" his tone was husky and flirtatious enough to be insulting. Shar ducked his head and took up Rian's place at Una's side. Once moderately alone, Rian's right hand lashed out so fast that Tam Lin's head snapped into the wall with a mild crack. His fingers flew to his offended cheek. "Ow! What in the *Hells* do you think—"

"Listen, you arrogant swine. For weeks and weeks, I've listened to you rant and rave, pout and instigate, prattle and prod— and kept my peace about it. Only when your outrageously overinflated self-love has attempted to harm someone else have I butted in. The stupid grudge between you and Ben, for one." Her chest heaved with the urge to smite this vainglorious creature on the spot. "But so help me, *Siora*, if you ever speak to or about Una that way again, I will kill you. Am I making myself clear? All that she has suffered for those of us in your presence, aside... she lost her father *today*. You will keep that insufferable narcissism in check, or I'll make you regret it."

She couldn't see his face anymore at all. "I'm—"

"I don't give a tenth of a shite who you bloody well are! You're a vain, spoilt, monstrous boil of a person, and I *despise* you." She wiped her mouth with the back of her hand. She could hear him breathing and hated that too. "Remember what I said."

"Come on then!" called Robin from the front. "We're about there."

Without another word, she spun on her good heel and limped toward her friends.

AT THE TERMINUS OF THE FORKED PASSAGE, A DUSTY WOODEN DOOR perched above a set of nail-starved stairs. The lanterns on either side were equally encrusted and disused. Robin slipped past Kaer Yin to take a closer look for himself. His iron stiletto once more slipped from his sleeve. He caught the lock before it fell. When the door creaked inward, he stuck his head in and looked around. He whispered over his shoulder, "Empty as a Kneeler's church."

Kaer Yin clapped him on the back, taking point. He drew a single lark and climbed into the moldy cellar first. Heaps of boxes, dusty crates, and assorted oddments filled the dingy chamber to the rafters. The only light came from a handful of barred, arched windows set at intervals in the brick exterior wall. They could hear the street traffic from the cobbles outside. The day rolled on, unaware of the handful of warriors and thieves busily spiriting their Duch's heir away, far beneath their feet.

He selected one with the tip of his blade. "That door, I presume?"

"Yeah." Robin mopped his brow with a sopping sleeve. "And up into the parlor from here. Across the hall to the other side, then to the sewer grate in the opposite wine cellar. The one way out, unseen."

Kaer Yin reached the door first and stretched his fingers toward the handle, but Rian caught his wrist. "Wait! You heard what Barb said about this place?"

"Greenmakers have been here before." Robin boasted from over her shoulder.

"Right. If you were invited to smuggle in goods, then I'd presume they'd keep it clear of clients and guests."

He stuck out his lower lip. "Well, yeah."

"Any way they'd mistake you for a guest, now?"

He fidgeted under her scrutiny, muddy face and all. "Probably not."

She shared a long, unspoken glance with Una, who relented after some hesitation. The pair retreated to a darker corner, each doffing garments from the muffled sounds they made. When they emerged again a few moments later, each wore the other's garb. Rian's fine linen tunic, and now dusty brown leggings had to be rolled up at the cuffs and cinched in at the waist. In Rian's case, she was thin enough to wear Una's gown but far too tall. In the dim, mottled light, it became apparent that the dress hugged curves no one had ever noticed Rian had.

Tam Lin picked invisible lint from a nonexistent cuff.

Kaer Yin rolled his eyes. "Why?"

"Because none of you can pass for someone who should be here, can you?"

Robin scratched the scar on his chin. "No, I 'spose not."

Kaer Yin noted Una's pinched expression.

He groaned, "It wasn't my idea this time. I swear."

"Right," she said dubiously. "I think the lot of you know more about brothels than anyone ought to."

Rather than answer, he jerked a thumb at Robin. "His plan."

Robin held up his hands beneath her imperious stare. "Barb's plan, actually."

Her face fell. "That's *loads* better, isn't it?"

"We should go," interrupted Tam Lin with a petulant scowl.

With a faint whimper, Rian bit her finger to produce a tiny spot of blood, which she smeared over her moon-pale cheekbones and across her lips. Once Una managed to unbraid and shake out her smooth, cornsilk hair, Rian looked very much like someone who might be employed upstairs. Hands on hips, Una took a step back to admire her work. "It'll do."

"I'll say," chuckled Robin appreciatively.

"Still look like a sallow guttersnipe, you ask me," snuffled Tam Lin.

Rian fixed him with a piercing blue eye. "You want another smack?"

He did not, insofar as far as Kaer Yin could tell.

"Barb said this place caters to a specific clientele," she said, making awkward progress toward the stairs. "Men that prefer their women a bit... odd."

"Rian, I think it might be better if—"Una attempted.

"No, it won't. It's you they're looking for. Robin?"

"Hm?" He stared openly. She ignored him.

"How far down the hall is the next door?"

"Four or five yards, give or take."

Inhaling and exhaling, she stood up as straight as she could. "Okay. Leave the door cracked and follow me when I wave. Ready?"

"Rian!" Una tried and failed to grab her wrist before Rian tottered through the door and into the gilded hall. Here, the floor shone a brilliantly polished grey marble, so dark it was nearly black. Red glass sconces adorned fine sateen wallpaper trimmed in gold thread. There were many heavy doors, and each was painted a glossy obsidian. The sconces between rooms were either lit, or the door lay wide open, beckoning occupants with its sumptuous, velveteen décor. The rooms with lit sconces were very much occupied.

Kaer Yin caught Rian's deeply embarrassed blush. He often forgot she was barely seventeen years old and had lived most of her life in deep seclusion. She'd never set foot in a slum before they met and certainly never a brothel.

He felt a bit bad right about then if he were honest.

He would have to wait his turn to worry over her, in any case. Una dashed ahead of him into the hall behind her. He muffled a curse. She stopped a few paces from Rian, waiting for her to crane her neck around the first turn. Rian waved them forward, her cheeks burning beneath her rudimentary rouge. Having passed the first of two adjoining halls, she approached the next with an audible breath. A hair before the last puddle of protective darkness in the distant corner, a door slammed open on the opposite side— the parlor, or so the most cursory glance confirmed. A servitor bore a tray piled high with delicate confections and tiny glasses of sweetly scented wine.

Rian flattened herself against the wall. As he passed, the servitor spouted hushed abuse at someone in the doorway behind him. He didn't see her. He then turned down the first hall, mumbling something under his breath. Rian met Kaer Yin's eyes over Una's head. He waved her on. Before she reached the next threshold, a couple burst through the parlor door, hands and mouths all over each other. As swiftly as they appeared, the couple disappeared into one of the empty rooms; its sconce suddenly bloomed red, lit from behind the closed door.

Kaer Yin knew a servitor would come and blow out the candle after a quarter-hour, though the mark would have paid for the entire hour: a simple trick to squeeze the local gentry of more coin. The savvy knew to bring their own or would demand to leave a servant in the hall. This customer was new to the game.

Robin sucked his teeth.

He and Kaer Yin shared the briefest of grins.

Una bloody saw, of course.

She whispered, "Rian, get moving before I murder this pair of ingrates."

Rian took a deep breath and peeled herself from the wall. She crept forward as quickly as she might, without making noise. She was near to the far side of the hall when a figure emerged from the parlor. Bleary-eyed with a drink that Kaer Yin could smell from nine paces and partially dressed, the fellow turned to retch into a potted plant near Rian's left elbow. She recoiled so fast that she half-tripped over her own feet. Wiping his mouth with the back of a mealy hand, the patron set a hand against the wall to steady himself. A slow smile broke over his mouth when his eyes finally fixed on her flushed face.

"Well, hello there," he belched. "That's a lovely, lovely dress."

Rian said nothing. She took a step backward.

With a burst of agility one might not expect from a fat, drunken sot like this, he reached out to grasp her wrist. He caught Una's, instead. Kaer Yin glared at her over the clod's head, his lark poised and ready to hamstring the bastard on the spot, but the light from within the parlor cast long shadows in the hall. She shook her head at him. Several people stood shy of that door. If the patron cried out, they'd be discovered, and their escape critically hampered.

Dry as parchment, Una broke in, "My Lady has another appointment. If you'll excuse us, milord?"

His clumsy hand slid over Una's left breast and squeezed. Una didn't move a muscle. Kaer Yin took a step forward. Again, she shook her head at him. "Oh, you're a piece!" tutted the patron. "Where's Janet been hiding you, love?" He did something to her that Kaer Yin couldn't see but vowed the fool had mere seconds to live if he persisted. The patron wrestled her around with a laugh. "It's novitiate today then? My favorite! There's an empty room over there. Why don't we see which of your holes is supposed to be fresh, hm?"

Kaer Yin had trouble keeping himself still.

While he'd no doubt they'd escape *The Butterfly* without much blood, the attention they'd bring to themselves might pour dozens of soldiers into the tunnels after them. He couldn't afford to risk everyone so soon. Robin placed a restraining hand on his shoulder; thus, he didn't see them move toward an unlighted doorway. The drunk menacingly leaned over her. "How about it?"

"By all means, lead the way," she replied flatly.

"You like it a bit rough, do you? Or do you prefer to do the hurting?" He rubbed her captive hand against the front of his breeches.

Rian failed to smother a gag.

"You know something," purred Una, as she maneuvered the patron through the open door, slipping her uncovered hand over his bulbous chin. "I absolutely *do*." An unseen force gripped his throat from the inside. Suddenly, he staggered sideways, clutching at his collar as his throat visibly caved in. She kicked him through the open door and gently closed the door behind him as he fell. Taking Rian by the hand, she tugged her along behind her toward the exit. "I've had enough of this place already. Kaer Yin?"

"Coming," he called after her, trying not to smile.

"What in the Hells was that?" demanded Tam Lin, horrified.

"I told ye she was scary," Robin said with a shrug.

"Dagda," Tam Lin breathed as he passed the door she had closed on their way down the hall. The patron gurgled slightly, on the other side. "I don't think I care much for the women of Tairngare, Master Gramble."

"I don't think *they* much care," hissed Rian, from the end of the hall.

Once they descended the stairs into the dry cellar, then latched and barricaded the door at their backs, Robin and Shar made short work of the sewer grate on the far side. Una wrinkled her nose at the noxious odors that swept into her face from its gaping maw.

"*Siora*. One nearly forgets how much fun our little adventures can be."

"Aye." Robin whistled to himself. "Something *has* died in this one, sure."

"No help for it, I'm afraid. Once they discover the gift Una has left for the proprietor, they'll search the place top to bottom," advocated Kaer Yin.

On cue, a riot of screams trilled overhead.

Una lifted a shoulder. "Too late."

AS A GROUP, THEY CLAMBERED FROM A STORM DRAIN SOMETIME LATER, which spilled directly into the Lee on the Northeast end of the city wall. Sputtering and freezing, they shuffled up the riverbank one by one, seeking the minimal shelter of a small copse of trees. Rian, now in Una's uselessly thin gown, suffered the worst of the Dor Cromna air. There were small chips of ice stuck to her eyelashes and woven throughout her long damp hair. Shar removed his own cloak and spoke a few words over it. It dried as he placed it over her quaking shoulders. He moved on to Una next, who mumbled indecipherable gratitude into her collar.

"Now w- what?" Her teeth chattered, looking out over the eastern plains. She saw nothing but rolling hills and farmland for leagues into the Midlands.

"Gerry and the others are a few miles west, waiting with our horses. They left the city last night. I wanted them well out of sight," Kaer Yin said, strapping his swordbelt around his waist.

Tam Lin scrubbed cobwebs and ice from his own scalp with a colorful Sidhe curse. "Yin, this has been a grand escapade thus far, one I'm sure we'll enjoy the telling of for many centuries to come... but we should take the Shadow Path."

Kaer Yin gave him a long look. "We've discussed this. It's no place for Milesians, cousin." He tossed Una a dagger, which she carefully slipped into the knot of hair she'd tied to the crown of her head. He raised his brows.

"What? I don't have a belt or a pack, idiot," she sniped.

"I'd thought they'd made an elegant lady of you, at court?"

"I'll make one of you, if you don't shut your mouth."

"Gods," moaned Tam Lin, clearly having the worst time of his life. "Which bloody way, then?"

Robin clapped him on the back. His answering curse was slightly less banal than before. "Through this thicket here, then we swing east afore the next village. 'Bout ten miles, as the crow flies."

After retrieving something from his pack, Tam Lin passed the overlarge satchel to Niall and marched up to Rian, whose lips had gone blue, with a dark scowl.

"Here," he grumbled, holding out a pair of thoroughly extravagant fur-lined gloves. She stared at him like he had two heads. "Well, take them already. Consider them a peace offering."

Several uncomfortable moments later, she slipped them on and tucked both hands within the folds of her now dry cloak. Rather than thank him, she strode over to Una, who tied the girl's gaping cowl together beneath her chin and fastened it with a small hairpin. Appropriately swaddled, the pair followed Kaer Yin and Robin through the trees. Tam Lin and Niall took up the back, each eying the city walls behind them with equal parts derision and wariness.

TWO HOURS OF INTERMITTENT FREEZING RAIN AND SIX MILES LATER, riders appeared on a far hill, silhouetted against the distant haze of the setting sun. Tam Lin exchanged a knowing look with his lieutenant, who sheathed his larks for the dash ahead. "Yin," he boomed, as Niall ran past. "We've company."

Kaer Yin stopped to squint behind them. There were hundreds of them, heavy cavalry from the glint of steel at their helms.

He spat. "He's early, damn it." With a distant snap of spurs, the mass of dark shapes began to descend in a flawless, lethal vanguard. He cursed long and low under his breath. "We have no choice. We'll never outrun them in this."

"I won't say I told you so," quipped Tam Lin, without mirth.

"Still, we ought to try."

"What are you talking about?" Una's eyes widened at the distant threat.

"If followed, we meant to lead them into a trap, My Lady," replied Shar. "But your kin is remarkably determined."

"A trap? Are you mad? Did you imagine we could outrun my father's destriers for four straight miles?"

Kaer Yin's brow darkened. "We weren't supposed to. Though, if you hadn't killed that fat pervert in *The Butterfly*, it would have taken them a great deal longer to figure out which way we'd gone."

"You're saying this is my fault?"

"He didn't need to die, did he?"

"Not now, you two!" screeched Rian.

Una opened and closed her mouth like a fish. "I didn't ask you to come, did I?"

Kaer Yin bared his teeth. "I'll forget you said that... damn you."

"I won't." She crossed her arms.

Gods above and below, help me not to murder the woman I...

"Yin? You know what choice we face. They gain. I'd rather not die in a muddy Souther field today," prodded Tam Lin, interrupting his train of thought.

A call went out among the riders. They turned sharply west, as a flock of birds might. Kaer Yin knew what they were doing before it played out. Rather than allow their quarry to dash ahead any further, Damek's cavalry would arch westward then turn again to hammer them from the North, a pincer move, which would block their exit and encircle them. With the bulk of Tam Lin's forces only four miles out, Kaer Yin had no choice.

"Herne, bloody damn your infuriating family, Una."

He reached deep within himself, willing the earth roll away beneath their feet; the sky opened up around them. The air, static and pregnant with purpose, halted the blood in his veins and sucked the sound from his ears. Time swept over and through him, then drifted away.

He spoke the words.

27

SERVED COLD

Grainne was displeased to see her, Aoife knew, but the fear in her eyes outweighed her aversion. Carn helped her from her saddle, watching the Fir Bolg princess advance upon their party. Aoife was exhausted and equally disinterested in anything Falan's sister might have to say. She'd been out riding and murdering in the High King's name for the better part of a month, thus couldn't care less what this spoilt bitch had to complain about. Grainne paused five paces from her, twisting her nose at Aoife's grooms. With a put-upon sigh, Aoife waved them away. Whatever this Mac Nemed fool wanted to say, she might as well get it out of the way in private. Aoife was hungry and meant to fuck Creahal until sleep finally claimed her. She preferred him to his brother, whose body worked miracles, but he had taken some fool notion of love into his head.

She had no time for such drivel.

"What? If you've come to order me back out, I'll have you know the work is all but done. You're welcome, by the way."

Grainne wrung her hands. "Nevermind that now. We have problems."

Aoife guffawed while she unlaced her tack. "What else is new?"

"Your attitude is unwarranted, girl."

"And your urgency is uninteresting. Step aside, *Highness*."

Grainne did not. Sweat dotted her burnished brow. That gave Aoife pause. Had the great Grainne Mac Nemed ever labored a day in her long, long life? What on earth could have the daughter of mighty Falan the Elder in such a lather?

"What?" she repeated.

Grainne appeared to struggle over the words. "It's my grandmother. She's... deviating."

"Deviating, how?"

Grainne craned her head around like the walls themselves had ears. Aoife knew, well enough, that they probably did. She inched closer, whispering, "She's broken with our lord."

Aoife snorted. "You'll have to work much harder than that, if you mean to make a traitor of me, cousin. I wasn't born a fool."

Grainne, growing ever more nervous, pulled Aoife below an awning, out of sight of the walls. "It's no ruse. I vow it, on Emain Macha." She placed a thumb over her heart. Instinctually, Aoife mirrored her. "She's had her minions in the Cloister draft a new gospel."

"Yes, that's to plan, is it not?"

"She makes no mention of the Ancestor's divine son... only the Queen Mother."

That was *not* to plan.

Aoife was silent for a few moments, mind racing. "She wouldn't."

"She *has*. Any who have dared to question her have been immolated, as you were. Two days ago, she filed a motion to have Siora's name stricken from all Patent of Maternas. In this absurd pantomime, you can imagine whose name is meant to take the Ancestor's place?"

That was... well. "She would never break with our lord for such a paltry platitude."

Grainne exhaled through her nose. "Many things I believe she'd never do, she has already done, and swiftly, I might add. The Fir Bolg who accompanied me into the Cloister have already been pressed into service or incarcerated. They won't even receive the benefit of a sham trial, I'm afraid. She's gone insane, Aoife. Drunk with power."

"Liadan Mac Nemed has never lacked for power, Grainne."

"She means to make herself a god. How else would you describe such behavior, except as madness?"

"What difference does it make if it's her or Falan we are meant to adore? Like grandmother, like grandson. Neither will be satisfied with one city to crush, and now that she's succeeded here, why should she hand it over? I don't care which of them means to rule here. They're two sides of the same hideous coin."

Aoife turned to leave but Grainne grasped her arm and squeezed, her eyes bright amethysts in the starkness of her thin face. She looked nearly... ill, like she had barely slept or eaten in days. There was hopelessness, anger, and terror in the directness of her gaze.

"He was here, you see, some weeks ago. He came to remind her whom she was meant to herald. Something changed in her that night, as if a dam was bursting. She will never bow to him, or anyone else again. I can feel it."

"Can't say I blame her, Grainne. Falan's always been a bit of a cunt, hasn't he? The single play he's ever made was to convince the world of his untimely demise in hopes of raising Innisfail against the High King from the shadows. Why not come at the Dannans directly, hm? Challenge Kaer Yin Adair for the throne?" Aoife giggled, wrenching her arm out of Grainne's bruising grip. "Because he knew he'd *lose*, that's why. All of this, every plan, every subterfuge, every murder and action— all of it— is built upon a precipice of ultimate failure. The only way the Mac Nemed's will rule again in Eire is to cheat. If Falan meant to turn the most powerful woman in the world into his faithful lapdog, one who not only birthed his line but also gave him the means and will to see it through— then more fool, he. If I were Liadan, I might have done the same thing."

Grainne drew in a breath. "Loyal even now, cousin? After everything she's done to you?"

"Oh, I hate her more than you ever will, princess. I don't care which of them takes power. Innisfail is in for a treat, whichever megalomaniacal beast is on the throne. Don't pretend we're suddenly allies just because old granny isn't playing by your rules anymore."

They stared each other down for half a millennium in a minute's passing. Grainne broke first, looking away with a huff. "I'm leaving, tonight. This is the last time I will extend my hand to you, Aoife Ap Sionnavar. Reject it now at your peril."

"Why do *you* support your brother, Grainne? What possible benefit is in it for you?"

Grainne's answering smile was cold and empty as a cavern. "You could never understand the importance of placing one's family above oneself, Aoife. You have none. You're as bereft of worth now as you've always been, *isasáeligh*. They should have strangled you in your crib, traitor that you are."

"As you're always so eager to point out, cousin— I'm no Mac Nemed. I don't give a shite what imaginary line you believe I should be toeing."

Grainne tugged her heavy cowl over her ears, leaving the burning derision of her violet glare. "Farewell, ungrateful wretch. When next we meet, I will have your skull polished and placed upon my mantle."

"Ooh," Aoife exaggerated a shiver. "I've been murdered many, many times, little princess... and here I stand. I wonder how long you'll hold up when it's your turn?"

With one last hateful smirk, Grainne took her leave. Once she was gone, Aoife allowed her grin to fade to a tight, concerned line. Carn appeared at her elbow like a faithful shadow. "If what she says is true, My Lady, I would fain encourage you to linger here. Her Dark Majesty will accept nothing less than your total subservience."

Aoife turned to wrap herself in his arms. His heartbeat tapped beneath her earlobe, warm, loyal, and wholly *hers*. She had planned to take his brother tonight as a reward for so many days and nights bathed in blood. But perhaps not? As soon as they were well clear of the city, she'd take them both, one at a time, or perhaps together? She pulled his head down for a lengthy, promising kiss. She could taste his love for her on his tongue—bloody fool.

"You are right, my love." She pressed her face into his neck. "I think someone else might appreciate us more."

"Your kinsman," he frowned, jealously. Poor soul. "He'll betray you again."

"If he lives so long," she smiled, running her nose against the drum of his pulse. He sighed. Men were so... easy. "You will protect me."

"We shall," declared his brother as he came up beside her, voice husky with caution and desire. Aoife recalled her youth spent in the half-light of the

Oiche Ar Fad with these two as her sworn keepers. Until Liadan summoned her to Court, they'd been her favorite toys. So they would be again. She was a great-granddaughter of Falan the Elder, great-great-grandchild of the mighty Eochaid Mac Nemed, who'd wed the fearsome daughter of Balor and united the Clans. No man on Macha's green earth could resist the song in her blood, once bonded.

Well, save for those who shared it.

"Good," she hummed, accepting Carn's hand into her saddle. "We should leave before we're announced. My cousin will need my help, if he's to usurp this abhorrent family."

Basa blinked at the flickering candles in her path, as if she stared directly into the sun. Inside, she cringed away from the merciless, soul-snatching light— reviled it as deeply as any shadow shrinks from illumination. Once her eyes cleared, she recoiled from the shape that emerged from that blinding, limitless brightness. Garbed in saffron, Vanna Nema spared her a garish, red grin. She stood at the edge of her newly constructed balcony, the very one she'd graced to pass sentence on the nobles of Tairngare. Beneath them, the Grand Arcade was silent and still as an etching: a ghost of its former use, and majesty.

Basa leaned heavily against her escort, who stared at an invisible point above their Doma's head. Now that her eyes had regained their ability to focus, she noted, not a single individual on that balcony had the gall to glance at her terrible Magnificence directly. Well, save for Basa, of course. What could this overdressed, self-important gash do to her now? Her family was gone. Her daughter's shriveled fingerbones rested against her breastbone. Basa's wealth and privilege were figments from a past life. She was a shade that could not die, a husk without solace. No, Vanna Nema had nothing to gain from her now. She couldn't even toss out the odd word of defiance. Nema had taken that from her too. Voiceless, humorless, careless— she raised her chin and radiated everything she lacked. Nema waved a grey-robed Secunda over to offer Basa a chair. She took it without a struggle. What point would there be?

Basa could glare death and defiance just as easily on her arse.

"You've lost a deal of weight, Basa, dear."

Tongueless, Basa could but sneer in return.

"I don't think I've ever seen you so thin, old friend."

We were hardly friends, you interloping bitch, her expression read.

"Lily, would you please remove that horrid decoration from her neck? It's quite pungent," Nema sniffed in disdain.

Basa closed her fingers over Ana's desiccated flesh, with a determined jut of her fragile chin. She'd sooner die than part with it now. The Secunda made a half-hearted attempt but backed away when Basa's three good teeth latched upon her reaching arm. "Ow!" she cried, leaping away.

"Now, now, Basa. Don't you wish to be rid of that thing?"

I wish you'd fuck yourself with a Bethonair sabre.

"Well, so be it. If you prefer to carry her with you, I shall have a craftsman make an appropriate housing for you. Would that please you?"

Basa cocked her head in confusion.

"Oh," Nema said. "Forgive me, I should have explained my summons. You're to be reinstated, my dear, with certain... stipulations, of course. Foremost among these would be your appearance. We cannot allow our Altas to wander these vaunted halls in such a state, can we?"

Reinstated?

Horseshite.

There was a game here, as sure as the moon would rise in the east. Nema did nothing by halves. Besides, Basa would never serve this power-hungry witch, no matter what boon she might dangle from her manicured claws.

Might as well kill me, old girl.

I'd sooner eat my daughter's mummified flesh.

Nema accepted a cup from a second lickspittle. She took a long sip. "You know, it isn't like you to be such a sore loser, Basa. In your youth, you'd have disassembled this palace stone by stone with your teeth, for such slights as I have shown you. That beaten dog in your eyes disappoints me. Where's your fire? Your rage? That clever, unrelenting shrew I know so well? She would never have sat quietly in a cell for so long, waiting to die. Do you accept defeat so easily?"

The heat this statement inspired, crept through Basa's veins— a thousand flames licking through the remnants of her heart.

I would smash your mind to pieces with one touch, did I have the strength, Your Eminence.

Nema gave her a mocking pout. "Look how far the mighty have fallen, Basa. Once queen of the Cloister in all but name." She shook her head. "What a shame. So, shall that be your legacy? A lifetime of fear and intimidation, ending in abject failure?"

Basa was ready to die.

This harpy had taken everything of value. Yet...

Nema sensed her hesitation. "Not you, Basa. Not the woman who famously defied her enemy on her appointed execution day, who refused to break, even as her daughter perished before her. Why pretend that I have cowed you, lessened you? You are more than a hobbled old woman without a name to cling to, aren't you?"

Basa narrowed her eyes to slivers.

I will never *serve you, Vanna.*

Kill me, imprison me, break me... never.

Nema's sigh was absolute. She brushed a stray feather from her sleeve. "As long as I've lived among mortals, some of you never cease to surprise me. You're all short-sighted and pigheaded without the proper motivation. That's always been true. Though," her voice took on a whimsical quality. "In the rare few, that pigheadedness speaks of something more. Something finer. I shudder to use the term 'courage,' but there it is, all the same."

Mortals?

"Yes," replied Nema, as if she'd understood Basa perfectly. "You Milesians are brute creatures, full of spite, need, and fury. It's very rare to find one who isn't the sum of its parts. I'm complimenting you, Basa, for your sense of self."

Milesians?

"Once, I thought to create a kingdom here for my kin. To remake Innisfail as it had been, long before the Dannan *curraghs* rocked ashore and destroyed the world. Return it to the paradise it had been ruled strictly by women, in Macha's name. There were no kings then, did you know? No word for them, either. Even when my father rose to power, he was no king, rather..." She searched the air for the equitable term. "A consort. My mother was queen, you see. She ruled the Fomor with a soft, but unyielding fist. Balor was brought to her at Beltane for her First Night. I was the result. A queen with no rivals: granddaughter to mighty Macha, daughter of Maeve, sister to Mabh. The Morrigan, they called me— '*the thrice death.*' I would have ruled all of Innisfail, had Eber Finn not plagued our shores."

Basa did not move, for fear this madwoman would launch from her place by the railing and flap about her head like a bat. What lunacy was this?! The Morrigan? What did a death goddess of the Tuatha De Dannan have to do with this tyrannical upstart? She would have the impudence to insist Basa believe she was the Dowager Queen of Armagh?

Basa tried to scoff but found it difficult to do without a tongue.

"Ah, but that is precisely what I intend you believe, Basa Alvra... as it is— and has always been— quite true."

It took a moment for the realization to sink in. Vanna *was* reading her thoughts! Shocked, Basa lumbered to her feet, breathing hard. Vanna's Manipulation exhibited through mind manipulation? No wonder! No bloody *wonder*. No amount of scheming had ever come close to diminishing Drem Moura's fiercest rival, not even Basa Alvra who once could crush an object with her will alone. Nema had known for *forty* years what she was working toward and how she would manage it. She'd used their own plans against them, the while.

Nema patted Basa's empty chair. "I suppose, in a crude way, you're correct. Although, I don't believe my grandmother would have denigrated our gifts with such a simplistic term. Your Siora never labeled her talents in this way. One of your Domas decided this distinction, if I recall. Many, many years before Tairngare ever incorporated. I believe I was mystified by the arrogance, whence first I heard it. As if you could boil such an art to its most fundamental element. Siora knew better. She was blood of my line, after all."

Basa sank into her chair like a brick. Her heart pounded against her ribs, like a captive sparrow.

You're telling me the truth... Vanna?

"I've never understood why none of you smart women ever put the core of my name together. 'Woman from nowhere' is fairly self-explanatory, I find. Especially for you, Basa. You studied Linguistics at the Libellum," she tsked. Had her teeth always been so white, so perfectly formed— did the green of her eyes always sparkle like a forest spring in sunlight? Basa clasped her hands together to keep them steady.

It cannot be.

"Can it not? Mortals used to say the same, before the Transition. You would have been appalled by the world at that time, Basa." She wrinkled her nose. "Great stinking machines rolled over every beautiful hill and dale, gorged themselves upon the earth and her minerals. Feasted upon our sacred trees and animals, spewed filth into the rivers and seas. It was a Hellscape of steel, rabid overpopulation, social decay, and decadence. Even from the confines of the Oiche Ar Fad, the bleakness of that world, the emptiness... I cannot accurately describe its horrors. Left unchecked, your kind will breed and breed, crave, demand, and plunder yourselves into extinction. You Milesians are a plague upon this realm, and always have been. That is not to say, however, that you do not have your uses— in strict moderation, of course."

She paused to observe Basa's thunderstruck features.

"Women, as it happens, bear your species' singular worth. Once you wrest control of your tribes away from greedy, selfish, warmongering males, there's promise for your race. That's why I chose you, chose Tairngare, the sole bright spot in Innish history, since the Fomor ruled this land. Through women, the natural order is restored. Men make much noise about being the more rational sex, yet in three millennia, I've never seen evidence to prove this. Rather, the opposite. They expend every effort to dominate and subjugate women as the 'lesser' creature, when it is quite the reverse. Siora's Acolytes prove this false, do they not? For only women may bear the power to rule the world."

Basa cleared her mind of all riotous thoughts, save one.

What do you want, Vanna?

Those swirling green eyes rested on her face for a long, breathless moment. "I want Tairngare to replace Bri Leith as capital of the civilized world, Basa. I mean to enslave all males on this Continent to our will, as it should always have been. I intend to break the cycle of war and conflict, of aggressive male dominance. The promise of Tairngare, which I've helped to foster these many decades, is peace, harmony, and women in their proper place. Help me. Help me build this world, this new Innisfail."

You murdered my daughter, my family, my friends, and servants.

Why you imagine you could enlist my aid now... you've gone mad, Vanna.

"Eva and Una are alive. Your line is not yet spent."

Basa unfurled her hands. Her eyes stung with tears she refused to shed. She knew her relief would be a tool Vanna would use to enlist her power and remaining influence with the Tairngare's disparate nobility.

"Of course I will," Vanna rejoined. "Why do you suppose you're still alive, after the trouble you and your family have caused me? A bent, broken old woman you may be, but your name means something to those who yet defy me. Your obeisance to the cause will bring a hundred thousand to the fold: an army of holy warriors, ready and willing to wipe the land clean of taint, and remake it anew."

With you on the sole throne: a living god.

Vanna gave a demure smile. "A vulgar misrepresentation of the greater good."

Greater good? Basa grunted.

You murdered the best Manipulators in the city, dismantled Parliament, scourged the Treasury, executed Judges, Merchers, Primas, and Altas who might ever challenge you. You say you did all this to vaunt Tairngare and her women? To make us the center of the world. What bollocks! You did this to elevate yourself, to make Vanna Nema the next High Queen. You hope to erase anything or anyone who stands in your way— and good luck! You've done your job so well, you're pandering your dreams of domination to an enemy, because you've run through all your allies. Isn't that right?

Vanna absorbed her unspoken speech with a faint tick in her upper right cheek. A gull called overhead, trilling like a scream.

Basa squinted at her. Beneath that ageless beauty were cracks in the veneer. Her lips were thin and dry as paper, nails dull and bloodless as glass. Faint lines hugged the curve of each eye, so fine, they were scarcely noticeable, but plentiful enough to suggest an ancient and endangered sort of porcelain. Her strength and power pulsed from her narrow frame, as a beacon on a far shore, yet, looking at her now— really looking— Basa knew her age, her fatigue, and fear.

You're dying, aren't you?

Nema didn't reply, which was answer enough.

Basa crossed her shaking arms.

How long have you got?

"Eons, years, weeks. Who knows?"

I didn't think your kind could die.

"A common misconception. It is the Oiche Ar Fad that sustains immortality. Without its benefit, our cells age and die, as yours do. The process is much slower... but ultimate, nonetheless."

Then, all of this— Basa waved a hand, encompassing all.

Was to cement your legacy? That must be a bad joke? You've murdered half of Tairngare and enslaved the other half to give yourself a last chance at immortality.

Why not return to the shadows, and leave us be?

"I cannot. I am no longer able to survive there, as you could not. It is not a place for... mortals."

Basa sat back, mystified.

Vanna went on, "With the time I've left, I mean to cure the world of the masculine plague. Return our tribes to their divine roots— in Macha's name. Help me do this, Basa. Together, we can bring a real, lasting peace to this continent, forever."

Tea, please.

Vanna glanced at her nearest servant. The girl launched herself at the larder so fast, Basa felt sure she would trip. With a trembling wrist, she handed her former Alta Prima a steaming cup of something rich and dark. It smelled faintly of Bretagn chocolate. Basa held it for a while, waiting for it to cool.

You knew I'd say no when I was brought here.

Tell me, what trick do you have in that sleeve, to force my hand?

"None. As you said, I have nothing left to barter with where you're concerned. I've taken from you and shall not beg forgiveness for that fact. Here, I hoped to appeal to you as a rational patriot, who loves Tairngare enough to help me save it."

Eva and Una?

"I see no reason why Eva ever need suffer her family's fate, if you join me. Una, on the other hand, must not be allowed to thrive. The girl will die."

Ah, we're getting to the point.

"How do you mean?"

When you say her name, I hear fear, Vanna.

She can stop you, can't she?

Vanna's lip curled. "She's an abomination, Basa. She should not exist. If Drem hadn't been so greedy for power, so eager to scar her mind and body to produce this 'prophesied child,' Una would never have been born to tip the balance. I might never have been forced to accelerate my plans to such an unfortunate degree."

So, she is Siora's heir? My young, bookish niece, who'd rather flee than rule this land as she was born to?

This girl is the reason you've lain waste to Tairngare?

"She too, is of my line, Basa. In case you haven't figured that out already. She was never meant to be born, never meant to carry such horrible power. If she rises to the throne of this land, many thousands will die. The ice will descend and bury us all. My grandson was meant to take the High King's throne, to lead us through the next Transition, but he has strayed from his path, as all men are wont to do. He fancies himself Midhir's equal, and my superior." She blew a long breath out of her nostrils. "Even he shall be lain low. If balance is not restored to this land, nothing shall survive— no one. The future of both our races is in question, my dear. I seek allies with the capacity to grasp an inconvenient truth, and the will to do what needs to be done to prevent calamity."

Una will destroy the world?

"If she takes power, Milesians will once again dominate Innisfail. You were not alive during the Transition, Basa. You did not see what these mortals did to each other, to the land, to *all* lands, in their desperation and stupidity. With my last breath, I will fight to prevent it happening all over again."

Basa sipped her tea, studying Vanna blankly. Her thoughts summoned and fixated on the sound of the bells dangling from her own balcony on the Ninth Floor, her home for four decades. She loved those bells and had always been soothed by them. Ana had grown laying beneath them reading, laughing, while she basked in the sun or stared out to sea. Basa ran her finger over her daughter's shriveled hand.

She set her cup down on the stone floor beside her chair. Inside her heart, she felt what was left of her Spark leap at her touch.

Perhaps she could help? Perhaps she *would.*

Vanna's narrow lips pulled back over a genuine smile. "I am pleased you are the reasonable woman I always thought you were."

Basa resumed her pleasant mien, filled with renewed vigor. Her gums vibrated with it. She didn't bother to stand; she'd have that much farther to fall, and if she were to do this, she'd do it with dignity. She clenched an arthritic fist, summoning every ounce of strength she had left. Vanna's eyes flew wide, a hair too late. From the core of each of Basa's cells, she unfurled her Spark. It flew from her as an arrow, lancing her enemy through the black chasm of her heart. Vanna's cup shattered against the tiles. She dropped to her knees, shrieking as her cheeks were torn open, divided from the inside by Basa's Spark. Next, her forehead, chest, and throat. A red line carved itself across Nema's neck.

Here is my answer, Vanna Nema, or whoever you truly are.

I curse you with failure at every turn.

You take from us today, steal from us tomorrow, and kill us at a whim— but that is all you will ever achieve.

Your descent is nigh, and it will be as swift and merciless as your rise... you villainous, lunatic cunt.

Basa had the extreme pleasure to watch Nema's pretty face open in widening gashes, hear her pitiful screams, before her Spark burned out. Empty of all but a lingering sense of joy at joining her beloved Ana in the Undying Lands, Basa grinned before she slumped from her chair and her head struck the ground.

28
FALLING STAR

Time and space stretched long and wide, popping his ears and stilling the blood in his veins. Beside him, Una lurched against him, unsteady as a reed. Rian gave a slight whimper as she, too, was nearly swept from her feet. Kaer Yin grasped Una's shoulders, pressing her heels into the earth. Suddenly, the group was alone in an ocean of gleaming grass beneath a sweet, summer wind. The air was ripe and fragrant as honey. A low-slung sun trailed over the whispering treetops ahead while the moon chased her from the twilit fields to the west. Bright stars glistened at either end of that rose and violet sky. Gone was the winter chewed Souther field. Their pursuers' whistles and spurs were snuffed out in a moment. Taking a deep breath, Una slid her hands over her knees.

"I can guess where we are, by how badly I want to puke."

Kaer Yin patted her back, feeling like the captain of a sinking ship. "More fun than the alternative, I'm afraid."

"Thank you, Yin," hooted Tam Lin, breathing a mite hard from all the running they'd been doing for the last few hours. "I was starting to get a stitch in my side."

"Have Shar find the others." Kaer Yin held his nose and blew out to clear his ears. It had been many, many years since he'd been in the Oiche Ar Fad. He'd all but forgotten how disorienting the shift could be.

Tam Lin waved his order away. "No bother. They'll find us. Fergal will have heard the bell. That was rather inelegantly done, cousin."

"I'm out of practice."

Shar held his ribs, sides heaving. He pawed at a tree for support. "I'll say."

Kaer Yin made a face at both of them. Robin spun around and retched into the grass. Ignoring him, Kaer Yin turned to check on Rian. She had color in her cheeks already. "We've been here before, Una and I."

"So, you have," he acknowledged. "Recently, too."

Una, also, perked up faster than everyone else. She wiped a hand over her nose and squared her shoulders. "Well, where to now?"

"Tir Falias," he sighed. "Not much choice."

"Where the hell is that?"

"Tech Duinn."

She paled. "Are you mad?"

"Do you want to go back?"

"No, I..." she searched Rian's face for affirmation.

The girl couldn't help.

Kaer Yin wasn't sure what exactly had occurred in that cabin on Samhain, but whatever had been, its recollection altered Una's entire demeanor. He watched as she seemed to deflate before his eyes.

"What did he do to you, Una?"

"He tried to— well, it isn't really what he did, rather what I..."

Her explanation trailed off, just as a flash of pealing light trailed across the sky like a falling star. The sound, like a balloon being filled and summarily popped by a large pin, made each person in their party flinch and cover their ears.

"Bloody Hells," grumbled Robin. "What was that?"

"A rider," Shar told him, green eyes on the horizon. He pointed. "There."

Indeed, a lathered warhorse perched against the terminally setting sun.

Kaer Yin clutched his pommel. "Son of a bitch."

"He's alone, at least," Tam Lin noted. "Even if I've no idea how he got here."

"I bloody well do."

"Well, grand. He's on his way over."

"Let him come."

Damek Bishop kicked his horse into a charge. As he neared, the hard determination in his eyes shone bright. Una made a move to shove to the front of the Greenmakers, but Kaer Yin elbowed her back. He drew his dagger and waited. If this arrogant, obsessive child wanted to play, by Herne, the Lord of the Wild Hunt was ready. Two months of unspeakable pain from wounds that had yet to fully heal, countless sleepless nights worrying over the fate of those he cared for, hours of discomfort and cold— low on uishge and ale— wondering what this poncey, overdressed fop was doing to Una... All of this broke over him like a fever.

"Ben, no!" cried Rian, but Kaer Yin couldn't care less.

He wanted this.

He'd wanted this since Samhain, the moment Bishop rode away with the woman he loved over his saddle, like a prized doe. Kaer Yin widened his stance. Nemain's pommel brushed his waiting fingertips.

Come on, you fool.

Come and die.

As Bishop neared, Una shouted, "Damek, no!" Ignoring her incredulous plea, he launched himself from his saddle mid-gallop, taking Kaer Yin to the ground with him. They rolled sideways, each pelting the other with bone-jarring blows. At first, Damek had the upper hand. He drove an elbow into Kaer Yin's jaw that set his ears ringing anew, but Kaer Yin grabbed the back of the young lord's head by the scruff and bashed his forehead into his nose. Damek skittered back onto his knees, coughing blood into his palms. Kaer Yin rocked to his feet, flicking the tip of his dagger toward his opponent's ear. Hissing in pain, Damek staggered to his feet, fumbling at his belt for the same weapon. Kaer Yin didn't give him too much time to recover. He drove him back toward his charger, which was much more unsettled by their surroundings than was his master. With a grunt, Damek dug his heels in, ducking under two of Kaer Yin's quick-stop thrusts. At the third, however, Damek managed to hook an arm around Kaer Yin's shoulders and slam his fist deep into the Crown Prince's right eye, before kicking him roundly in the chest.

Kaer Yin backed off, if only to breathe through the fresh fury that surged through his nerves with the pain. Glaring at Bethany's beloved Lord Bishop, he slid his fingers over Nemain's pommel. Four eager Sidhe took their places behind their prince, larks raised.

Damek choked out a dry laugh, drawing his sabre and using it to point at Tam Lin. "I knew, if that really is the Prince of Connaught, there was no way you'd have missed the chance to press your luck. Glad you could make it, Prince Adair. Truly. There's so much I didn't get to say, last time."

"Damek, please stop. Go back," pleaded Una, genuine sorrow in her voice.

Damek's facial muscles twitched at her voice; otherwise, he kept his full attention on the Prince of Innisfail. That was as well. Kaer Yin wanted things simple. He cracked his knuckles. "You heard her. Go home, boy."

"You know, I saw you once, at Dumnain— *from* a distance, of course. The way the old men whispered fear of you, you might have been some kind of god."

"I am no god," observed Kaer Yin, wiping blood from his own mouth.

"Obviously. Gods don't bleed, do they?" Damek flexed his fingers over his hilt, eyeing Kaer Yin carefully. "Give her back."

"I am not her keeper, and you are not her jailer."

Silence stretched between them.

"How did he get here, anyway?" Tam Lin asked, aside.

"His father," Una told him. "He was like you."

Tam Lin recoiled. "Ugh, *another* faerie?"

Rian shot O'Ruiadh a look that should have boiled his tongue from his skull. He quickly shut his mouth with an audible snap of his jaws.

"He looks a bit too human if you ask me," ruminated Shar.

Damek ignored them all, his focus on Kaer Yin. "Fight me for her, then."

Una groaned, "Damek, go home!"

Finally, he met her eyes. Watching them both carefully, what Kaer Yin saw in her returned gaze burned. Deep, complex feelings were not something he hoped to witness in her expression, but there they were, all the same.

"Not without you," Damek promised her. He unbuttoned his doublet very casually, as if fear were the furthest emotion from his mind.

Kaer Yin's smile was forced. "I won't mind killing you, Bishop, but I think someone here would rather not have your death on their conscience. Last chance."

Damek flung his doublet and cloak away, brandishing his sabre with a flourish. "I'll pass. Shall we?"

"Kaer Yin," Una said softly. "He's blood. Please, don't—"

"I'll try," he heaved a heavy sigh. Truthfully, he wished no one was in that meadow save for him and Bishop. Then, he'd have the pleasure of bleeding the arrogant little prick, drop by drop.

"He couldn't," boasted Damek. "No need to worry, Una. We've fought before, you see. I know his footwork by rote. Tell your men to stay out of it, Adair."

Tam Lin said, "Boy, if you manage to land a single blow, I'll congratulate you by taking each of your grubby hands off at the wrists.

"Tam Lin, tóg na cailíní agus lean ort. Gabhfaidh mé suas?"[21] asked Kaer Yin.

"Ithe cac, col ceathrar,"[22] Tam Lin declined.

"I'll catch up."

"I said no, you grimy blighter."

Kaer Yin wasn't granted freedom to argue. Damek rushed him, and it seemed he was everywhere at once. Kaer Yin dodged, parried, rolled, and leapt under, over, and around each thrust— but the attacks wouldn't stop coming and were much, much more skillful than they should have been. *Neithana.* Not only did the Lord Bishop know how to handle a longsword, he did so in pure Sidhe fashion. Someone had taught this young man to fight like one of Kaer Yin's own. Someone good. He'd sparred with this man a mere two months previously, and already, his skills had raced so far ahead.

How? Where in the *Hells* did Bishop learn to fight like this?

"Herne," avowed Tam Lin, mouth agape. "That's—"

"I know!" Kaer Yin broke out in a real sweat, busy putting every effort into defending his vitals for each eyeblink it took for Bishop to attack.

"Stop dancing around and fight back!" Damek jibed, leaning right to swat Nemain's tip away with the flat of his blade. A heartbeat later, his knuckles crashed into Kaer Yin's nose. Kaer Yin staggered a few paces, leaning against Nemain to catch a break. Through the red haze in eyes, he barely marked the meadow, the group, or the sword in his own hand. All he could see was the triumphant smirk on the Lord of Clare's petulant mouth.

---

21   "Tam Lin, take the girls and go ahead."
22   "Eat shite, cousin."

"You've done it now, lad. I hope you feel good about your chances," called Tam Lin, knowing very well what that look meant.

"That's a dead fellow, or I'm buggered," whistled Robin.

"Good! Come on!" Damek roared.

Kaer Yin Adair answered.

He came.

Damek, now on the defensive, was in awe of the speed, calculation, and brutal grace the Prince of Innisfail forced into every stroke. His footwork was intricately, inhumanly precise, and maddening. Damek considered himself a master of every sword form he could study. In fact, he'd always had such an affinity for steel, he could garner a fair understanding of each discipline after one or two bouts. His father had told him his talent was a gift of his blood, but Damek didn't care about the particulars. He knew he wasn't merely good: he was excellent and knowing it didn't encourage false humility. He had an intuition, an aptitude that most swordsmen could never hope to match.

Though, in the Prince of Innisfail's case, Damek could but marvel. For the second time, he realized there had never lived a man more skilled with a sword.

Neithana, as with all other styles Damek had studied, bore a specific formula. Once he mastered the complex foundation, from there it was only a matter of time before the art came to him as naturally as breathing. Neithana, all said, took lifetimes to properly conquer. Watching Kaer Yin move, feeling the power behind each stroke, he finally understood. Even after having fought the prince once before in the wilds of Northern Eire, he'd never seen such measured skill in his life. Not even Damek's father had it, and he had once been lauded as the greatest swordsman in Armagh.

It wasn't simply the fluidity, the practiced motion without thought that shocked him most, rather the complete dissolution of self that all sword masters speak of, and none have ever achieved. To become the blade itself, to merge with it as an extension of one's own will— *that* is what made Kaer Yin a peerless opponent.

In two minutes, Damek was already sweating heavily and taking hacking breaths that sounded terribly reminiscent of an old man attempting a sprint. With a grunt that cost him something deep in his gut, he lurched away, putting a fair distance between the prince and himself. The bastard didn't even appear winded. "Damn!" He couldn't help but laugh. Kaer Yin didn't seem to share his amusement. His silver eyes gleamed like ice chips in a storm. "They weren't kidding when they said you were the best Dannan swordsman alive." This was a genuine compliment.

Tam Lin snickered from the sideline.

Robin scratched at his scar. "Best leave it at that, yer lordship. I've seen him cut through scores o'fellas with that face on him. I'd get on, were I ye."

Damek shrugged. "Let's try a different tack." He slid his feet toward the opposite position: one foot slipping forward, the other behind.

He lifted his sabre into a high guard.

"Godsdamnit," muttered Tam Lin.

"Adrac," Shar concurred.

"What's that?" Una asked, lost.

"Armagh's private discipline," he replied. "Fir Bolg stuff, very complicated."

"That explains a great deal. Yin," bellowed Tam Lin. "You'd better quit messing about and kill that faerie cunt. He's a fucking Mac Nemed!"

"I knew that already," Kaer Yin snapped. "Stop distracting me."

Tam Lin threw up his hands.

"You ready?"

Damek grinned. He was having the time of his life, regardless of the outcome. If he died fighting the greatest swordsman in the world, he couldn't think of a better ending. If, however, he won... He launched himself again, giving everything he had.

Adrac lacked the sinuous beauty of Neithana, but made up for form with function, patience, and kinetic power. Neithana was clean, hard to follow with the eyes, and always presented a moving target. Adrac was the opposite. Using the inertia of an opponent against itself, it took lethal advantage of any gaps in one's endurance.

Damek Bishop was good. Again, far too damned good.

Even a faerie lad who'd embraced his Sidhe heritage would scarcely have the time and training to achieve such skill in this discipline— *let* alone, the permission to do so at the behest of the Mac Nemed Clan. Yet, Kaer Yin sensed no magic in his talents. They simply... were. It seemed the boy had a gift. He must be the first true prodigy Kaer Yin had ever encountered. He was too good to be just anyone's son. Once, many, many years ago... Kaer Yin fought a man who very nearly carved his heart out in a drunken duel. That man, as it happened, was to die on the battlefield at Dumnain, decades later. There wasn't a shred of doubt in Kaer Yin's mind who this boy's father might be. Again, Damek had him on the defensive, pressing his advantage of surprise. When Kaer Yin redoubled his efforts by attempting to make a steel wall, Damek took a low guard, sweeping up from the ground and leaping around Kaer Yin to jerk Nemain's tip backward. That opened up a vicious gash in Kaer Yin's right arm.

"There went your hands, Lord Bishop!" sang Tam Lin, with honest concern.

He'd never seen his cousin lose a bout before— *especially* to a faerie Souther who fought for the likes of Patrick Donahugh. Kaer Yin shot him a glare. Well, he wasn't about to see it happen now, either. The good Lord Bishop had a flaw in his footwork... and when he'd come in too close once before, Kaer Yin saw the ogham stone sticking out of Damek's damp tunic.

No wonder the lad had been able to chase them into the Oiche Ar Fad so effortlessly. He had a bloody key.

Oblivious, Damek glowed with martial fervor. He moved back into a high guard, as if winding a clock. "Are we done playing now, Highness?"

Kaer Yin flashed Una an apologetic glance.

"Yes." He moved, dogging every step Damek took, swallowing up every space he'd meant to slide into. Before he could fix his heels, Kaer Yin pushed him back. Again, and again Kaer Yin pressed him this way, until Damek faltered a bit on advance, temporarily stymied by the speed with which his adversary attacked. When Damek reared left to get under his elbow, Kaer Yin suddenly turned, leaning in to clutch Damek's sword arm from below. A single vicious jerk, and Bishop cried out, dropping his sword. Then for the second time, Kaer Yin's forehead smashed into Bishop's nose, then he hefted him by the collar and threw him bodily over his own shoulder. Damek struck the earth with a dry thud.

He howled in pain and, no doubt, rage.

A broken arm and nose will do that to a man.

Kaer Yin kicked Damek's sword away from his grasping fingers, and knelt beside him, leaning against Nemain for support.

"Don't," Una repeated, from somewhere behind him.

Kaer Yin exhaled long and hard. "Do you hear that, Lord Marshal? Una alone kept you alive today. Perhaps you'll remember that when next you decide to take a woman against her will." With that, he reached into Damek's tunic and ripped the *ogham* stone away, as if from a naughty child.

Only when Bishop disappeared from the meadow altogether did Kaer Yin meet Una's eyes. She knelt before him, tucking herself into his arms. She didn't speak a word— she didn't need to.

He understood.

Over Una's head, he looked up at Tam Lin, his arm burning like someone had stuffed his skin full of nettles. "That was a lot fucking harder than it should have been." He turned the *ogham* stone over in his free hand, as if spinning an entirely new threat in his mind.

LATER, WHEN THEY WERE PACKED AND READY TO MEET THE OTHERS some miles hence, Kaer Yin pulled Una aside. He knew what he had to do, though he had no desire to do it. If he didn't say it now, he never would.

"Una," he began, hesitating. "Where do you want to go? Truly?"

Her brow gathered. "I thought—"

"No. That's what *I* wanted, why I came here. I hoped... well, it doesn't matter now. I don't need to know what I want: I want to know what you do."

She stared off at the distant treetops waving in the mild summer wind. Her eyes were bright with tears, though they did not fall. "I want to make up my own mind. I want to live my own life, be my own woman. I want to be free."

His heart clenched. "That's what I thought. I can— I will take you anywhere you want to go, Una. Alba, Bretagne, Kernow, Hells, I'll even take you to Iberia, if you're feeling adventurous. Wherever you want to go, whoever you want to be, I'll give it to you. I want you to be happy. You deserve to be."

He let her fingers go; resolved, even if it killed him.

"You know," her voice broke. "My grandmother always says freedom is a choice you make every day. I never really understood that till right now."

"I don't follow."

"I *am* free, Kaer Yin. Finally, free to choose for myself."

He felt like drinking himself dead, right about then. "So, what do you choose?"

"You're really stupid, you know that?" Her hand slid over his cheek. She pulled him in so close, her nose brushed against his. He flinched— bloody hurt for the number of times he'd recently taken a punch— but didn't budge. "This is freedom, Kaer Yin. Freedom to follow my heart."

When her lips met his, this time, he didn't allow her to dart away.

29
BLOOD MAGIC

Melba was unceremoniously dragged through a garish room decorated in silver plate and ugly red gemstones. The room stank of incense and mold, and something sweeter— bolder, which left a sour taste at the back of her throat. She gagged. Before she could locate the source of the rot, she was thrown to the floor by a dark-haired man who was obviously Sidhe and seemed too large for the space. It took several seconds to gain her bearings, and a sharp boot to force her to her knees.

Her guard backed off after a last brutal kick for good measure.

After several sucking breaths, Melba could focus on her own filthy hands against the expensive silk carpet beneath her. She couldn't help but flinch. This was the first time she'd been outside of her cell in weeks. Had it been so long that her skin should look like the shrunken husk of a fish's belly? She imagined she must smell even worse, though with the pervading scent of decay so prominent a feature in this enclosed space, her hygiene might be of least concern. She pushed herself upright, eyes level with a broad, walnut desk.

Flinching a bit in the invasive lanternlight from the far corner of its smooth surface, she didn't see the shriveled occupant of the room until she caught a haggard reflection in the polished wood.

Melba recoiled.

Nema? But how?

The figure cackled, drawing Melba's gaze to the real thing above.

The sight was startling, to say the least.

Though there was no discounting the identity of the individual seated behind that desk, her appearance was far removed from the face that haunted Melba's dreams. Where once Nema had been stately, regal, and quite handsome to look upon, now she was painfully thin and overly pale. Her eyes had shrunken into her skull and her once beautiful ochre skin sagged from her bones. Though, this was not the worst of it. A jagged gash had opened the tissues of her face from her right eyebrow to the line of her throat. Melba could plainly see through the torn skin, yellow fat, and shiny muscle, to Nema's browning teeth.

Melba felt her airways constrict.

How long have I been imprisoned?

"Not long," answered Nema, as if she had plucked the thought directly from Melba's mind. "Have you had time to rethink your hasty words, Melba my dear?"

Melba had read about a serpent once that would issue a rattle when it prepared to strike. The rasping quality of Nema's voice reminded her of this now. She cleared her dry, dusty throat. "Yes. I have, Eminence."

Nema's smile was a horror that turned Melba's empty stomach. "Excellent. Then you will sign and merge Alba's interests with our own?"

"I will," Melba replied, and hated herself. Truth be told, strong though she might have been, she had not prepared herself for internment. Confinement and darkness had done unspeakable things to her mind. She would readily admit that she would sign away her own children at that point, if to be spared that long, cold, dark a second time. "Gladly."

Nema waved a withered hand and Melba felt herself shoved into the desk. The guard laid a scrap of vellum before her, and a sharp quill was crammed into her shaking fist. She didn't even care to read it. With tears in her eyes, she clenched her teeth and signed her country away. Before she might recant her decision, the document jerked away, even as her ink was wet on the page.

Not everyone is a mountain, she told herself.

Siora will forgive me.

Nema's laugh felt like a lash against her skin. "Not likely. You see, Siora was a bit of a fanatic about these things. I should know. I made her."

Melba's embattled heart raced anew. "You can read my mind?"

Nema shrugged. "Most times. Some people broadcast more loudly than others. Your thoughts are like a shout underwater, but I can gather the gist."

Melba opted to remain silent and stifle her thoughts. They might betray her. Nema drew her heavy fur stole more tightly around her shoulders. The room was too small to accommodate braziers and was therefore quite cold. "Have you any requests for me, now that you've seen the proverbial light?"

Melba didn't hesitate. "I want to go home."

"Perhaps something less... demonstrative?"

Silence stretched between them, and Melba let out a breath. "I've done as ye asked. You have no further opposition from Alba, Eminence."

"Nor will I again, Mistress." The macabre grin alarmed Melba once more. "You see, I can't have you returning to power with that troublesome family of yours. You'd make a poor influence and would surely convince yourself and others that this concession was made under duress."

Some of Melba's old fire leapt in her belly. "It *has* been made under duress, Eminence. Ye killed my men and imprisoned me for daring to debate yer terms. To pretend otherwise would be disingenuous."

"Hm." Nema grinned again. "If only your hand bore the same courage as your mouth, no?"

Melba shrank into herself.

Equal parts rising panic and boiling fury commingled in her breast.

You're going to die.

Do something!

"Alba will rise against ye, with me or without me. If ye spare me now, I vow to plead yer case to my people and vote to uphold yer interests."

Nema ignored her comment and nodded to the tall guard behind Melba. "Bring her to me, Raes."

Melba was allowed a momentary breath of perfect fear before she was wrenched to her feet then forcibly prostrated before Nema. She struggled against her captor, to little effect. He delivered a blow to her left ear that made the room spin around her, Nema's glowing green eyes loomed at the edge of her spinning vision. A scream built deep in her chest.

"There now," Nema said, reaching out and digging her sharp nails into Melba's delicate collarbone. The bones beneath that hand trembled with some unknown current. Instantly, Melba felt the oxygen whisk from her lungs.

What is happening?

To her rising horror, Melba watched the flesh around Nema's damaged cheek begin to stitch itself together, and the hollows of her eye sockets fill with sudden vigor. Simultaneously, Melba felt her body crumple beneath Nema's hand. Her muscles collapsed while her veins drained of fluid. Her throat closed up when no blood or water was left to hold its passages open. She felt her eyes wither in their sockets, and she let out a pathetic gurgle that should have been a scream.

She's eating me!

"That's a crude way to put it, Melba dear," purred Nema in Melba's weakening ears. "I like to think of it as a 'repurposing' of useless organic material. Sounds much more elegant that way, don't you think?"

AUTHOR'S NOTE

2022
Sunny Florida

THIS SERIES WAS THE CULMINATION OF 24 YEARS OF HARD WORK, SELF-doubt, disbelief, giddy anticipation, relationship strife, stolid determination, depression, sidetracks, renewed hope, disappointment, stubbornness, imposter syndrome, begrudging self-respect, supportive peers, toxic peers, success, failure, and love.

In 24 years, Kaer Yin and I have stormed many castles, lost many battles, and found that inner peace we thought would forever lay just beyond our grasp. We weathered every negative thought and comment, each self-fulfilling prophecy, and every 'yeah, but what do you *really* do' question.

Kaer Yin and I have been together a long, long time. You might say we grew up together. Thank you for joining us on this journey.

We'll be back.

L.M. Riviere

www.lmriviere.com

Social: @LMRiviereAuthor

ABOUT THE TEXT

This series leans heavily on Irish Gaelic. As a student of the language, I have done my level best to include the appropriate usage of every term and phrase, from syntax to punctuation. That said, I am not entirely fluent, and there are bound to be mistakes in the text.

Additionally, most of the terms I use were derived from the most archaic forms, as the characters and place names are meant to reflect a time period and etymology that precedes written alphabet by at least a thousand years. In that order, there are bound to be minor variations in spelling and pronunciation. Some terms I changed to suit myself and the rolling language I hear in my head when my characters speak... and I daresay, that is my prerogative in a fantasy novel.

For example, there a few obvious 'me-isms', like the use of '*Tuatha Dé Dannan*', which is historically spelled '*Danaan*', or '*Danann*'. I elected to place a hard focus on the interior 'n' to aid its pronunciation for non-Gaelic speakers.

If there are any mistakes or unbearable abuses of the language that distract from the text, please keep in mind that this story exists in a (semi) fictional continent a thousand years from now. A few liberties were taken.

GLOSSARY

Innish names, phrases and terms; in alphabetical order:

A

- *Aenghus Mac Og*- (Aynn-guss-mack-Oh-ge) Dannan god of the Western Sea, love and poetry. Comparable to the Greek god Dionysus.
- *Aes Sidhe*- (Ayess-Shee) "Land of the ever-living', or 'Land of the Sidhe'. Northernmost region of Innisfail, home of the Immortal High King, and his people. Comprised of two major tribes; the Tuatha De Dannan, in Bri Leith and the Fir Bolg in Armagh.
- *Agrea*- (Ah-gray-ah) The Agriculturists Guild in Tairngare, run directly by the House of Commons in Tairnganese Parliament.
- *Alta*- (All-tah) A priestess second in rank to the Doma, in the Cloister of the Eternal Flame, in Tairngare.
- *Amer Gin Gluingel*- (Ahmer-genn-glonn-gall) "Amer the White kneed". A son of Mil Espanga, bard, druid and magician. Helped his brother Eber Finn, conquer Innisfail, and defeat the Tuatha De Dannan.
- *Aoife*- (Eee-Fah) "Radiant one".
- *Ard Ri*- (Ardh- Ree) "Highest King".

- *Ard Tuaithe*- (Ardh-too-ah-hee) "Highest Landsman". A common way to address a Sidhe noble. "Tuaithe", simply means 'countryside'.
- *Ard Tiarne*- (Ardh-tee-arh-nah) "Highest Lord, or Prince". A title reserved for the Crown Prince of Innisfail.
- *Armagh*- (Arr-mah) Capital of the Kingdom of Ulster, and seat of the ancient Kings of the Fir Bolg. As the Fir Bolg's power has waned over the centuries, the Kingdom of Ulster is less than one-third its size in ancient times. Ruled by the Mac Nemed Clan (House of the Black Bull).

B

- *Badh*- (Bae-ve) Sidhe goddess of discord, disharmony and dread. Pestilence and famine are also her domain. One of three divine sisters. SEE MORRIGAN AND MACHA. Her herald is the crow.
- *Ban*- (Bahn) "White", "Light" or "Bright". As in "Ban Lug"— or the Month of Midsummer (formerly August).
- *Ban Sidhe*- (Bahn-shee) "White Spirit" or "Good Folk". A term reserved for the higher classification of Sidhe (or Immortal Ones). The Tuatha De Dannan and Fir Bolg, belong to this class, on whole. See *DAOINE SIDHE*, for nobility.
- *Bel*- (Ball) The Sidhe sun god. Considered a male figure, but otherwise one of the few non-personified deities in the Sidhe pantheon, save for Samn, his mate.
- *Beltane*- (Ball-tinna) A festival celebrated on the first of the Month "Ban-Bela" (Bahn-balla), formerly 'May'. A celebration for seeding crops, full spring, and fertility.
- *Bethany*- (Beth-ahn-nee) The Southernmost Kingdom in Innisfail, and second-most powerful city in Eire. Ruled by the Donahugh Clan, under their line of ancestral Duchs. Seat of Duch Patrick Donahugh, fervent enemy of Aes Sidhe. Sometimes called the 'Machine City', for their use of cannons and other siege devices in warfare.
- *Bodhran*- (Bode-ran) A circular frame drum made from animal hide and polished wood. The Sidhe carry bodhrans into battle.
- *Bov Mac Nuada Dearg*- (Bove- mack- new-ah-dah-derrck) King of Connaught, and former High King of the Tuatha De Dannan, in pre-Celtic times. Known as 'Bov the Red', for his famous temper, and rash behavior. Rules from his capital at Croghan. Brother to the High King, Midhir.
- *Breccan*- (Breck-ahn) "Freckled one".
- *Brehon*- (Breh-honn) "Teacher" or "Knowing One". Brehons are the highest ranking magic users in Innisfail. They are considered 'holy men', for the

ability to commune with both spirits and nature itself. Their advice is sought by Sidhe leaders before any major commitment, such as war, marriage, treaties, or policy making. They are as feared as they are respected, for to incur a Brehon's wroth is to endure all manner of travesties. It is illegal to harm a Brehon, and they are immune to Common Law. A Brehon may gainsay even the High King, without fear of repercussion.

- *Bretagne*- (Breh-tan-ee) A peninsula jutting into the Southern sea, from the old kingdom of Francia. A major sea power in its own right, and one of the few remaining kingdoms free of Innish over-rule.

- *Brida*- (Bree-dah) The Sidhe goddess of the dawn. The Dagda named one of his own daughters for her, who died in ancient times. The horse, is her herald— speed and strength, are her creed.

- *Bri Leith*- (Bree-leyth) "Highest Realm", or "Foremost Hall". Capital of Aes Sidhe, and home of the High King, Midhir. Ruled by the Adair Clan (House of the White Stag).

- *Bru Na Boinne*- (Broo-nah-boyne) A valley of ancient hillforts at the Northern border of Eire, along the river Boyne (*Boinne*, in old Innish). The passage tombs of Newgrange, Dowth, and Knowth— gird the river from the North, in Aes Sidhe. The passage tombs are older even than the Sidhe, having been built many thousands of years before the Invasion Cycles of Innish history. The Sidhe call these first peoples 'Fomorian', or sometimes 'Stone People'; for the complex network of standing stones, passage tombs, dolmens, and hillforts they left behind. Considered the holiest site in Innisfail, by the Sidhe.

C

- *Clare*- (Clayre) A sea province along the South-Western Coast of Eire. Ruled by Lord Damek Bishop.

- *Connaught*- (Cuhn-aught) Westernmost kingdom in Aes Sidhe. Ruled by King Bov, 'The Red'.

- *Croghan*- (Crew-Hahn) Capital of the Kingdom of Connaught, and seat of Bov Dearg, and the Marshal of the West. Ruled by the Dearg Clan (The House of the Red Eagle).

- *Cu Chulainn*- (Cu-hoo-linn) An ancient Innish hero, and champion of a Milesian King of Eire.

- *Crom Dagda*- (Cruhm- dagh-dah) The 'good father'. First King of the Tuatha De Dannan, and also a Skysinger of unimaginable power. Sacrificed his own eye to save Nuada's life after the battle at Magh Tuiredh, against the formidable Fomorian King, Balor. And years later, sacrificed his own life to save his people from the onslaught of the Milesians, after Nuada's death. He is honored at Cromnasa, each midwinter. Opened a path into the Otherworld with his own sacrifice, which granted all Sidhe tribes everlasting life.

- *Cromnasa*- (Cruhm-nah-sa) "Festival of Crom" or "Crom's Feast". Celebration of the Dagda's sacrifice for the Immortality of the Sidhe. Midwinter festival, celebrated on the Longest Night of the year.

- *Cymru*- (Kim-ree) An ancient Kingdom at the Easternmost reaches of Innisfail, having once been called 'Wales', before The Transition. A mineral rich country, for its mountains and hills are filled with precious ores. In the West of the Kingdom, their major export is wine, which is grown largely in the South, toward the capital at Swansea. Cymru is a Tairnganese colony but pays homage and tithes to Aes Sidhe. Over the Cyrmian mountains in the far east of the Kingdom, lies a region known as the 'Wastes', for its inhospitable, uninhabitable, and arid landscape.

- *Cymrian*- (Kim-ree-ahn) One who dwells in Cymru.

D

- *Dagda*- SEE CROM DAGDA, under 'C'.
- *Danu*- (Day-new) The goddess of the earth, in pre-Innish Europe. The patron goddess of the Tuatha de Dannan, who claim to be descended from her and her mate Donn, the god of death.
- *Daoine Sidhe*- (Doone-Shee) A term reserved for the upper echelons of Ban Sidhe society. The nobles and royalty of Aes Sidhe.
- *Dearg*- (Derckk) "The Red".
- *Damek Bishop, Lord of Clare*- (Dahm-eck) Alis Donahugh's illegitimate son, fathered by an unknown Sidhe lord. Adopted by Duch Patrick Donahugh after his mother's death. An accomplished soldier and statesman. Commander of Bethany's armed forces.
- *Dian Cecht*- (Diahn-caysht) Sidhe ancestor god, son of the Dagda. Forged Nuada's Golden Hand, after the battle at Maigh Turiedh. The Sidhe consider him the father of healing.
- *Diarmid Mac Nuada Dubh*- (Derr-mett-mack-nu-ah-dah-duvv) King of Tech Duinn, and Lord of the *Oiche Ard Fad*. Called *Fiachra Ri*, by the Sidhe- or Raven King, in Eire. A Skysinger, like his father Crom Dagda; and Brehon of the Tuatha De Dannan. He is the only member of his house, as he rules a kingdom of the dead. All lesser Sidhe call him 'King', including the Lu Sidhe, and Dor Sidhe- which would unleash themselves upon mortal kind, did he not guard the gates of the Otherworld with a firm hand. Brother to Midhir, the High King. An ambitious, mercurial man, whose loyalty can

never truly be counted upon. Also known as "Diarmid, The Black". Servant of Donn- the god of the dead; and Donn's daughter, Morrigan.

- _Doma_- The title of the High Priestess of the Cloister of the Eternal Flame, in Tairngare. The theocratic and secular ruler of Tairngare. Holds a seat on the High King's Council, and the highest-ranking official in Eire. Currently held by Drem Moura.

- _Donn_- "Dark One", the Sidhe god of the dead. Mate of Danu, goddess of the earth. Donn is the only god the Sidhe and Milesians shared before the Invasions. Donn, was also the name of one of Mil Espagna's seven sons. He died after cursing his brother Ir. Diarmid as a Skysinger and Brehon, is his servant.

- _Dor_- (Door) "Black" or "Darkest", see also 'dorchas'. As in "Dor Samna" (Door-Sawa), or the Month of Winter's Birth (formerly, October).

- _Dor Sidhe_- (Door-shee) "Darkest Spirits", or "Evil Folk". A term to describe the darker denizens of the Otherworld. Unnatural beasts and spirits that harm and hunt mortals for food or sport. They only exist within the Otherworld, or sometimes on the fringes of the border with Aes Sidhe- where the veil between worlds is thinnest. Often roam wild in Eire on Samhain, when the veil vanishes altogether, once a year. Goblins, selkies, pookas, trolls, ghasts, giants, and gnomes- all belong to this classification.

- _Drem Moura_- (Drehm-More-Ah) The High Priestess of Siora, the Ancestor; in the Cloister of the Eternal Flame at Tairngare. Head of the wealthiest and most influential family in Eire, and most powerful woman on the continent. Not well-loved by the common people, for her frequent attempts to crown members of her own family Queen of the Commons; in order to shore up absolute power for the Moura Clan. Mother of Arrin Moura, and grandmother to Una.

- _Donahugh_- (Donnah-hew) The ruling clan of Bethany, and the greater South of Innisfail.

- _Dubh_- (Duvv) "Black".

- _Duch_- (Duke) A lord second only to a king in rank— but far removed from a High King, who rules over all lesser kings and lords equally.

- _Dumnain_- A village in the lower Midlands of Eire, which was destroyed by the Crown Prince Kaer Yin Adair, during the war with Bethany in '84. The site of one of the bloodiest battles in Innish history, and the very place Duch Donahugh lost his right to a seat on the High King's Council, in exchange for his life. Due to this battle, the Kingdom of Bethany pays the highest tithes and taxes in Innisfail, in reparation for the horrors inflicted on the Eirean people for Bethany's warmongering. Also, the site where the High King's son was exiled from Aes Sidhe for war crimes, after the extreme measures he took to safeguard his own troops.

E

- *Eber Finn*- (Everr-Feen) A Milesian King, son of the King Mil Espagna. The first 'celtic' king of Innisfail.
- *Eire*- (Ay-err) The Milesian (mortal) region of Innisfail. It borders Aes Sidhe at the Boyne in the Midlands and ends at the Bretagn Straits in the far South. Straddles the Straits of Mannanan in the East. Cities like Tairngare and Ten Bells have colonies in Cymru and Kernow (formerly Wales, and Cornwall).
- *Emain Macha*- (Aavvinn-mash-ah) A holy hillfort, in the Kingdom of Ulster.
- *Eochaid Mac Nemed*- (Yoh-hee- mack- nehm-ehd) Ancient King of the Fir Bolg. Slain by Nuada, king of the Tuatha De Dannan for his throne and the right to rule in Innisfail. Married to his cousin Liadan, by their Fomorian Grandfather, Balor. Was a just ruler, and fearsome warrior.
- *Eri Mac Midhir Bres*- (Ayre-ee-mack-med-heer-bray) Daughter of Midhir and Etain, Princess of Innisfail, and Queen of Scotia. Married to Jan Fir Bres, King of Scotia; and Lord of Skye.
- *Eriu*- (Ayr-yoo) One of the Dagda's daughters, for which Eire was named. Died in ancient times.

F

- *Faerie*- (Fare-ee) "Doomed One", or "Touched by Doom". A racial slur for those of half-Sidhe blood. Also used to denigrate people born with deformities, mental disorders, or those whom suffer from depression or madness. It is believed that the blood of the Sidhe is a curse for mortal kind, and often leaves its progeny unnaturally lovely, but usually deficient in every other area. Faeries (whether real or slandered) are largely reviled in Eire.
- *Fainne*- (Feene) The literal gold standard, upon which all Innish currency is based. Also called "Crowns", or "Royals".
- *Falan*- (Fahl-ahn) The given name of two members of the Armagh royal family, Falan the Elder, and Falan the Younger, respectively. An ancient Bolgish name.
- *Fiachra Ri*- (Fee-ah-cruh-ree) "Raven King". Refers to Diarmid Mac Nuada Dubh, the King of *Tech Duinn*— or the Land of the Dead.
- *Fir Bolg*- (Feer-Bolck) A tribe of Sidhe warriors, descended from the ancient warrior Nemed. They fought with the Fomorians for several generations, and

were expelled for a time to Southern Europe, where they were enslaved by the Greek tribes in Macedon. Forced to carry bags of stone up and down ladders into mines, before their escape back to Innisfail, they became known as the "Bag Men". Close cousins of the Tuatha De Dannan from their mutual ancestor, Nemed- but dark complected, where the Dannans are fair. Sometimes called, "dark elves" for this trait. Their last stronghold in Innisfail is the city of Armagh, ruled by the Mac Nemed Clan.

- *Fodla*- (Fole-ah) One of Crom Dagda's wives.
- *Fomorians*- (Fov-or-ee-ahns) Ancient people whom lived in Innisfail before the first invasions. Worshipped dark gods of earth and stone, harvest and reaping, until a Comet known as Lug of the Long Arm came sailing out of the west, bringing calamity, and famine. They began to build stone circles and passage tombs to mark the heavens after this, to honor their new god. Defeated by the Fir Bolg in ancient times. The Tuatha De Dannan revere them as wise ancestors and keep their holy places sacred. They also adopted several of the Fomorian gods, like Lug of the Long Arm, Bel the sun god, and Samn the moon goddess. Also known as the "Stone People".

G

- *Geis*- (Gay-ehss) "Unbreakable Vow". A curse, taboo, or restriction placed upon an individual of power, to restrict their actions. In a Dannan warrior's case, it is an obligation one cannot break, without great personal sacrifice.

H

- *Hamish*- (Hay-mesh) A soldier from Bethany.
- *Herne*- (Hurnn) The White Stag, or God of the Forest. The patron god of House Adair.

I

- *Imbolg*- (Em-bolk) A festival in high winter, to summon spring. Celebrated on the first day of the Month of Blinding White, "Dor Imba" (Formerly February).
- *Innisfail*- (Enn-ess-fay-ehl) "Land of Destiny". A small continent at the rim of the Northern Ice Flows, comprising much of what was once Ireland, Scotland, Wales, and Cornwall. Much of what was England has largely become tundra, or inhospitable wastes; due to catastrophic climate change, and trace human corruptions of the land. In many places, the soil is either frozen under two feet of ice, or simply too toxic from long-forgotten nuclear reactors that have leached radiation into the soil. Innisfail is the last bastion of

relative habitable land in what was Europe. Parts of Northern France, Spain and Portugal, are similarly liveable- but not as biodiverse. This biodiversity and ecological prosperity are due in large part, to the Sidhe, whom have reclaimed dominance over the land.

J

- *Ian Fir Bres*- (Yahn-feer-bray) King of Scotia, and Lord of Skye. Descended from the Half-Fomorian king Bres, whom married one of the Dagda's daughters, and emigrated to Skye. Second cousin to the High King and married to his daughter Eri.

K

- *Kaer Yin Mac Midhir Adair*- (Kayer-eeann-mack-med-eehr-ah-dare) The *Ard Tuiathe* of the *Tuatha De Dannan*, and Crown Prince of Innisfail. Son of Midhir and Etain, he was the first Dannan to be born in Innisfail after The Transition. Grand Marshal of the Wild Hunt, and Commander of Aes Sidhe's standing armies. Slayed Kevin Donahugh in single combat, during the first Bethonair War, and ended the war of '84, at Dumnain with another victory over the Donahugh Clan. Prince of Eire, and Cymru. A cold, unfeeling character, who values martial might over all other virtues.

L

- *Libella*- Tairngare's elite class of nobles. To be a member of the Libella, and its House in Parliament, one must hold a Patent of Maternas, which must be traced back at least three generations, in the Cloister of the Eternal Flame. Also, refers to the House of Nobles in Parliament.
- *Libellum*- (Ly-bell-uhm) Founded by the Tairnganese aristocractic class. The Educator's Guild in Tairngare, also a collection of schools, in which all Tairnganese citizens (even those whom live in the Colonies) may study free, although to earn a degree in any field, one must pass a series of aptitude tests before and after each school term, to assure the student is devoted to his or her craft. The schooling might be free, but each school requires a sizeable donation from the family to ensure employment afterward. Most students who are not from Aristocratic families, often take secondary education in the Agrea for agriculture, or buy into the Merchanta to apprentice for a trade. The Libellum educates all children not accepted in the Cloister, until the age of 16, when the more expensive secondary education begins. Usually specializing in Law, Engineering, Rhetoric, or Medicine.

- _Liadan Mac Nemed_ (formerly, Mac Balor) (Lee-ah-dann-mack-neh-mehd) Queen of the Fir Bolg in ancient times, and Dowager Queen of Armagh, after The Transition.
- _Lir_ (Leer) A Sidhe ancestor god. His children were changed into swans by his second wife and were forced to languish in these forms for hundreds of years.
- _Lug-_ (Lew) Lug of the Long Arm, was a Fomorian sky deity that the Dannans appropriated when they conquered Innisfail in ancient times. He is represented as a traveling god, who comes only once every eighty years or so— sometimes bringing fortune, and others, calamity. The Sidhe pray to him for luck and guidance. Often considered the God of Law, and Chance.
- _Lugnasa-_ (Lew-nah-sah) Festival of the sky god Lug; to curry Lug's blessings upon the Harvest, and to guard the living from the coming starving season. Lugnasa is the time of year in which the Sidhe's major policies, treaties or major martial and agricultural matters are decided. Trials are held during Lugnasa, children are named, and funerals are held. Property may change hands or be gifted at Lugnasa. Celebrated at the start of Ban Lug, or 'The Month of The Bright Sky' (formerly, August 1).
- _Lu Sidhe-_ (Lew-shee) Less powerful, wise, or long-lived denizens of the Otherworld. Some share blood with the Ban Sidhe, but many are simply spirits or other mischievous creatures who assume a human-like shape. Often, faeries and other half-bloods are classified as Lu Sidhe. Such as: Slyphs, satyrs, Pixies, Niskies, Dryads, Nymphs and Brownies.

M

- _Mac-_ (Mack) "Son of", or "Daughter of".
- _Macha-_ (Mah-sha) Sidhe goddess of strategy, ambition, and courage. She is associated with sovereignty. One of three divine sisters. See also: Badh and Morrigan. Her herald is the eagle.
- _Maeve-_ (Mae-ve) Sidhe goddess of wisdom, magic, and mystery. Her herald is the Owl. SEE BABH, the goddess of discord, strife, and pestilence.
- _Magh Tuiredh-_ (Moy-teer-ah) Site of two ancient battles, the first of which was waged on the Fir Bolg by the Tuatha De Dannan. The Dannans took control of Innisfail at the end but granted the Fir Bolg their own corner of the land to rule— Ulster. The second battle was fought between the resurgent Fomorians, where Nuada of the Golden Arm was killed.
- _Manipulation-_ A form of magic studied by the _Siorai_ acolytes of the Cloister of the Eternal Flame, in Tairngare. Using one's own body energy (or Spark_), one can force particles to join or separate, and even build unnatural chains which change an objects trajectory, composition, or shape.

- *Mannanan Mac Lir*- Sidhe god of the Eastern Sea. Son of the god Lir.
- *Merchanta*- (Merr-cant-ah) The Merchant's Guild of Tairngare, run directly by the House of Commons in Parliament.
- *Midhir Mac Nuada*- (Mehd-eer-mack-nu-ah-dah) *Ard Ri* of the Tuatha De Dannan, and High King of Innisfail. Brought his people out of the Otherworld at the end of the Third Age of Man- also known as The Transition. Conquered the surviving mortals and brought them firmly under unified Sidhe overrule. A kind and compassionate ruler, if distracted and detached.
- *Mil Espagna*- An ancient 'celtic' king, hailing from the Iberian plateau. Forced to search for a new home when climate, war, and famine struck his people; they came to Innisfail— a lush, green, fertile land— in such numbers and with far superior weapons than anything the Sidhe could muster. His victories forced the Sidhe into the Otherworld and began the long period of Gallic rule. To the present, all Sidhe refer to mortal men and women as 'Milesians'
- *Morrigan*- (More-ah-gahn) Sidhe goddess of war, bloodlust, fury and pride. One of three divine sisters. (Equivalent to the Greek Fates). Her herald is the raven.

N

- *Navan*- (Nah-vahn) A small town on the river Boyne, at the border with Aes Sidhe.
- *Nemain*- (Neh-mayne) Sidhe goddess of the waterways and springs. It was said that her beauty drove men to madness for desire of her, but her kiss was poison and tortuous death. Kaer Yin's longsword is named for her. Her sister Niamh is the goddess of purity and love.
- *Nemed*- King of the first Innish invaders, in ancient times. Mortal grandson of the earth goddess Danu, and her mate, Donn— the god of death. Their daughter Brida took a mortal lover, from the tribe of Abraham. An accomplished sailor and adventurer, Nemed led his sea-faring tribe around the Mediterranean before a storm swept them out into the ocean, to Innisfail. Nemed fought the Fomorians for almost thirty years, before his death. His people divided and fled in separate directions. One half went South and were enslaved in Macedon; the Fir Bolg. The others took their ships far into the north and west, battling gods and monsters, until they returned with 300 ships, to oust their cousins from Innisfail- The Tuatha De Dannan.
- *Niall*- (Nay-all) A Dannan warrior, in Tam Lin's retinue.

- _Niamh_- (Neh-ve) Sidhe goddess of purity and love. Dwells in the waterways and springs, with her corrupted sister, Nemain.
- _Norther_- One whom dwells in Northern Eire.
- _Nova_- An initiate of the Cloister of the Eternal Flame, in Tairngare.

O

- _Oiche Ar Fad_- (Eesha-arh-fah) The Otherworld. A realm that exists just below the mortal. The Sidhe retreated to this realm for thousands of years, until the Milesians nearly purged themselves from the world. Only the Sidhe may come and go from this realm unmolested. To humankind, it holds mainly horror, forgetfulness, or death.

P

- _Porter_- A game of cards and two-sided dice.
- _Prima_- (Preema) A tertiate acolyte of the Cloister of the Eternal Flame, in Tairngare.

R

- _Ri_- (Ree) A king, or high lord.
- _Ruiadh_- (Roo-ah) "Red".

S

- _Samn_- (Sow) Sidhe goddess of the moon. Bel, god of the sun, is her mate.
- _Samhain_- (Sow-ahn) Festival of the moon, and the onset of winter. Celebrated (or mourned, considering perspective) at the end of the Month of Oncoming Night or Winter, or "Dor Samna". Samhain is the passage of life into death, and of autumn to winter. It is the one night of the year, in which the dead and all manner of Otherworld creatures may wander free of its borders— to trouble, torment, or comfort the living.
- _Scota_- (Skoh-tah) "Fierce One". The Queen of the Milesians in ancient times. Wife of Mil Espagna. Died fighting on the beach during the first Milesian invasion. Her son Amer Gin, who led his own men across the sea of Mannanan, named the land east of Skye after her (formerly Scotland).
- _Secunda_- (Seh-koon-dah) An intermediate in the Cloister of the Eternal Flame, in Tairngare.
- _Shannon_- The longest, widest river in Innisfail.
- _Sidhe_- (Shee) "Ever-Living", Describes the Immortals who dwell or dwelt in the Otherworld. Some are powerful and human-like, the Ban Sidhe; and some merely aspire to take human form— or never wish to.

- *Siora*- Patron goddess of Tairngare, also known as the 'Ancestor'. A goddess of unity, knowledge, and feminine power.
- *Siorai*- Acolytes of the Cloister of the Eternal Flame. Considered witches, by most of the peoples of Innisfail.
- *Souther*- One who dwells in Southern Eire.
- *Spark*- The life-force, or energy within one's body, that can be harnessed to manipulate the actions and properties of an object's compositional particles.

T

- *Tara*- (Tare-ah) A midling-sized town in Eire, south of the Boyne. In ancient times, it was a hillfort, fortress and castle— belonging to the High Kings of old Eire. Site of the *Lia Fail*, or "Stone of Destiny", before which all Kings of Eire were crowned. Now, it is a hub of the Merchanta— or Merchant's Guild, in Tainrgare.
- *Tairngare*- (Tare-ehn-gare) A matriarchal city in the Northeast of Eire, at the mouth of the Boyne (formerly Drogheda). A city run by a religious order of women, and a Parliament elected from noble families and commoners. Founded by a woman named Siora, a former prostitute who had magical abilities she shared only with the women who swore their supreme loyalty to the nameless earth goddess she claimed to have been born of. She vanished after the women took over the city. They call her the 'Ancestor'.
- *Tech Duinn*- (Teck-Doon) "House of Donn", or "Realm of Donn". The god of death in pre-Innish Europe, also the mate of Danu, goddess of the earth. His realm is the land of the dead, and all whom share his blood (Such as the Tuath De Dannan, Fir Bolg, and Milesians alike), must come to his realm after death. In the Otherworld, Diarmid is the king of Tech Duinn, and Donn's servant. All whom are given the god of death's name, are said to be cursed, or bring misfortune to their families. Such as the son of Mil, whom was angered by his brother Ir's rowing abilities, and cursed him, causing the oar to snap and both boys to die. The realm of Tech Duinn is a peaceful but solemn one within the otherworld, and only once a year on Samhain, are the dead given reprieve to wander outside its confines.
- *Tir Na Nog*- (Teer-nah-noge) "Land of the Undying Ones". The realm of the Sidhe gods. Only great heroes or those with divine blood, may enter when they die. All else must go to Tech Duinn
- *Tir Falias*- A Sidhe city in the Otherworld.
- *Transition*- SEE TUATHA DE DANNAN.
- *Tuatha De Dannan (or Tuatha De Danaan, or De Danann)*- (Too-ah-ha-day-dahn-ahn) "Children of Danu". A half-divine tribe of warriors descended

from the demi-god and adventurer Nemed. Unlike their Fir Bolg cousins, the Tuatha De fled Innisfail in ships, toward the north and west. They traveled from Isle to Isle, fighting monsters, hostile tribes, and brushing elbows with the gods. When they returned to Innisfail in ancient times, they defeated the Fir Bolg for supremacy over the land; then defeated the Fomorians, the old Fir Bolg enemy. They ruled in peace for many seasons, until they were defeated by the crafty Milesians from the Iberian Peninsula. Their greatest Brehon, Crom Dagda, sacrificed his life to the god of death— Donn, to give all those whom shared the Dagda's blood immortality, and a piece of the Otherworld to rule. They remained there for thousands of years, vowing to return when the rule of Mil's spawn failed. In N.E. 1, when the Milesians were fast becoming extinct, the Dannans came back to reconquer what was stolen from them in ancient times. This is known as the 'Transition'.

U

- *Uishge*- (Whisk-ey) "Water of Life". An ancient, amber colored spirit.
- *Ulster*- (Ull-Sterr) Kingdom in the north of Aes Sidhe, its capital is Armagh. Ruled by the remaining Fir Bolg nobility, the Mac Nemed Clan. Has been one of the chief Innish kingdoms since ancient times.
- *Una Moura Donahugh*- (Ooh-nah-more-ah-donnah-hew) "Bright One". Prima of the Cloister of the Eternal Flame. Reigning Domina of House Moura, and proposed Queen of the Commons, in Parliament. Studying to ascend to Alta Prima, and being groomed to succeed Drem as Doma. Daughter of Arrin Moura and Patrick Donahugh.

V

- *Vanna Nema*- (Vah-nah-Nee-mah) Alta Prima, Mistress of the House of Commons in Parliament, and second-in-command to the Doma.

DRAMATIS PERSONAE

EIRE

TAIRNGARE

- *Drem Moura*- Doma, high priestess of the Cloister of the Eternal Flame. Highest ranking noble in Tairngare. Represents all of Eire in the High King's Council.
- *Vanna Nema*- Alta Prima, Mistress of the House of Commons in Parliament, and second-in-command to the Doma.
- *Arrin Moura*- (Deceased) Former Alta Prima of the Cloister of the Eternal Flame. Former Queen of the Commons, appointed by the Doma, her mother. Taken from a market by Duch Patrick and made Duchess of Bethany, against her will. Committed suicide in *N.E. 487*, when her daughter was but two years old.
- *Una Moura Donahugh*- Prima of the Cloister of the Eternal Flame. Reigning Domina of House Moura, and proposed Queen of the Commons, in Parliament. Studying to ascend to Alta Prima, and being groomed to succeed Drem as Doma. Daughter of Arrin Moura and Patrick Donahugh.
- *Aoife Sona*- Prima of the Cloister of the Eternal Flame. Servant of Vanna Nema. Rumored to hold Fir Bolg blood.

- *Eva Alvra*- Member of the Libella, and Domina of House Alvra. Servant of the Doma, and former Prima of the Cloister of the Eternal Flame.
- *Pors Yma*- High ranking member of the Libella. A staunch opponent of the House of Commons.
- *Mel Carra*- Member of the Mercher's Guild, and highest-ranking member of the House of Commons. Ardent supporter of Vanna Nema.
- *Fawa Gan*- Steward, to Vanna Nema

BETHANY

- *Duch Patrick Donahugh*- Ruler of the South. Ardent opponent of the High King in Aes Sidhe. Instigator of two wars, which cost him many men and most of his fortune— as well as his seat on the High King's Council. Chafes under Sidhe rule, and plots to take the throne for himself. Kidnapped Una's mother from a market in broad daylight and forced her into a loveless marriage of convenience. Una's father; he means to conquer all of Eire, and rule in her name.
- *AlisDonahugh*- (Deceased) Kidnapped by an unknown Sidhe lord in *N.E. 474*, returned home several months later, heavy with child and mad. After the child was born, she threw herself from the north parapet. Some say, her death prompted the battle at Dumnain, ten years later.
- *Henry Fitz Donahugh*- Patrick's illegitimate half-brother. Attempted to overthrow Patrick after his failure at Dumnain. Banished to the wastes of Cmyru, for nearly twenty years. A fervent Kneeler.
- *Damek Bishop, Lord of Clare*- Alis' illegitimate son, fathered by an unknown Sidhe lord. Adopted by Patrick after his mother's death. Accomplished soldier and statesman. Views himself as Patrick's rightful heir, and plots to conquer the whole of Eire to force his uncle to legitimize his claim to the throne. Commander of Bethany's armed forces.
- *Martin O'Reardan*- Lord Marshal at Arms, of Bethany. Damek's self-appointed right-hand man, and protector. Damek reveres him as a father figure and close confidant.
- *Wallace Cunningham*- Major of Bethany's Steel Corps (formerly, Captain, (Heavy Cavalry). An accomplished tracker, and talented swordsman.
- *Killian*- A lieutenant
- *Hamish*- A corporal
- *Douglas*- A sergeant
- *Dawes*- A corporal

- *Blane*- A ranger

ROSWEAL

- *Barb Dormer*- Madam of the tavern and pleasure house, *The Hart and Hare*. A former Nova in the Cloister of the Eternal Flame. Mistress of the Greenmakers' Guild. Aims to be the Town Headwoman, and dreams of modernizing their backwater town.
- *Robin Gramble*- A poacher, and town crime boss. Master of the Greenmakers' Guild, answers only to Barb, his undeclared mistress. Well-respected by his men, and greatly feared by his enemies.
- *Ben Maeden*- A drifter, and sometime poacher. Mysterious origins, and curious loyalties. Fond of drink, dicing, and women.
- *Matt Gilcannon*- A bootlegger, distiller of illegal spirits, and whoremaster. Owner of the *Black Corset*. A bordello of ill-repute. Fond of using the sons of his whores to do his dirty work. Desirous of destroying the Greenmakers' monopoly on trade, and opening new revenue streams outside of the North.
- *Solomon Trant*- A brewer and tavernkeeper, in the Greenmakers' Quarter. Member of the Greenmakers' Guild.
- *Samuel Trant*- A butcher, tanner and crime underboss. Brother to Solomon Trant, but not a member of the Greenmakers' Guild.
- *Gerrod Twomey*- A competent woodsman, and member of the Greenmakers' Guild, despite his youth and optimism.
- *Colm*- Tavernkeeper at the *Hart and Hare*, member of the Greenmakers' Guild. Barb's right-hand man.
- *Seamus*- A tracker and woodsman. A member of the Greenmakers' Guild.
- *Dabney*- Barb's dimwitted bodyguard.
- *Dean*- A bouncer at the *Hart and Hare*, and sometime hired thug.
- *Paul*- A hired thug, sometime member of the Greenmakers' Guild.
- *Rose*- A prostitute at the *Hart and Hare*, from a disgraced Tairnganese noble family. Soft-spoken and loyal.
- *Violet*- A prostitute from the Midlands.
- *Tansy*- A prostitute.
- *Vick*- One of Matt Gilcannon's street toughs.

FERNDALE

- _Arthur Guinness_- (Deceased) Physician. Once a triage doctor for the Tairnganese forces in the war of '84.
- _Aednat Guinness_- (Deceased) His wife. Sidhe half-blood.
- _Rian Guinness_- Took over her father's practice after his death. Reviled by all whom seek her out for her faerie blood. Methodical, practical and intelligent- if not overly friendly.

aes sidhe

BRI LEITH
(house of the white stag)

- _Nuada of the Golden Arm, Nuada Mac Crom_- (Deceased) Ancient ancestor of the House Adair (White Stag). Son of the Dagda, and King of the _Tuatha De Dannan_. Defeated the armies of Balor the One-Eyed, King of the Fomorians. Defeated the Fir Bolg King, Eochaid Mac Nemed in single combat for the title of _Ard Ri_. Slain by Eber Finn, son of Mil Espagna- a mortal man.
- _Crom Dagda_- The 'good father'. First King of the _Tuatha De Dannan_, and also a Skysinger of unimaginable power. Sacrificed his own eye to save Nuada's life after the battle at Magh Tuiredh, against the formidable Fomorian King, Balor. Years later, sacrificed his own life to save his people from the onslaught of the Milesians, after Nuada's death. He is honored at Cromnasa, each midwinter.
- _Midhir Mac Crom_- _Ard Ri_ of the _Tuatha De Dannan_, and High King of Innisfail. Brought his people out of the Otherworld at the end of the Third Age of Man- also known as The Transition. Conquered the surviving mortals, then brought them firmly under unified Sidhe overrule. A kind and compassionate ruler, if distracted and detached.
- _Etain_- (Deceased) Midhir's Queen. Died in childbirth, or some say, retreated to _Tir Na Nog_ on the other side of _Tech Duinn;_ to await her beloved in peace. Long believed to be the daughter of the sun god Bel, and Danu, the earth goddess. Midhir's winning of her hand, is its own tale.
- _Kaer Yin Mac Midhir Adair_- The _Ard Tiarne_ of the _Tuatha De Dannan_, and Crown Prince of Innisfail. Son of Midhir and Etain, he was the first Dannan to be born in Innisfail after The Transition. Grand Marshal of the

Wild Hunt, and Commander of Aes Sidhe's standing armies. Killed Kevin Donahugh in single combat, during the first Bethonair War, in (408), and ended the war of '84, at Dumnain with another victory over the Donahugh Clan. Prince of Eire, and Cymru. A cold, unfeeling character, who values martial might over all other virtues.

- *Eri Mac Midhir Bres*- Daughter of Midhir and Etain, Princess of Innisfail, and Queen of Scotia. Married to Jan Fir Bres, King of Scotia; and Lord of Skye.
- *Fionn*- Lord Protector of Aes Sidhe, and Midhir's sworn Sword.
- *Ysirdra*- High Priestess of Danu, and trusted advisor to the High King.

CROGHAN
(house of the red eagle)

- *Bov Mac Crom Dearg*- Son of Nuada of the Golden Arm, and King of Connaught. Called Bov 'The Red', by his people, for his fiery hair and disposition. Some call him the 'Red Boar of Connaught', behind his back- for his stubborn pride, short temper, and devotion to the hunt. A peerless warrior in battle, but too hotheaded to make much of a commander. Brother of Midhir, the High King.
- *Grainne Mac Eochaid*- Bov's Queen. A Former Fir Bolg Princess, daughter of Eochaid Mac Nemed, and his wife, Liadan Mac Nemed- also, his first cousin. She was married into the *Tuatha De Dannan* as part of a peace treaty with Armagh, after Nuada slew Ecohaid, and took his throne. She and Bov have a stormy relationship.
- *Tam Lin Mac Bov Dearg*- Prince of Connaught, and Marshal of the West. Son of Bov and Grainne, making him the only living Dannan prince who is also half Fir-Bolg. Beloved nephew of the *Ard Ri,* Midhi— and Commander of Croghan's Blood Eagles; an elite fighting force, second only to Bri Leith's Wild Hunt (*An Fiach Fian).* Favorite cousin and trusted friend of Kaer Yin Adair.
- *Shar Lianor*- Tam Lin's First Lieutenant, and right-hand man.
- *Niall*- A Blood Eagle
- *Oisin*- A Blood Eagle

TECH DUINN
(house of the raven)

- *Diarmid Mac Crom Adair*- King of Tech Duinn, and Lord of the *Oiche Ard Fad*. Called *Fiachra Ri*, by the Sidhe- or Raven King, in Eire. A Skysinger, like his grandfather Crom Dagda; and a Brehon of the Tuatha De Dannan. He is the only member of his house, as he rules a kingdom of the dead. All lesser Sidhe call him 'King', including the Lu Sidhe, and Dor Sidhe- which would unleash themselves upon mortal kind, did he not guard the gates of the Otherworld with a firm hand. Brother to Midhir, the High King. An ambitious, mercurial man, whose loyalty can never truly be counted upon.

ARMAGH
(house of the black bull)

- *Eochaid Mac Nemed*- (Deceased) Ancient King of the Fir Bolg. Slain by Nuada, king of the *Tuatha De Dannan* for his throne, and the right to rule in Innisfail. Married to his cousin Liadan, by their Fomorian Grandfather, Balor. Was a just ruler, and fearsome warrior.

- *Liadan Mac Nemed*- Queen of the Fir Bolg in ancient times, and Dowager Queen of Armagh, after The Transition.

- *Falan (the elder) Mac Eochaid*- King of the Fir Bolg, and lord of the ancient city of Armagh. A notorious philanderer and by all accounts, a terribly irresponsible ruler. Often wanders the *raths* of his Sworn Shields, to seduce their wives and avail themselves of their forced hospitality.

- *Falan (the younger) Mac Nemed*- (Deceased) Prince of Armagh, and former Marshal of the North. Despised his father so much, he took his grandfather's surname. Believed to have been the mightiest warrior in Armagh, and the greatest swordsmen in Innisfail— until he was defeated by Kaer Yin Adair at a tourney, years before his death. Slain at Dumnain, by a nameless Milesian soldier from Bethany.

- *Grainne Mac Nemed*- Princess of Armagh, and daughter of Falan the Elder and his third wife, Taliu. Half-sister to Falan the Younger, and an astute pupil of the Dowager Queen. Named for her aunt Grainne, whom married Bove Dearg in ancient times.